A Joyous Season

HISTORICAL ROMANCE FROM PINNACLE BOOKS

A JOYOUS SEASON

FERN MICHAELS

JENNIFER BLAKE

HANNAH HOWELL

OLGA BICOS

ZEBRA BOOKS
KENSINGTON PUBLISHING CORP.
http://www.zebrabooks.com

ZEBRA BOOKS are published by

Kensington Publishing Corp.
850 Third Avenue
New York, NY 10022

First Printing: November, 1996
10 9 8 7 6 5 4 3 2 1

Printed in the United States of America

Contents

Merry, Merry

Fern Michaels

One

Andi Evans stared at the light switch. Should she turn it on or not? How many kilowatts of electricity did the fluorescent bulbs use? How would it translate onto her monthly bill? She risked a glance at the calendar; December 14, 1996, five days till the meter reader arrived. The hell with it, the animals needed light. She needed light. Somehow, someway, she'd find a way to pay the bill. On the other hand, maybe she should leave the premises dark so Mr. Peter King could break his leg in the dark. Breaking both legs would be even better. Like it was really going to happen.

Maybe she should read the letter again. She looked in the direction of her desk where she'd thrown it five days ago after she'd read it. She could see the end of the expensive cream-colored envelope sticking out among the stack of unpaid bills. "Guess what, Mr. Peter King, I'm not selling you my property. I told that to your forty-seven lawyers months ago." She started to cry then because it was all so hopeless.

They came from every direction, dogs, cats, puppies and kittens, clawing for her attention, their ears attuned to the strange sounds coming from the young woman who fed and bathed them and saw to their needs. They were strays nobody wanted. This was what she'd gone to veterinarian school for. She even had a sign that said she was Andrea Evans, D.V.M. Eleven patients in as many months. She was the new kid on the block, what did she expect? Because she was that new kid, people assumed they could just dump unwanted animals on her property. After all, what did a vet with only eleven patients have to do?

Andi thought about her student loans, the taxes on her house and three acres, the animals, the bills, the futility of it all. Why was she even fighting? Selling her property would net her a nice tidy sum. She could pay off her loans, go to work for a vet clinic, get a condo someplace and . . . what would happen to her animals if she did that? She wailed louder, the dogs and cats clambering at her feet.

"Enough!" a voice roared.

"Gertie!"

Tails swished furiously; Gertie always brought soup bones and catnip. Andi watched as she doled them out, something for everyone. She blew her nose. "I think they love you more than they love me."

They love what I bring them. I'd like a cup of tea if you have any. It's nasty out there. It might snow before nightfall."

"Where are you sleeping tonight, Gertie?"

"Under the railroad trestle with my friends. Being homeless doesn't give me many choices."

"You're welcome to stay here, Gertie. I told you the cot is yours anytime you want it. I'll even make you breakfast. Did you eat today?"

"Later. I have something for you. Call it an early Christmas present. I couldn't wait to get here to give it to you." Gertie hiked up several layers of clothing to her long underwear where she'd sewn a pocket. She withdrew a thick wad of bills. "We found this four weeks ago. There it was, this big wad of money laying right in the street late at night. Two thousand dollars, Andi. We want you to have it. We watched in the papers, asked the police, no one claimed it. A whole month we waited, and no one claimed it. It's probably drug money, but them animals of yours don't know that. Better to be spent on them than on some drug pusher. Doncha be telling me no now."

"Oh, Gertie, I wouldn't dream of saying no. Did you find it in Plainfield?"

"Right there on Front Street, big as life."

Andi hugged the old woman who always smelled of lily of the valley. She could never figure out why that was. Gertie had to be at least seventy-five, but a young seventy-five as she put it. She was skinny and scrawny, but it was hard to tell with the many layers of clothing she wore. Her shoes were run-down, her gloves had holes in the fingers, and her knit cap reeked of moth balls. For a woman her age she had dewy skin, pink cheeks, few wrinkles and the brightest, bluest eyes Andi had ever seen. "Did you walk all the way from Plainfield, Gertie?"

Gertie's head bobbed up and down. "Scotch Plains ain't that far. I left my buggie outside."

Translated, that meant all of Gertie's worldly possessions were in an Acme shopping cart outside Andi's clinic.

"Here's your tea, Gertie, strong and black, just the way you like it. It's almost Christmas; are you going to call your children? You should, they must be worried sick."

"What, so they can slap me in a nursing home? Oh, no, I like things just the way they are. I'm spending Christmas with my friends. Now, why were you bawling like that?"

Andi pointed to her desk. "Unpaid bills. And a letter from Mr. Peter King. He's that guy I told you about. His forty-seven lawyers couldn't bend me, so I guess they're sending in the first string now. He's coming here at four-thirty."

"Here?" Gertie sputtered, the teacup almost falling from her hand.

"Yes. Maybe he's going to make a final offer. Or, perhaps he thinks he can intimidate me. This property has been in my family for over a hundred years. I'm not selling it to some lipstick mogul. What does a man know about lipstick anyway? Who cares if he's one of the biggest cosmetic manufacturers on the East Coast. I don't even wear lipstick.

These lips are as kissable as they're going to get, and his greasy product isn't going to change my mind."

"I really need to be going now, Andi. So, you'll tell him no."

"Gertie, look around you. What would you do if you were me? What's so special about this piece of property? Let him go to Fanwood, anywhere but here. Well?"

"Location is everything. This is prime. Zoning has to be just right, and you, my dear, are zoned for his needs. I'd tell him to go fly a kite," Gertie said smartly. "I hear a truck. Lookee here, Andi, Wishnitz is here with your dog food."

"I didn't order any dog food."

"You better tell him that then, 'cause the man's unloading big bags of it. I'll see you tomorrow. Greasy, huh?"

"Yeah. Gertie, I wish you'd stay; it's getting awfully cold outside. Thanks for the money. Tell your friends I'm grateful. You be careful now."

"Hey you guys, I didn't order dog food."

"Bill says it's a gift. Five hundred pounds of Pedigree dog food, sixteen cases of cat food and two bags of birdseed. Sign here?"

"Who sent it?"

"Don't know, ma'am, I'm just the driver. Call the store. Where do you want this?"

"Around the back."

Andi called the feed store to be sure there was no mistake. "Are you telling me some anonymous person just walked into your store and paid for all this? It's a fortune in dog and cat food. No name at all? All right, thanks."

A beagle named Annabelle pawed Andi's leg. "I know, time for supper and a little run. Okay, everybody *SIT!* You know the drill, about face; march in an orderly fashion to the pen area. Stop when you get to the gate and go to your assigned dishes. You know which ones are yours. No cheating, Harriet," she said to a fat white cat who eyed her disdainfully. "I'm counting to three, and when the whistle blows, *GO!* That's really good, you guys are getting the hang of it. Okay, here it comes, extra today thanks to our good samaritan, whoever she or he might be."

"Bravo! If I didn't see it with my own eyes, I wouldn't have believed it. There must be thirty dogs and cats here."

"Thirty-six to be exact. And you are?" Andi looked at her watch.

"Peter King. You must be Andrea Evans."

"Doctor Evans. How did you get in here? The dogs didn't bark." Andi's voice was suspicious, her eyes wary. "I'm busy right now, and you're forty-five minutes early, Mr. King. I can't deal with you now. You need to go back to the office or come back another day." The wariness in her eyes changed to amusement when she noticed Cedric, a Dalmatian, lift his leg to pee on Peter King's exquisitely polished Brooks Brothers loafers.

The lipstick mogul, as Andi referred to him, eyed his shoe in dismay. He shook it off and said, "You might be right. I'll be in the waiting room."

Andi raised her head from the sack of dog food to stare at the tall man dwarfing her: Thirty-six or -seven, brown eyes, brown unruly hair with a tight curl, strong features, handsome, muscular, unmarried; no ring on his finger. Sharply dressed. Pristine white shirt, bold, expensive tie. Very well put together. She wondered how many lipsticks he had to sell to buy his outfit. She debated asking until she remembered how she looked. Instead she said, "You remind me of someone."

"A lot of people say that, but they can never come up with who it is." He started for the waiting room.

"It will come to me sooner or later." Andi ladled out food, the dogs waiting patiently until all the dishes were full. "Okay, guys, go for it!" When the animals finished eating, Andi let them out into their individual runs. "Twenty minutes. When you hear the buzzer, boogie on in here," she called.

Andi took her time stacking the dog bowls in the stainless steel sink full of soapy water. She'd said she was busy. Busy meant she had to wash and dry the dishes now to take up time. As she washed and dried the bowls, her eyes kept going to the mirror over the sink. She looked worse than a mess. She had on absolutely no makeup, her blond hair was frizzy, her sweat shirt was stained and one of her sneakers had a glob of poop on the heel. She cleaned off her shoe, let the dogs into their pens, then stacked the dishes for the following day. "When I'm slicked up, I can look as good as he does," she hissed to the animals. The beagle threw her head back and howled.

"I have five minutes, Mr. King. I told your forty-seven lawyers I'm not selling. What part of no don't you understand?"

"The part about the forty-seven lawyers. I only have two. I think you mean forty-seven letters."

Andi shrugged.

"I thought perhaps I could take you out to dinner . . . and we could . . . discuss the pros and cons of selling your property." He smiled. She saw dimples and magnificent white teeth. All in a row like matched pearls.

"Save your money, Mr. King. Dinner will not sway my decision. You know what else, I don't even like your lipstick. It's greasy. The colors are abominable. The names you've given the lipsticks are so ridiculous they're ludicrous. Raspberry Cheese Louise. Come *onnnnn.*" At his blank look she said, "I worked at a cosmetic counter to put myself through college and vet school."

"I see."

"No, you don't, but that's okay. Time's up, Mr. King."

"Three hundred and fifty thousand, Dr. Evans. You could relocate."

Andi felt her knees go weak on her. "Sorry, Mr. King."

"Five hundred thousand and that's as high as I can go. It's a take it or leave it offer. It's on the table right now. When I walk out of here it goes with me."

She might have seriously considered the offer if the beagle hadn't chosen that moment to howl. "I really have to go, Mr. King. That's Annabelle howling. She has arthritis and it's time for her medication." She must be out of her mind to turn down half a million dollars. Annabelle howled again.

"I didn't know dogs got arthritis."

"They get a lot of things, Mr. King. They develop heart trouble; they get cancer, cataracts, prostate problems, all manner of things. Do you really think us humans have a lock on disease? This is the only home those animals know. No one else wanted them, so I took them in. My father and his father before him owned this kennel. It's my home and their home."

"Wait, hear me out. You could buy a new, modern facility with the money I'm willing to pay you. This is pretty antiquated. Your wood's rotten, your pens are rusty, your concrete is cracked. You're way past being a fixer-upper. You could get modern equipment. If you want my opinion, I think you're being selfish. You're thinking of yourself, not the animals. The past is past; you can't bring it back, nor should you want to. I'll leave my offer on the table till Friday. Give it some thought, sleep on it. If your decision is still no on Friday, I won't bother you again. I'll even raise my price to $750,000. I'm not trying to cheat you."

Andi snorted. "Of course not," she said sarcastically, "that's why you started off at $200,000 and now you're up to $750,000. I didn't just fall off the turnip truck, Mr. King. Let's cut to the chase. What's your absolute final offer?"

It was Peter King's turn to stare warily at the young doctor in front of him. His grandmother would love her. Sadie would say she had grit and spunk. Uh huh. "A million," he said hoarsely.

"That's as in acre, right? I have a little over three acres. Closer to four than three."

King's jaw dropped. Annabelle howled again. "You want three million dollars for this . . . hovel?"

"No. Three plus million for the *land*. You're right, it is a hovel; but it's my home and the home of those animals. I sweated my ass off to keep this property and work my way through school. What do you know about work, Mr. Lipstick? Hell, I could make up a batch of that stuff you peddle for eight bucks a pop right here in the kitchen. All I need is my chemistry book. Get the hell off my property and don't come back unless you have three million plus dollars in your hand. You better get going before it really starts to snow and you ruin those fancy three hundred dollar Brooks Brothers shoes."

"Your damn dog already ruined them."

"Send me a bill!" Andi shouted as she pushed him through the door and then slammed it shut. She turned the dead bolt before she raced back to the animals. She dusted her hands dramatically for the animals' benefit before she started to cry. The animals crept from their cages that had no doors, to circle her, licking and pawing at her tear-filled face. She hiccupped and denounced all men who sold lipstick. If he comes up with three million plus bucks, we're outta here. Then we'll have choices; we can stay here in New Jersey, head south or north, wherever we can get the best deal. Hamburger and tuna for you guys and steak for me. We'll ask Gertie to go with us. I'm done crying now. You can go back to sleep. Come on, Annabelle, time for your pill."

Andi scooped up the pile of bills on her desk to carry them into the house. With the two thousand dollars from Gertie and the dog and cat food, she could last until the end of January, and then she'd be right back where she was just a few hours ago. Three million plus dollars was a lot of money. So was $750,000. Scrap that, he'd said a cool million. Times three. At eight bucks a tube, how many lipsticks would the kissing king need to sell? Somewhere in the neighborhood of 375,000. Darn, she should have said two million an acre.

It might be a wonderful Christmas after all.

Peter King slid his metallic card into the slot and waited for the huge grilled gate to the underground garage of his grandmother's high rise to open. Tonight was his Friday night obligatory dinner with his grandmother. A dinner he always enjoyed and even looked forward to. He adored his seventy-five-year-old grandmother who was the president of King Cosmetics. He shuddered when he thought of what she would say to Andrea Evans' price. She'd probably go ballistic and throw her salmon, Friday night's dinner, across the room. At which point, Hannah the cat would eat it all and then puke on the Persian carpet. He shuddered again. Three million dollars. Actually, it would be more than three million. The property on Cooper River Road was closer to four acres. He had two hard choices, pay it or forget it.

Who in the hell was that wise-assed girl whose dog peed on his shoe? Where did she get off booting him out the door. Hell, she'd pushed him, shoved him. She probably didn't weigh more than one hundred pounds soaking wet. He took a few seconds to mentally envision that hundred pound body naked. Aaahh. With some King Cosmetics she'd be a real looker. And she hated his guts.

"Hey, Sadie, I'm here," Peter called from the foyer. He'd called his grandmother Sadie from the time he was a little boy. She allowed it because she said it made her feel younger.

"Peter, you're early. Good, we can have a drink by the

fire. Hannah's already there waiting for us. She's not feeling well." Sadie's voice turned fretful. "I don't want her *going* before me. She's such wonderful company. Look at her, she's just lying there. I tried to tempt her with salmon before and she wouldn't touch it. She won't even let me hold her."

Peter's stomach started to churn. If anything happened to Hannah, he knew his grandmother would take to her bed and not get up. He hunched down and held out his hand. Hannah hissed and snarled. "That's not like her. Did you take her to the vet?"

Sadie snorted. "He went skiing in Aspen. I don't much care for all those fancy vets who have banker's hours and who don't give a damn. Hannah is too precious to trust to just anybody. Let's sit and have a drink and watch her. How did your meeting go with Dr. Evans?"

"It was a bust. She wants a million dollars an acre. She means it, too. She booted my ass right out the door. I have a feeling she's a pretty good vet. Maybe you should have her take a look at Hannah. One of her dogs squirted on my shoe."

"That's a lot of money. Is the property worth it?"

"Hell yes. More as a matter of fact. She ridiculed my lowball offer. Hey, business is business."

"We aren't in the business of cheating people, Peter. Fair is fair. If, as you say, Miss Evans' property is the perfect location, then pay the money and close the deal. The company can afford it. You can be under way the first of the year. I know you had the attorneys do all the paperwork in advance. Which, by the way, is a tad unethical in my opinion. Don't think I don't know that you have your contractor on twenty-four-hour call."

"Is there anything you don't know, Sadie?"

"Yes."

Peter eyed his grandmother warily. God, how he loved this old lady with her pearl white hair and regal bearing. It was hard to believe she was over seventy. She was fit and trim, fashionable, a leader in the community. She sat on five boards, did volunteer work at the hospital and was an active leader in ways to help the homeless. Her picture was in the paper at least three days a week. He knew what was coming now, and he dreaded it. "Let's get it over with, Sadie."

"Helen called here for you about an hour ago. She quizzed me, Peter. The gall of that woman. What do you see in her? I hesitate to remind you, but she dumped you. That's such an unflattering term, but she did. She married that councilman because she believed his PR campaign. She thought he was rich. The man is in debt over his ears, so she left him. Now, she wants you again. She's a selfish, mean-spirited young woman who thinks only of herself. I thought you had more sense, Peter. I am terribly disappointed in this turn of events."

He was pretty much of the same opinion, but he wasn't going to give his grandmother the pleasure of knowing his feelings. She'd been matchmaking for years and was determined to find just the right girl for him."

"We're friends. There's no harm in a casual lunch or dinner. Don't make this into something else."

"I want to see you settled before I go."

"You can stop that right now, Sadie, because it isn't going to work. You're fit as a fiddle, better than a person has a right to be at your age. You can stay on the treadmill longer than I can. You aren't going anywhere for a very long time. When I find the right girl you'll be the first to know."

"You've been telling me that for years. You're thirty-six, Peter. I want grandchildren before . . . I get too old to enjoy them. If you aren't interested in Helen, tell her so and don't take up her time. Don't even think about bringing her to your Christmas party. If you do, I will not attend."

"All right, Sadie!"

Sadie sniffed, her blue eyes sparking. "She just wants to

be your hostess so she can network. Men are so stupid
sometimes. Tell me about Dr. Evans. What's she like?"

Peter threw his hands in the air. "I told you she kicked
me out. I hardly had time to observe her. She has curly
hair, she's skinny. I think she's skinny. She had this look
on her face, Sadie, it . . . Mom used to look at me kind of
the same way when I was sick. She had that look when she
was with the animals. I was sizing her up when her dog
squatted on my shoe. The place is a mess. Clean, but a
mess."

"That young woman worked her way through school. She
worked at a cosmetic counter, did waitressing, sometimes
working two jobs. It took her a while, but she did it. I approve
of that, Peter. That property has been in her family for a long
time. Both her parents were vets, and so was her grandfather.
No one appreciates hard work more than I do. Take a good
look at me, Peter. I started King Cosmetics in my kitchen. I
worked around the clock when your grandfather died and I
had three children to bring up. I read the report in your office.
I can truthfully say I never read a more comprehensive report.
The only thing missing was the color of her underwear. I felt
like a sneak reading it. I really did, Peter. I wish you hadn't
done that. It's such an invasion of someone's privacy."

"This might surprise you, Sadie, but I felt the same way.
I wanted to know what I was up against, financially. For
whatever it's worth, I'm sorry I did it, too. So, do we buy
the property or not?"

"Are you prepared to pay her price?"

"I guess I am. It's a lot of money."

"Will she hold out?" Sadie's tone of voice said she didn't
care one way or the other.

"Damn right. That young woman is big on principle.
She's going to stick it to me because she thinks I tried to
cheat her."

"You did."

"Why does it sound like you're on her side? What I did was an acceptable business practice."

"I'm a fair, honest woman, Peter. I don't like anything unethical. I wish this whole mess never happened. Why don't you invite Dr. Evans to your Christmas party. If you got off to a bad start, this might shore up things for you. I think you're interested in the young woman. I bet she even has a party dress. And shoes. Probably even a pearl necklace that belonged to her mother. Girls always have pearl necklaces that belonged to their mothers. Things like pearl necklaces are important to young women. Well?"

"Before or after I make the offer?" Jesus, he didn't just say that, did he?

"If you're going to make the offer, call her and tell her. Why wait till Monday? Maybe you could even go over there and take Hannah for her to check over. That's business for her. Then you could extend the invitation."

Peter grinned wryly. "You never give up, do you?"

"Then you'll take Hannah tomorrow."

"For you, Sadie, anything. What's for dinner?"

"Pot roast," Sadie said smartly. "I gave the salmon to Hannah, but she wouldn't eat it."

"Pot roast's good. We settled on the three million plus then?" His voice was so jittery sounding, Sadie turned away to hide her smile.

"I'd say so. You need to give Dr. Evans time to make plans. Christmas is almost here. She'll want to spend her last Christmas at her home, I would imagine. She'll have to pack up whatever she's going to take with her. It's not much time, Peter. She has to think about all those animals."

"Three million plus will ease the burden considerably. She can hire people to help her. We're scheduled to go, as in go, the day after New Years. I hate to admit this, but I'm having second thoughts about the contractor I hired. I think I was just a little too hasty when I made my decision, but I signed the contract so I'm stuck. Time's money, Sadie. If the young lady is as industrious as the report says, she'll have it under control."

Sadie smiled all through dinner. She was still smiling when she kissed her grandson good night at the door. "Drive carefully, Peter, the weatherman said six inches of snow by morning. Just out of curiosity, do you happen to know what kind of vehicle Dr. Evans drives?"

"I saw an ancient pickup on the side of the building. It didn't look like it was operational to me. Why do you ask?"

"No reason. I'd hate to think of her stranded with those animals if an emergency came up."

"If you want me to stop on my way home, just say so, Sadie. Is it late? Why don't I call her on the car phone on the way?"

"A call is so impersonal. Like when Helen calls. You could tell Dr. Evans you were concerned about the animals. The power could go out. She might have electric heat. You could also mention that you'll be bringing Hannah in the morning. If she doesn't like you, this might change her mind."

"I didn't say she didn't like me, Sadie," Peter blustered.

"Oh."

"Oh? What does oh mean?"

"It means I don't think she likes you. Sometimes you aren't endearing, Peter. She doesn't know you the way I do. The way Helen did." This last was said so snidely, Peter cringed.

"Good night, Sadie." Peter kissed his grandmother soundly, gave her a thumbs-up salute, before he pressed the down button of the elevator.

As he waited for the grilled gate to open, he stared in dismay at the accumulated snow. Maybe he should head for the nearest hotel and forget about going home. What he should have done was bunk with Sadie for the night. Too late, he was already on the road. The snow took care of any visit he might have considered making to Scotch Plains.

He eyed the car phone and then the digital clock on the Mercedes walnut panel. Nine o'clock was still early. Pay attention to the road, he cautioned himself.

In the end, Peter opted for the Garden State Parkway. Traffic was bumper-to-bumper, but moving. He got off the Clark exit and headed for home. He could call Dr. Evans from home with a frosty beer in his hand. When the phone on the console buzzed, he almost jumped out of his skin. He pressed a button and said, "Peter King."

"Peter, it's Helen. I've been calling you all evening. Where have you been?"

He wanted to say, what business is it of yours where I was, but he didn't. "On the road," he said curtly.

"Why don't you stop for a nightcap, Peter. I'll put another log on the fire. I have some wonderful wine."

"Sorry, I'm three blocks from home. The roads are treacherous this evening."

"I see. Where were you, Peter? I called your grandmother, and she said you weren't there."

"Out and about. I'll talk to you next week, Helen."

"You're hanging up on me," she said in a whiny voice.

"Afraid so, I'm almost home."

"I wish I was there with you. I didn't get an invitation to your Christmas party, Peter. Was that an oversight or don't you want me there?"

Peter drew a deep breath. "Helen, you aren't divorced. I know your husband well. We play racquet ball at the gym. He's a nice guy and I like him. He's coming to the party. It won't look right for you to attend."

"For heaven's sake, Peter, this is the nineties. Albert and I remained friends. We're legally separated. He knows it's you I love. He's known that from day one. I made a mistake, Peter. Are you going to hold it against me for the rest of my life?"

"Look, Helen, there's no easy way to say this except to say it straight out. I'm seeing someone on a serious basis.

You and I had our time, but it's over now. Let's stay friends and let it go at that."

"Who? Who are you seeing? You're making that up, Peter. I would have heard if you were seriously seeing someone. Or is she some nobody you don't take out in public? I bet it's somebody your grandmother picked out for you. Oh, Peter, that's just too funny for words." Trilling laughter filled Peter's car.

Peter swerved into his driveway just as he pressed the power button on the car phone, cutting Helen's trilling laughter in mid-note. He waited for the Genie to raise the garage door. The moment the garage door closed, Peter's shoulders slumped. Who *was* that woman on the phone? Jesus, once he'd given serious thought to marrying her. He shook his head to clear away his thoughts.

How quiet and empty his house was. Cold and dark. He hated coming home to a dark house. He'd thought about getting an animal, but it wouldn't have been fair to the animal since he was hardly ever home. He slammed his briefcase down on the kitchen counter. Damn, he'd forgotten the report on Andrea Evans. Oh, well, it wasn't going anywhere. Tomorrow would be soon enough to retrieve it.

Peter walked around his house, turning on lights as he went from room to room. It didn't look anything like the house he'd grown up in. He leaned against the banister, closing his eyes as he did so. He'd lived in a big, old house full of nooks and crannies in Sleepy Hollow. The rug at the foot of the steps was old, threadbare, and Bessie, their old cocker spaniel had chewed all four corners. She lay on the rug almost all her life to wait for them to come home, pooping on it from time to time as she got older. When she died, his parents had buried her in the backyard under the apple tree. Jesus, he didn't think there was that much grief in the world as that day. He thought about the old hat rack with the boot box underneath where he stored his boots, gloves and other treasures. The hat rack and boot box were

somewhere in the attic along with Bessie's toys and dog
bones. He wondered if they were still intact.

Peter rubbed at his eyes. He'd loved that house with the
worn, comfortable furniture, the green plants his mother
raised, and the warm, fragrant kitchen with its bright colors.
Something was always cooking or baking, and there were
always good things to eat for his friends and himself after
school. The thing he remembered the most, though, was his
mother's smile when he walked in the door. She'd always
say, "Hi, Pete, how's it going?" And he'd say, "Pretty good,
Mom." They always ate in the kitchen. Dinner hour was
long, boisterous and memorable. Even when they had meat-
loaf. He tried not to think about his younger brother and
sister. He had to stop torturing himself like this. He banged
one fist on the banister as he wiped at his eyes with the
other. He looked around. Everything was beautiful, decorated by a professional whose name he didn't know. Once
a week a florist delivered fresh flowers. The only time the
house came alive was during his annual Christmas party or
his Fourth of July barbecue. The rest of the time it was just
a house. The word nurture came to mind. He squeezed his
eyes shut and tried to imagine what this perfectly decorated
house would be like with a wife, kids and a dog. Maybe
two dogs and two cats.

"Five thousand goddamn fucking square feet of *NOTH-
ING.*" He ripped at his tie and jacket, tossing them on the
back of a chair. He kicked his loafers across the room. In
a pique of something he couldn't define, he brushed at a
pile of magazines and watched them sail in different directions. Shit! The room still didn't look lived in. Hell, he
didn't even know his neighbors. He might as well live in a
damn hotel.

On his way back to the kitchen he picked up the portable
phone, asking for information. He punched out the numbers
for the Evans Kennel as his free hand twisted the cap off
a bottle of Budweiser. He wondered if her voice would be

sleepy sounding or hard and cold. He wasn't prepared for
what he did hear when he announced himself.

"I don't have time for chit-chat, Mr. King. I have an
emergency on my hands here and you're taking up my time.
Call me on Monday or don't call me on Monday." Peter
stared at the pinging phone in his hand.

Chit chat. Call or don't call. *Emergency.* Sadie's dire
warnings rang in his ears.

Peter raced up the steps. So there was a sucker born every
minute. Sadie would approve. He stripped down, throwing
his clothes any which way as he searched for thermal
sweats, thick socks and Alpine boots. His shearling jacket,
cap and gloves were downstairs in the hall closet.

Emergency could mean anything. She was handling it.
Oh, yeah, like women could really handle an emergency.
Maybe his mother could handle one, or Sadie, but not that
hundred pound prairie flower. He raced to the garage where
all his old camping gear was stored. Blankets and towels
went into the back of his Range Rover. He threw in two
shovels, his camp stove, lanterns, flashlights. The last things
to go in were Sterno lamps and artificial fire logs. What
the hell, an emergency was an emergency.

It wasn't until he backed the 4 by 4 out of the garage
that he questioned himself. Why was he doing this? Because . . . because . . . he'd heard the same fearful tone in
Dr. Evans' voice that he'd heard in his mother's voice the
day Bessie couldn't get up on her legs anymore.

Driving every back street and alley, over people's lawns,
Peter arrived at the Evans Kennel in over an hour. Every
light appeared to be on in the house and the kennel. There
were no footprints in the snow, so that had to mean the
emergency was inside the house. Even from this distance
he could hear the shrill barking and high-pitched whine of
the animals that seemed to be saying, intruder, intruder.

Peter walked around to the door he'd been ushered out
of just hours ago. His eyebrows shot up to his hairline when

he found it unlocked. He felt silly as hell when he bellowed above the sound of the dogs, "I'm here and coming through!"

In the whole of his life he'd never seen so many teeth in one place—all canines. "You need to lock your goddamn doors is what you need to do, Dr. Evans!" he shouted.

"You!" She made it sound like he was the devil from hell making a grand entrance.

"Who'd you expect, Sylvester Stallone? You said it was an emergency. I react to emergencies. My mother trained me that way. I brought everything. What's wrong?"

Andi, hands on hips, stared at the man standing in front of her, the dogs circling his feet. She clapped her hands once, and they all lay down, their eyes on the giant towering over them.

"I had to do a cesarian section on Rosie. Her pups were coming out breach. Come here. Mother and puppies doing just fine, all eight of them. God, eight more mouths to feed." Andi's shoulders slumped as she fought off her tears.

"I'll take two. Three. I love dogs. It won't be so hard, I'm going to meet your price. Three million plus, whatever the plus turns out to be. It's fair. You'll be able to do a lot if you invest wisely. I can recommend a pretty good tax man if you're interested. You might even want to give some thought to taking payments instead of one lump sum. You need to talk to someone. Am I getting girls or boys? Make that four. I'll give one to my grandmother. That's another thing, her cat Hannah is sick. I was going to call you in the morning to ask if you'd look at her. Their regular vet is away on a winter vacation."

"Oh, my. Listen, about this afternoon . . ."

"You don't have to apologize," Peter said.

Andi smiled. "I wasn't going to apologize. I was going to try and explain my circumstances to you. I appreciate you coming back here. It's the thought that counts. Are you serious about the pups?"

Was he? "Hell yes. Told you, I love dogs. Isn't it kind of cold out here for the new mother and my pups?"

"No. Actually, dogs much prefer it to be cooler. I was going to take Rosie into the kitchen, though. I leave the door open, and if the others want to come in, they do. At some point during the night, when I'm sleeping, three or four of them will come in and sleep outside my door. There's usually one outside the bathroom when I shower, too. They're very protective; they know when you're bathing and sleeping you're vulnerable. It's really amazing."

"Bessie was like that. Do you want me to carry the box?"

"Sure. Can I make you some coffee? I was going to have a grilled cheese sandwich. Would you like one or did you have your dinner?"

Peter thought about how he'd pigged out on his grandmother's pot roast. "I'm starved. Coffee sounds good, too. I brought a lot of blankets and towels with me. I thought maybe your heat went out."

"I could really use them. My washer goes all day long, and like everyone else in this house, it's getting ready to break down. My furnace is the next thing to go."

Peter's face turned ashen. "Your furnace? Don't you check it? You need to call PSE&G to come and look at it. My parents . . . and my brother and sister died from carbon monoxide poisoning. Turn it off if it's giving you trouble. Use your fireplace. I can bring you electric heaters. Is the fireplace any good?"

Andi stared at the man sitting at her table, a helpless look on her face. "I . . . I 'm sorry. I don't know the first thing about the furnace except that it's very old. The fireplace is in good condition; I had it cleaned in September. I'd probably be more at risk using electric heaters; the wiring and the plumbing are . . . old. I guess I just have to take my chances. It's only another two weeks. You said you wanted to . . . start . . . whatever it is you're going to do right after the first of the year."

"Tomorrow when I bring Hannah I'll bring you some of those detectors. I have one in every room in my house. I was away at school when it happened. All you do is plug them in."

"I appreciate that. I won't charge you for Hannah, then."

"Okay, that's fair." He wasn't about to tell her each detector cost eighty-nine dollars. She would need at least four of them for the sprawling house and kennel.

Want some bacon on your sandwich? Ketchup?"

"Sure."

"I made a pie today. Want a piece?"

Peter nodded. "Your house smells like the house I grew up in. It always smelled like apples and cinnamon. At Christmastime you could get drunk on the smell. Speaking of Christmas, I give a party once a year, would you like to come? I think you'll like my grandmother. It's next Thursday."

"I don't know . . . I hate to leave the animals. I haven't been to a party in so long, I don't think I'll remember how to act. Thank you for asking, though."

"Don't you have a pair of pearls?" he asked, a stupid look on his face.

"What do pearls have to do with it?"

"Your mother's pearls." Jesus, he must have missed something when Sadie was explaining party attire. She was staring at him so intently he felt compelled to explain. "You know, pearls to go with the dress. Your mother's pearls. If you have that, you don't have to worry about anything else. Right? Can I use your bathroom?"

"Upstairs, third door on the right. Don't step on the carpet at the bottom of the steps. Annabelle lies there all the time. She pees on it and I didn't have time to wash it. She chewed all the fringe off the corners. She's getting old, so I can't scold her too much."

Peter bolted from the room. Andi stared after him with puzzled eyes. She scurried into the pantry area where a mirror hung on the back of the door. She winced at her appearance. She didn't look one damn bit better than she had looked earlier. "What you see is what you get," she muttered.

Andi was sliding the sandwiches onto plates when Peter entered the room. "This must have been a nice house at one time."

Andi nodded. "It was a comfortable old house. It fit us. My mother never worried too much about new furniture or keeping up with the neighbors. It was clean and comfortable. Homey. Some houses are just houses. People make homes. Did you know that?"

"Believe it or not, I just realized that same fact today. Every so often I trip down memory lane."

"I don't do that anymore. It's too sad. I don't know how I'm going to walk away from this place. My mother always said home was where your stuff was. Part of me believes it. What's your opinion? By the way, where do you live?"

"In Clark. It's a new, modern house. Decorated by a professional. Color-coordinated, all that stuff. I don't think you'd like it. My grandmother hates it. I don't even like it myself. I try throwing things around, but it still looks the same."

"Maybe some green plants. Green plants perk up a room. You probably need some junk. Junk helps. I'll be throwing a lot away, so you can help yourself."

"Yeah? What kind of junk? My plants die."

"You need to water plants. Get silk ones. All you have to do is go over them with a blow dryer every so often. Junk is junk. Everybody has junk. You pick it up here and there, at a flea market or wherever. When you get tired of it you throw it away and buy new junk."

Peter threw his head back and laughed until his eyes watered. "That's something my grandmother would say. Why are you looking at me like that?"

"I'm sorry. You should laugh more often. You take your-self pretty seriously, don't you?"

"For the most part, I guess I do. What about you?" He leaned across the table as though her answer was the most important thing in the world. She had beautiful eyes with thick lashes. And they were her own, unlike Helen's.

"I've been so busy scrambling to make a go of it, I haven't had the time to dwell on anything. I guess I'm sort of an optimist, but then I'm a pessimist, too, at times. What will be will be. How about some pie? I can warm it up. More coffee?"

"Sure to everything. This is nice. I haven't sat in a kitchen . . . since . . . I left home. We always ate in the kitchen growing up."

"So did we. Are you married?"

"No. Why do you ask? Do you have designs on me?"

"No. I just want to make sure Rosie's pups get a good home. Who's going to take care of them when you work?"

"I already figured that out. I'm going to hire a sitter. I'll have her cook chicken gizzards and livers for them. My mother used to cook for Bessie. She loved it. You're very pretty, Dr. Evans. Why aren't you married?"

"Do you think that's any of your business, Mr. King?"

"As the owner of those dogs of which I'm taking four, I should know what kind of person you are, marital status included. Well?"

"I was engaged, not that it's any of your business. I wanted to come back here; he didn't. He wanted to work in a ritzy area; I didn't. He was in it for the money. I wasn't. I don't know, maybe he was the smart one."

"No, you were the smart one," Peter said quietly. "It's rare that the heart and mind work in sync. When it does happen, you know it's right."

"Your turn."

Peter shrugged. "I run my grandmother's business. She tells me I'm good at it. She's the only family I have left, and she's up in years. I always . . . take . . . introduce her to the women I, ah, date. I value her opinion. So far she hasn't approved of anyone I've dated. That's okay; she was on the money every single time. Guess I just haven't met the right girl. Or, maybe I'm meant for bachelorhood. Would you like to go out to dinner with me to celebrate our deal?"

"Under other circumstances, I'd say yes, but I have too much to do. I also want to keep my eye on Rosie and the pups. If you like, you can come for dinner tomorrow."

"I'll be here. I'll bring in the towels and blankets and shovel you out before I leave."

"I'll help you. Thanks."

It was one o'clock in the morning when Andi leaned on her shovel, exhaustion showing in every line of her face. "I'm going to sleep like a baby tonight," she panted.

"Yeah, me, too. Tell me, what's it like when you operate on one of the animals, like you did tonight?"

"Awesome. When I saw those pups and when I stitched up Rosie, all the hard years, all the back-breaking work, it was worth every hour of it. Guess you don't get that feeling when you label Raspberry Cheese Louise on your lipsticks."

Suddenly she was in the snow, the giant towering over her. She stretched out her foot, caught him on the ankle and pulled him down in an undignified heap. He kissed her, his mouth as cold and frosty as her own. It was the sweetest kiss of her life. She said so, grinning from ear to ear.

"Sweet?" he asked.

"Uh huh?"

"Didn't make you want to tear your clothes off, huh?"

"You must be kidding? I never do that on a first date."

"This isn't a date." He leered at her.

"I don't do that on pre-dates either. I don't even know you."

"I'll let my hair down tomorrow, and you can *really* get to know me."

"Don't go getting any ideas that I'm easy. And, don't think you're parading me in front of your grandmother either."

"God forbid."

"Good night, Mr. King. You can call me Andi."

"Good night, Dr. Evans. You can call me Peter. What are we having for dinner?"

"Whatever you bring. Tomorrow is bath day. I'm big on fast and easy. What time are you bringing Hannah?"

"How about ten? Our attorney will be out bright and early for you to sign the contract. Is that all right with you?"

"Okay. Good night?"

"I enjoyed this evening. Take good care of my dogs."

"I will." Suddenly she didn't want him to go. He didn't seem to want to go either. She watched the 4 by 4 until the red taillights were swallowed in the snow.

He was nice. Actually, he was real nice. And, he was going to give her over three million dollars. Oh, life was looking good.

The following morning, Andi woke before it was light out. She threw on her robe and raced down the stairs to check on Rosie. "I just want you to know I was having a really, that's as in really, delicious dream about Mr. Peter King." She hunched down to check on the new pups, who were sleeping peacefully, curled up against their mother.

While the coffee perked, Andi showered and dressed, taking a few more pains with her dress than usual. Today she donned corduroy slacks and a flannel shirt instead of the fleece-lined sweats she usually wore in the kennel. Today she even blow dried her hair and used the curling iron. She diddled with a jar of makeup guaranteed to confuse anyone interested in wondering if she was wearing it or not. A dab of rouge, a stroke of the eyebrow pencil and she was done. She was almost at the top of the steps when she marched back to her dressing table and spritzed a cloud of mist into the air. She savored the smell, a long-ago present from a friend. She told herself she took the extra pains because it wasn't every day she signed a three million plus deal. As she drank her coffee she wondered what the plus part of the contract would net her.

Andi thought about Gertie and her friends under the railroad trestle. Where did they go last night during the storm? Were they warm and safe? As soon as everything was tended to and she checked out Hannah the cat, she would drive into Plainfield and try to locate Gertie and her friends. Now that she had all this money coming to her, she could rent a motel for them until the weather eased up, providing the manager was willing to wait for his money.

The notebook on the kitchen table beckoned. Her list of things to do. Call Realtor, make plans to transport animals. Her friend Mickey had an old school bus he used for camping in the summer. He might lend it to her for a day or so. She could pile Gertie and her friends in the same bus.

Andi's thoughts whirled and raced as she cleaned the dog runs and hosed them out. She set down bowls of kibble and fresh water, tidied up the kennel, sorted through the blankets and towels. The heavy duty machines ran constantly. Her own laundry often piled up for weeks at a time simply because the animals had to come first. She raced back to the kitchen to add a note to her list. Call moving company. She wasn't parting with the crates, the laundry machines or the refrigerator. She was taking everything that belonged to her parents even if it was old and worn-out. The wrecking ball could destroy the house and kennel, but not her *stuff*.

She was on her third cup of coffee when Peter King's attorney arrived. She read over the contract, signed it and promised to take it to her attorney, Mark Fox. Everything was in order. Why delay on signing. The plus, she noticed, amounted to $750,000. That had to mean she had three and three-quarter acres. "Date the check January first. I don't want to have to worry about paying taxes until ninety-seven. Where's the date for construction to begin? Oh, okay, I see it. January 2, 1997. We're clear on that?"

"Yes, Dr. Evans, we're clear on that. Here's my card; have Mr. Fox call me. Mark is the finest real estate attorney in these parts. Give him my regards."

"I'll do that, Mr. Carpenter."

The moment the attorney was out of her parking lot, Andi added Mark Fox's name to her list of things to do. She crossed her fingers that he worked half days on Saturday. If not, she'd slip the contract, along with a note, through the mail slot and call him Monday morning.

Andi's eyes settled on the clock. Ten minutes until Peter King arrived with his grandmother's cat. She busied herself with phone calls. Ten o'clock came and went. The hands of the clock swept past eleven. Were the roads bad? She called the police station. She was told the roads were in good shape, plowed and sanded. Her eyes were wet when she crouched down next to Rosie. "Guess he just wanted my signature on the contract. My mother always said there was a fool born every minute. Take care of those babies and I'll be back soon."

At ten minutes past twelve, Andi was on Park Avenue, where she dropped the contract through the slot on Mark Fox's door. She backed out of the drive and headed down Park to Raritan and then to Woodland, turning right onto South Avenue, where she thought she would find Gertie and her friends. She saw one lone figure, heavily clad, hunched around a huge barrel that glowed red and warm against the snow-filled landscape. Andi climbed from the truck. "Excuse me, sir, have you seen Gertie?" The man shook his head. "Do you know where I can find her? Where is everyone?" The man shrugged. "I need to get in touch with her. It's very important. If she comes by, will you ask

her to call me? I'll give you the quarter for the phone call."
She ran back to the truck to fish in the glove compartment
for her card, where she scrawled, "Call me. Andi." She
handed the card, a quarter and a five-dollar bill to the man.
"Get some hot soup and coffee." The man's head bobbed
up and down.

Her next stop was Raritan Road and her friend Mickey's
house. The yellow bus was parked in his driveway next to
a spiffy hunter green BMW.

Mickey was a free spirit, working only when the mood
struck him. Thanks to a sizable trust fund, all things were
possible for the young man whose slogan was, "Work Is A
Killer." She slipped a note under the door when her ring
went unanswered. Her watch said it was one-thirty. Time to
head for the moving company, where she signed another
contract for her belongings to be moved out on December
22nd and taken to storage on Oak Tree Road in Edison.
Her last stop was in Metuchen, where she stopped at the
MacPherson Agency to ask for either Lois or Tom Finneran,
a husband/wife realty team. The amenities over, she said,
"Some acreage, a building is a must. It doesn't have to be
fancy. I'm going to build what I want later on. Zoning is
important. I was thinking maybe Freehold or Cranbur. You
guys are the best, so I know you can work something out
that will allow me to move in with the animals the first of
the year. Have a wonderful holiday."

There were no fresh tire tracks in her driveway and no
messages on her machine. "So who cares," she muttered
as she stomped her way into the kennel. The kitchen clock
said it was three-thirty when she put a pot of coffee on to
perk. When the phone shrilled to life she dropped the wire
basket full of coffee all over the floor. She almost killed
herself as she sprinted across the huge kitchen to grapple
with the receiver. Her voice was breathless when she said,
"Dr. Evans."

"Andi, this is Gertie. Donald said you were looking for me. Is something wrong?"

"Everything's wrong and everything's right. I was worried about you and your friends out in the cold. I wanted to bring you back here till the weather clears. I signed the contract this morning. For a lot of money. Oh, Gertie, what I can do with that money. You and your friends can come live on my property. I'll build you a little house or a big house. You won't have to live on the street, and you won't get mugged anymore. You can all help with the animals, and I'll even pay you. I'll be able to take in more animals. Oh, God, Gertie, I almost forgot, Rosie had eight puppies. They are so beautiful. You're going to love them. You're quiet, is something wrong?"

"No. I don't want you worrying about me and my friends. I'll tell them about your offer, though. I'll think about it myself. How was . . . that man?"

"Mr. King?"

"Yeah, him."

Last night I thought he was kind of nice. He came back out here later in the evening and shoveled my parking lot. He was starved, so I gave him a sandwich and we talked. I invited him to dinner tonight. He was supposed to bring his grandmother's cat for me to check and he was a no show. I even let him kiss me after he pushed me in the snow. You know what, Gertie, I hate men. There's not one you can trust. All he wanted was my signature on that contract. He had this really nice laugh. We shared a few memories. As far as I can tell the only redeeming quality he has is that he loves his grandmother. Oh, oh, the other thing was he was going to bring me some carbon monoxide things to plug in. He was so forceful I agreed and said I wouldn't charge for Hannah. That's the cat's name. He even invited me to his Christmas party, but he never even told me where he lived. Some invitation, huh? I should show him and turn up in my rubber suit. He acted like he thought I didn't know how to dress and kept mumbling about my mother's pearls. You're still coming for Christmas, aren't you? You said you'd bring all your buddies from the trestle. Gertie, I don't want to spend my last Christmas alone here in this house with just the animals. If they could talk, it would be different. Promise me, okay?"

"I can't promise. I will think about it, though. Why don't you hold those negative thoughts you have for Mr. King on the side. I bet he has a real good explanation."

Andi snorted. "Give me one. Just one. The roads are clear. Alexander Bell invented this wonderful thing called the telephone, and Mr. Sony has this machine that delivers your messages. Nope, the jerk just wanted my signature. I'll never see him again and I don't care. Do you want me to come and get you, Gertie? It's supposed to be really cold tonight."

"We're going to the shelter tonight. Thanks for the offer. Maybe I'll stop by tomorrow. Are the pups really cute?"

"Gorgeous. That's another thing; he said he was taking four, three for him and one for his grandmother. On top of everything else, the man is a liar. I hate liars as much as I hate used car salesmen. You sound funny, Gertie, are you sure you're all right?"

"I'm fine. Maybe I'm catching a cold."

"Now, why doesn't that surprise me? You live on the damn streets. I'll bet you don't even have any aspirin."

"I do so, and Donald has some brandy. I'll talk to you tomorrow, Andi. Thanks for caring about me and my friends. Give Rosie a hug for me."

"Okay, Gertie, take care of yourself."

Andi turned to Rosie, who was staring at her. "Gertie was crying. She's not catching a cold. She's the one who is homeless, and she's the one who always comes through for us. Always. I can't figure that out. She's homeless and she won't let me do anything for her. I hope somebody writes a book about that someday. Okay, bath time!"

Andi ate a lonely TV dinner and some tomato soup as she watched television. She was in bed by nine o'clock. She wanted to be up early so she could begin going through the attic and packing the things she wanted to take to storage. If her pillow was damp, there was no one to notice.

Less than ten miles away, Peter King sat on the sofa with his grandmother, trying his best to console her. He felt frightened for the first time in his life. His zesty grandmother was falling apart, unable to stop crying. "I thought she would live forever. I really did. My God, Peter, how I loved that animal. I want her ashes. Every single one of them. You told them to do that, didn't you?"

"Of course I did, Sadie. I'm going to bring them by tomorrow. Do you want—"

"Do not touch anything, Peter. I want all her things left just the way they were. I wish I'd spent more time with her, cuddled her more. Sometimes she didn't want that; she wanted to be alone. She was so damn independent. Oh, God, what am I going to do without Hannah? She kept me going."

"It can't be any worse than when Bessie died. I still think about that," Peter said past the lump in his throat.

"She just died in her sleep and I was sleeping so soundly last night. What if she needed me and I didn't hear her?"

"Shhhh, she just closed her eyes and drifted off. That's how you have to think of it."

"Don't even think about getting me another cat. I won't have it, Peter. Are you listening to me?"

"I always listen to you, Sadie."

"Did you call Dr. Evans?"

"No. She'll understand. She loves animals. She's nice, Sadie. I really liked her. She forced a sandwich on me and I ate it to be polite. I shoveled her parking lot and pushed her in the snow." At Sadie's blank stare, his voice grew desperate. "I kissed her, Sadie, and she said it was a sweet kiss. Sweet! It's too soon to tell, but I think she might be *the one*. Did you hear me, Sadie?"

"I'm not deaf."

"I invited her to the party, but she doesn't want to come. I screwed up the pearl thing. She thought I was nuts." Sadie's eyes rolled back in her head. "Okay," Peter roared, "that's enough, Sadie, pets die every day of the week. People and children grieve, but they don't go over the edge. You're teetering and I won't have it."

Sadie blinked. "Oh, stuff it, Peter. This is me you're talking to. I need to do this for one day for God's sake. Tomorrow I'll be fine. Why can't I cry, moan and wail? Give me one damn good reason why I can't. I just want to sit here and snivel. You need to make amends to that young veterinarian, and don't go blaming me. I didn't ask you to stay here with me. You didn't even like Hannah and she hated you. Hannah hated all men. I never did figure that out. Go home, Peter. I'm fine, and I do appreciate you coming here and staying with me. It might be wise to send the young lady an invitation. I'd FedEx it if I were you."

"Do you want me to call that guy Donald you're always talking about?"

"Of course not. He's . . . out and about . . . and very hard to reach."

"Why don't you get him a beeper for Christmas."

"Go!"

"I'm gone."

Peter had every intention of going home, but his car seemed to have a mind of its own. Before he knew it he was on the road leading into the driveway of Andi's clinic. What the hell time was it anyway? Ten minutes past ten. It was so quiet and dark he felt uneasy. Only a dim light inside the clinic could be seen from the road. The rest of the house was in total darkness. If he got out to leave a note, the animals would start to bark and Andi would wake up. Did he want that? Of course not, his mother had raised him to be a gentleman. He felt an emptiness in the pit of his stomach as he drove away. He couldn't ever remember being this lonely in his entire life. Tomorrow was another day. He'd call her as soon as the sun came up, and maybe they could go sleigh riding in Roosevelt Park. Maybe it was time to act like kids again. Kids who fell in love when they were done doing all those wonderful kid things. One day out of their lives, and it was a Sunday. Just one day of no responsibilities. He crossed his fingers that it would work out the way he wanted.

Andi rolled over, opening one eye to look at the clock on her nightstand. Six o'clock. How still and quiet it was. Did she dare stay in bed? Absolutely not. She walked over to the window and raised the shade. It was snowing. Damn, her back was still sore. Maybe she could call one of the companies that plowed out small businesses.

She was brushing her teeth when the phone rang. Around the bubbles and foam in her mouth, she managed to say, "Dr. Evans."

"This is Peter King. I'm calling to apologize and to invite you to go sleigh riding. Hannah died in her sleep. I spent the day with my grandmother. I'm really sorry. Are you there?"

Wait." Andi rushed into the bathroom to rinse her mouth. She sprinted back to the phone. "I was brushing my teeth."

"Oh."

"You should have called me. It only takes a minute to make a phone call." Hot damn, he had a reason. Maybe . . .

"I came by last night around ten; but everything was dark, and I didn't want to stir up the animals so I went home."

He came by. That was good. He said he was sorry. He was considerate. "I went to bed early. It's snowing."

"I know. Let's go sledding in Roosevelt Park. My parents used to take me there when I was a kid. I have a Flexible Flyer." He made it sound like he had the Holy Grail.

"No kidding. I have one, too. Somewhere. Probably up on the rafters in the garage."

"Does that mean you'll go? We could go to the Pancake House on Parsonage Road for breakfast."

"Will you pull me up the hill?"

"Nope."

"I hate climbing the hill. Going down is so quick. Okay, I'll go, but I have things to do first. How about eleven o'clock?"

"That's good. What do you have to do? Do you need help?"

This was looking better and better. "Well, I have to clean the dog runs and change the litter boxes. I was going to go through the things in the attic. You could see if you can locate someone to plow my parking lot and driveway. Don't even think about offering. I know your back is as sore as mine, and my legs are going to be stiff if we climb that hill more than once. It's going to take me at least two hours to find my rubber boots. Is your grandmother all right? I have some kittens if you're interested."

"It was a real bad day. She doesn't want another cat. Hannah is being cremated so she'll have the ashes. She'll be okay today. Sadie is real gutsy. I know she'll love it when I give her one of Rosie's pups. She'll accept the dog but not a cat. I understand that."

"Yes, so do I."

"What did you have for supper last night? I'm sorry about standing you up. I mean that."

"Tomato soup, a TV dinner and a stale donut. If you do it again, it's all over." She was flirting. God.

She was flirting with him. Peter felt his chest puff out. "Bundle up."

"Okay. See you later."

"You bet. Don't get your sled down; I'll do that."

"Okay." A gentleman. Hmmnn.

Peter kicked the tire of his Range Rover, every curse known to man spitting through his lips. How could a $50,000-year-old truck have a dead battery? He looked at his watch and then at the elegant Mercedes Benz sitting next to it. The perfect vehicle to go sledding. "Damn it to hell!" he muttered.

He was stomping through the house looking for his keys when the doorbell rang. Expecting to see the paperboy, he opened the door, his hand in his pants pocket looking for money. "Helen!"

"Peter! I brought breakfast," she said, dangling a Dunkin Donuts bag under his nose, "and the *New York Times*. I thought we could curl up in front of a fire and spend a lazy day. Together."

He wanted to push her through the door, to slap the donut bag out of her hand and scatter the paper all over the lawn. What did he ever see in this heavily made up woman whose eyelashes were so long they couldn't be real. "I think one of your eyelashes is coming off. Sorry, Helen, I have other plans. I'm going sledding."

"Sledding! At your age!" She made it sound like he was going to hell on a sled.

"Yeah," he drawled. "Your other eyelash is . . . loose. Well, see you around."

"Peterrrrr," she cried as he closed the door.

He was grinning from ear to ear as he searched the living room, dining room and foyer for his keys. He finally found them on the kitchen counter right where he'd left them last night. She really did wear false eyelashes like Sadie said. He laughed aloud when he remembered the open-toed shoes she had on. "My crazy days," he muttered as he closed the kitchen door behind him.

In the car, backing out of the driveway, he realized his heart was pounding. Certainly not because of Helen. He was going to spend the whole day with Andrea Evans doing kid things. He was so excited he pressed the power button on his car phone and then the number one, which was Sadie's number. When he heard her voice he said, "Want to go sled riding? I'll pull you up the hill. I'm taking Dr. Evans. You won't believe this, but she has a Flexible Flyer, too. So, do you want to come?"

"I think I'll pass and watch a football game. Don't forget to bring Hannah's ashes. I don't want to spend another night without her. I don't care, Peter, if you think I'm crazy. Be sure you don't break your neck. Are you aware that it's snowing outside? I thought people went sled riding when it *stopped* snowing."

"I don't think you're crazy at all. I know it's snowing. I think there's at least three inches of fresh snow. You know how you love a white Christmas. I'll be sure not to break my neck, and I think you can go sledding whenever you want. Mr. Mortimer said I could pick up the ashes after five this afternoon. I'll see you sometime this evening."

"Peter, does this mean you're . . . interested in Dr. Evans?"

"She's a real person, Sadie. Helen stopped by as I was leaving—I'm talking to you on the car phone—and she had open-toed shoes on, and both her eyelashes were loose at the ends. How could I not have seen those things, Sadie?"

"Because you weren't looking, Peter. Do you think Dr. Evans is interested in you?"

"She agreed to go sledding. She wasn't even mad about yesterday. I like her, Sadie. A lot."

"I love June weddings. Six months, Peter. You have to commit by six months or cut her loose. Women her age don't need some jerk taking up their time if you aren't serious."

"How do you know her age?"

"Well . . . I don't, but you said she put herself through vet school and the whole education process took ten years. That should put her around thirty or so."

"I don't remember telling you that."

"That's because you were rattled over Helen. It's all right, Peter, I get forgetful, too, sometimes. Now, go and have a wonderful time."

Peter pressed the end and power buttons. He decided his grandmother was defensive sounding because of Hannah. He wished the next eight weeks were over so he could present her with one of Rosie's pups.

Peter was so deep in thought he almost missed the turnoff to the Evans Kennel. He jammed on his brakes, the back end of his car fishtailing across the road. He took a deep breath, cursing the fancy car again. Shaken, he crawled into the parking lot and parked the car. He wondered again if the Chevy pickup actually worked.

"I saw that," Andi trilled. "It's a good thing there was no one behind you. Where's your truck?"

"Dead battery."

"We can take my truck. It's in tip-top shape. Turns over every time. No matter what the weather is. It was my dad's prized possession. The heater works fine and we can put our sleds in the back." Andi dangled a set of car keys in front of him. She was laughing at him, and he didn't mind one damn bit. "Those boots have to go. When was the last time you went sled riding?"

"Light years ago. These boots are guaranteed to last a lifetime."

"Perhaps they will. The question is, will they keep your feet dry? The answer is no. I can loan you my father's Wellingtons. Will you be embarrassed to wear yellow boots?"

"Never!" Peter said dramatically. "Does the rest of me meet with your approval?"

Andi tilted her head to the side. Ski cap, muffler,

gloves . . . well, those gloves aren't going to do anything for your hands. Don't you have ski gloves?"

"I did, but I couldn't find them. Do you have extras?"

"Right inside the yellow boots. I figured you for a leather man. I'm a mitten girl. I still have the mittens my mother knitted for me when I was a kid. They still fit, too. When you go sled riding you need a pair and a spare. I bet you didn't wax the runners on your sled either."

"I did so!"

"Prove it." Andi grinned.

"All right, I didn't. It was all I could do to get the cobwebs off."

"Come on," Andi said, dragging him by the arm into the garage. Neither noticed a sleek, amber-colored Mercury Sable crawl by, the driver craning her neck for a better look into the parking lot.

"Here's the boots. They should fit. I'm bringing extra thermal socks for both of us, extra gloves and mittens. There's nothing worse than cold hands and feet. I lived for one whole winter in Minnesota without central heat. All I had was a wood-burning fireplace."

"Why?"

"It was all I could afford. I survived. Do they fit?"

"Perfectly. You should be very proud of yourself, Andi."

"I am. My parents weren't rich like yours. Dad wasn't a businessman. There's so much money on the books that was never paid. He never sent out bills or notices. I'm kind of like him, I guess."

"My parents weren't rich. My grandmother is the one with the money. My dad was a draftsman; my mother was a nurse. You're right, though; I never had to struggle. Did it make you a better person?"

"I like to think so. When you're cold and hungry, character doesn't seem important. You are what you are. Hard times just bring out the best and worst in a person. Okay, your runners are ready for a test run."

"Do you ski?"

"Ha! That's a rich person's sport. No. I'm ready."

"Me, too," Peter said, clomping along behind her.

"You look good in yellow," Andi giggled.

"My favorite color," Peter quipped.

"That's what my mother said when she presented my father with those boots. The second thing she said was they'll never wear out. My dad wore them proudly. How's your grandmother today?"

"Better. I promised to stop by this evening with Hannah's ashes. My grandmother is a very strong woman. She started King Cosmetics in her kitchen years ago after my grandfather died. I'd like you to meet her."

"I'd like that. Do you want to drive or shall I?"

"I'll drive. Sleds in the back," he said, tossing in both Flexible Flyers.

An hour later they were hurtling down the hill, whooping and hollering, their laughter ringing in the swirling snow.

On the second trek up the hill, Peter said, "Have you noticed we're practically the only two people here except for those three kids who are using pieces of cardboard to slide down the hill?"

"That's because we're crazy. Cardboard's good, so is a shower curtain. You can really get some speed with a shower curtain. A bunch of us used to do that in Minnesota."

Peter clenched his fists tightly as he felt a wave of jealousy river through him. He wanted to slide down a hill on a shower curtain with Andi, not some other guy, and he knew it was a guy on the shower curtain next to Andi. He asked.

"Yeah." He waited for her to elaborate, but she didn't.

"Hey, mister, do you want to trade?"

Peter looked at Andi, and she looked at him. "The cardboard is big enough for both of us to sit on. Wanna give it a shot?" he asked.

"Sure. You sit in the front, though, in case we hit a tree."

"Okay, kid." He accepted their offer, then turned to Andi. "Did you notice they waited till we dragged these sleds to the top of the hill," Peter hissed.

"I don't blame them. I think this is my last run. My legs feel numb."

"Sissy," Peter teased. "Cardboard's easy to drag. We've only been here two hours."

"It seems like forever," Andi said. "I can't feel my feet anymore. How about you?"

"Hey, mister, where'd you get them yellow boots?" one of the kids asked.

"Macy's. Neat, huh?"

"They look shitty," the kid said.

"That, too. You kids go first and we'll follow."

"Nah, you go first. You might fall off and we'll stop and pick you up. You might break a leg or something. You're *old.*"

Peter settled himself on the slice of cardboard that said Charmin Tissue. "Hang on, Andi, and sit up straight."

They were off. Andi shrieked and Peter bellowed as they sailed down the steep hill. Midway down, the cardboard slid out from under them. They toppled into the snow, rolling the rest of the way down the hill. The kids on the sleds passed them, waving and shouting wildly. Andi rolled up against Peter, breathless, her entire body covered in snow.

"Now *that* was an experience," Peter gasped as he reached for Andi's arm to make sure she was all right.

"I feel like I'm dead. Are we?"

"No. Those little shits are taking off with our sleds!" Peter gasped again.

"Who cares. I couldn't chase them if my life depended on it. Every kid needs a sled. Let them have them."

"Okay. Are you all right?"

"No. I hurt. This wasn't as much fun as I thought it would be. God, I must be getting old. My eyebrows are frozen to my head. They crunch. Do yours?"

"Yep. C'mon, lets get in the truck and go home. The first

run was fun. We should have quit after that." He was on his feet, his hand outstretched to pull Andi to her feet. "Ah, I bet if I kissed your eyebrows they'd melt."

"Never mind my damn eyebrows, kiss my mouth, it's frozen."

"Hmmmnn. Aaahhh, oh, yes," Andi said later.

"Was that *sweet?* I have a kiss that's a real wake-up call."

"Oh, no, that one . . . sizzled. Let's try it out," Andi said.

"Oh, look, they're kissing. Yuk. Here's your sleds, Mister."

"I thought you stole those sleds. Your timing is incredible. Go away, you can have the sleds."

"My mother ain't never gonna believe you gave us these sleds. You gotta write us a note and sign your name."

"Do what he says." Andi giggled as she headed for the truck, and Peter hastily penned a note.

"Guess you're gonna have to wait for my wake-up call," he said when he caught up to her.

"How long?"

Peter threw his hands in the air. "I have all the time in the world. You just let me know when you're ready."

"Uh huh. Okay. That sounds good. I had a good time today, Peter, I really did. I felt like a kid for a little while. Thanks. Time to get back to reality and the business at hand."

"How about if I drop you off, go pick up Hannah's ashes, take them to my grandmother and come back. We can have dinner together. I can pick up some steaks and stuff. I want to get those carbon monoxide units for you, too."

"Sounds good."

"It's a date, then?"

"Yep, it's a date."

"I'll see you around seven-thirty."

Inside the kennel the animals greeted their owner with sharp barks and soft whines, each vying for her attention. She sat down on the floor and did her best to fondle each one of them. "I smell worse than you guys when you get wet," she said, shrugging out of her wet clothes. "Supper's coming up!"

With the door closed to the outside waiting room, Andi paid no mind to the excessive barking and whining from the animals; her thoughts were on Peter King and spending the night with him. She had at least two hours, once the animals were fed, to shower and change into something a little more *romantic*.

Outside, Helen Palmer watched the dinner preparations through the front window. When she was certain no one else was in attendance, her eyes narrowed. She walked back to the office, a manila folder in hand, the detective's report on one Dr. Andrea Evans that she'd taken from Peter King's car when she backtracked from Roosevelt Park where she'd spied on her old lover.

She eyed the messy desk with the pile of bills. On tiptoe, she walked around the back of the desk to stare down at the piles of bills. With one long, polished nail, she moved the contract to the side so she could see it better. Three million, seven hundred and fifty thousand dollars! For this dump! She tiptoed back to the door and let herself out. Miss Girl Next Door would know there was no manila envelope on the desk. Better to drop it outside where Peter's car had been parked. "She'll think it fell out when he got out of the car. Perfect!" she muttered.

Her feet numb with cold, Helen walked out of the driveway to her car parked on the shoulder of the road in snow up to her ankles. She'd probably get pneumonia and all of this would be for naught. One way or another she was going to get Peter King for herself.

Inside the house, Andi climbed the stairs to the second floor to run a bath. She poured lavishly from a plastic bag filled with gardenia bath salts. It was the only thing she consistently splurged on. She tried to relax, but the dogs' incessant barking set her nerves on edge. What in the world was wrong with them today? Maybe they were picking up on her own tenseness in regard to Peter King. And she was tense.

"I hardly know the man and here I sit speculating on what it would be like to go to bed with him." The bathtub was the perfect forum for talking to herself. She loved this time of day when she went over her problems, asked questions of herself aloud and then answered them in the same manner. She wondered aloud about what kind of bed partner he would make. "Shy? No way. Lusty? To a degree. Wild and passionate? I can only hope. Slap bam, thank you, ma'am? Not in a million years. A man with slow hands like the Pointer Sisters sang about. Oh, yeahhhhh."

Puckered, hyped and red-skinned, Andi climbed from the tub, towel dried and dressed. She fluffed out her hair, added makeup sparingly. The gardenia scent stayed with her.

Andi eyed the bed. When was the last time she changed the sheets? She couldn't remember. She had the bed stripped and changed inside of eight minutes. "Just in case."

Downstairs the dogs milled around inside the house, running back and forth to the waiting room and her tiny office area. Susy, a long-haired, fat, black cat, hissed and snarled by the door, her claws gouging at the wood. "Okay, okay, I get the message, something's wrong. Let's do one spin around the parking lot. When I blow this whistle, everyone lines up and comes indoors. Allow me to demonstrate." She blew three short blasts. "Everybody line up! That's the drill. If you don't follow my instructions, you're out for the night. Let's go!" She stood to the side as the dogs and cats stampeded past her. She'd done this before, and it always worked because Beggin Strips were the reward when everyone was indoors. She waited ten minutes, time for everyone to lift their leg or squat, depending on gender. The floodlights blazed down in the parking lot, creating shimmering crystals on the piled-high snow. Now it was speckled with yellow spots in every direction.

Andi blew three sharp blasts on the whistle as she stepped aside. One by one, the animals fell into a neat line and marched to the door. "C'mon Annabelle, you can do it!" Andi called encouragingly. "You can't sit down in the middle of the parking lot. All right, all right, I'll carry you. Move it, Bizzy," she said to a cat with two tails. The cat strolled past her disdainfully. Andi gave one last blast on the whistle for any stragglers. Satisfied that all the animals were indoors, she walked over to Annabelle to pick her up. She noticed the folder then and picked it up. She stuck it under her arm as she bent to pick up the beagle. "I swear, Annabelle, you weigh a ton."

Inside, she did one last head count before she doled out the treats, the folder still under her arm. "My time now!"

Andi did her best not to look at the clock as she set the table and layered tin foil on the ancient broiler. Candles? No, that would be too much. Wineglasses? She looked with disgust at the dust on the crystal. How was it possible that she'd been here almost a year and a half and hadn't used the glasses, much less washed them? That was going to change now. The wineglasses were special, and there were only two of them. She remembered the day her father had presented the Tiffany glasses to her mother and said, "When we have something special to celebrate we'll use these glasses." To her knowledge, nothing special had ever occurred. Well, tonight was special. She liked the way they sparkled under the domed kitchen light. Peter probably used glasses like this to gargle with every day.

He was late. Again. Her insides started to jump around. What should she do now to kill time? What if he didn't show up? "Oh, shit," she muttered. No point in letting him think she was sitting here biting her nails waiting for him. Only desperate women did things like that. In the blink of an eye she had the dishes back in the cabinet and the wineglasses in their felt sacks with the gold drawstrings. She refolded the tablecloth and stuck it in the drawer. She eyed the manila folder as she slid the drawer closed. It must have fallen out of Peter's car because it wasn't hers and no one else had been at the kennel today.

Eight o'clock.

Andi moved the folder. She moved it a second time, then a third time. She watched it teeter on the edge of the kitchen counter. She brushed by it as it slid to the floor. Now she'd have to pick up the papers and put them back in the folder. When she saw her name in heavy black letters on the first page, she sucked in her breath. Her heart started to pound in her chest as she gathered up the seven-page report. Twenty minutes later, after reading the report three times, Andi stacked the papers neatly in the folder. From the kitchen drawer she ripped off a long piece of gray electrical tape. She taped it to the folder and plastered it on the door of the clinic. She locked the doors and slid the deadbolt into place. She turned off all the lights from the top of the steps. Only a dim hall light glowed in the house.

She made her way to the attic. The small window under the eaves was the perfect place to watch the parking lot. Sneaky bastard. The report chronicled her life, right down to her bank balance, her student aid, her credit report, and her relationships with men. Her cheeks flamed when she remembered one incident where her landlady said Tyler Mitchel arrived early in the evening and didn't leave for three days. The line in bold letters that said "THE LADY USES A DIAPHRAGM" was what sent her flying to the attic. That could only mean someone had been here in her house going through her things. Unless Tyler or Jack or maybe Stan volunteered the information.

"You son of a bitch!"

Headlights arched into the driveway. Andi's eyes narrowed. Down below, the animals went into their howling, snarling routine.

Andi nibbled on her thumbnail as she watched Peter walk back to his car, the folder in his hand. Her phone rang on the second floor. She knew it was Peter calling on his car phone. She sat down on the window seat and cried. The phone continued to ring. Like she cared. "Go to hell, Mr. Lipstick!"

When there were no more tears, Andi wiped her eyes on the sleeve of her shirt. She had things to do. Empty cartons beckoned. She worked industriously until past midnight, packing and sorting, refusing to go to the window. Tears dripped down her cheeks from time to time. At one-thirty she crept downstairs for a soda. She carried it back to the attic and gulped at it from her perch on the window seat. He was still there. He was still there at four in the morning when she called a halt to her activities.

Andi curled herself into a ball on top of the bed with a comforter where she cried herself to sleep. She woke at seven and raced to the window. "We'll see about that!"

With shaking hands, Andi dialed the police, identified herself and said in a cold, angry voice, "I want you to send someone here right now and remove a . . . person from my parking lot. He's been sitting there all night. You tell him he's not to dare set foot on my property until January. If I have to sign something, I'll come down to the police station. Right now. I want you to come here right now. My animals are going crazy. I have a gun and a license to use it," she said dramatically. "Thank you."

Her heart thundering in her chest, Andi raced back to the attic. She knew the dirt and grime on the window prevented Peter from seeing her. She clenched her teeth when she saw the patrol car careen into her driveway, the red and blue lights flashing ominously. She just knew he was going to give the officers a box of Raspberry Cheese Louise lipsticks for their wives.

Five minutes later the Mercedes backed out of her parking lot. It didn't look like any lipstick had changed hands.

"He's probably going to mail them," she snorted as she raced down the steps to answer the door, the din behind her so loud she could barely hear the officer's voice.

"Do you want to file a complaint?"

"You're damn right I do," Andi screamed.

"All right, come down to the station this afternoon."

"I'll be there."

Andi closed the door and locked it. She tended to the animals, showered and ate some cornflakes before she resumed her packing. "You are dead in the water, Mr. Lipstick," she sniveled as she started to clean out her closet and dresser drawers.

At ten o'clock she called the Finnerans. "You really and truly found something in Freehold! . . . I can move in on Sunday? That's Christmas Eve! . . . Move in condition! Fifteen acres! A heated barn for the animals. God must be watching over me. How much is fenced in? . . . Great. That's a fair price. . . . The owners are in California. . . . I knew you could do it. . . . Okay. I'll drive down this afternoon and look at it. . . . The last of their things will be out by Saturday. I'm very grateful, Tom." She copied down directions. Her sigh of relief was so loud and long she had trouble taking a deep breath.

Andi's second call was to her friend Mickey. "Can you bring the bus by today? Thanks Mickey. I owe you one."

Her third call was to her attorney, who admonished her up one side and down the other for signing the contract before he had a chance to go over it. "You're lucky everything is in order. Congratulations. I'm going to set up a payout structure you'll be able to live with." Andi listened, made notes, gave the attorney her new address and told him to check with information for her new phone number.

The phone started to ring the moment she hung up from the attorney. The answering machine clicked on. If it was a patient she'd pick up. A hang up. Mr. Lipstick. "Invade my privacy, my life, ha! Only low-life scum do things like that. Well, you got your property, so you don't have to continue with this charade. It doesn't say much for me that I was starting to fall for your charms." Her eyes started to burn again. She cuddled a gray cat close to her chest, the dogs circling her feet. "So I made a mistake. We can live with it. We'll laugh all the way to the bank. The new rule is, we don't trust any man, ever again."

The elaborate silver service on the mahogany table gleamed as Sadie King poured coffee for her nephew. "You look like you slept in a barn, Peter. Calm down, stop that frantic pacing and tell me what happened. You've never had a problem being articulate before. So far all I have been able to gather is someone stepped on your toes. Was it Dr. Evans? I'm a very good listener, Peter."

"Yesterday was so perfect it scared me. She felt it, too, I could tell. Somehow, that goddamn investigative report fell out of my car and she found it. When I went back later for dinner, after I left you, she had it taped to the door. Obviously she read it. I called on the car phone, I banged on the door, but she didn't want any part of me. I sat in her parking lot all night long. This morning the police came and ran me off her property. Their advice was to write her a letter and not to go back or they'd run me off. I think I'm in love with her, Sadie. I was going to tell her that last night. I think . . . thought she was starting to feel the same way. My stomach tightens up when she laughs and her laughter shines in her eyes. She gave me her father's boots that were bright yellow, and his gloves. She's so down to earth, so real. I even started to wonder how our kids would look. What should I do? How can I make her understand?"

"A letter isn't such a bad idea. You could enclose it with the invitation to your Christmas party and send it Federal Express or have a messenger deliver it. I'd opt for the messenger because he could deliver it today. If you choose Federal Express she won't get it until tomorrow."

"What's the use, Sadie? I don't blame her. Jesus, the guy even . . . a diaphragm is pretty goddamn personal. I didn't want that kind of stuff. I didn't ask for it either. All I wanted was her financials and a history of the property. I have that same sick feeling in the pit of my stomach I used to get when I was a kid and did something wrong. I could never pull anything over on my mother, and Andi is the same way."

"There must be a way for you to get her to listen to you. Apologies, when they're heartfelt, are usually pretty good. Try calling her again."

"I've done that. Her answering machine comes on. I know she's there listening, but she won't pick up. I told you, I don't blame her."

"Maybe you could disguise yourself and ride up on a motorcycle with . . . someone's animal and pretend . . . you know, it will get you in the door. She'll have to listen if you're face-to-face."

"Sadie, that's probably the worst idea you ever came up with. Andi Evans is an in-your-face person. She'll call the cops. They already gave me a warning. I don't want my ass hauled off to jail. They print stuff like that in the papers. How's that going to look?"

Sadie threw her hands up in the air. "Can you come up with a better idea?"

"No. I'm fresh out of ideas. I have to go home to shower and shave. Then I have to go to the office. I have a business to run. I'll stop by on my way home from the office." Peter kissed his grandmother goodbye, his face miserable.

Sadie eyed the urn with Hannah's ashes on the mantel. "Obviously, Hannah, I have to take matters into my own hands. Men are so good at screwing things up, and it's always a woman who has to get them out of their messes. I miss you, and no, I'm not going to get maudlin. I now have a mission to keep me busy."

Sadie dusted her hands before she picked up the phone. "Marcus, bring the car around front and make sure you have my . . . *things*. Scotch Plains. The weather report said the roads are clear." She replaced the receiver.

"They're meant for one another. I know this in my heart. Therefore, it's all right for me to meddle," Sadie mumbled as she slipped into her faux fur coat. "I'm going to make this right or die trying."

Andi had the door of the truck open when she saw Gertie picking her way over the packed-down snow. "Gertie, wait, I'll help you. If you tell me you walked all the way from Plainfield, I'm going to kick you all the way back. You're too old to be trundling around in this snow. What if you fall and fracture your hip? Then what? Where's your shopping cart?"

"Donald's watching it. I wanted to see Rosie and her pups. Can I, Andi?"

"Of course. Listen, I have some errands to run. Do you want to stay until I get back? I can drive you home after that."

"Well, sure."

"Rosie's in the kitchen, and the tea's still hot in the pot. Make yourself at home. I might be gone for maybe . . . three hours, depending on the roads. You'll wait?"

"Of course."

"Gertie, don't answer the phone."

"What if it's a patient?" Gertie asked fretfully.

"If it is, you'll hear it on the machine. Pick up and refer them to the clinic on Park Avenue. My offices are closed as of this morning. I called the few patients I have and told them."

"All right."

"I'll see you by mid-afternoon."

Ninety minutes later, Andi pulled her truck alongside Tom Finneran's white Cadillac. "Oh, it's wonderful, Tom! The snow makes it look like a fairy land. I love the old trees. Quick, show me around."

"Everything is in tip-top shape. Move in condition, Andi. The owners' things are packed up ready for the mover. All the walls and ceilings were freshly painted a month ago. There's new carpet everywhere, even upstairs. Three bathrooms. A full one downstairs. Nice modern kitchen, appliances are six years old. The roof is nine years old and the furnace is five years old. The plumbing is good, but you do have a septic tank because you're in the country. Taxes are more than reasonable. I have to admit the road leading in here is a kidney crusher. You might want to think about doing something to it later on. Fill the holes with shale or something. It's a farmhouse, and I for one love old farmhouses. A lot of work went into this house at one time. Young people today don't appreciate the old beams and pegs they used for nails back then."

"I love it," Andi said enthusiastically.

"The owner put down carpeting for warmth. Underneath the carpeting you have pine floors. It was a shame to cover them up, but women today want beige carpets. The blinds stay, as do the lighting fixtures and all the appliances. You'll be more than comfortable. Take your time and look around. I'll wait here for you. The owner agreed to an end of January closing, so you'll be paying rent until that time."

"It's just perfect, Tom. Now, show me the barn."

"That's what you're really going to love. It's warm and there's a mountain of hay inside on the second floor or whatever they call it in barns. Good electricity, plumbing, sinks. There's an old refrigerator, too, and it works. The stalls are still intact. You can do what you want with them. There's a two-car garage and a shed for junk. The owner is leaving the lawnmower, leaf blower and all his gardening stuff. Any questions?"

"Not a one. Where do I sign?"

"On the dotted line. You can move in on Sunday at any time. I probably won't see you till the closing, so good luck. Oh, Lois took care of calling the water company, PSE&G and the phone company. Everything will be hooked up first thing Monday morning. You can reimburse us at the closing for the deposits."

Andi hugged the realtor. She had to remember to send him a present after she moved in.

The clock on the mantel was striking five when Andi walked through the doors of the kennel. "I'm home," she called.

Gertie was sitting at the kitchen table with three of the pups in her lap. "Rosie is keeping her eye on me. It almost makes me want to have a home of my own. Did you give them names?"

"Not yet. Did anyone call?" Andi asked nonchalantly.

"Mr. King called; his message is on the machine. He sounded . . . desperate."

"And well he should. Let me tell you what that . . . lipstick person did, Gertie. Then you tell me what you think I should do. I hate men. I told you that before, and then I let my guard down and somehow he . . . what he did . . . was . . . he sneaked in. I let him kiss me and I kissed him back and told him I liked it. Do you believe that!"

Gertie listened, her eyes glued to Andi's flushed face. "Well?"

"I agree, it was a terrible thing to do. Andi, I've lived a long time. Things aren't always the way they seem. Everything has two sides. Would it hurt you to hear him out? What harm is there in listening to him? Then, if you want to walk away, do so. Aren't you afraid that you're always going to wonder if there was an explanation? You said he was nice, that you liked him. He sounded like a sterling person to me."

"Listen to him so he can lie to my face? That's the worst kind of man, the one who looks you in the eye and lies. That's what used car salesmen do. Sometimes lawyers and insurance men do it, too. I called the police on him this morning. He sat in my parking lot all night, Gertie."

"How do you know that?"

"Because I watched him. You know what else? I even changed the sheets on the damn bed because I thought . . . well, what I . . . oh, hell, it doesn't matter."

"Obviously it does matter. Your eyes are all red. You really sat up watching him sit in your parking lot! That's ridiculous!"

"I was packing my stuff in the attic. I looked out from time to time," Andi said defensively. "I guess he wasn't who I thought he was. I swear to god, Gertie, this is it. I'm not sticking my neck out, ever again."

"Don't business people do things like that, Andi? I'm not taking sides here; but think for a moment, if the situation was reversed, wouldn't you want to get the best deal for your company?"

"Does that mean he and his company need to know about my love life, that I use a diaphragm? No, it does not. He had no damn right."

"Maybe it's the detective's fault and not Mr. King's. Maybe Mr. King told him to do a . . . whatever term they use, on you, and the man took it further than he was supposed to. That's something to think about," Gertie said, a desperate look on her face.

"Whose side are you on, Gertie? It sounds like you favor that war paint king."

"I believe in giving everyone a fair hearing."

"Is that why you refuse to call your children and live in a ditch?"

"It's not the same thing, and you know it."

"There's no greater sin in life than betrayal. I could . . . can forgive anything but betrayal."

Gertie's tone turned fretful. "Don't say that, Andi. There's usually a reason for everything if you care enough to find out what it is. I've lived a long life, my dear, and along the way I learned a few things. An open mind is a person's greatest asset in this world."

"I don't want to hear it, Gertie, and my mind just shut down. I know his type; he was just playing with me in case I changed my mind about selling. I would have gone to bed with him, too. That's the part that bothers me. Then, one minute after the closing, it would be goodbye Andi."

"He's not like that at all, Andi. You're so wrong." At Andi's strange look she hastened to explain. "What I meant was . . . from everything you said, from what I've seen in the papers, Mr. King is a gentleman. You said so yourself. I really should be going. Someone's pulling into your driveway. I'm going to walk, Andi. I've been cooped up too long in the shelter." Gertie held up her hand. "No, no, I do not want a ride. You still have packing to do. Thanks for the tea and for letting me hold these precious bundles. When are you going to name them?"

"I was thinking of giving them all Christmas names. You know, Holly, Jingle, et cetera. Just let me get my coat; it's too cold, and there's ice everywhere. I refuse to allow you to walk home, wherever home may be today."

"I'm walking and that's final," Gertie said, backing out the door. "Besides, I have some thinking I have to do. I do thank you for caring about this old woman. I'll be fine. It's a messenger, Andi, with a letter. I'll wait just a minute longer to make sure it isn't an emergency."

Andi stared after her, a helpless look on her face. She knew how important it was for the seniors to feel independent. She reached for the envelope and ripped at it. "Ha!" she snorted. "It's an invitation to Mr. Lipstick's Christmas party."

"Guess that makes it official. Change your mind and go. Is there a note?"

"Yep. It says he's sorry about the report and all he had requested were the financials, none of the personal stuff. He said he meant to destroy it once he met me, but time got away from him. He also says he had more fun yesterday than he's had in twenty years, and he thinks he's falling in love with me. He's very sorry. Please call."

"So call and put the poor thing out of his misery. That certainly sounds contrite to me. Everyone makes mistakes, Andi, even you. I would find it very heartwarming to hear someone tell me they think they're falling in love with me. Think about that, Andi. Have a nice evening."

"Goodbye, Gertie. Be careful walking."

"I will, my dear."

Andi read the note and the invitation until she had them both memorized. She ran the words over and over in her mind as she finished packing up the attic. At one point, as she descended the attic steps, she put the words to music and sing-songed her way through her bedroom as she stuffed things in cartons.

Andi stopped only to feed the animals and eat a sandwich. The telephone continued to ring, the answering machine clicking on just as the person on the other end hung up. At eleven o'clock she carried the last of the boxes downstairs to the garage where she stacked them near the door. By three o'clock she had her mother's china packed as well as all the pictures and knickknacks from the living room sealed in bubble wrap. These, too, went into the garage.

At three-thirty, she was sitting at the kitchen table with a cup of tea, the invitation to Peter King's party in front of her and his letter propped up against the sugar bowl. Believe or not believe? Go to the party, don't go to the party? Call him or not call him? Ignore everything and maybe things would turn out right. Like thirty-year-old women with thirty-six animals were really in demand. Was Gertie right? Was she acting like some indignant teenager?

There were no answers in the kitchen, so she might as well go to bed and try to sleep. Was this how it felt to be in love? Surely love meant more than a sick feeling in the stomach coupled with wet eyes and a pounding headache.

Andi felt as old as Gertie when she climbed the stairs to the second floor. She blubbered to herself as she brushed her teeth and changed into flannel pajamas. She was asleep the moment she pulled the down comforter up to her chin.

Even in her dream she knew she was dreaming because once before, in another lifetime, she'd slid down the hill on a plastic shower curtain with a colleague named Tyler. The same Tyler she'd had a two-year relationship with.

She fell sideways, rolling off the frozen plastic, to land in a heap near a monstrous holly bush. The wind knocked out of her, she struggled to breathe.

"You okay, Andi?"

"Sure. Bet I'm bruised from head to toe, though. How about you?"

"I'm fine. You really aren't going with me tomorrow, are you?"

"No. I'll miss you. Let's stay in touch, okay?"

"People promise that all the time, they even mean it at the time they say it, but it rarely happens. I'll be in Chicago and you'll be in New Jersey. I want the big bucks. I could never be content living in some rural area counting my pennies and practicing veterinarian medicine for free. Right now you're starry-eyed at taking over your family's old practice, but that's going to get old real quick. You're gonna be the new kid on the block. Who's going to come to your clinic? Yeah, sure, you can board dogs, but how much money is there in that? Not much I can tell you. Let's go home and make some magic. We're probably never going to see each other again. We'll call at first and even write a few letters, and then it will be a Christmas card once a year with our name printed on it. After that it will be, Tyler who? Andi who?"

"Then why do you want to go to bed with me?"

"Because I think I love you."

"After two years you *think* you love me? I want to go home and I want to go by myself. I don't want to go to bed with you either because you remind me of someone I don't like. He makes greasy lipstick. I changed the sheets and everything, and then he found out, probably from you, that I use a diaphragm. That was tacky, Tyler, to tell him something that personal."

"I never told him any such thing."

"Liar, liar, your pants are on fire. Get away from me and don't think I'm going to your stupid Christmas party either. Take this damn shower curtain with you, too."

"All right, all right. You came with me, how are you going to get home?"

"I have two feet, I'll walk. When you're homeless that's how you get around. I hope you make your three million plus. Goodbye, Peter."

"My name isn't Peter, it's Tyler."

"Same thing, birds of a feather flock together. All you're interested in is money. You don't care about me. The fact that you're taking this so well is suspect in my eyes. And another thing, I wouldn't let you see me wear my mother's pearls even if you paid me my weight in gold. One more thing, don't for one minute think I'm giving one of Rosie's pups to you to give your grandmother. She'll sneeze from all of that Lily of the Valley powder."

Andi rolled over, her arm snaking out to reach the phone. She yanked it back under the covers immediately. Six-thirty.

She'd only had two and a half hours of sleep, and most of that had been dream time. Damn.

Andi struggled to remember the dream as she showered and dressed.

The animals tended to, Andi sat at the table sipping the scalding hot coffee. She frowned as she tried to remember what it was in her dream that bothered her. It didn't hit her until she finished the last of the coffee in the pot. Lily of the Valley. Of course. "When you're stupid, Andi, you're stupid." A moment later the phone book was in her hands. She flipped to the Ks and ran her finger down the listing. She called every S. King in the book until she heard the voice she was expecting. She wasn't sure, but she thought her heart stopped beating when she heard Gertie's voice on the other end of the line. *Sadie King, Peter King's grandmother, was the homeless Gertie.*

Blind fury riveted through her. Shaking and trembling, she had to grab hold of the kitchen counter to steady herself. A conspiracy. If the old saying a fool is born every minute was true, then she was this minute's fool. Of all the cheap, dirty tricks! Send an old lady here to soften me up, to spy on me so I'd spill my guts. You son of a bitch!

Andi fixed another pot of coffee. Somewhere in this house there must be some cigarettes, a filthy habit she'd given up a year ago. She rummaged in the kitchen drawers until she found a crumpled pack pushed way in the back. She lit one, coughed and sputtered, but she didn't put it out.

Promptly at nine o'clock she called King Cosmetics and asked to speak to Peter King. "This is Dr. Andrea Evans and this call is a one-time call. Tell Mr. King he doesn't get a second chance to speak with me. It's now or never."

"Andi, is it really you? Listen I'm sorry—"

"Excuse me, I called you, so I'm the one who will do the talking. Furthermore, I'm not interested in any lame excuses. How dare you send your grandmother to spy on me! How dare you! Homeless my ass! She said her name was Gertie and I believed her. I didn't get wise till this morning. It was that Lily of the Valley. *That always bothered me.* Why would a homeless lady always smell like Lily of the Valley? She should have had body odor. All those good deeds, all those tall tales. Well, it should make you happy that I fell for it. You have to sink pretty low to use an old lady to get what you want. Don't send her back here again either. My God, I can't wait to get out of here so I don't ever have to see you or your grandmother again. She actually had me feeling sorry for her because her children, *she said,* wanted to slap her in a nursing home. This is my R.S.V. P. for your party. I'll leave it up to you to figure out if I'm attending or not."

"What the hell are you talking about. Who's homeless? My grandmother lives in a penthouse, and she works to help—"

Andi cut him off in mid-sentence, slamming down the phone. She zeroed in on Rosie, who was watching the strange goings-on with puzzlement. Her owner rarely raised her voice. It was rarer still that she cried. "Do I care that his grandmother lives in a penthouse? No, I do not. Do I care that she sneaked in here and . . . took care of us? No, I do not. I bet that old lady came here in a chauffeur-driven limousine and parked it somewhere, and then she trundled over here in her disguise. I am stupid, I admit it. Well, my stupid days are over."

Andi cried then because there was nothing else for her to do.

"Sadie!" The one word was that of a bellowing bull.

"Peter! How nice of you to come by so early. Did you come for breakfast?"

"Sadie, or should I call you Gertie? What the hell were you trying to do, Sadie?"

"So you found out. I only wanted to help. Who told you?"

"Guess!"

"Not Andi? Please, don't tell me Andi found out. So, that was who called this morning and hung up without speaking. I thought it might be Donald."

"Who the hell is Donald?" Peter continued to bellow.

"He covered for me. He's a homeless man I befriended. How did she find out?"

"I have no idea. She said something about you always smelling like Lily of the Valley."

"Yes, I guess that would do it. Was she very upset?"

"Upset isn't quite the word I'd use. She thinks I put you up to it. She thinks we had a conspiracy going to get her property."

"Well, I certainly hope you explained things to her. I'll go right over there and make amends."

"I wouldn't do that if I were you. I couldn't explain; she hung up on me. Don't meddle, Sadie. I mean it."

"She's so right for you, Peter, and you're perfect for her. I wanted you two to get together. When the men found homeless animals, I had them take them to Andi. They told me how nice and kind she was. I wanted to see for myself what kind of girl she was. I want you to get married, Peter, and I don't want you marrying someone like Helen. That's why I did it."

"Couldn't you trust me to find out for myself, Sadie? Why couldn't you simply introduce me or in this case leave me to my own devices? I met her on my own."

"No, I couldn't trust you. Look how long it took you to figure out Helen wore false eyelashes." She watched her grandson cringe at her words. "I just wanted to help so you would be happy. I'm sorry, but I'm not taking all the blame, Peter. You screwed it all up with that report."

"That's another thing. That report was on the back seat. The day we went sledding I didn't have anything in the back seat. I didn't even open the back door. All my stuff was in the trunk. How'd it fall out?"

"It doesn't matter now how it fell out. It did, and Andi found it and read it. End of story," Sadie said.

"I'm not giving up. I like her spunk."

"She hates your guts," Sadie said. "By the way, she isn't going to your party. I was there when the messenger brought your invitation. Peter, I'm so sorry. I just wanted to help. Where are you going?"

"To correct this situation."

"Peter, Andi is very angry. Don't go on her property again unless you want to see yourself and this company on the six o'clock news."

"Then what the hell am I supposed to do?"

"Does that mean you want my advice?"

"Okay, I'll try anything."

"Go to the police station and increase your Christmas donation to the Police Benevolent Association. Then ask them if they'll loan you one of their bullhorns. Talk to her from the road. She'll have to listen, and you aren't breaking any laws. I'm not saying it will work, but it's worth a try."

"Sadie, I love you!" Peter said as he threw his arms around his grandmother.

Peter King, the bullhorn next to him on the front seat, pulled his car to the curb. He felt stupid and silly as he climbed from the car. What to say? How to say it? Apologize from the heart. You know Spanish and French and a smattering of Latin. Do it in four languages. That should impress her. Oh yeah.

Peter took a deep breath before he brought the horn to his mouth. "Dr. Evans, this is Peter King. I'm outside on the road. I want you to listen to me. When I'm finished, if you don't want me to bother you again, I won't, but you need to hear me out. You can't run and hide, and you can't drown this out."

Peter sensed movement, chattering voices and rock music. Disconcerted, he turned around to see a pickup truck full of skis, sleds, and teenagers, pulling a snowmobile, drive up behind his parked car. "Shit!" Like he really needed an audience. Tune them out and get on with it.

"Andi, listen to me. Don't blame my grandmother; she only wanted to help. She wants to see me married with children before she . . . goes. I didn't know she was pretending to be a bag lady, I swear I didn't. As much as I love her, I wanted to strangle her when I found out."

"That's nice, mister," shouted a young girl in a tight ski suit and hair that looked like raffia. "You should always love your mother and grandmother. You're doing this all wrong. You need to appeal to her basic instincts."

"Shut up, Carla," a pimple-faced youth snarled. "You need to mind your own business. Yo, mister, you need to stand tall here and not beg some dumb girl for . . . whatever it is you want out of this scene."

"Listen, Donnie, don't be telling me girl stuff. You're so ignorant you're pathetic. Listen to me, mister, tell her she has eyes like stars and she's in your blood and you can't eat or sleep or anything. Tell her all you want in life is to marry her and have lots of little girl kids that look just like her. Promise her anything, but you better mean it because us women can spot a lie in a heartbeat."

Peter turned around. "She thinks I cheated her or tried; and then I did something really stupid, but I didn't know it was stupid at the time. Well, I sort of knew, but I didn't think anyone would ever find out. How do I handle that one?" he asked the girl with the three pounds of makeup and raffia hair.

"Tell her what you just said to me. Admit it. It's when you lie and try to cover up that you get in trouble."

"Don't listen to Carla, man, that chick in there is gonna think you're the king of all jerks."

"You're a jerk, Donnie. Listen to me, mister, what do you have to lose?"

Peter cleared his throat. "Andi, I'm sorry for everything. I was stupid. I swear to God, I'll never do another stupid thing again. I tried to explain about the business end of things. I want to marry you. I'll do anything you want if you'll just come out here and listen to me or let me come in and talk to you. Sadie says we're meant for each. She's hardly ever wrong. What's ten minutes out of your life, Andi? I admit I'm dumb when it comes to women. I don't read *Cosmo,* and I don't know diddly squat about triple orgasms and such stuff; but I'm willing to learn. I'll use breath mints, I'll quit smoking, I'll take the grease out of the lipstick. Are you listening to me, Andi? I goddamn well love you! I thought I was falling in love with you, but now I know I love you for real."

"Mister, you are a disgrace to the male race," Donnie said.

"Oh, mister, that was beautiful. You wait, she's coming out. Give her five minutes. No woman could resist that little speech. You did real good, mister. My sister told me about triple orgasms. I can explain . . ."

"Oh, Jeez, look, she's coming out. That's who you're in love with?" There was such amazement in the boy's face, Peter grinned.

"Oh, she's real pretty, mister. I know she loves you. You gonna give her something special for Christmas?"

"Yeah, himself," Donnie snorted.

"You know what, kid, they don't come any better than me. You need to get a whole new attitude. Carla, we're looking for teenage models at King Cosmetics. Here's my card; go to personnel and arrange a meeting with me for after the first of the year. Dump that jerk and get yourself a real boyfriend. Here's the keys to my car. My address is in the glove compartment. Drop it off for me, okay? That way she'll have to take me home or else allow me to stay. Thanks for your help. Can you drive?"

"Now you got it, mister. I can drive. Remember now, be humble, and only the truth counts from here on in."

"Got it," he said as he moved toward the house.

Inside the kennel, Andi said, "You got the dogs in a tizzy. I'm in a tizzy. You're out of your mind. I never heard of a grandmother/grandson act before."

"It wasn't an act. Everything I said was true. I do want to marry you."

"I hardly know you. Are you asking me so the three million plus stays in the family?"

"God, no. I feel like I've known you all my life. I've been searching for someone like you forever. My grandmother knew you were the one the moment she met you. She adores you, and she feels terrible about all of this. Can we start over?"

Well . . . I . . . we're from two different worlds. I don't think it would work. I'm not giving up my life and my profession. I worked too hard to get where I am."

"I'm not asking you to give up anything. I don't much care for the life I move around in now, but it's my job. I can make it nine-to-five and be home every night for dinner. If you're busy, I can even cook the dinner or we can hire a housekeeper."

"I'm moving to Freehold Christmas Eve."

"Freehold's good. I like Freehold. It's not such a long commute. Sunday's good for me. I'm a whiz bang at putting up Christmas trees. Well?"

"Were you telling me the truth when you said you couldn't eat or sleep?"

"Just look at the bags under my eyes. How about you?"

"I cried a lot. I would have cried more, but the animals got upset so I had to stop."

"So right now, this minute, we're two people who are starting over. All that . . . mess, it never happened. Your money will always be your money. That was a business deal. What we have is personal. So, will you marry me? If you don't have pearls, Sadie will give you hers. This way they'll stay in the family. That kid who took my car knows more than I do. I'll tell you about her later. Was that a yes or a no?"

"It's a maybe. We haven't even gone to bed yet. We might not be compatible."

"Why don't we find out."

"Now? It's morning. I have things to do. How about later?"

"Where we're concerned, later means trouble. Now!"

"Okay. Now sounds good. I put clean sheets on the bed on Sunday. You were a no show. That didn't do anything for my ego," Andi said.

"I dreamed about it," Peter said.

"You said you didn't sleep."

"Daydreamed. There's a difference. In living color."

"How'd I look?"

"Wonderful!" Peter said. "Want me to carry you upstairs?"

"No. I'm the independent type. I can be bossy."

"I love bossy women. Sadie is bossy. People only boss other people around when they love them. Sadie told me that."

"You are dumb." Andi laughed.

"That, too. I sleep with my socks on," Peter confided.

"Me, too! I use an electric blanket."

"You won't need it this morning." Peter laughed.

"Pretty confidant, aren't you?"

"When you got it you got it."

"Show me," Andi said.

"Your zipper or mine?"

"Oh the count of three," Andi said.

Zipppppppp.

He showed her. And was still showing her when the sun

set and the animals howled for their dinner. And afterward, when the kennel grew quiet for the long evening ahead, he was still showing her. Toward midnight, Andi showed him, again and again. He was heard to mutter, in a hoarse whisper, "I liked that. Oh, do that again."

She did.

"I hate to leave. Oh, God, I have to borrow your truck, do you mind?"

"Of course I mind. You sport around in a fifty thousand dollar truck and a ninety thousand dollar car and you want to borrow my clunker!"

"I'll have someone drive it back, okay. Is this going to be our first fight?"

"Not if I can help it. I do need the truck, though. I have some errands to do, and I'm not driving that bus."

"Are you going to call Sadie?"

"Not today. She needs to sweat a little. Are you going to tell her?"

"Not on your life. Well, did that maybe turn into a yes or a no? What kind of ring do you want?"

"I don't want an engagement ring. I just want a wide, thick, gold wedding band."

"Then it's yes?"

Andi nodded.

"When?"

"January. After I get settled in."

"January's good. January's real good. Jesus, I love you. You smile like my mother used to smile. That's the highest compliment I can pay you, Andi. She was real, like you. I don't know too many real people. When you stop to think about it, that's pretty sad."

"Then let's not think about it," Andi said as she dangled the truck keys under his nose.

"I can't see you till tomorrow. I'll call you tonight, okay?

Some clients are in town, and the meetings and dinner are not something I can cancel. You're coming to the party?"

"Yes."

"What about the pearls?" Peter asked fretfully. "You have to explain that to me one of these days."

"I have my mother's pearls."

"God, that's a relief"

He kissed her then until she thought her head would spin right off her neck.

"Bye."

Andi smiled, her eyes starry. "Bye, Peter."

Thursday morning, the day of Peter King's Christmas party, Andi climbed out of bed with a vicious head cold. Her eyes were red, her nose just as red. She'd spent the night propped up against the pillows so her nasal passages would stay open. If she slept twenty minutes it was a lot. The time was ten minutes to eight. In her ratty robe and fleece-lined slippers she shuffled downstairs to make herself some hot coffee. She ached from head to toe. Just the thought of cleaning the dog runs made her cringe. She shivered and turned up the heat to ninety. She huddled inside the robe, trying to quiet her shaking body as she waited for the coffee to perk.

Cup in hand at fifteen minutes past eight, she heard the first rumblings of heavy duty machinery in her parking lot. The knock on the door was louder than thunder. She opened the door, her teeth chattering. "What are you doing here? What's all that machinery? Get it out of here. This is private property. Is that a wrecking ball?"

He was big and burly with hands the size of ham hocks, the perfect complement to the heavy duty monster machinery behind him. "What do you mean what am I doing here? I'm here to raze this building. I have a contract that says so. And, yeah, that's a wrecking ball. You gotta get out of here, lady."

"Come in here. I can't stand outside; I'm sick as you can

see, and I'm not going anywhere. I, too, have a contract, and my contract says you can't do this. Mine, I'm sure, supersedes yours. So there. I have thirty-six animals here and no place to take them until Sunday. You'll just have to wait."

"That's tough, lady. I ain't comin' back here on Sunday; that's Christmas Eve. I have another job scheduled for Tuesday. Today is the day for this building."

"I'm calling the police; we'll let them settle it. You just go back outside and sit on that ball because that's all you're going to do with it. Don't you dare touch a thing. Do you hear me?" Andi croaked. She slammed the door in the man's face. She called the police and was told a patrol car would be sent immediately.

Andi raced upstairs, every bone in her body protesting as she dressed in three layers of clothing. She had to stop three times to blow her runny nose. Hacking and coughing, she ran downstairs to rummage on her desk for her contract to show the police. While she waited she placed a call to both Peter and Sadie and was told both of them were unavailable. Five minutes later, her electricity and phone were dead.

Two hours later, the electricity was back on. Temporarily. "I don't know what to tell you, ma'am. This man is right and so are you. You both have signed contracts. He has every right to be here doing what he's doing. You on the other hand have a contract that says he can't do it. Nobody is going to do anything until we can reach Mr. Peter King, since he's the man who signed both these contracts."

"Listen up, both of you, and watch my lips. I am not going anywhere. I'm sick. I have thirty-six animals in that kennel, and we have nowhere to go. Based on my contract, I made arrangements to be out of here on Sunday, not Saturday, not Friday and certainly not today. Now, which part of that don't you two men understand?"

"The part where you aren't leaving till Sunday. This is a three-day job. I can't afford to lose the money since I work for myself. It's not my fault you're sick, and it's not my fault that you have thirty-six animals. I got five kids and a wife to support and men on my payroll sitting outside in your parking lot. Right now I'm paying them to sit there drinking coffee."

"That's just too damn bad, mister. I'm calling the *Plainfield Courier* and the *Star Ledger.* Papers like stories like this especially at Christmastime. You better get my phone hooked up again and don't think I'm paying for that."

The afternoon wore on. Andi kept swilling tea as she watched through the window. The police were as good as their word, allowing nothing to transpire until word came in from Peter King. Her face grew more flushed, and she knew her fever was creeping upward.

Using the police cell phone, Andi called again and again, leaving a total of seven messages on Sadie's machine and nine messages in total for Peter at King Cosmetics. The receptionist logged all nine messages, Mr. King's words ringing in her ears: "Do not call me under *any* circumstance. Whatever it is can wait until tomorrow. Even if this building blows up I don't want to know about it until tomorrow."

At five o'clock, Andi suggested the police try and reach Mr. King at his home. When she was unable to tell them where he lived, the owner of the wrecking equipment smirked. It wasn't until six o'clock that she remembered she had Peter's address on the invitation. However, if she kept quiet she could delay things another day. Besides, his party was due to get under way any minute now. He would probably try and call her when he realized she wasn't in attendance.

The police officer spoke. "You might as well go home, Mr. Dolan. We'll try and reach Mr. King throughout the evening and get this thing settled by morning."

Cursing and kicking at his machinery, Dolan backed his equipment out of the parking lot. The officer waited a full twenty minutes before he left. Andi watched his taillights fade into the distance from the kitchen window. The yellow bus was like a huge golden eye under her sensor light. Large, yellow bus. Uh huh? Okay, Mr. Peter King, you have this coming to you!

"Hey you guys, line up, we're going to a party! First I have to get the location. Second, you need to get duded up. Wait here." The Christmas box of odds and ends of ribbon and ornaments was clearly marked. Spools of used ribbon were just what she needed. Every dog, every cat, got a red bow, even Rosie. The pups smaller, skinnier ribbon. "I'm going to warm up the bus, so don't get antsy. I also need to find my mother's pearls. I don't know why, but I have to wear them." Finally, wearing the pearls, wads of tissue stuck in the two flap pockets of her flannel shirt, pups in their box in hand, Andi led the animals to the bus. "Everybody sit down and be quiet. We're going to show Mr. Peter King what we think about the way he does business!"

Thirty-five minutes later, Andi swung the bus onto Brentwood Drive. Cars were lined the entire length of the street. "This indeed poses a dilemma," she muttered. She eyed the fire hydrant, wondering if she could get past it and up onto the lawn. Loud music blasted through the closed windows. "It must be a hell of a party," she muttered as she threw caution to the wind and plowed ahead.

Andi grabbed the handle to open the door. "Ooops, wait just one second. Annabelle, come here. You, too, Cleo.'" From her pocket she withdrew a tube of Raspberry Cheese Louise lipstick and painted both dog's lips. Annabelle immediately started to lick it off. "Stop that. You need to keep it on till we get to the party. Okay, you know the drill, we move on three. I expect you all to act like ladies and gentlemen. If you forget your manners, oh, well." She blew her nose, tossed the tissue on the ground and gave three sharp blasts on the whistle. "We aren't going to bother with the doorbell, the music's too loud."

"PARTY TIME!"

"Eek!" "Squawk!" "Oh, my God! It's a herd!" "They're wearing lipstick! I don't believe this!"

"Hi, I'm Andrea Evans," Andi croaked. "I think I'd like a rum and coke and spare the coke." Her puffy eyes narrowed when she saw her intended lounging on a beautiful brocade sofa, his head thrown back in laughter. He laughed harder when Cedric lifted his leg on a French Provincial table leg. Not to be outdone, Isaac did the same thing. Annabelle squatted in the middle of a colorful Persian carpet as she tried to lick off the lipstick.

"Now, this is what I call a party," Peter managed to gasp. "Ladies and gentlemen, stay or go, the decision is yours. It ain't gonna get any better than this! Wait, wait, before you go, I'd like to introduce you to the lady I'm going to marry right after the first of the year. Dr. Andrea Evans, meet my guests. I don't even want to know why you did this," he hissed in her ear.

"You said you wanted a lived-in house. Myra is going to get sick from all that paté. Oh, your guests are leaving. By the way, I parked the bus on your lawn."

"No!"

"Yep. Don't you care that your guests are leaving? I'm sick."

"And you're going right to bed," Sadie said, leaning over Andi. "You can forgive me later, my dear. Oh, my, you are running a fever. Isn't this wonderful, Peter? It's like we're a real family. Your furniture will never be the same. Do you care?"

"Nope," Peter said, wrapping his arm around Andi's shoulder. Do you want to tell me what prompted this . . . extraordinary visit?"

Andi told him. "So, you see, we're homeless until Sunday."

"Not anymore. My home is your home and the home of these animals. Boy, this feels good. Isn't it great, Sadie? That guy Dolan is a piece of work. It's true, I did sign the contract, but it was amended later on. I don't suppose he showed you a copy of that."

"No, he didn't. It doesn't matter. I thought you'd be angry. I was making a statement."

"I know, and I'm not angry. You did the right thing. You really can empty a room. Look, the food's all gone."

"Do you really love me?"

"So much it hurts."

"I'm wearing my mother's pearls. I think I'd like to go to bed now if you don't mind. Will you take care of Rosie and her pups?"

"That's my job," Sadie chirped. "Peter, carry this child to bed. I'll make her a nice hot toddy, and by tomorrow she'll be fine. Trust me."

Andi was asleep in Peter's arms before he reached the top of the steps. He turned as he heard steps behind him. "Okay, you can all come up and stand watch. By the way, thanks for coming to the party. I really like your outfits and, Annabelle, on you that lipstick looks good."

Peter fussed with the covers under Sadie's watchful eye. "I meant it, Sadie, when I said I love her so much it hurts. Isn't she beautiful? I could spend the rest of my life just looking at her."

"Ha! Not likely, you have to work to support all of us," Andi said sleepily. "Good night, Peter. I love you. Merry Christmas."

"Merry Christmas, Andi," Peter said, bending low to kiss her on the cheek.

"Ah, I love it when things work out," Sadie said, three of Rosie's pups cradled against her bony chest. I think I'd like five grandchildren. Good night, Peter."

"Thanks, Grandma. It's going to be a wonderful life."

"I know."

A Vision of
Sugarplums

Jennifer Blake

One

He was the kind of man who made up his mind in two seconds, max. Masculine assurance was as much a part of him as his wide shoulders and dark, close-cropped hair. Ordinarily, Meghan Castle thought, he would know what he wanted the instant he spotted it, would point, pay, and be out of the store before the average shopper even started looking. So why was he having trouble now?

Meghan paused in her task of closing out the back cash register for the day, tucking the shining honey-blond bell of her hair behind her ear as she watched the customer. Her usual response would be to go over and offer her help. She had the feeling, however, that this guy might prefer doing things on his own.

He seemed to want a Christmas tree, since he was standing in front of the row of decorated display trees which was a feature of the Silver Bells Christmas Store. That was comparatively normal, even if he had left it a little late. Yet it was hard to believe he was actually interested in the Sugarplum Fairy Tree that he was scowling at with such fierce deliberation.

Meghan hadn't noticed him when he came in. It must have been during the mad frenzy an hour ago when the store was crowded by customers seized with holiday spirit as the last minutes of shopping time ticked down. Still, he had been hard to miss as people began to clear out.

It was not just his impressive height, the iridescent sheen

in the neat waves of his hair, or eyes so intensely blue their color was apparent clear across the store. No, it was the indefinable sense of presence he wore like a comfortable old shirt. It seemed to fill the place to its far corners, impressing itself upon her against her will. She was acutely aware of his frustration and impatience, aware enough that she was having trouble totaling the cash and credit card slips in the register drawer.

It was too bad she had already sent her store manager home to enjoy what was left of Christmas Eve with her family. Yvonne would have bustled over, all cheer and motherly, admiring smiles as she steered this final customer toward something more suitable, such as the Scots Tartan Tree, the Denim Special, or maybe the Camouflage example on its rustic stand. Yvonne could get away with things like that because she liked macho hunks and made no bones about it, in spite of being married to the same lovable teddy bear for forty years. More than that, she was big-hearted and genuinely filled with the spirit of the season. Meghan had none of these things going for her. She had no particular appreciation for hunks, and wanted nothing so much as to have Christmas Eve over at last.

Regardless, she had to admit that it was pretty brave of this rugged, construction worker type in his scruffy leather bomber jacket, jeans and work boots to venture into the Silver Bells. The usual customer for Meghan's year-round Christmas store was a female bent on making her home festive; holiday decorating seemed to be exclusively a woman thing, at least in North Louisiana. He might, of course, have been sent by his wife or girlfriend along with instructions either too vague or fancy for his taste. That would account for his uncharacteristic indecision. The only thing wrong with that idea was that he didn't seem the kind of man to run any woman's errands.

Meghan glanced at her wristwatch. Fifteen minutes past closing time. Yvonne had put out the Closed sign and locked the entrance leading into the mall behind her as she left. Meghan had used her key to let the last few shoppers out of the store after they paid for their purchases. These hints had gone unnoticed by the man in front of the Christmas trees.

She probably shouldn't be checking the receipts while he was still around, Meghan thought. For all she knew, he could have stayed behind to rob the place. It was just that she was so anxious to get home. She needed to rest and relax, needed desperately to have the season behind for another year, even if the store itself was a constant and aching reminder of loss.

The main thing standing between her and her goal was the macho hunk. He had to go, one way or another.

Pressing her lips together in a determined line, Meghan felt for her shoes with her toes and slipped them on her aching feet. She stuffed the cash register receipts into a bank bag and locked them away, then reached to flip off the switch of the compact disc player that had been cycling endlessly through a collection of Victorian Christmas music box tunes. In the abrupt and blessed silence, she slid off her stool and moved toward the front of the store.

It was as Meghan was passing the giant Christmas tree that dominated the center of the store during the holidays that she heard the noise. It was a soft cooing, a low and almost musical sound, yet it stopped her dead in her tracks.

The tree was a Silver Bells trademark, an extravagant showpiece to draw attention to the store. Hundreds of people traipsed through every December to see what had been devised to astonish them. Meghan's mother, who had first opened the shop fifteen years ago, had always wracked her brain for new ideas and combed the Dallas gift market every July for products. Meghan had done the same when she took over some seven years before, though no one was ever more amazed by the results each year than she was herself.

Her heart simply hadn't been in it this year, or for the

past four years for that matter. She had opted for the cherubs which seemed to be everywhere, then added the basic recurring motif of silver bells. These ornaments were richly carved Medieval-style pieces thickly gilded in gold or encrusted with silver. Added to them were swaths of gold lamé or silver gauze that wove their way through dark green fir branches flocked with iridescent fairy dust. The somberly magnificent tree soared to the fluorescent lights in the ceiling, while underneath it lay a myriad of boxes in gold and silver wrapping paper topped by bows of iridescent gauze. Customers had been mildly appreciative, but not especially impressed. Meghan didn't blame them.

The noise she had heard, like a sweet hum touched with the humorous certainty of attracting attention, seemed to come from beneath the tree. The source of it was somewhere among the packages piled under the low-hanging tree branches.

Meghan didn't want to look. An instinct she had thought almost forgotten warned her of what she was going to find. Yet she was forced to investigate by that same sure instinct.

A baby.

A living cherub in pink and white perfection. With pale gold curls, autumn-sky blue eyes, chubby yet delicate features. It had an angelic smile showing two small pearls for bottom teeth. And it was looking straight up at her.

Strapped into a carrier, the baby had been pushed well back under the tree, wedged between a box covered in silver brocade and one in gold foil. Bright-eyed and imperious, the small being kicked blanket-wrapped feet and waved dainty hands, cooing again in a request to be picked up.

Meghan's breath caught in her throat. Her heart shifted, aching, in her chest. Her eyes burned. The urge to back away, turn and run, surged into her brain.

It was not possible. Against her will, she knelt in slow, inevitable adoration. Her fingers shook as she reached out to drag the carrier forward. As if compelled, she released the straps that held the baby in place, slipped her fingers carefully around the small, warm body, and lifted the lovely, living doll in her hands.

The baby was a girl, judging by her rosebud mouth, fragile build, and also the pink and aqua jacket she wore with a pair of pink knit rompers. She appeared well cared for, with the sweet, unforgettable scent of a clean and healthy baby.

As she cleared the side of the carrier, a small rag doll slid out of her blanket, falling to the floor with the brief musical tinkling of a lullaby. Carrier, clothing, and toy were all of excellent quality. The precious mite didn't seem at all the kind of child that someone would abandon on Christmas Eve.

Meghan forced her trembling lips into a smile. Her voice tender and not quite steady, she said, "Well, hello. Hello there, my little love."

The smile on the round, cherubic features faded, becoming solemn. The baby reached out with pink and white starfish fingers. Clutching a handful of Meghan's shining hair, she pulled her face forward with determined effort and planted a moist, open-mouthed kiss on the point of her chin.

A choked, watery laugh caught in Meghan's throat. Then she folded the small, warm being carefully into her arms and rocked her with a gentle motion while she bent her head and squeezed her eyes shut.

Across the store, Rick Wallman stood transfixed, his gaze fastened on the two under the Christmas tree. There was such naked love and longing in the woman's face that he felt almost ashamed, as if he had stumbled on something sacred, something he had no business seeing. The lady and baby were a matched pair, both soft, gentle, and beautiful. They belonged together. There was no doubt about it.

And he was excluded. It was a sensation he didn't care for at all. He hated it, in fact.

Funny. Or maybe not so funny.

What would it take to change things? Rick considered

that question with the single-minded concentration he brought to most problems. At the same time, he began walking toward the pair under the tree in the middle of the store. By the time he reached them, he had the first glimmerings of an idea.

"Not the best place to stash a kid," he said with a trace of amused interest in his voice. "But then, I guess maybe she's used to it?"

The lady glanced up, her rich, fudge-chocolate brown gaze so startled it was plain she had forgotten his existence, assuming she had ever noticed it in the first place. Chocolate was Rick's favorite flavor in all the world. He felt the smile that tilted his mouth widen.

The lady gasped as she watched his lips, a small, winded sound that was amazingly soothing to his ego. Looking away, she said, "She doesn't—she isn't—I mean I don't have the faintest idea how this baby got here."

"She's not yours?" He arched a skeptical brow even as he checked out the fact that the lady wore no wedding band. Fantastic.

"Of course not!" she said indignantly as a flush of color spread across her cheekbones.

His appraisal was judicious before he replied, "She looks like you."

"She has blue eyes, too, but I don't suppose that makes her yours!"

"No way!" He retreated a quick step, holding up a hand.

"I thought not." She glanced pointedly from his rough appearance to the baby's dainty perfection. An instant later, her look of vindication was replaced by a frown. "You didn't see who left her, did you?"

He shook his head. "Didn't see a thing."

"But who would just go off and desert her? Who could possibly do such a thing?"

"People do it all the time." Rick watched her face, mesmerized by the emotions registering in quick succession.

"Oh, I know parents leave kids in the video arcade or toy stores for other people to baby-sit," she answered with scorn, "but this is ridiculous."

"Guess you look like a trustworthy soul," he offered with a small shrug. "Or a motherly one."

Her gaze was vulnerable and edged with pain before she looked away. She moistened her lips, a movement that made him draw a deep, silent breath. "Well—well, I can't help that. I'll have to call the police."

"Yeah? And what if the mother comes back, screaming hysterically, two minutes after they get here? What if she thought the daddy had the kid, and the daddy thought she had her? It can happen."

"Or maybe I should contact the child protection hot line at Community Services," the lady continued as if he hadn't spoken. "Yes, that might be best. They can take care of everything."

"Some Christmas spirit you have," he drawled, his disappointment giving his voice a distinct edge.

Her glance was wide and vulnerable. "I fail to see what that has to do with it."

"No? You want to let this pretty little thing spend the night in a lonely crib? You want her to wake up in the morning to strange faces and no presents, no Santa Claus in sight?"

Exasperation crossed her lovely features, though she cuddled the baby in a touchingly protective gesture. Her tone acid, she said, "Just what do you suggest then? I can't stay here all night on the off chance somebody will suddenly remember they misplaced their child."

"No problem," Rick said with more nonchalance than he felt. "Put a note on the door and take the kid home with you."

"Are you out of your mind!"

At the sharp tone, the baby began to cry. Rick reached

out instinctively to chuck her under the chin. "Hey, take it easy, Annie, honey. It's going to be all right, sugarplum."

"What did you call her?" The lady's brown gaze was sharp.

"Sugarplum?"

"No, the other name."

"Honey?" It was a play for time.

"You know what I mean," she said in distinct warning.

"Annie," he said, feeling foolish and frowning to cover it. "You know. As in Little Orphan, et cetera? We have to call her something."

The look in her rich brown eyes was scathing, though she made no direct answer. She began to rock the baby, murmuring, trying to comfort her. Tilting her head at an angle to look into the small, screwed-up face resting on her shoulder, she appeared for all the world as if she would burst into tears herself.

The lady holding the baby was dressed in a black and cream dress that made her look competent and sophisticated and a bit severe. It wasn't at all what he would have chosen. He'd love to see her dressed in bright red or rich blue or clear yellow, something, anything, that had a little color to it.

Of course, nothing at all, except maybe a bright, rich, clear smile for him alone, would be even better.

He had lost it. He was gone.

Before he could speak again she said in thick tones, "I don't know what to do, really. I don't have diapers or formula or baby food. Besides, I'm not sure I can take care of a baby."

"Tell you what," Rick said, thrusting his hands into the back pockets of his jeans as he eyed the wailing kid. "Since we're sort of in this together, so to speak, I could maybe give you a hand."

She looked at him, her gaze startled, as if she was really seeing him for the first time. Meeting her eyes without evasion, Rick felt himself sinking into the deep, velvety sweetness of them, and he didn't give a damn if he went clean under. She moistened her lips, and he could almost taste them, almost feel their tender texture, their heat and moisture. And he felt the drawing of a desire so virulent and hungry it was like nothing he had ever known. It was not simple lust, though that was a part of it. It was a deep, sweet yearning for forever, or maybe a glimpse of it.

She swallowed, a convulsive movement in the smooth line of her throat, as she looked away. "It's Christmas Eve. You must have some other place to go, something better to do."

He shook his head. It was the most he could manage.

"Family? Relatives?"

"Out of town." It was the exact truth.

"Possibly a woman friend expecting you somewhere, then?"

"She ran out on me two days ago, so I'm fresh out of female company. Guess Annie will have to do." He didn't include the woman who held her, but that was understood. He hoped.

A tiny frown pleated the skin between her eyes. "Don't you think it would be a little strange?"

It would be a lot strange, but he didn't intend to let that stop him. Rick lifted a forbidding brow. "Why?"

"You don't know me, I don't know you. Neither of us has any connection whatever with this child. Why should we get involved?"

"Why shouldn't we?" Because he couldn't stand to hear the baby cry a minute longer, Rick reached out for her, easily overcoming the brief resistance of the woman who held her. He tossed little Annie up once, twice, laughing into her eyes. She gasped, chortled, and reached to grasp a fistful of his hair. Magically, the crying stopped.

Rick flashed the lady a look of triumph; he just couldn't help it. Turning back to the baby, he said, "Well, now, Annie, my sweet thing, my name's Rick Wallman, but you can call me Uncle Rick. And this lady is . . ." He paused, sending the lady an expectant look.

She gave him the name.

He grinned in secret triumph. "This lady is Meghan Castle, but you can call her Aunt Meg."

"Meghan, not Meg. But why? We aren't her aunt and uncle." She folded her arms over her chest.

"Annie doesn't know that," he said reasonably. "Besides, it's a good old southern tradition. Makes people seem familiar so kids are more comfortable."

"If you say so," Meghan answered dubiously.

"Right. So what do you say, Annie? Shall we all go shopping?"

The baby gurgled and clutched his shirt as she tried to pull herself up to stand on his hard forearm. He turned to Meghan. "See? She likes the idea."

Abruptly, she shook her head so the soft bell of her hair swung against her cheeks. "I can't."

Rick's smile faded while his thoughts moved with rapid precision. Voice pensive, he said, "The way I see it, you can't get out of it. What if the mother really has abandoned her, but has second thoughts and comes back—only you've called the police? I'll tell you what happens. The mother gets arrested for neglect and thrown in jail. Annie is left to the mercy of the courts, which means an institution, or maybe foster parents if she's lucky. No family for Annie anymore."

"That would be . . . terrible," she said with a frown.

"Right," he agreed. "So what's wrong with giving things a little time? Just a day or two? Or do you have something better to do?"

She bit her lip. "No. Not—really."

"Well, then?"

"You don't understand—" she began.

"No, I don't," he said, the words hard. "Do you think Annie does? Or that she will when she grows up?"

The woman running the Silver Bells met his gaze, her own intent, searching. She shut her eyes so tight her long lashes meshed; then she opened them again and gave a slow nod. "All right, you win. But you get to hold her until I close."

"Great," he said. "That's great."

At least, Rick thought it might be. With just a little luck.

Two

The three of them looked like a family group as they walked around the discount supercenter with Annie on Rick's arm while he pushed the shopping cart piled high with baby things. It made no difference, of course; still Meghan was disturbed. She kept glancing at the man and the baby; she couldn't help herself. Rick seemed so natural with little Annie, so at ease. She wasn't the only one who noticed it. The man and the child attracted their share of attention from other customers. Meghan saw also, with a certain glacial humor, that the glances of most of the women who passed lingered on the man.

Rick was totally oblivious; she had to give him that much. The major portion of his attention was given to Annie as he tried to keep her pacified. He talked to her in a constant running commentary, even directing his comments to Meghan through her. It was distracting and a bit disturbing, as if the three of them really were interconnected.

She was also troubled by the sight of his long, brown fingers splayed over the baby's back to support her while he reached for this or that. There seemed such tender strength, such security, in his grasp. She wondered, in the briefest of flashes, what it would be like to feel his hands on her own skin. Hard on the thought, she was engulfed in a wave of heat that coalesced in the lower part of her body. She fought it, amazed. It had been so long since such awareness had troubled her that it felt unnaturally erotic, far too extreme for comfort.

They had reached the baby formula section. As they paused in front of it, she gave Rick a considering look as she said, "You like children, don't you?"

"Kids, dogs, cats, strays of all kinds," he said in humorous agreement. "Don't you?"

"I suppose." His denim blue gaze was so warm and intent it was difficult to sustain. "But I don't make a practice of taking them all in."

"No? Maybe you should try it more often."

Maybe she should at that, she thought as she studied the strong planes of his face, the crinkles at the corners of his eyes, and the firmly molded lines of his mouth.

She was staring. Realizing it, she hurriedly directed her gaze to the different varieties of baby formula. In offhand tones, she said, "You know, we have no idea what kind of formula this child is used to taking. How are we supposed to choose?"

"Humm." He reached out and picked up a can in his large, square hand, turning the label to show it to Annie. "What do you think, sweetie?"

The baby blinked without any particular recognition.

"Nope." He put it back, then chose again. "This one?"

Meghan found herself watching Annie, measuring her lack of enthusiasm. As she recognized what she was doing, she made a soft sound of exasperation. "Come on! This child no more knows what she's been drinking than the man in the moon. And it could upset her stomach if we choose the wrong thing."

"Going hungry could upset her more," Rick said with maddening logic. "Not to mention us, if we have to listen to her yell." He replaced the can, took another one. The baby chortled and waved her hand at the bright aqua label. "Aha!" he said, and began to dump cans into the shopping cart.

"Wait a minute!" Meghan protested, laughing even as she reached out to stop him. "You can't do things that way."

He cocked an eyebrow at her. "Got a better idea?"

She didn't, though she refused to admit it.

At least they knew what type of bottle to get. One like it had been tucked into the back of the baby carrier along with a pacifier and a spare diaper. All three items had been extremely useful in helping to return Annie to what was apparently her normal sunny disposition on the drive to the supercenter. They moved from the formula to the bottles, and from there to the baby food.

"What else?" Rick asked, scanning the grocery aisles as he wheeled the cart along at a fast clip, one that required Meghan to extend her stride to keep up.

"I don't know."

"Think," he said, then slowed as if putting on the brakes as he noticed her breathless pace. "You're the female. You're supposed to know about these things."

She gave him an acerbic look. "It doesn't come with the genes."

"You're doing fine so far."

She felt as if she had been given a major accolade. The pleasure that flooded her was as disconcerting as it was unwelcome. Flushing, she avoided his gaze as she began to count off items on her fingers. "Clothes, pajamas, diapers, wipes, baby soap, baby food, formula, bottles, dish and spoon, sipping cup. Oh, yes, and toys." She sighed and pulled a wry face. "I think we've got most of what's needed."

"Great," he said, then added instantly. "So have you given any thought to what the grown-ups need? Food, for instance?"

The stare she swung on him was blank. "You're hungry?"

"Just starving is all."

"I didn't realize I was expected to feed you, too."

He lifted a thick, dark brow. "No? Actually, I thought

we'd try it the other way around. I'll feed you, since I don't imagine you've had a chance to eat this evening."

"You don't have to do that."

"I know, but I want to do it," he said with strained patience. "It's a bit late for a restaurant, especially with Annie in tow. But we can pick up something to cook while we're here at the store, or fast food on the way to your house. Your choice."

Instant decisions were not only his specialty, but what he expected from other people. She should have known. She said, "Since you're buying, you choose."

"How do I know what you like?" He waited.

She gave him an exasperated glare, then realized that cooking was the last thing she felt like doing at that moment. Through tight lips, she said, "Pizza to go. Pepperoni."

"Fine," he said in easy acceptance. "Why don't you find a phone and place the order while I head for the checkout line."

She stared at him a moment. She was being maneuvered, though it was for her own comfort and convenience. Or was it?

Then realizing at least a part of what was going on, she said, "But if you check out, you'll wind up paying for all this." She reached for her shoulder bag. "Here, let me give you—"

"No."

She looked up, caught by the implacable sound of his voice. A frown darkened her eyes. "But that isn't fair. I'm the one who found Annie. She was left in my store."

"It's not only fair, it's the way it's going to be."

"Oh, sure. Man, the great provider."

"You got it right," he said, and had the nerve to grin.

Her lips tightened with the instinct for battle. Then she noticed the amused attention they were attracting. She needed a way out. One came to her almost immediately.

"Fine," she abruptly. "This was your idea, after all." She

turned on her heel and headed for the bank of phones near the entrance.

"Fine," he repeated behind her, and she thought she heard him let out his breath in relief.

It was raining when they came out of the supercenter, the kind of endless steady drizzle that could last all night, all week, or even longer in Louisiana. It was turning colder, too, with a wet, biting chill that would probably drop below the freezing mark before morning to cause icing on bridges and overpasses. Rick insisted that Meghan go back inside and wait with Annie while he brought her car around. She set her jaw, but didn't argue, mainly because of the baby.

They had driven over to the supercenter together, so had to swing back by the mall to pick up his Bronco before heading for the apartment complex where she had a town house. She gave him the address, then took the baby with her. He followed as far as the pizza place, where he peeled off to pick up their dinner. Even so, he reached the town house in time to help her unload their purchases. It was just as well, since Meghan was exhausted from lugging Annie and her carrier up the outside stairs of the New Orleans style structure that was built with the living quarters above the laundry and two-car garage. As he took the heaviest bags from her, she realized with grim humor that there might be advantages to macho maneuvering.

An hour later, the three of them were still sitting at the polished dining table amid a litter of pizza crusts, crumpled napkins, baby food jars, and multicolored splotches of goo.

"We should have bought a high chair," Meghan said wryly as she wiped strained peas from her eyelid.

Rick lifted his arm to look at the pea green and carrot orange combination that decorated the underside of his shirt-sleeve. "First thing tomorrow morning."

Meghan's smile faded. "Maybe. If Annie is still here. And if anything is open on Christmas Day."

He agreed. In the silence that followed, they watched Annie as she did her best to transfer peas and carrots to her mouth with both hands at the same time.

The baby had shown herself well able to sit up on Meghan's lap, and had given her new baby spoon a good try before discarding it in favor of the utensils nature had provided at the ends of her arms. She had also displayed an iron will, refusing to eat unless she fed herself.

Her age, Meghan thought, must be around nine months. She was not only old enough to sit alone, but also to crawl after a fashion when put on the floor, and to wiggle and squirm and reach for what she wanted with bright-eyed determination. Old enough to be a handful and then some.

After a moment, Rick looked away, scanning the apartment, most of which could be seen from the table because of the great room concept of its construction. In curious tones, he said, "You don't have much in the way of Christmas decorations."

She shook her head as she searched for a clean napkin to wipe a sliding avalanche of peas from Annie's chin.

"I guess you see more than enough of it at the shop?"

"You could put it that way."

He leaned back in his chair, the blue of his eyes clear as he studied her. The pose was easy, relaxed and confident. It also drew his chambray shirt taut across the firm muscles of his chest. Meghan looked away as quickly as she could without being obvious about it.

Voice deep and low, he said, "So how come a woman like you isn't married?"

"I'm a widow," she said shortly. To forestall further questions, she added, "What's your excuse?"

He shrugged. "All work and not much play. The wrong woman a couple of times."

"You're divorced, then."

"Never got as far as the marrying part." His smile was a little crooked as he held her gaze for long, intent moments.

It was strange having a man in her apartment. He looked rugged and incredibly male against her soothing cream and taupe color scheme with its silk, satin, and brocade textures. She had chosen the decor, imminently suitable for a single woman, when she moved in six months ago. Before that, there had been a house in a nice subdivision close to a good school. She had sold it because too many haunting memories had been collected there.

Annie chuckled and waved her spoon, a movement that embellished the dining table with another wash of mottled green. It was a welcome distraction. As Meghan used her napkin to wipe up some of the mess, she said, "So what do you do?"

"Construction. In partnership with my brother."

Something clicked in Meghan's mind. She gave him her full attention as she said, "Wallman & Wallman Construction? You built the mall. And didn't you just complete the new wing for the hospital north of town?"

"We had the contracts for the jobs," he agreed with a steady look.

"But—surely you don't do the actual labor?"

He lifted a brow as he followed her gaze which brushed over his rough clothes. "Sometimes. When the mood strikes or a man fails to show up. Why not?"

"No reason," she answered hastily. "I guess I was just surprised."

"My brother, Brad, and I are both architects, but we learned the practical side of building from our dad, who was an old-time, hammer-and-nails carpenter. Most of the time, I draft or modify plans, figure bids for projects, round up special materials, keep an eye on the jobs, that kind of thing. But I like working with my hands now and then."

Meghan was quiet for a moment. Her thinking required some serious readjustment, which served her right for judging the man across from her by the clothes he wore. Wallman & Wallman was one of the largest companies of its kind in the tri-state area of Louisiana, Texas and Arkansas. If Rick Wallman wanted to take in strays and orphans, he could certainly afford it.

"Anyway, I was just thinking it would have been nice," he said in musing tones as he glanced around again, "if there had been a Christmas tree for Annie to wake up to in the morning."

Meghan avoided his direct look by beginning once more to clean up after the baby. "I don't suppose she'll miss it, being so little. We did buy the toys for her."

"Still . . ."

He was pushing for an answer to his earlier question, and she didn't think he would give up until he got it. He had that kind of single-minded concentration. She compressed her lips, uneasily aware that she owed him at least a little consideration after all his help. Finally, she said, "I don't have a tree or a wreath because I don't care for Christmas. Okay?"

A startled look flashed into his eyes. "But you own a Christmas shop!"

"My mother started it before my dad retired. She turned it over to me when the two of them decided to take off in their travel trailer for a year. They enjoy life on the road so much they still haven't come home, and—well, I had to have something to do after . . ." She trailed off, unwilling, even unable, to explain further.

"After your husband died."

"Yes." As the baby in her lap gave a prodigious yawn, Meghan snatched at the excuse to change the subject. "Annie has had it, I think. I'll give her a quick bath, then a bottle. It must be long past her bedtime."

His face was impassive for long seconds before he accepted the evasion. Inclining his head, he said, "I expect I'd better be going then. It must be your bedtime, too."

"Going?" She looked up, startled. "But you can't."

His dark brows drew together as he got to his feet. "You certainly don't want me to stay?"

"You have to!" Panic threaded her voice as she watched him reach for his jacket which hung over the back of his chair. "You promised to help."

Little Annie, staring from one to the other of them, became ominously quiet, though they hardly noticed.

"I did and I have," Rick answered, his gaze on Meghan's taut features. "But you look like you've got everything under control."

"Well, I don't, not by a long shot," she answered shortly. "You cannot leave me here alone with this baby."

Annie's pink bottom lip began to quiver. She whimpered, a distinctly unhappy sound.

Rick looked from one to the other with incredulity in his eyes. "Are you inviting me to bed down here?"

"I don't know that I'd put it like that, exactly," Meghan said. "But it's just like a man to try to run out on a woman after it's too late."

"I have never," he said with rough emphasis, "run out on anybody or anything in my life."

"Well, good, because I don't intend for you to start now!"

A muscle stood out in his jaw. "What I was trying to do is show a little consideration. I didn't figure you for the kind of woman who would let a man sleep over."

"I most certainly am not," she declared stoutly. Then ruined it by adding, "But this is different."

"I'm a man, in case you haven't noticed." The words were grim.

"Of course I noticed!"

"Good." His stance lost a little of its rigidity. "Look, I'll be back. Really. Bright and early in the morning."

"No, you won't, darn it all, because you aren't going anywhere! And that's final!"

He shook his head in slow bemusement. "But what will the neighbors think?"

"I don't care what they think," she said above Annie's rising cries. "You started this, and by all that's holy, you're going to finish it."

Humor appeared, unexpectedly, to brighten the dark blue of his eyes. "Careful with the language there, or you just might cuss me out."

"Don't think I can't," she told him, her own eyes narrowing.

"I'd love to see it."

She thought he meant exactly what he said, which was disconcerting to say the least. "Try sneaking out of here again and you certainly will."

There was measuring speculation and a species of strain in his face as he met her defiant gaze. Annie's screams were piercingly loud in the sudden silence between them. Then his lashes came down, shuttering his expression.

"Fine," he said, throwing his jacket back across the chair. "I'll clear up here while you give Annie her bath and put her to bed. Will that suit you?"

Her relief was instant, but not without reservations. "It'll be fine—for a start."

He paused as he picked up the oil-stained pizza box. "What does that mean? Once she's asleep, you shouldn't need me anymore."

"Maybe. We'll see." Standing up with the crying baby, Meghan headed for the bathroom.

Rick watched her retreating back for long seconds. Then he gave a slow, disbelieving shake of his head while a slow grin tilted his mouth.

Three

Annie wouldn't stop crying.

She didn't want her bottle. She didn't want her pacifier. She didn't want to rock, but was unhappy sitting still. She didn't want to be put down, but also didn't want to be carried. Red-faced, tears streaming from her drowned, woe-begone blue eyes, she screamed in a frenzy of nerves while she threw herself back and forth in Meghan's arms.

The sound was driving Meghan frantic. Pacing the floor, trying to hold the sobbing child, she felt her own tears gathering with acid heat against her burning eyelids.

"What's wrong with her?" Rick's voice held doubt and concern as he came to stand in the door of the bedroom where Meghan strode up and down with the crying baby.

"Heavens, I don't know what's wrong!" Meghan shouted above the din. "She's in a strange house, in strange pajamas, with strange people who ask stupid questions. What on earth could possibly be the matter with her!"

"Let me have her." He moved forward, reaching as if he meant to take Annie out of her arms.

Meghan twisted away from him. "You think you can do better with her than I can?"

"I'm not likely to do any worse." This time he closed his hand on Meghan's upper arm, swinging her around to face him. "Look," he went on in tones of firm reason, "it's late. You're dead-tired. Both you and Annie have gone about as far as you can go. So give it a rest. Get a hot bath and try to relax while I see what I can do with the kid."

It was perfectly reasonable. Unfortunately, that wasn't how she felt. "You think she likes you better."

"Little girls tend to go for men," he said with a crooked smile. "They respond to the size and authority. Sometimes big girls do the same."

Meghan could imagine. But she wasn't one of them. Refusing to meet his gaze, she said, "She's bound to cry herself to sleep in a few minutes."

"Probably," he agreed, his lips thinning with tested patience. "But can you stand to hear it?"

It was disconcerting to be understood so well. She could feel the tears gathering in warm, salty wetness along her lower lashes.

"I thought so," he said. "Even if you could stand it, I don't think I can. Come on, now. Let me have her."

She gave up the baby. What else could she do? Still, it felt like a failure on her part. It was even worse when, a few minutes later, while she lay soaking in the tub, she realized that Annie was no longer crying.

She couldn't do this; she just couldn't. Yet what other choice did she have? She had started it, and now she couldn't get out of it. If she tried, Rick Wallman would think she was heartless and cruel. Which was ironic when the problem was too much heart and tenderness instead of too little. Not that she cared what he thought. He was a stranger to her, after all.

A stranger in her house in the middle of the night. And she had not only invited him in, but insisted he stay when he tried to leave.

Annie liked the man, drooled all over him, in fact. Not surprising, when she herself was ready to do the same. Meghan wasn't ready to accept the judgment of a nine-month-old girl over her own, of course, but wasn't there supposed to be something special about the instincts of dogs and children?

She didn't think Rick would try anything. He wasn't the type, as far as she could see. She sensed he was solid, dependable, highly trustworthy. He was also outrageously sexy and knock-you-dead gorgeous, not that the last mattered. He was there for Annie's sake. Nothing more. Which was just a tiny bit depressing, or would be if she let herself think about it.

When Meghan emerged from the connecting bath a short time later, Rick was lying on the king-size bed in her darkened bedroom. She stopped, skimming her gaze along his lean form. He had removed his boots and thrown the comforter that served as a bedspread back out of the way. He had, in fact, made himself quite at home, so comfortable and at home that he had fallen asleep with his dark head cushioned on her spare pillow.

As she took a step into the room, however, the light from behind her fell across his body. She saw at once that he had only lain down on the bed with Annie. The baby was sleeping peacefully, supported in the crook of his arm, her thumb in her mouth and her musical rag doll held against her.

Rick roused as the light spilled across his face. He opened his eyes and turned his head toward it.

Meghan was standing near the bed with her body backlit perfectly by the glow from inside the bathroom. The sight of her lovely, slender curves seen through white silk took his breath and jarred his heart into a hard, unnatural rhythm. The scent of her drifting toward him, warm and womanly and overlaid by the fresh clean fragrance of lavender soap, made his stomach muscles tighten.

He wrenched upward in abrupt, involuntary self-protection. Annie tumbled from his shoulder, and promptly set up a wail.

"Stay where you are," Meghan commanded in a low hiss.

"No, it's all right," he whispered, even as he rolled Annie

to her stomach and began to pat her between the shoulder blades, urging her back to sleep. "I've got to go."

But as he tried to slide away from Annie, the baby flopped over toward him again, burrowing into his side with small grunting, whimpering noises.

"I don't think so," Meghan said in dry humor. Swinging around, she moved back to the bathroom to flip off the light switch.

Rick watched every swaying step she made; he couldn't help himself. Even after the room was plunged into darkness again, he could see her graceful progress in shadow as she moved around the foot of the bed and climbed in on the other side.

He knew he should get up. Should go. He would, too, just as soon as he regained his self-control.

In the meantime, he settled back down, trying to relax as he felt the shift of the mattress under Meghan's slight weight. Lying perfectly still with every nerve in his body tingling, he heard the soft rustling of the covers as she settled herself, her quiet sigh of tiredness as she stretched full length.

He closed his eyes, concentrating on keeping his breathing somewhere in the neighborhood of steady. With determination, he switched his attention to the rain still murmuring on the roof and pecking on the sill of the bedroom window. The wind. The faint click of a digital clock turning over its numbers on the table beside the bed. Anything. Everything.

As he listened, he tried to be sensible. This was not good strategy, staying here, sleeping in Meghan Castle's bed; he knew that beyond a doubt. Somehow, it didn't matter. It felt right.

It was too right, that was the main trouble with it. He closed his eyes, savoring the comfort, the pleasure. The rightness. He could stay here forever, and would with just a little encouragement. Only a little.

He came awake abruptly, every sense zinging with razor-sharp alertness. Something was wrong.

The rain had stopped. The heating system for the town house was running, a steady drone that suggested it had turned much colder outside. Annie had squirmed around in her sleep to lie across the mattress with her head toward him and her feet toward Meghan. Moving quietly, he tucked the down comforter that covered the bed more closely around the baby's small, warm body. It must have been some sound or movement she had made that disturbed him.

Then he felt it again, the slight quiver of the mattress. At the same time, he heard Meghan draw a strangled, difficult breath. Another shaking movement and choked-off gasp. She swallowed, an audible sound caused by tight throat muscles.

She was crying. Weeping silently in the dark, she was trying not to let him hear.

"Meghan? What is it?" Without thinking, he reached across the bed as he spoke.

His fingertips brushed a smooth, warm shape. Silky soft yet resilient, it was the rounded side of her hip he touched as she lay with her back to him.

She flinched away at the same instant that he jerked his hand back. Voice thick, she said, "Nothing. It's—nothing."

His fingers tingled all the way to his elbow. Doing his best to ignore the sensation, he whispered, "I'm sorry, I didn't mean . . ." He abandoned explanations, started again. "There must be something wrong if you're crying."

"It doesn't concern you. Go back . . . to sleep."

"I can't," he said simply as he heard the catch in her voice. Levering up on one elbow, he lay staring at her slight shape across the width of the mattress. He could just barely make it out in the faint beam of the complex security lights glowing beyond the bedroom curtains.

She turned to her back and lifted an arm, using it to cover her eyes. "It's Christmas Eve," she said thickly, stumbling a little over the words. "I told you I don't like Christmas."

"Why?"

"It's something I have to . . . to get through every year, something I have to get over. I . . . my husband was killed on Christmas Eve four years ago."

"I'm sorry." Such an inadequate response, but better than nothing. "What happened? Tell me."

For long moments, he thought she wasn't going to answer. Then the night and the darkness, and perhaps the odd bond caused by Annie lying between them, seemed to force the words from her.

"I was working late, as usual. James, my husband, picked up my little boy—ours—at day care. There was an accident. The other driver had been drinking, celebrating early. He was going too fast, crossed the center line. All three—died instantly."

"Your little boy." It was not a question. He knew what was coming, knew it with sick, aching dread because it explained so much that had not been quite right. He knew, too, that there was no way to stop it.

"Jimmy. He was only a baby, eight months old." She gasped, a harsh sound of anguish. "Just like, almost like, Annie." Her voice broke and the tears came in a hard, rough torrent.

Rick didn't stop to think. Easing Annie out of the way, he slid over on the mattress, then reached to drag Meghan into his arms. She resisted for an instant, her muscles stiff with reluctance. "Easy. Take it easy," he whispered in low compassion. "Just hold on to me."

Resistance left her in a rush. Body jerking with tremors, sobs shaking her, she rolled against his chest, melting into him, fitting curves to hollows with perfect fidelity before she pressed her wet face into his shoulder.

Forget it! Forget she's a beautiful woman. Forget the rightness. Forget her softness. Don't think. Forget it.

He chanted the words to himself in admonishment even as he inhaled with hoarse difficulty, dragging breath deep into his lungs. He closed his eyes tight as he tried to think of her as a larger version of Annie, just another tender female creature who sought comfort and a broad bulwark between herself and the pain of living.

Meghan only accepted what he offered because it was all that was available; he knew that without question. He was glad to provide it. It was the least he could do. No matter how much it might cost him.

The price was going to be high. That much, too, he knew all too well.

He had made a mistake, a bad one. He had fallen headlong, no holds barred, in love with Meghan Castle the minute he saw her with Annie. The decision to get close to her, to worm his way into her heart and home and stay there a lifetime was immediate. The only question had been how to go about making her see how necessary it was, how necessary he could become to her.

It had seemed natural, a bit of perfect timing, that Annie was on the scene. He had used the baby to get to the lady.

It was the wrong thing to do. He ached inside as he saw what a mistake it was, and how terribly wrong it could turn out.

Little Annie was too sweet, too adorable, and Meghan was half-crazy about her already. To lose her was going to be a blow, like losing her own baby all over again. He and Annie, between them, were going to hurt Meghan more than she could bear. If they hadn't already.

It had to happen, because in just one week little Anne Kathryn Wallman's mother and father would be coming home from their ski trip to Colorado, coming back to claim their darling Annie who had not been abandoned at all. And they might not take it too kindly if their only child had been handed over to another woman, given away by the brother of Annie's father, the uncle who was supposed to be taking such good care of her.

Annie's doting uncle who had left her sleeping under a Christmas tree while he made up his mind whether she would like having a Sugarplum Fairy Tree on Christmas morning.

Her Uncle Rick.

Four

"Want to see a miracle?"

The deep-voiced question echoed in Meghan's head with such warm promise that it seemed part of an ongoing dream. She opened her eyes, though she lay quite still. No one, particularly no man, should be in her town house, much less in her bedroom.

Or should he? Yes, she did remember. Too well. Including a few other things that brought varying degrees of pleasure and embarrassment.

A slow wave of color made its way to her forehead. She turned her head.

He was just as she remembered, only better. With the soapy scent of a shower and shave clinging to him, his square, even features, assured manner, and easy, unshadowed smile were just too much. She felt her heart contract in her chest.

He lifted a brow as he handed her a white silk robe, the one that went with the nightgown she wore. "Annie and I had about decided you were going to sleep all day. Wouldn't matter, except it would be a shame if you missed the sights."

"Where is Annie?" The question seemed natural. At least it was seminormal and far better than asking how he had remembered what her nightgown was like well enough to find a match for it in her closet. Or inquiring just how long she had slept in his arms.

For an answer, Rick only pointed toward the floor at his feet. Leaning over the edge of the bed, Meghan saw Annie rounding the end in a fast and efficient G. I. Joe crawl. As she saw Meghan looking down at her, the baby broke into a wide grin and redoubled her efforts.

Meghan could not have stopped the smile that spread over her face if her life had depended on it. She didn't even try. Murmuring a soft greeting and a great deal more nonsense as well, she slid from the bed to the floor and reached to pull the little girl onto her lap.

"Careful," Rick said. "She might get the remains of her breakfast oatmeal on you."

"As if I cared," Meghan returned, laughing as Annie grabbed at once for the silk rosettes on her robe. What he said struck her then, and she gave him a quick glance. "Breakfast? Just how long have you two been up?"

"Ages," he answered ruefully. "You wouldn't believe how long. Annie seems to be an early riser."

"You should have woke me."

He shook his head. "You needed your zees. Besides, we had things to do."

"Such as?" She spared him another brief look even as she tickled Annie for the pleasure of hearing her laugh.

"Playing Santa Claus, since you and I never got around to it last night."

"What?" He had her full attention. She even raked her hair back and tucked it behind her ear with one hand, the better to see him.

"For Annie. You know the drill. A tree? Presents?" He looked uneasy yet expectant as he stood over her.

Meghan was not at all sure she liked the compassion she saw as she searched the dark blue depths of his eyes. Nor was she sure she wanted to participate in a scene of Christmas morning joy. She was positive she didn't, in fact, since she wasn't at all certain she could stand it.

Returning her gaze to Annie, she said, "Where did you get a tree?"

"Best place I could think of. I borrowed your keys, talked the security guard into letting me in the back door at the mall. Silver Bells is minus one display, I'm afraid, but I didn't know where to find the boxed trees."

In blank disbelief, she said, "You've been to the store?"

"I left my credit card imprint to take care of what I carted off. Hope you don't mind."

"Would it make the tiniest bit of difference if I did?" she demanded.

He had the grace not to answer that. Instead, he extended his hand to help her and Annie up from the floor. "Come see what I found."

The Sugarplum Fairy Tree, complete with a myriad of fairy figures with pale green and gold wings, artificial, gold-streaked purple plums, marzipan candies and twinkling fairy lights, sat in the corner of her living room. Stacked under it was an impressive array of wrapped boxes that she recognized as being part of her store decorations. Since these were no longer quite as crisp or perfectly pristine as they had been, she could only assume they now held the toys bought the evening before.

That wasn't all. The smell of fresh-brewed coffee was in the air, and a plate heaped with croissants warm from the bakery sat on the table.

A lump formed in Meghan's throat as she stared at everything. Rick had gone to so much trouble, getting out so early, taking the baby with him, setting everything up so quietly. Who would have thought he could manage it? Or that he would bother?

"Why?" she said, almost to herself.

"For Annie," he answered. "Christmas and kids go together."

"Yes, I guess so." She drew a shaky breath. "I'll have to say it's a miracle, all right."

"Oh, this isn't as good as it gets," he said, smiling as he clapped his hands and held them out to Annie. As the baby leaned toward him and stretched out her small arms to be plucked from Meghan's grasp, he added, "Look outside."

The glance she gave him was both wondering and wary. Still, she moved toward the window he indicated and drew back the draperies on one side.

Snow.

It was a clean blanket of white that muffled sound, softened the edges of the world, and sparkled like angel hair in the clear morning sunlight. A white Christmas in Louisiana.

Meghan drew in a soft breath of astonishment. Snow was rare. A scant inch or two in late winter every three years or so here in the northern part of the state was about as much as could be expected, with even less farther south around New Orleans. Thick snowfall, and as early in the winter as Christmastime especially, was something that happened once in fifty years. It was something to remember, something people talked about for the rest of their lives.

It was dangerous.

There was no snow removal equipment in Louisiana, no preparations for dealing with it or the ice caused by the freezing of the first layer of melted snow that was sure to lie underneath. Most people didn't know how to drive in the stuff, had little experience with the inevitable skids, yet the very rarity of it made them want to get out and look at it.

Turning slowly to the man who had come to stand beside her, she stared at him in chill accusation. "You took Annie out with you in this?"

"The Bronco has four-wheel drive," he said. "And I do a lot of work in the Texas Panhandle where bad weather comes with the territory. I'm used to snow and ice. Annie and I were perfectly safe. We made it just fine."

She watched him with parted lips for long seconds before

she looked away, then drew a quick breath. "I—yes, I suppose so. That's about as much a miracle as everything else."

It was an acknowledgment of a great deal more than she realized, he thought. She accepted what he said. She trusted him.

A smile tugged at his mouth. To cover it, he looked at Annie with a wink. "Right, and we won't tell her about stopping to winch the guy out of the drainage ditch, will we, sugar? We might get ourselves permanently grounded."

Annie gurgled happily. It was a good thing she couldn't talk, he thought, since she seemed to be reminding him that there had actually been a couple of folks who had needed a nudge back onto the highway. "So what do you say, little pal?" he went on as he hefted her higher against his chest. "Do you think the grown-ups can have their coffee while you're tearing into the presents?"

The suggestion met with hand-waving approval.

The kid was a pro at the business. She ripped paper, snatched bows, and flung the pieces right and left. The contents of the boxes were of passing interest, but the wrapping was a high treat that she babbled about, tasted, and did her best to share by creeping over to where the adults sat on the floor and trying to stuff fistfuls down the front of Rick's shirt. She also tried to push a handful down the front of Meghan's nightgown—a fascinating operation, at least from his point of view. Meghan didn't seem to get quite the same kick out of it.

She did enjoy Annie's antics, however, even laughing out loud from time to time with the sheer pleasure of them. Before it was over, they were all sprawled out beside the tree, waist deep in paper, toys, and croissant crumbs. The last were no problem, since Annie obligingly crawled around retrieving anything the pair of them dropped and crammed it into her mouth.

In the middle of the proceedings, Annie yanked the paper off the package with the one-step camera. "Hey, whoa, honey," Rick exclaimed as he reached to save the distinctive yellow-and-black box. "That one belongs to the old folks."

"Ours?" Meghan said, looking up from trying to open a plastic bucket holding magnetic blocks. "What do you mean?"

"Ours, as in yours and mine. Our present to each other." He busied himself with removing the camera and its film cartridge from their packaging so he wouldn't have to look at her.

"Why? What for?"

"Because it's Christmas, why else?" he said with suppressed exasperation. "We didn't get each other anything last night, so I found this at a twenty-four-hour drug store."

"We didn't need anything."

He glanced up then, wondering if she could have any idea how close he had come to routing a friend of his out of bed at dawn to open up his jewelry store for a major purchase. It was just as well he hadn't, he thought. Meghan was the kind of woman who would have refused to take a valuable gift, and not just because she felt guilty she had nothing for him in return. Quickly, he said, "You don't buy presents because people need them."

"Profound, very profound," she replied with irony. "But I thought you said Christmas was for kids."

"It is. It's watching and remembering their fun that's for grown-ups. So this is for instant memories." Flipping open the camera back, he slapped the film into place, then brought the camera up and clicked the shutter.

"Don't!" she exclaimed, turning her head away from the flash.

"Too late," he said, and laughed because he knew exactly how true the words were, at least for him.

Annie, attracted by the light and whirring noise as the developing picture ejected into the closed back, came crawling over to them. Meghan reached and pulled the baby into her lap almost as if for protection, then bent her head to drop a quick kiss on the fine blond curls.

It was too good a shot to miss. Rick snapped it.

Later, when the wrapping paper had been gathered up and disposed of and the remains of breakfast cleared away, Meghan retreated to her bedroom to change clothes. Rick had suggested that she wear the red cashmere sweater that had been a gift from her parents, and he couldn't wait to see if she complied.

In the meantime, he was watching out for Annie. He ran a quick eye over her where she was busily tossing the magazines from Meghan's wicker holding basket and replacing them with her blocks. Since it didn't look like she could hurt herself or destroy anything really valuable, he took the developed photographs he had made from their cache in the camera back and spread them out to look at them.

Pure Madonna and child. Especially the one of Meghan kissing Annie. He hadn't realized he had taken so many shots of the two of them together. Shaking his head in slow wonder, he studied them one by one, absorbing the love and longing in Meghan's face and the perfect, unparalleled harmony between woman and child.

He felt like the biggest rat in the western world.

He hadn't meant for it to turn out this way. He had been floored, almost literally, seeing Meghan with Annie.

Realizing she thought the baby under the tree was abandoned, he had let the idea run. Some guys swore by a warm puppy or big, friendly mutt for attracting women. Using Annie to get close to the only woman to turn him on in ages had seemed a play along the same lines, one that was perfectly natural. He had expected to let things proceed long enough to prove he was a nice guy, a good prospective helpmate and father. Then he would confess the joke and they would have a good laugh over it.

The joke was on him. He felt as if somebody had clamped his heart in a vise, trying to see how much blood and bitter regret they could squeeze out of it. For when Annie went out of Meghan's life, Meghan would go out of his; it could be no other way. Now, the more time he spent in her company, the more he saw just how much he had to lose.

What was he going to do about it?

What in God's name was he going to do?

What?

He stared at the photographs, eyes burning, mind churning as he searched for a way out. Then it came to him, an idea so powerful that he gave a soft grunt as it struck, as though it packed the punch of a hard right to the solar plexus.

Born of the pure, snow-white glory of the season, it was so simple. So perfect. Simply perfect.

Did he dare? Hell, did he have the pure, unmitigated gall it would take?

No. Yes. Maybe.

Yes, and maybe he was kidding himself. Maybe the notion was the weird product of a deranged and sexually frustrated mind. Maybe he was nuts if he thought he could manage it.

Yes, and maybe he was setting himself up for a giant fall. A terminal error. One that could tear his heart to shreds.

It wasn't what he would prefer, not by a long shot. He would dearly love to be wanted for himself as well as needed for his protection, his name. No matter. He would take what he could get and be glad.

What other choice was there?

He looked toward Annie, who had crawled over to the Christmas tree and yanked off an ornament to take a taste. Moving quickly, he rescued the fragile piece, tucking it into his palm as he picked up the baby and hefted her close against his chest.

What he needed was another miracle, he thought as he

clenched his fingers on the ornament in his free hand, a sugarplum fairy vision of the perfect Christmas present.

He had a week, give or take, to pull this one off. A week for a desperate gamble, his one chance to catch and hold the happiness he could feel slipping away.

Was that enough?

Maybe. Just maybe.

How long did it take, anyway, to do what he had dared to plan?

Five

It was the middle of the morning when it occurred to Meghan that it had been some time since Rick had said a word about leaving. Perversely, she began to wonder why, and also just how long he thought she would allow him to stay.

A part of her concern was caused by the duffel bag she had discovered in her bathroom, one holding his personal articles and a couple of changes of clothes. He had apparently gone by wherever he lived for it while he was out. The black nylon bag had a disturbingly permanent look about it, sitting there beside her lavatory sink.

Not that she really wanted him to go or intended to send him out into the weather. After a scant hour of sun, just enough to form a sheet of ice on every street in town, it had turned overcast, then begun to snow once more.

It was still sifting down in huge, wet flakes. No traffic moved outside the apartment. The town was shut down, for all practical purposes. At this rate, they were likely to be iced in for at least twenty-four hours, possibly longer.

Yet Meghan realized, after examining the problem for a while, that the main thing bothering her was not that Rick had ceased trying to leave. It was, rather, that he might be remaining for entirely the wrong reason.

The two of them were trying to be as quiet as possible just now. Annie was napping on a quilt folded into a pallet and spread on the far side of the living room. Rick had built a fire in the flimsy metal firebox of her town house fireplace, then found a football game on television that he could watch with the volume turned almost off. After putting on a pot roast with potatoes and carrots, and also a frozen apple pie, Meghan had picked up her needlework and moved to join him. The meal would not be traditional holiday fare, but it was all she wanted or had on hand.

As the silence stretched with only the crackling of the fire and mutter of the television, Meghan cleared her throat. "About last night," she began, then stopped, uncertain exactly how to go on.

Rick turned his head on the back of the sofa where he lay stretched out beside her. "What about it?"

There was entirely too much awareness in his eyes. She looked down at the piece of needlepoint in her hands. Voice tight, she murmured, "Nothing."

He watched her long seconds. When she said no more, he returned to his game.

Outside, the wind moaned around the eaves with a chill sound. The smell of rich brown gravy seasoned with onion and garlic mingled with the scents of spiced apples and wood smoke that circulated in the room with the warm draft from the heating system. The fire leaped and snapped in homey comfort as it threw dancing shadows across the floor. On television, the home team made a touchdown, calling for prolonged cheers and several instant replays.

Rick transferred his gaze to the fire, then took a deep breath. With a crooked smile and a quick glance in her direction, he said, "I could get used to this."

So could she, Meghan knew, far too easily. The quiet companionship, the safe feeling caused by his presence, the sight of his powerful frame lying in easy, masculine repose satisfied some need deep inside that she had not known was there.

She bit her lip, not quite meeting his eyes. "You don't have to stay, you know, not really. I mean—I realize I was a little emotional about the whole thing last night, but I expect I can—"

"I want to stay." He added, "If you don't mind."

"No, of course not," she said quickly, perhaps too quickly. "Still, if it's out of pity, I would just as soon—"

"It isn't pity!" He sat up, swinging around toward her and bracing his wrists on his knees. "How in the name of heaven could you think it might be?"

"You were nice enough to let me cry all over you last night."

"Nice?" His expression was pained.

"Kind, very kind," she amended, repressing an all too clear vision of the other things he had been: strong, gentle, extremely controlled. "But I wouldn't want you to think I'll go to pieces if you leave me alone with Annie."

"You had every reason to be upset—and to resent having her pushed on you, if it comes to that. What I feel, if you want to know the truth, is responsible."

"There was nothing else to be done except take her with us; you were right about that," she said with a quick shake of her head. She was silent a moment. "Regardless, I keep thinking we should be doing something more to find out who she belongs to. I turned her clothes inside out looking for a name tag or any kind of clue—"

"Find anything?" he interrupted.

He almost sounded as if he was afraid she might have, Meghan thought, giving him a swift glance. He must honestly be enjoying their odd Christmas Day.

With a shake of her head and a negative grimace, she went on. "I don't mind looking after her now that I've gotten used to it. It's lovely, really. But I worry about the mother out there somewhere trying to find her baby. I mean, just think how she must be feeling if leaving her was an accident. She must be going out of her mind. And what if she reports Annie missing? You and I could be charged with kidnapping."

A wry smile came and went across his face. "I don't think it will come to that."

"You never can tell," she said darkly.

"You left a note, didn't you? We're keeping her safe and happy. Don't worry about it."

"I can't help it." The corners of her mouth tightened an instant before she tried to smile.

The planes of his face were gilded by firelight as he watched her, yet the wavering dance of the flames made his expression unreadable. Then he sighed. "Yes, I can see you can't. I guess maybe there's something I should tell you—"

He halted as a cry came from the direction of the pallet. They both turned in that direction. Annie had turned over on her stomach and lifted her head to watch them.

"Short nap," Rick said with something like relief in his voice.

Meghan lifted a shoulder in helpless resignation as she jumped up to get the baby. By the time she returned, Rick was engrossed in the football game once more. Whatever he had meant to say seemed forgotten.

She handed Annie to him to hold while she checked the food that was cooking. Afterward, she came back and took the baby away again to change her. Returning, she sat on the floor playing with her for some time. She looked up once to find Rick watching them with an odd expression on his face, like a combination of pleasure and yearning. Yet he only smiled as he caught her eyes, and looked away again almost immediately.

The day went fast after its slow start. Annie kept them occupied for the most part. It was amazing the time and effort required to keep her fed and clean, or to repair the ravages she left behind in her path of general destruction. She also entertained them. She was a natural monkey, clowning for their benefit, enticing one or both of them down to her level to play. She crawled and tumbled over them like a tiger cub testing the good nature of a semi-comatose tiger and tigress. And for their indulgence, she rewarded them indiscriminately by falling on them and saluting various parts of their faces with her bountiful, drooling affection.

Later, when they had eaten a combination lunch and dinner, Meghan lay down in the middle of the king-size bed with the baby in the hope of persuading her to take a longer afternoon nap. Surprisingly, Annie lay perfectly still beside her without protest. Watching the baby grow drowsy as she sucked her thumb and mauled her rag doll, smiling at the silky doll-like lashes as they fluttered shut, Meghan felt a deep, burgeoning feeling of indescribable warmth and gratification.

She was growing attached to Annie. She knew it, knew the danger in it, but couldn't help it.

In all truth, she wasn't sure she wanted to stop it. She had tried to remain numb these past few years, as if that would make the loss of James and little Jimmy easier to bear. It hadn't. Maybe letting herself feel and acknowledging the pain was the better choice. Something, perhaps her tears in the night and the comfort she had found, made her willing to take the risk.

Pondering this phenomenon, she drifted half-in, half-out of sleep. Tired, she was still so tired. She really should force herself off the bed, though. It wasn't polite to leave a guest alone while she indulged in a nap like a child. She would get up in a minute, but first she was going to close her eyes. For just a second.

The room was dim with the approach of evening when she surfaced again from some deep well of rest. Annie was still asleep in a warm sprawl.

They were not alone in the bed.

Meghan turned to her back to find Rick lying on his side behind her. The movement brought her closer to the warmth of his body since his weight was tilting the mattress in his direction. He looked as if he had been there for some time, as he lay propped on one elbow with his head resting on his palm. His eyes were heavy-lidded, his hair ruffled where he pushed his fingers through it. The urge to roll closer, to press against him and hold him close, was so strong that Meghan went absolutely still while she fought the treacherous impulse.

Rich humor rose to sparkle in the smoke blue depths of Rick's eyes. His mouth curved in a movement that was fascinating to watch. Then with a glance at Annie's supine form, he said softly, "I don't think I ever saw two such sleepyheads in my whole life."

His naturalness released the tension that held Meghan. A yawn caught her unaware then, though she lifted a hand to smother it. "Sorry," she murmured, veiling her gaze. "I didn't mean to desert you."

"I'm not complaining. It gave me an excuse to join you, after all."

"You slept, too?"

"I did, though I've been lying here awhile, thinking." His voice was tentative.

"About what?" She relaxed still more, willing to be entertained as she noted the warmth in his eyes.

He indicated the bed with a brief nod. "There was a time when our position here would have been called compromising, extremely compromising."

"I suppose," she said as he paused. Her gaze was watchful, serious.

"The consequences would have been clear and inescapable. I'd have been forced to propose. You would have been forced to accept. There would have been a nice, quick wedding."

"So much for the good old days," she quipped, her laugh a little hollow.

"They had their advantages," he allowed. "We could revert, if you just say the word. Want to give it a try?"

For one vivid, heart-stopping instant, she thought he meant it. Then she realized how impossible that was, saw the dry consideration in his gaze, remembered his ready sense of humor.

Her disappointment was shocking. With a strained smile and her best imitation of a Victorian belle, she murmured, "Oh, sir, I am deeply honored, dear sir, but this is so sudden. We are barely acquainted."

His thick lashes came down, hiding his expression. "I suppose so. Guess that means we'll just have to continue the trial marriage."

"Oh, is that what this is?"

"Close enough. A lot of couples who have known each other far longer couldn't have spent a better day together."

She felt a flush of pleasure and confusion spreading across her face. In quick, mocking defense, she said, "Well, you might have warned me."

"And scared you off?" he said, lifting a brow. "I've got better sense than that."

"Good, because you had me worried there for a second."

He met her gaze, his own dark yet with an impression of heat in its depths. "Yes, well, don't get too cocky. It could happen yet."

He rolled from the bed then in a smooth movement of well-oiled muscles and left the room without looking back. Meghan stared after him with a frown between her eyes. She didn't move until Annie began to stir awake.

The memory of the odd exchange would not go away. It hovered somewhere between them as the evening wore on, while they watched a movie and the late news, including the weather that promised freezing rain. Remnants of it were still palpable as they both got sopping wet trying to give Annie a bath. It was there in an uneasy awareness as Meghan emerged from the bathroom later in her nightclothes.

Annie was not asleep, which was no great surprise, all

things considered. In fact, she was ready to play. They were going to have to do something about adjusting her schedule, or so they agreed as they alternately fended off her attempts to climb over them where they hemmed her in on the mattress or watched her roll around clutching her toes.

Finally, Meghan glanced at the damp splotches that made Rick's shirt cling to his chest. "You should get out of those wet things. Didn't you bring any pajamas?"

"Yeah, sure." His glance flickered over her, brushing her form so clearly outlined by the drape of her gown and robe, before he looked away again. "But I guess I'd better bed down on the sofa tonight."

"There's plenty of room here." She wished the words unsaid the minute they left her mouth. It wasn't that she was that naive, just that it had begun to seem natural to have him so close. She added quickly, "Anyway, Annie might roll off with no one on the other side of her."

He put his big hand on the baby's stomach, giving her a small shake as he grinned down at her. "She might at that. She flips and flops like a whale and kicks like a mule. Don't you, sweet thing?"

Annie laughed up at him.

He quirked a brow. "But I'd still better sleep on the sofa, hadn't I, my honey, because otherwise this trial marriage might get to be too much of a trial. Wouldn't want the nice lady to kick us both out."

Annie cooed.

"Right." He leaned over the baby. "Give us a good night kiss, then, sugarplum, and be good for Aunt Meghan."

Annie grabbed a handful of his hair, yanking unmercifully as Rick brushed his lips across her forehead and under each plump cheek. Meghan, wincing in sympathy, rolled closer to grab the baby's hand and unwrap the naturally sticky little fingers, releasing Rick so he could remove himself from the bed. It was then necessary to unwind the silky black hair caught on Annie's thumb. Engrossed in her task, Meghan only looked up as a shadow swooped across her.

"Good night to you, too, sweet lady," Rick said, smile crooked and voice husky as he leaned over her. Putting a knuckle under Meghan's chin to tip it up, he pressed his mouth to hers.

It was a warm and vibrant assault on the senses, one that carried a coded message. He wanted her and didn't care if she knew it. He was aware that she could want him if she would just allow it.

The startling suggestion of intimacy set off a thousand bursting roman candles of half-forgotten excitement inside her. She melted into the smooth and gentle pressure of his lips, absorbing the sensual intent behind them, and the warning.

Sweet, he tasted so sweet. She could sense the molten heat inside him, like boiling syrup brought to the candy stage. Or like a banked fire that promised to take her up in flames yet keep her warm and safe from the cold, forever. And in that moment, she didn't care if she might also get burned.

He broke the contact, lifting his head with what seemed slow reluctance. His gaze lingered on her half-parted lips for a fleeting instant. Then he was gone.

Six

It was the small hours of the morning when Annie started crying. Rick levered himself to one elbow on the sofa. He cocked his head to listen as he tried to decide whether to go and get her or wait to see what happened.

Within seconds, he heard Meghan's voice in a soothing murmur. The wailing died down to fretful whimpers. He eased back down on his pillow, but lay staring into the dimness of the living room lighted only by mercury vapor beams through the windows.

It wasn't long before he heard the soft scuff of footsteps on the great room carpet. Meghan, carrying the baby on her hip, ghosted through the living area on her way to the kitchen. The refrigerator door opened, throwing a wedge of light across the room. In its glow, he could see Meghan's worried frown and Annie's small face screwed up in distress.

Meghan took out a bottle and closed the refrigerator, then went through the now familiar motions of warming the milk a few seconds in the microwave. She moved with grace and competent ease in the semidarkness. He felt a smile curve his lips from the pure pleasure of watching her.

He waited until she had replaced the nipple on the bottle and started back to the bedroom. As she came even with the sofa, he said, "What's the problem?"

She barely flinched. It was possible she had a better understanding of what he was like than he thought.

Her voice was tight with her concern as she answered, "I'm not sure. Annie may just be hungry, but she feels a little warm to me."

"Fever?" he asked, sitting upright.

"Maybe. I wish I had one of those instant thermometers."

He flung back the covers. "Want me to go get one?"

"This time of night?" Her voice registered startled inquiry.

"Something is bound to be open."

Meghan rocked the crying baby in her arms as she considered it. She was silent so long that Rick really began to worry. Finally, she said, "I just don't know. She doesn't seem to have a cold. Do you think maybe she's teething?"

Relief washed over him as he recalled some mention of that possibility in the instructions left behind by his sister-in-law. "Yeah, I expect that's it. She has her two bottom teeth, but might be getting the top ones."

There had been a teething ring and medicine for pain in the bag of emergency provisions he had been given; he remembered seeing them. They were, of course, at his house on the far side of town. He was almost sure one of those thermometers Meghan was talking about had been thrown in for good measure. His brother's wife, Christy, had been pretty thorough, probably because she hadn't been too happy at leaving Annie. Christy had never cared for Stacy, Rick's girlfriend, who was supposed to be helping him baby-sit. Turned out she was right. Stacy had suddenly discovered other plans when she learned her Christmas holidays were going to be complicated by a nine-month-old girl. He wondered what Christy would think of Meghan.

Even as these thoughts flashed through his head, he said, "Tell me what you think Annie needs, and I'll make sure she has it."

"I suppose we can try the bottle first. If that doesn't work . . ." Meghan didn't finish the sentence as she turned away with the whimpering child, moving back toward the bedroom.

Rick was far too antsy to lie back down or even to stay in the living room. Rising to his feet, he followed them. As Meghan sat down on the bed, he reached to drag the pillows over and pile them against the headboard for her so she could lean back with Annie in her arms. She smiled her thanks as she eased down against them.

He felt so helpless—not to mention guilty for separating Annie from the things she might need. He hovered over her and Meghan, on the verge of offering one more time to make the run to a drugstore. Annie's crying trailed away, however, as she accepted the bottle. Maybe he could wait a few more minutes. He dropped down on the mattress just beyond Meghan's feet.

In the silence that followed, he realized the light in the connecting bathroom had been left on with the door almost closed to create a night light. He could make out the gleam of Meghan's hair and the white sheen of her nightgown. In her hurry to pick up Annie, she had failed to slip into her robe. The silk material she had on was so sheer he could make out the circular shadow that was the aureole of a breast and even the tiny bud of her nipple.

She could also see him. She could plainly tell he had avoided the pajamas he seldom wore to sleep in his briefs. He felt his neck and the tops of his ears burning. It was not that he was particularly modest, but he did have a few manners. He would have slipped on his jeans if he hadn't been so worried about Annie.

Beating a quick retreat had a powerful appeal. He let it go mainly because it seemed likely to add to the problem instead of solving it.

"What's that you're wearing?" she asked in quiet curiosity.

For a stunned heartbeat of time, he thought she meant the briefs. Then he saw that her gaze was directed considerably higher. Reaching up, he touched the chain at his neck. "This? Just a gold coin. Comes from the Isle of Man; St. Michael on one side, the queen on the other."

"I hadn't noticed it before."

"I'm not much on wearing it so it shows." He gave an uneasy shrug. "It's sort of a talisman, a Christmas gift a couple of years back from my sister-in-law. She knows I collect coins. Besides which, she's Catholic and I think she felt I could use the protection."

"From the patron saint of soldiers?"

He lifted a brow, pleased at her knowledge as well as intrigued by her interest. "Soldiers, policemen, firemen, fighters of all kinds. She thinks I interfere in other people's business too much, always trying to help get rid of their demons."

"And do you?"

"I don't know. It's not always easy to see the difference between helping and pushing in where you don't belong."

He saw too late where the subject might lead. If he had any hope that she would fail to make the connection, however, it died as soon as she spoke.

"So it's not only because you like children that you're taking care of Annie?"

"I don't have any mandate to right the wrongs of the world, if that's what you mean." The words were defensive and he knew it.

"Only the ones you can do something about?"

The heat in the back of his neck spread to the top of his head. "Don't make me out to be all noble, because I'm not. I like babies, as I said before, and I don't exactly hate spending Christmas with a gorgeous woman like you. If there's any deep, dark reason for trying to take care of Annie, it's because I once—" He stopped, appalled at what he had been about to say to the quiet, lovely woman sitting across from him on the bed, her face shadowed in near darkness.

"You once what? I told you my secrets. It isn't fair to hint that you have one and then keep it to yourself."

"It's not something I like remembering."

"There would be no point in keeping it secret if you did, would there?" The words were soft and simple, yet cut to the heart of the matter.

She was perfectly right. He took a deep breath and let it out in a rush. Voice compressed, he spoke before he could change his mind. "I once had—almost had a son. The girl I was living with was a television reporter with big ideas. She found out she was pregnant at the same time a job offer came up in Chicago. I wanted her to stay, get married. She didn't like the idea, so she got rid of the baby. But she made sure I knew it was a boy." His voice roughened, almost went away. "I had a son, but I never knew him."

"Oh, Rick," Meghan whispered in vibrant compassion. "I'm sorry, so sorry."

"So am I," he said, clenching his hands into fists. "I shouldn't have said anything, didn't mean to remind you."

"Yes." She paused, drew a quick breath. "It almost makes it easier, you know, in a way. I suppose misery really does love company. Or maybe it just helps to have the reminder that we're all walking wounded."

He moved a shoulder as if easing a burden, even as his lips twisted in a wry smile. "I can't think of anybody I'd rather have hiking along for company."

She made no immediate reply. He watched the pale oval of her face, wishing he could see her eyes. Wishing, too, that things were different so he didn't have to press quite so hard. She needed time, and it was something he could not afford to give her.

Maybe what he had in mind was all wrong. Here in the lowest hours of the night it seemed unlikely, if not downright impossible, that it would work. Yet he had to try. It was his only chance.

He had never been much for bed hopping. Slick moves

and one-night stands weren't his style. Whatever predatory instincts he might have were reserved for business. If he met a woman he liked, he asked her out. If things proceeded to the point where it seemed natural to go to bed, and the lady was agreeable, well, then he went. But he didn't use women, and he tried not to raise hopes he couldn't satisfy.

He had discovered over time that he required a certain amount of warmth and affection, otherwise sex was no good. His long-term arrangements had been few, a grand total of two in fact, but he had never gone into one without thinking along permanent lines. No, or feeling regret when it didn't pan out. In general, he liked the idea of marriage.

Christy claimed his relationships didn't work because he had poor judgment when it came to women. Being so strong himself, he couldn't resist the needy ones who latched on to him. He might look as tough as the nails he used, she informed him once, but his heart was like a caramel: soft, rich, and incredibly sweet. He didn't much care for the sound of that description himself, sounded kind of sticky-gooey. It was far more likely that he was just soft in the head.

Still, he did envy his brother his family. And he had often wondered if he would ever meet anyone who was as close a match for himself as Christy was for Brad.

Now he had. He had met his perfect mate, the one he wanted beside him his whole life through. He would give anything if she could want him as well as need him, but if he couldn't have it that way, then he'd take whatever he could get.

It was all he could expect, really, because he had screwed up royally. He had this one chance to fix it, the way he saw it, and he was going to have to take it soon.

Too bad he couldn't come up with a few of those slick moves now when he needed them.

Meghan, sitting in the semidarkness with the warm weight of the baby in her arms, could not stop looking at the golden glint of the small coin half-hidden in the dark hair on Rick's chest. Nor could she keep her gaze away from the white, winglike shape of his briefs, the only thing covering him. In the dim light, he appeared perfectly formed, hard-muscled, like a bronze of some ancient warrior-god.

He was very real, however. She could feel his body heat against the soles of her bare feet. The least shift of his long form on the mattress sent a shiver of awareness along her nerves.

It was Annie who distracted her. The baby nursed for only a few minutes before she began to make piteous whimpering noises again. As she refused the bottle, Meghan set it on the nightstand, then got up and began to pace up and down. Annie's crying increased.

Babies in pain always sounded desperate, Meghan knew. Still, the sound raked along her nerves. What if Annie weren't teething after all?

"Do you think she could really be sick?" she said with an anxious glance toward Rick.

"Sick how?"

His voice was calm yet alert, though his muscles appeared tense. Meghan wished she could see his expression more clearly, could tell if he was as unconcerned as he sounded.

She replied shortly, "I don't know. Maybe the milk we bought has upset her stomach."

"She's been doing fine on it until now."

"Maybe she's coming down with a cold, then, or some kind of twenty-four-hour virus. Maybe she has some strange disease, and that's why her mother deserted her. Do you think we should take her to the emergency room?"

He stared at her a long moment while his jaw tightened. Finally, he said, "We don't have a last name for her or a birth date. We don't know her pediatrician, have no idea where her medical records are stored. Any doctor who sees her would have to put her through a whole battery of tests just to bring her up to speed. That would be a bit drastic, don't you think, if all that's wrong with her is she's cutting teeth?"

Meghan flung him a look of desperation even as she continued to walk up and down with the wailing child. His measured approach was all very well, but it could be annoying, too. "Yes, I can see that, but what if she has measles or pneumonia? Or maybe it's something worse like—scarlet fever or typhoid or—or AIDS? Maybe the mother was depending on me to get help for her? We can't just do nothing because we don't know who Annie belongs to!"

"We can't panic, either," he said sensibly.

Trouble was, he sounded too damned reasonable. It made her wonder if he really recognized the dangers. Swinging away so her back was to him, Meghan spoke with difficulty. "Yes, but what if she—dies?"

He was on his feet in an instant, coming up behind her and wrapping his long arms around both her and the crying baby. His voice was near her ear, his breath warm in her hair as he spoke. "She isn't going to die."

"But if she did, I would be responsible. I couldn't stand that. I couldn't." She rested the back of her head against his collarbone for an instant, long enough that she could feel the contrasts between them, her softness and his hard strength, her trembling doubts and his steady assurance.

"You wouldn't be responsible," he answered firmly. "Look, I'm going to get what Annie needs. Right now. Will you be all right?"

"I . . . yes, I suppose. You really think she's just teething?" She wanted to believe it, wanted it so much that unconsciously she leaned into the support of his arms. There was such limitless confidence there, such comfort and incredible rightness in the feel of them around her.

"I'm positive. You won't do anything until I get back?"

"Not if you hurry." She pushed erect. Then she spun

around. "No, wait! Forget I said the last part. The streets are too icy for hurrying. I just—"

"I know," he said, laying his fingers on her lips. "I won't be a minute longer than I have to be."

He smoothed the tender surface of her mouth with his thumb in a reassuring caress. Then the warm, encompassing strength of his presence was removed. She was left alone.

Meghan listened to him sliding into his clothes in the living room, finding his jacket and Jeep keys, letting himself out of the house. She shivered a little and rubbed her face against the baby's soft hair as the door closed behind him. In truth, she wasn't sure who she was trying to comfort, Annie or herself.

Yes, she would wait. She would wait and she would pray that Rick was right and Annie wasn't really ill. But she didn't know how much more of this she could take.

Something was going to have to be done to find the person this precious child really needed most, her own mother. If Rick wouldn't do it, Meghan thought in determined resolution, then she would have to see to it herself.

And she would, too.

First thing in the morning.

Seven

Rick simply went to the nearest all-night drugstore and threw himself on the mercy of the woman behind the counter. He returned loaded up with enough stuff to open his own pediatric clinic, but that was better than being minus something essential.

The lighted instrument used for looking into Annie's ears indicated no sign of redness that might signal infection. The instant digital thermometer showed only the low fever to be expected with teething. The gel for her swollen gums quieted her down enough that she finished her bottle. And the liquid pain killer put her out like a light.

As the dawn began to break, Annie was sound asleep. Rick and Meghan, on the other hand, were now wide awake.

"So how were the roads?" Meghan asked, propping one elbow on the table where they sat. As the sleeve of her robe slipped back, she barely caught it in time to keep it from dipping into the coffee cup in front of her.

Rick glanced at her blue-veined wrist as she pushed the sleeve aside. The need to press his mouth to the pulse that beat there came winging out of nowhere. His lips and tongue tingled while his stomach muscles clenched. Amazing. Her hair was tousled, she was pale from fatigue and had dark circles under her eyes only partially caused by smudged mascara, yet he had never seen anything more beautiful in his life. Or anything he wanted more.

"The roads? Not too good," he answered her question

almost at random. "The interstate and several secondary roads are closed because of ice on the overpasses and bridges. About all I saw moving were police and emergency vehicles, plus a delivery van or two with chains. Looks like you get another day off from work."

She rubbed at the frown between her eyes. "I really should get to the store. We usually have an after-Christmas sale that does well."

"Not much point in opening up if customers can't get there," he said reasonably.

"I suppose."

If he believed in such things, Rick thought, he would almost say divine providence was lending him a hand. Roads closed. Businesses closed. Life at a stand-still. He and Meghan were stuck in the apartment with Annie. Nobody coming, nobody going. He loved it.

What he didn't care for was the pressure of having to stage some kind of seduction scene. If it wasn't for his own stupid mistake, he could take it nice and easy. Slow down and enjoy every stage. Like constructing a great architectural project, he could build with careful and meticulous inevitability to what would be a once-in-a-lifetime experience. God, but it would have to be if what he felt right this minute was any indication.

The whole thing was beginning to seem far too important to rush. He didn't want to take the place of her dead husband, but to make one of his own. Didn't want to be accepted only because he might be the father of her child, but because she wanted him for himself.

And the last thing he wanted to do was blow it. He already had more than his share of explaining to do. Another strike against him could be too much to overcome.

Extra time might also weight the odds in his favor. Associating with babies was supposed to make a woman more susceptible to becoming pregnant, wasn't it? Hormones and instinct kicked in, or something. Just look at all the women who tried for years to start a family without any luck. Then the month after they finally gave up and brought home an adopted child? Boom.

Anyway, he owed it to Meghan not to mess up. She needed an Annie, if not the real thing, then at least a substitute along the same lines. Odds were any child of theirs would look much the same. Annie's mother, Christy, had coloring similar to Meghan's, while he and Brad were basically alike, give or take a scar or two and a few gray hairs. He had thought Brad's graying was due to advanced age, since his brother was some three years older. Now he knew it was all Annie's fault. Still, he was looking forward to earning his own silver decorations. In more ways than one.

It might be a good idea if he got his mind out of the sack. As he looked around for inspiration, his gaze landed on a photograph in a silver frame that sat on the fireplace mantel, the picture of a man in horn-rimmed glasses holding a yawning baby and sitting in an armchair. It was obviously the husband and child Meghan had lost.

He had competition here, he ought to remember that. The past that had such a grip on Meghan could well get in his way. The more he knew about it, the better he would be able to fight it. At least finding out about her dead husband should go a long way toward lowering his own male hormone level.

Taking a deep breath, he said, "Tell me about—I think you called him James. What kind of man was he?"

For a long moment, he thought she wasn't going to answer as she gazed at him with wariness and restraint warring on her features. Then she looked away, moistening her lips in a quick gesture that made him tingle to his toes.

Voice almost too soft to hear, she said, "He was the quiet type, a college dean, English department." She smiled, a sad curving of the lips. "He read Chaucer to little Jimmy while I was pregnant. He actually liked mowing the lawn, edging the walk. He called himself a neat-freak, and he was right about that. He dressed preppy because it suited him, not because it was stylish. He was . . . a gentle man."

"You miss him." It hurt him to say the words. It wasn't pleasant to discover that he could be jealous of a dead man.

"I did, for a long time. Now it seems as if it was almost another life, another lifetime ago. Sometimes . . ." She stopped, tried again. "Sometimes I have trouble remembering exactly what he looked like."

The constriction in Rick's chest eased a fraction. Nodding at the photograph, he said, "The boy was like him."

"Yes," she said quietly. "Jimmy, I remember. It helps."

He swallowed, hard. "I don't know what to say. I can't imagine what it must have been like to be told they were gone."

She turned her head to look at him, her gaze open. "I think you may be one of the few who can."

She was right, he could. Knowing she realized it was like the forging of a bond. He wondered if she felt it, too, or if it was only in his own mind.

But this was cutting a little too close to the bone. She would not appreciate being reminded of past pain, and he wasn't sure how much of it he could stand without reaching out and pulling her close. Though he wasn't at all certain whom he would be comforting, her or himself.

As the silence stretched, he said, "Right. So if work is out for both of us, what's on the agenda for today?"

"I hadn't really thought," she answered as she followed his lead with a careful smile. "Laundry, I suppose, since Annie is fast catching up with the wardrobe we got for her."

"Right. I can give you a hand there."

The look she gave him was dubious. "I'm a little behind in general around here after all the late closings with the Christmas rush." She gave a small shrug. "After that, I don't know. I could pay some bills, get the books for the store ready for the accountant since it's almost the end of the year."

"Work and more work," he said with a wry grimace. "Don't you ever quit?"

"You can come up with something better?"

"Without half trying." The words were positive.

She seemed skeptical, but not unwilling to be diverted. "Such as?"

"Well, we can start by playing in the snow. After the laundry, of course."

She stared at him a moment, then a smile rose in her eyes. "You've got a deal."

While they washed and folded clothes, they talked about everything under the sun, from the problems in Washington to the latest movies. Afterward, they had to cook the big breakfast of pancakes and sausage they suddenly decided they couldn't do without. Halfway through the process, Annie woke up, and eating became secondary to watching her stuff herself with syrup-and-butter-soaked bits of pancake. That last fun-filled process made it necessary to give Annie another bath and wash the buttery stickiness from her hair.

A crunching walk in the snow, then building a snowman in the front drive of the town house took up what was left of the morning. Annie was intrigued by the way the white stuff disappeared in her hand and into her mouth, and was particularly delighted by the reaction created when she dripped handfuls of it down the necks of the grown-ups. Her favorite thing, however, was the snow ice cream made with fluffy scoops from a clean drift stirred together with sugar, vanilla, and milk. The treat interfered not at all with her lunch, of course, though chasing bits of ham and cheese around on her plate was an exhausting business that called for a long nap.

Dusting and polishing and waiting for Annie to wake up again so they could run the vacuum pretty much rounded off the day. At some time during mid-afternoon the weather turned traitor, for the sun came out and caused a meltdown of the snow and ice. By nightfall, nothing was left except muddy slush.

There was no question that Meghan would go to work on the following day. As usual, she dressed for the store as soon as she got out of bed. That was an error, of course. By the time she had fed, bathed and dressed Annie, she had to change her own clothes again.

Rick would also be going to work, but he saw no need for day care or any such arrangement for Annie. He had leg work to do for a couple of jobs, so would be spending a lot of time in the Bronco. Annie could ride around with him. If he needed to change a diaper or warm a bottle, he could always run by his office. If he got things rounded up, he would be back at the town house in time for her afternoon nap. If not, she could sleep in her new car seat. No problem.

It might not be the best solution, Meghan thought, but she didn't doubt he could handle Annie for one day. By tomorrow, it shouldn't be necessary any longer. Meghan hadn't made that call to Community Services the day before, but she would this morning. Without fail.

Rick was shaving as she left for work, since he had stayed out of the bathroom until he was certain she was done. Meghan picked up Annie and hugged her close, closing her eyes as she pressed a kiss to her forehead. There were tears in her eyes when she finally put the squirming baby down and let herself out of the apartment.

"Oh, honey," Yvonne said, her hazel eyes dark with concern in her soft, wrinkled face as Meghan told her what had happened on Christmas Eve and what she meant to do about it. "Do you have to?"

"You know I do," she said. "It's not only the responsible thing to do, but it's a matter of survival."

"What's Rick Wallman going to say?"

Meghan's smile was wry. "I don't know, but I wouldn't be surprised if it turned the air blue."

The older woman sighed as she leaned on the counter, abstractedly running a pen through her silver-white curls. "It seems such a shame."

"The shame is that anyone would abandon a baby, much less an angel like Annie. I can't believe there wasn't someone here this morning, or at least an answer to my note on the door. How anyone could just walk off and leave her, I can't begin—" Meghan stopped, folding her lips over words she had already said too often.

Yvonne gave her a look of calculation. "I was thinking more about this Rick of yours. It seems such a shame to waste good husband material like that. You wouldn't want to wait on finding Annie's mama so you can keep him around a little longer?"

The temptation was not new, but her conscience wouldn't let her take that course, even if there weren't other things at stake. "That wouldn't be right, now would it?"

"I suppose not. Pity." Yvonne pursed her lips. "You know, I've got to meet this guy who's so crazy about a found baby that he won't hear of turning her in."

"Come on, you make it sound like I'm a stool pigeon," Meghan protested.

The older woman looked at her with a glimmer of humor. "Aren't you? But don't change the subject. I was talking about your Rick."

"He isn't mine!"

"Yes, well. But I was just thinking that I've never heard of a man who wasn't all thumbs with a baby. Are you positive he's not the father? You sure he's not stringing you along because he's on the lookout for a mother for Little Orphan Annie?"

Meghan laughed; she couldn't help it. The idea of pink

and white cherubic Annie belonging to rough, tough Rick
was too funny for words.

Except that he wasn't as rough or as tough as he looked.
And she had misjudged him before.

Was it possible? Annie certainly responded to him, even
seemed to prefer being held by him, especially when she
was tired. He was amazingly at ease with her. Nothing was
too good for Annie, nothing too much trouble.

No. It didn't make sense. Hadn't Rick thought Annie was
hers that night when he first saw them?

Besides, if Rick Wallman were the father and wanted a
mother for his child, he wouldn't have to stoop to such a
clumsy subterfuge. All he had to do was pick out the woman
and ask. No female in her right mind was going to refuse.
Even she might consider . . .

Good grief, what was she thinking?

"I really don't want to talk about it anymore!" Meghan
said in strung-out finality. "I've made up my mind and
that's that."

"Whatever you say," Yvonne replied with a shrug as she
turned back to her job of marking down Santa Claus figures. "It's your funeral."

Those last words might be too apt entirely, Meghan
thought as she pictured herself confessing to Rick that she
had made the call. But she made it anyway. She had no
other choice.

Rick noticed the message light blinking on Meghan's answering machine when he walked into the town house. He
dismissed it in his concentration on putting Annie down for
her nap, then making himself a fresh pot of coffee. Cup in
hand, he sat down at the kitchen table and took a sheaf of
papers and blueprints from the portfolio he had brought in
with him. He had some catching up to do while things were
quiet.

It was hard to concentrate on business there in the town
house. Evidence of Meghan was everywhere he looked. He

smiled as he realized how much of her taste and style was reflected in the furnishings. Simple and warm yet elegant, comfortable but neat and clean, it was the home of a woman who knew exactly who she was and what she liked.

The blinking light on the answering machine drew his attention to it again. Curious, he got to his feet and strolled over to where it sat on a side table half-hidden by her discarded needlework. Four messages. The lady was not without friends.

He should leave it alone, he knew; it had nothing to do with him. Yet Meghan had known he might be coming back there in mid-afternoon. It was possible she had left a message for him about Annie or what they might do for dinner. He could hope, couldn't he? It would be nice to have some sign of interest, and even nicer to hear her voice. He reached out and punched the button.

What he heard were two hang-ups for wrong numbers and a plea to take out a newspaper subscription. Then came a brief message from a Mrs. Purdy at Community Services. She was sorry, but she was unable to fit the investigation of the found child into the work schedule for today after all. Several case workers had called in sick, and those who had come in were behind schedule due to the holiday and bad weather. She was sure Mrs. Castle understood. If she would return the call, their appointment could be rescheduled for tomorrow evening after five, or whenever might be more convenient. Beep.

Rick saw red. Literally. A blood haze of rage.

He couldn't believe Meghan would go behind his back to bring officialdom with all its rules and regulations and petty interference into what was a private affair. How could she do this to Annie? What the hell was she thinking? He raked his fingers through his hair, then set his fists on his hip bones while he cursed for a full minute.

Abruptly he fell silent.

It was stupid to rant and rave. If he used the brain God gave him, it wasn't hard to see what Meghan was thinking.

She wanted Annie out of her life, not because she didn't care what became of her, but because she was beginning to care too much.

The fault, then, rested squarely on his own shoulders. Every second he waited to admit his deceit made it that much more likely that he was going to come out of this a loser.

Thank God, he had caught that message. He would call bright and early in the morning and explain to Mrs. Purdy that the mother of the "found child" had only been temporarily mislaid. He was getting pretty good at lying through his teeth. He should to be able to handle an underpaid social worker without too much trouble.

That would take care of Community Services, but then he had to deal with Meghan. She might have placed the call to the agency, but she had no way of knowing what had been done about her report. And she wouldn't, not if he could help it.

Punching the button to erase the messages, he watched the counter blink back to zero. At the same time, he shook his head at the depths to which he was descending out of hope and cowardice. It was really pitiful.

Still, he had no choice. He needed every angle he could manage to gain, every single ounce of emotional weight he could swing in his favor. Because when the chips were down, it was going to take more than fast talking to get him out of this one. He needed to be close to Meghan, as close as he could possibly get. He needed her in his bed. Or he needed to be in hers.

Yes, and there was one thing more. The message was proof that he was fast running out of time.

Nice and easy just wasn't going to cut it.

Eight

The first thing Meghan saw when she walked in the door was the brand-new high chair sitting in the kitchen. That sign of semipermanence cut across her heart like a lash. She stood still, staring at it.

Then a small movement on the sofa caught her attention. Swinging in that direction, she saw Rick lying full length on the cushions, held down by Annie, who was sprawled, sound asleep, across his chest.

The appointment Meghan had made with Community Services had been for late afternoon, about the time Annie should have been getting up from her nap. Somewhere in the back of her mind, she had hoped that if she worked late enough the case worker would come and take Annie away before she got home. That way, she wouldn't have to say goodbye or watch her go.

With no reason left to stay, then, Rick might also have disappeared. Or perhaps he would be so livid he would never want to see her again. Either way, she had half expected both of them to be gone.

It hadn't happened.

She closed the door behind her, took off her coat and put it in the closet. Taking a deep breath, she walked slowly into the living area.

"Sorry I'm late," she said in tones of strained quiet. "Has she been asleep long?"

He shook his head. A moment later, he raised a brow as

he motioned toward the end of the sofa, then toward Annie. He wanted Meghan to spread the quilt so he could put the baby down.

Meghan did as he indicated, though she put the makeshift baby bed well out of the way in the bedroom. If there was going to be shouting, Annie would be better out left of it.

Yet Rick didn't seem angry when he rejoined her after putting the baby down. His smile perfectly easy, he said, "Hard day?"

"Fairly," she agreed, her gaze watchful as she waited for the explosion. At the same time, she felt an ache of regret somewhere deep inside. What a lovely homecoming this would be if the situation between them were real.

"Dinner's ready, if you are."

"You cooked?" The words were husky as she spoke through the tightness in her throat.

His smile was rueful. "Not exactly, but I brought it home with my own two hands."

So he had, and not fast food, either. The covered containers bore the label of an upscale gourmet food shop. Inside were étouffée rich with crab and shrimp, white asparagus, and fresh-baked bread. The addition of a perfect tossed salad and a chilled bottle of Chardonnay made it a nice meal indeed.

While Meghan ran the food through the microwave to reheat it, Rick set the table. He then found the matches and lit the candles that were a part of the permanent Capo-di-Monte centerpiece. That done, he turned toward the refrigerator to take out the wine.

Meghan, leaning against the cabinet with her arms folded over her chest as she watched him, thought he moved around her kitchen with the same competence and economy of motion that he might use in his own home. Anticipating his request as he swung toward her with the wine bottle in hand, she reached into a drawer to pull out a corkscrew and handed it to him. His smile of thanks warmed a place inside her she had not even realized was chilled.

He was different tonight. He had traded his work clothes for a pair of pressed chinos worn with a cream-colored oxford dress shirt open at the neck and his work shoes for loafers. The freshness of a recent shower and shave made an appealing aura around him, one heightened by a hint of spice and wood from an expensive aftershave. Yet it was more than these things. His attitude was purposeful. The look in his eyes was sharper, more compelling, and there was a subtle caress in his voice as he spoke.

If it hadn't seemed too far-fetched, she could almost believe he was setting her up for a seduction scene. Giving herself a mental shake for such a ridiculous idea, she said, "If you stay around much longer, I'm going to be hopelessly spoiled."

His lips curved, though he kept his attention on the wine he was opening. "Would that be so bad?"

"I could get used to it." The answer was supposed to be a joke, but somehow it didn't come out quite that way.

"So could I," he said. And smiled with devastating frankness, straight into her eyes.

She wanted to be wary. She needed to keep some kind of distance since she knew that whatever was growing between them could not last.

She didn't have a chance. He held her chair when the time came to sit down to their meal, then took the seat across from her. He was interested in everything she had done all day, everything she had said, and most of the thoughts that had run through her mind. They laughed and talked and drank their wine. They argued over whether the end of the French bread was called the heel or the nose, then divided it between them and ate it without settling the dispute. They polished off the individual dishes of chocolate mousse he produced for dessert and, still talking, put the dishes in the dishwasher.

There was only one bad moment. As they moved back into the living room, he picked up the remote control and clicked through the available television programs, stopping on the late weather. While he was busy, she wandered toward the answering machine on its side table. There was nothing on it; the counter was on zero. She usually had at least a couple of hang-ups from electronic solicitation calls. And surely there should have been some contact from Mrs. Purdy.

Over her shoulder, she said, "Did you check the messages, by any chance?"

"It's your machine."

He barely glanced her way as he spoke, yet something in his voice made her look at him again. He seemed absorbed in the forecast, however, with no other thought in his head. She let it pass.

Rick clicked off the TV when the weather was over, then reached for a news magazine. She thought of picking up her needlework, but it was getting late and she was tired. A shower might give her a little more energy, enough so she could consider dragging on a robe or caftan and coming back to talk a little longer.

He was waiting for her when she stepped from the lighted bedroom into the living room. Or perhaps that was too strong a word for it. Actually, he was only lying in the dark on the sofa that he had made down into a bed. His shoes were off and his hands propped under his head.

She had seen him there before, of course. Somehow this was different.

She didn't know how it was different, or even what made her think it might be. She only knew it was. And because of it, she was abruptly aware that she was naked under her worn and comfortable peach silk caftan.

He slid off the sofa and moved toward her with slow, animal grace. "That's exactly the way I saw you that first night," he said softly. "In silk, with the light behind you. I wanted you then. But I want you more now."

She knew what was going to happen. She could see it in his eyes, his voice, the way he moved. Perhaps she had even sensed it from the minute she walked in the door. That instinct, she thought, could even be the reason she had taken her bath, made herself ready.

She could stop it, stop him, with a single word; that much she also knew.

She couldn't find it. In a flashing moment of truth, she realized she didn't even want to search for it. She had asked him to stay, even demanded that he stay. Had it been for this? Had she recognized somewhere inside that such a moment would come between them? Was it what she had wanted, then and now?

She didn't know, and it didn't matter. It seemed so right as he took her in his arms. To feel them close around her, fitting their bodies together, was like finding the long lost pieces of an intricate, internal puzzle.

The sofa bed was only a step away. So convenient. The surface was softly yielding as they sank down on it. She sighed, closing her eyes, inhaling his scent into her lungs, her being.

The feel of his skin against her face gratified some need she had not known existed. The faint roughness of the beard at his jaw sent a prickling wave of desire over the surface of her skin. She spread her hands, gliding the sensitive palms over his shoulders, his back, the nape of his neck. She traced the smooth, liquid length of the gold chain he wore with its sliding coin, absorbing the warmth of his body that it held, absorbing also the essence of him so she would know him always by touch, even in the dark.

She felt so feverish, melting, as malleable as heated wax to the slightest press of his hands. Inclinations too deep for easy recognition shifted inside her like ancient tides. Her need was so vast it threatened to engulf her. And him. Help-

less, hopeless, she craved him for who he was and also as
bulwark and defense against coming loss. With an inarticu-
late murmur, she pressed closer.

He answered her desire with his own, moving convul-
sively against her. Whispered words feathered over her skin,
tingling at the sensitive hollow below her ear. They were
followed by the warm caress of his mouth, the wet, fleeting
flick of his tongue.

He tasted her, breathed her, moved against her and over
her with slow, compelling friction. The heated length of his
body was a long, devouring embrace.

He took her mouth, giving sweetness, consuming the flavor and texture of her, testing her desire. His tongue swirled
around hers, initiating her into the manner and meaning of
his deep passion for her, inciting her to show him what she
was, how she wanted him to be.

Open, she was so open to him. With courage and trusting
grace, she gave him access to her greatest depths. She held
nothing in reserve, needed nothing. For otherwise, her love
for him would have been less.

She loved his strength and tempered care, his humor, his
kindness, his immutable assurance, his easy, boundless affection for a child, and his passion. And more, so much
more that she sensed without being able to catalog. It was
enough for now, this deep affection. She required nothing
in return.

His hands held such rough yet tender magic. She pressed
into them while he gently kneaded the nipples of her
breasts. A low moan escaped her as he bent his head to
lick and suckle, tasting them through the thin silk of the
caftan as if they were small, hard Christmas candies. Writh-
ing with the sudden rush of stinging pleasure, she pressed
closer, wanting more, needing to become a part of him.

God.

Prayer and plea, Rick echoed the single word inside his
head as he caught fire from her consuming surrender. Every

muscle in his body shuddered as he clamped down, controlling the surge of his blood, the dark heat of his yearning. She was so perfect, so soft, so warm and giving. He wanted nothing so much as to sink into her hot, moist depths and stay until he became a part of her.

Yet he could not get enough of her mouth or the firm, sweet curves of her body. He wanted to hold her inescapably, to touch so intimately that he could never be erased. He wanted to reach deep and contain her innermost being.

He wanted her naked against his naked body. With quick, hard hands, he stripped away the thin silk of the loose robe she wore, shucked off his pants, his shirt, his underwear. Hot skin to hot skin. Smooth to rough. Soft to hard. Yes, please God. Heaven on earth. Always.

A miracle. His miracle.

She was his match, his mate. She held him to the last atom in her tender grasp. She was his love, the woman he would worship all his days. Whether she willed it or not, allowed it or denied him.

Nothing else mattered, not sweet, sleeping Annie, not mistakes made or resolutions decided upon. Not making a child, having a child, giving a child.

Gone were reasons, needs, fears. He wanted her, needed her, would die, shivering and soulless, if he could not have her. Soon. Endlessly. And forever.

God . . .

Her skin was on fire. Her heart rattled against the walls of her chest. The surge of her blood was a distant thunder in her ears, a throbbing vibration in her veins. Her lips were swollen, pulsing. She arched under his touch, giving, opening still more, as he trailed a burning path with lips and tongue from her breasts to her navel. His tongue dipped in, swirled, moved on. Her abdomen clenched, quivering, as he drifted lower, parted her thighs, explored her feminine folds as if marveling at some hot, tropical flower. And probed, heated, wet, thorough, deep into its heart. She moaned, shuddering into ecstasy with the invasion, and with the soft scrape of his beard stubble along the tender skin of her inner thighs.

She wanted him. She drew him up with frantic hands, whispering her need in the age-old phrase of courteous desperation, *Please, please . . .*

And she touched him out of that need, using delicate fingertips to explore the hot, swollen length of him. She marveled at the silky heat, the weight, the throbbing life of him. Circling with a careful grasp, she held him so the beat of his heart that she felt against her palm thundered into her, through her.

He drew a hard, tried breath. Shivering, he snatched at control, breaking out in chill bumps with the effort of it. Rolling, he settled over her, pressing her into the mattress with his strength, his welcome weight, and his power.

She moved infinitesimally in invitation. He probed gently, entered with a slow twist of his hips, then sank deep in a single slick and heated slide.

The world fell away. He surged, pushing it farther, higher, wider. Faster. He was power and hope, hard glory, fast, pounding magic. She was absorbing grace, spreading splendor, pulsing, internal silk that clasped, welcomed.

Striving, panting, they stared into each other's faces, met in each other's eyes. It was wondrous, and they knew it. It was heady, exploding grandeur. It was perfect union. Forever.

Soft, deep cries, formless words, bound them. They caught each other with desperate hands, their hearts aching as they held tight. Time retreated, leaving bright, beneficent immortality.

Or if they did not hold the secret of eternal life in their joined grasp, they came so close it touched them.

Nine

Meghan woke in Rick's arms. Actually there were three of them lying together, nested like spoons in graduated sizes. Annie had her small bottom snuggled into Meghan's stomach, while Meghan's was pressed against something considerably more firm.

It had been an eventful night. In addition to its exertions, she and Rick had been forced to get up just before dawn with Annie and her brand-new pearly-white top tooth. That was when they had all moved to the comfort of the king-size bed. Stretching a little, Meghan flashed a glance over her shoulder that was warm with remembrance.

Rick was awake, lying with his head propped on the heel of his hand as he watched. He nudged her suggestively even as he gave her a grin that could only be described as incredibly sexy.

Gasping a little in spite of herself, Meghan whispered, "You're insatiable!"

"Me?" he protested, keeping his voice low also. "What female was it, I ask you, who ravished my poor tired body this morning at three A.M.?"

"I have no idea. Who?"

"Well, let me see," he said, his free hand roaming under the cover. "I think she was about your size right here. And here. Yes, and the most incredible things happened when I touched her in this particular spot. Oh, yes," he added as she inhaled and arched against him, "exactly like that."

"If you don't behave yourself," she said in dire, if breath-less, warning, "you're going to get into more trouble than you can handle."

"God, I hope so," he muttered fervently against the sen-sitive lobe of her ear.

Why not? She was suddenly faint and fiery with longing. Annie was still comatose. The bed was huge. And it wasn't time to get up yet. Not quite.

In a less than successful attempt at sternness, she said as she turned languorously and rolled over against him, "Okay. But just remember that you asked for it."

"Begged is more like it," he whispered.

The bedroom was basically quiet again for at least a half hour. The mattress was not particularly still, however, and Annie roused at last. She was immediately ready to play, though for some strange reason she seemed to think the best game was bouncing up and down on the bed as if it were a trampoline.

The days that followed were just as warm and bright and frilled around the edges with laughter. They developed a morning routine for getting off to work, and an evening routine for chores and dinner. Some days Rick took Annie with him; the others Meghan kept her at the store. At Silver Bells, Yvonne, being her grandmotherly, indulgent self, spoiled the child every chance she got. She and Meghan between them indulged Annie outrageously, giving her the run of the office and letting her climb in and out among the Christmas trees, dumping reindeer and elves out of the peck-size baskets which held them. They allowed her to use the heads of gingerbread men carved from natural maple for teething, and watched benignly as she pulled a long strand of tinsel from a tree and trailed it behind her while she crawled up and down the aisles.

The customers were charmed by Annie as well, cooing

and gooing and talking the most ridiculous baby talk to her until even Yvonne and Meghan rolled their eyes. Annie, however, was delighted with the attention. She gave all communication her wide-eyed consideration and made intelligent noises in return. So many people waved and told her bye-bye as they left that she was soon flapping both arms and babbling bye-bye at everybody who passed through the doors, regardless of whether they were coming or going. Business, unaccountably, increased.

One morning in the middle of the week, Yvonne swore the baby said "Aunt Meghan," as plain as she could speak. Meghan refused to believe it, being mindful of the fact that Annie's speech, while obviously meaningful to Annie, was really not plain at all. That was until she heard the words herself later that evening. To her ears, however, they sounded suspiciously like "Aun' Mama." Swooping down on Annie, Meghan picked her up and kissed her a dozen times in quick succession under her little double chin, to the giggling delight of them both.

Several times, as the days passed, Meghan thought of her call to Community Services, and wondered what had become of the case worker Mrs. Purdy was supposed to send. She even went so far as to reach for the phone once or twice, on the verge of finding out. But each time she did, Annie smiled or planted a huge wet kiss on her cheek, or else crawled over and sat on her feet where she was working at her desk, and Meghan forgot it.

Occasionally, the thought of Annie's mother crossed Meghan's mind, and she frowned and shook her head. And other times she thought of what it might be like if the woman never turned up again. Brief glimpses of the life she and Rick and Annie might have then trailed through her mind, though she hastily switched them off. She couldn't allow herself to let such daydreams linger. Too much could happen to prevent them, none of it good.

Still, when no one was looking Meghan would sometimes

pick up Annie and hold the sweet, warm body close, turning her slowly back and forth with her eyes squeezed tightly shut. She was such a precious child, with so much loving personality and intelligence. A tiny person slowly unfolding like a miraculous flower.

Annie permitted herself to be held, often resting her head on Meghan's shoulder and sighing with contentment. Or else she looked into Meghan's eyes, pure, unclouded blue into chocolate brown, then reached a small, sure baby hand to touch her face. And her heart.

Suddenly New Year's Eve was upon them. Partying to the midnight hour would have been difficult with Annie around, but Meghan and Rick didn't even consider it. Loud noise and music, inane jokes, and too much to drink had no appeal. Neither of them cared much for that kind of thing in the ordinary way, and now their pleasures had become entirely domestic. The most they felt like doing to celebrate was eating out, and it was a toss-up whether even that might not be too much trouble.

It was Rick who finally settled it. Meghan needed the break, he said. She was working too hard between the shop and caring for Annie, and not getting enough sleep. He didn't regret the last too much, but he would do his part to relieve the work load. All she had to do was decide what kind of food she wanted, and he would handle the reservation and transportation.

She chose Italian, a *ristorante* on the other side of town that had recently become popular, one that Rick seemed to know well. It turned out to be a pleasant place with green-and-white striped awnings, brass doors and rustic tables under a canopy of silk grape leaves on arbors. The delicious smells of garlic, tomatoes and fresh-baked yeast bread were so hearty that they reached out into the parking lot and dragged diners in by their taste buds.

Inside, the family-owned eating place was crowded. It was also noisy with diners talking happily over their food instead of treating it with the hushed reverence of more upscale places. The full-bodied house wine everyone was pressed to order may have had something to do with the conviviality, of course, but it seemed to stem in the main from a general dedication to the pleasure of good food.

Annie was a hit without a doubt. She wowed the rotund hostess, made the waiter her slave, and even attracted the white-haired owner with his Italian accent from his office. She loved the garlic bread, and could only be prevented from choking down a piece as big as her fist by prompt action from Meghan. Buttery, garlicky fingers grasping, she then tried to take Rick's from him. Her fierce frown when he ate it was comical to see. Foiled there, she twisted around to beg a piece from the spare, gray-haired gentleman seated at the table directly behind her high chair, using all her grinning wiles. She would have got what she wanted, too, if Rick hadn't intervened The little moocher was only distracted from the bread, finally, by the fun of chasing lengths of spaghetti in a finger-paint thick tomato sauce around her high chair tray, slurping down the longer ones with riotous precision and using the shorter bits to decorate her hair.

Meghan tried for a short while to keep Annie moderately clean. After the third request for a clean napkin, she gave it up. Instead, she relaxed and enjoyed the baby's antics while concentrating on her own food, the wine, and the man across the table. Meeting Rick's gaze while they shook their heads over Annie gave her such a sense of completion that she felt warm all over with it. At the same time, she was frightened as she thought how easily it could all vanish.

They had reached their dessert, made-on-the-spot Neapolitan ice cream with marzipan, when a man and woman weaving their way from the rear of the restaurant approached their table. The woman glanced in their direction. Tall and trim in close-fitting jeans and a sequined vest over a long-sleeved tee, her hair was thick and dark and gypsy

wild. And the smile that suddenly spread across her face
was as wide as Texas.

"Rick!" she cried, bearing down on them with her male
companion in tow. "I can't believe it's really you!"

"Stacy," Rick said, his voice grim as he started to rise.

"Don't get up," the woman said, putting a familiar hand
on his shoulder as she came to a halt beside him. She gave
Meghan a friendly nod before turning back to Rick. "What
a shocker, to see you out and about. And darling little Annie, too. I thought you were stuck at home with her for the
duration."

Meghan felt her heart contract in her chest. The woman
knew Annie. But that was impossible. Wasn't it? She sent
Rick a glance of interrogation.

He returned her gaze, his face tight-lipped and pale. Sick
fatalism lay in his eyes as he performed the brief introduc-
tions.

"A pleasure," the other woman said, her gaze flickering
back and forth between them as she registered the strained
atmosphere. "But Rick, honey, I am truly hurt at how fast
you found a substitute baby-sitter." She directed a conspira-
torial wink in Meghan's direction. "Such a guy, never at a
loss, no problem too big that it can't be fixed. I bet you
even like children!"

"Meghan, I was going to tell you—" Rick began.

But Meghan wasn't listening. To the dark-haired woman,
she said in grim politeness, "Since you're a friend of Rick's,
perhaps you'd like to join us?"

"Oh, Keith and I were on our way out," she said, waving
at the man behind her. "I just had to come over and see
how Rick was doing. I've felt downright mean about letting
him down with Annie, but was just so outdone over missing
the ski trip. I mean, Rick and I could have gone with Brad
and his wife if he hadn't been so determined to play daddy
for a week."

"Play daddy," Meghan repeated, her tone hollow. She felt as if she had been kicked in the stomach.

"For Annie. He's crazy about her, isn't he?" The other woman put a hand on her hip as she tossed her mane of hair behind her shoulders. "I like kids as well as the next woman, but I told him he could darn well get himself another girl to be mama. Looks like that's just what he did. Or are you a friend of Christy's?"

"I don't believe I know Christy." The response was tight.

"Annie's mother, of course. Jeez, didn't he tell you anything?"

Dazed, not quite certain she was putting the rapid-fire revelations together as they should be, Meghan shook her head. "Apparently not."

"Christy is my sister-in-law," Rick rapped out. "My brother's wife."

Meghan turned her dark gaze on him. "But that makes you—" She couldn't say it.

"Annie's uncle," he agreed with swift impatience. "Look, I'll explain everything when we get home. I was going to anyway, I promise. I just didn't want to spoil the evening."

"Oh, dear," Stacy said contritely as she stared from one to the other. "And here I've gone and done it for you, haven't I? I guess it doesn't make a lot of difference, though, does it? Aren't Christy and Brad due back tomorrow?"

Meghan pushed to her feet, propelled by sheer horror and the pain that was exploding inside her. Annie was no orphan, no discarded child. She was Rick's niece.

Rick had lost the girlfriend he had expected to help him with baby-sitting Annie for a week while her parents were away. Needing a substitute, he had found one, and also found a simple yet terrible way to make sure Meghan took on the job.

Still, that had not been not enough, not for Rick. He had moved in with her, too. He had made her love him, love

Annie, and now it was over. He didn't need her anymore. No doubt he had been planning to tell her so tonight.

"Meghan, wait," Rick commanded as he surged upright and flung down his napkin. "Let me take care of the check and get Annie out of her seat, then we'll go."

The baby was watching her, eyes big, lips trembling. "Aun' Mama," she said, her voice rising in distress. "Aun' Mama."

That sweet, small voice cut into Meghan like jagged glass. The agony of it was vicious, slashing, inconsolable. She backed away.

"Meghan, listen—"

"No," she said faintly, then again with greater strength. "No! It's all right. I'm going home. Now. Since we came in my car, perhaps your friends will take you . . . wherever you need to go."

Stacy nodded with misery in her face. Behind her, the man she had called Keith looked acutely embarrassed.

"Don't do this," Rick said with an edge of rough appeal. He was taking out his wallet to fling money on the table, then reaching for Annie. "It isn't the way it looks."

Meghan backed away from him. "How does it look? Silly, maybe? Incredibly stupid? Then it's exactly the way it looks!"

She felt betrayed, used. Sickness gathered inside her. She was so weak she was not sure her legs would hold her. She had to get away before she shattered into a million brittle pieces. Or before she did something dumb like maybe listening to the man who had played a cruel joke on her on Christmas Eve, then lied again and again since then. The man who might never have stopped if someone else hadn't forced him.

"Wait, Meghan. Annie needs you. I need you!"

But they didn't, either of them. They never had. And they never would, which was the final, most hurtful truth.

She began to walk away.

"Aun' Mama," Annie whimpered, beginning to cry. "Aun' Mama . . ."

The sound was so plain, so achingly sweet. The name was one she had no right to hear, one she would never know again. That knowledge burst inside Meghan, burgeoning into unbearable pain. It pressed upward, tearing at her throat, burning its way behind her eyes.

Blinded by tears, she put her head down and ran.

Ten

Hearts and flowers, flowers and hearts. It was almost Valentine's Day, therefore merchandise with red satin and velvet, with white lace, pink silk, Cupids, bows and kissing lips, were literally everywhere.

Silver Bells, far from fading away after Christmas was over, catered to the full round of holiday celebrations. Meghan had been unpacking hearts and flowers and other symbols of romance for weeks now. She and Yvonne had hung and draped and scattered the frothy confections in displays until the very sight of them made her feel sick to her stomach.

But then, it didn't take much to make Meghan feel sick these days.

She was kneeling, grimly refilling the floor-level display of boxed gourmet chocolate hearts with caramel centers, when she heard the soft chime that indicated someone had entered the store. Yvonne, she knew, was busy in the back, unpacking a shipment of the St. Patrick's Day shamrocks and Easter bunnies that would take the place of the Valentine's Day merchandise before the week was out. Rising to her feet, she glanced around for the customer to see if any help was required.

A woman was wandering down the main aisle, pushing a baby stroller. Petite, elegantly turned out in tan slacks and a navy blazer, she had silvery blond hair and eyes the color of old sherry. As she caught sight of Meghan, she smiled and her footsteps quickened. Voice well-modulated, layered with satisfaction and a trace of humor, she said, "You must be Meghan Castle. Or should I say Aun' Mama?"

A golden-haired little girl was in the stroller the woman pushed. Eyes bright blue and dancing with delight, she was bouncing up and down on the stroller's springs, grinning for all she was worth and holding out her small hands to be picked up.

The store shifted, grew dim. Meghan's head swam. From far away, she watched the strange woman's smile fade, and felt her catch her arm in a firm clasp as she exclaimed, "Oh, my goodness!"

In the next instant, Meghan's vision began to clear. She grasped the counter beside her as she gave a shaky laugh. "Whoa. I . . . must have stood up too fast."

"Probably," the other woman said, though the look in her eyes said she was unconvinced. "Anyway, I'm Christy Wallman. I wanted to talk to you for a few minutes, if you have the time."

"If Rick sent you—" Meghan began.

"He didn't." The denial was instantaneous and obviously sincere. A moment later, the other woman went on. "I won't say I haven't come on his behalf, however. Rick is one of my favorite people in the world, and I hate seeing him in pain. You won't open the door to him, won't take his calls, refuse his flowers, return his letters. He's going crazy trying to find some way to make you listen to him."

"I'm sorry," Meghan said stiffly, "but we have nothing to say to each other."

"I'd hate to think that's true," the petite blonde said seriously. "He isn't sleeping, you know, and I'm not sure he's eating. He works day and night to keep himself sane. Worst of all, he's avoiding Annie because she reminds him too much of what he doesn't want to remember. So you're also hurting my child, because Rick is one of Annie's favorite people. And I don't stand for anyone hurting those who belong to me."

"I—can't help that," Meghan said, looking away from Rick's sister-in-law.

Her gaze dropped to Annie, who was making imperious demands for attention. As if forced, she sank down to the baby's level and reached to cup her small, sweet face in her hands. Leaning, she brushed the soft baby cheek, inhaling the sweet scent of her as if it were the air she needed to live.

Christy Wallman watched her for a long moment. When she spoke again, her voice was softer. "Look, I know what Rick did wasn't too smart. He told us, Brad and me, all about it, and I can't believe someone of his intelligence would even begin—well, never mind that. The point is, Rick didn't set out to harm you in any way. He wasn't thinking with his head, but with his heart."

"Or some other part of his anatomy," Meghan said in strained rejoinder.

Christy gave a quick laugh. "All right, that, too. There's no doubt he was extremely attracted to you. He thought he had found a unique way to meet a lady he wanted to know, by pretending Annie was a foundling to someone who obviously loved babies. The prank went wrong, so very wrong. But once he discovered what was so terrible about it, he didn't know how to put it right without losing you."

"I worked out what happened. You don't have to come here and tell me." There was asperity in the glance Meghan gave her.

Christy tilted her head. "Oh, that wasn't the only reason I came. The truth is I was curious to meet the woman who brought my brother-in-law to his knees. Rick isn't the man to be bowled over by a pretty face. You have to be something special."

"Hardly." The word was compressed.

The other woman ignored the comment. "Then there's

Annie. I had to see the female so warm and real she could care for another woman's child, see her through cutting a major tooth, teach her some of her first words, and indulge her to the point that she developed some sleeping and eating habits that still linger a month and a half later. The woman who captivated my daughter to such an extent in one short week that she cried after her for days."

"Don't!" Meghan exclaimed. Then she said again in near inaudible entreaty, "Please, just . . . don't."

Christy sighed as she looked away. "Yes, I suppose that was unfair."

Annie was a lot like her mother, Meghan saw, but she also favored the men in her family. She had her uncle's firm chin, also his habit of lifting one brow slightly higher than the other. Or perhaps she had these things from her father. Still, they were such poignant reminders of moments Meghan had thought put behind her that she felt her heart shift inside her.

"Why couldn't Rick have told me the truth?" she asked. "Why did he have to take it so far? Did he think all he had to do was climb into my bed and I would overlook whatever he had done?"

"A lot of things were in his mind, I would imagine," the other woman said frankly. "He's a man, after all. Of course, being a man, and a private one at that, he hasn't said much about that part of it, at least not in front of me. Still, he did mention something about needing to make everything up to you in the only way he knew how. He wanted, he said, to give you something truly precious." She paused, tilting her head. "How was it he put it? Oh, yes. He meant you to have the one gift from him that might mean something to a woman for whom every day is Christmas."

Meghan frowned, sitting back on her heels and glancing around the Silver Bells Christmas Store. "What do you suppose he meant?"

"I thought you might understand, or at least make a

guess. Whatever it is, I do know that he's worried sick about it. And he's also worried about you because of it."

Unconsciously, Meghan put her hand on her stomach. Could he possibly have meant . . . ?

No. There was no way. Was there?

Surely not. He wouldn't deliberately . . .

Would he? Could he have dared do such a thing?

He would and could. Rick Wallman would dare anything.

On that first night of sexual fireworks he had used no birth control. She had been caught unprepared herself, and assumed it was more or less the same for him. The two of them had never discussed it. The one time she had tried, there had been some distraction, real or otherwise. She had not been assertive enough, or certain enough of her position, to press the issue.

What if he had refrained from protection for good reason? Could he have purposely avoided the subject during the few days and nights they had spent together?

No, it wasn't possible. She refused to believe Rick had wanted her to become pregnant. The idea was simply too far-fetched to be possible.

With a firm tilt of her chin, she said, "Rick doesn't have to worry about me. I'll be fine."

"That's good, I suppose," Christy said. "But you know, I'm not sure Rick will. He acts like a man who has lost the woman he loves. But there's something else bothering him, something he's not talking about. And I have a strong suspicion that you could help, if you only would."

"I seriously doubt it. Rick hasn't called in at least two weeks." Meghan came to a halt, biting her bottom lip as she saw how she had given herself away.

"What can you expect?" Christy gave a light shrug. "He gave up, finally. But I'm sure you could fix that, too."

Could she? Did she want to try?

If Christy was wrong, Meghan wasn't sure she could stand seeing Rick, leaving herself open to all the pain again.

She didn't know if she would be able to bear hearing, after this tiny ray of hope, that it was well and truly over after all.

Before she could answer, Christy spoke again. "You can at least think about it, can't you? For Annie's sake if nothing else."

Meghan looked again at Rick's little niece who was playing with her fingers. "Don't you have shopping to do in the mall? I could watch Annie for you."

"Oh, I couldn't ask you to do that," Christy answered. "Really, I feel guilty enough for leaving her with Rick and causing all this trouble in the first place."

Meghan smiled, a brief movement of the lips as she rubbed her thumb over the baby's knuckles. "I know she can be a bit of a handful—Can't you, sweet thing?—so I'm sure you needed to get away awhile, spend some time with your husband. Anyway, there was . . . no real harm done. I would love to have her—watch her—for just a little while."

"Well." The other woman's gaze was thoughtful, even cunning. "If you're really sure you don't mind."

The moment Christy was gone, Meghan released Annie from her stroller and took her to see Yvonne. They barely had time for a rapturous greeting filled with baby talk and a quick game of patty-cake before the chime for the store entrance rang out. Yvonne scowled, but went to see to the customer. Meghan and Annie remained in the storeroom.

"Aun' Mama," Annie said, happily patting Meghan's cheeks and pulling her hair before giving her a wet kiss on the nose.

"Oh, sugarplum," Meghan said softly, and hugged her close.

As she held the child to her, rubbing her cheek over the fine baby hair, Meghan had a flashing vision of Rick and the way he had held Annie. She thought, too, of how he had pulled her, a much bigger girl, into his strong arms on that first night as she cried for James and Jimmy. She could almost hear the deep, aching sympathy that had been in his voice then, feel the security of being wrapped against him.

Hard on the heels of that moment came a replay of the evening when he had told her about the son he never knew. That loss had sliced deep inside him, leaving barely healed scars. He was a man of bone-deep emotions, and with a limitless ability to care. He had proven as much by the way he looked after Annie. Night and day, days on end, he had been patient and concerned, helpful and loving, so loving.

He had also been more: strong and patient, considerate, courteous, kind. Passionate.

It was possible he deserved better from her than to be closed out of her life. Especially now.

He would make a wonderful father.

"Well, Annie," Meghan said quietly as she stared over the baby's head. "What do you think? Should I go and see Uncle Rick?"

Annie drew back to look at her. Her face was solemn, her blue eyes candid. Then she gurgled a happy laugh and clapped her small hands, holding them tightly together. Meghan laughed, too, though tears rimmed her eyelids.

It was as good a reason as any for making a decision.

The offices of Wallman and Wallman Construction were clean-lined and modern in brick and glass, and conveniently located four streets over and seven blocks down from the mall. Meghan made the drive there during her lunch hour. If Rick was in his office, perhaps he would not be busy at that time. If he wasn't there, then she could leave a message.

She hoped it was the latter. She might manage a nice impersonal message, but wasn't too sure she was up to a face-to-face meeting.

Her heart was kicking her ribs as she got out of her car and approached the entrance. Her hands were shaking so badly she had a hard time opening the heavy glass door. She felt sick as she approached the receptionist, ill enough that she was afraid the first words out of her mouth were going to have to be a request for the rest room.

She shouldn't have come. It was foolish to think Rick might want to see her, stupid to think that it would make a difference. She was angry with herself for letting Christy Wallman put her in this position. She was a silly, sentimental fool for letting herself think she had any reason to be here, and a total idiot for being influenced by a ten-and-a-half-month-old baby who could speak no more than a half dozen words.

"You want to see Rick?" the middle-aged woman behind the desk said when Meghan inquired if he was in. "That's his office on the end. Go right in."

Rick was sitting at a drafting table with the light from wide corner windows falling over his left shoulder. Face absorbed, he was drawing minute lines in the squares of what appeared to be a floor plan. The blue-white light made his face appear thinner, and was merciless in picking out the faint half-moon shadows of weariness under his eyes. Wearing navy slacks and a blue dress shirt rolled to the elbows, he looked competent and assured, every inch the businessman. And not much at all like a father.

Meghan, standing in the doorway, turned quickly to leave. Rick glanced up at the movement.

"Meghan!" he exclaimed, dropping his pencil and sliding off his hardwood stool in a single movement. "Where are you going?"

She jerked back around. "You're busy. I don't want to disturb you."

"Please," he said, his lips curving in a slow smile as he came forward. "Please, disturb me. All you want."

Irritation at his choice of words brushed her, helping to steady her nerves, though an instant later she was certain the innuendo was only in her own mind. She looked away, and her gaze landed on the drawing table. As an idea came to her, she squared her shoulders and set her lips in a firm line.

Speaking quickly, before she lost courage, she said, "This isn't a personal visit. I'm—here on business."

The gladness drained out of his face, leaving it white under his light winter tan. With considerably less warmth in his voice, he said, "I see." Turning toward the oak desk in the office center, he indicated the leather chair in front of it. "Sit down. Tell me what I can do for you."

She took the chair because it was better than falling down, though she knew it would also make it more difficult to leave when she wanted. He did not move around to the desk chair as she expected, but perched on the corner of the polished oak surface in front of her. It was far too close for comfort.

Moistening her lips, she stared at the windows that extended behind his shoulder as she said, "I would like Wallman and Wallman to build a house for me."

Rick was silent for so long that she flicked him a nervous glance. He was watching her with speculation in his eyes, and something more that left her distinctly wary.

"A house," he repeated at last. "We usually do commercial construction, you know."

She swallowed hard. In deflated tones, she said, "You don't do houses, family dwellings?"

A muscle at the corner of his eye flickered, and his gaze rested on her flushed cheekbones. Abruptly, he said, "We don't as a rule, but for you we'll make an exception. So what do you have in mind?"

Relief made her feel a little giddy, even as she thought rapidly. "Something suitable for the country, that's the main thing. Bright and airy with lots of windows. And a porch, yes, or possibly a deck. Nothing too modernistic," she elaborated, warming to her theme. "Rather traditional really, but livable and comfortable."

"You don't have a floor plan?" His expression was closed in, watchful but intrigued.

She glanced at him and away again. "No, I . . . I thought it would be better if I outlined what I needed and let someone—you—design it for me."

He reached across the desk to pick up a note pad and pen. "How many square feet?"

"I don't know." She looked down at her hands clenched in her lap. "Fairly large, I suppose."

"How many bedrooms?"

"Five, I think."

He gave her a hard stare before he made a note on the pad he held on his knee. "Bathrooms?"

"Three. No, four. One near the back door, in case—"

He looked up. "In case of what?"

She tightened her lips, then opened them again. "In case the kids need it, when they run in from playing, or whoever is working outside can wash up before meals. Whatever."

"Do you want the master bedroom near the other bedrooms, or off to itself?" He kept his head down now, busily writing.

"To itself," she said, and swallowed against the huskiness in her throat.

"Den and living room both, or just a living room?"

"I—don't know, I think just one big room. With maybe French doors out onto the deck. And a fireplace."

"If there are to be kids, I'm assuming you'll have a husband? Have you agreed on the usual brick fireplace front, or would he prefer something more rustic in stone? What does he think about an entertainment wall? Or maybe an entertainment room for large screen television, surround sound, computer?"

Sick misery moved over her at his businesslike tone, but she choked it down. "I haven't asked him."

"Don't you think you should?" He looked up again, his gaze keen.

"I can't think it will matter a great deal to him one way or the other."

"He must be easy to get along with."

"Yes," the word came out as a whisper.

He returned to his pad. "Is there anything special you want in the bedrooms? I mean, do they need soundproofing or music systems? Maybe intercoms? Should one of them be designed for boys and the other for girls? Or should one of them be set up, possibly, as—a nursery?"

"Yes," she said faintly, staring at the way his dark, close-cropped waves clung to his bent head, remembering the way they felt under her fingers. Her heart turned over inside her, and there was nothing she could do about it.

He looked up suddenly to meet her eyes. Voice soft, he said, "Yes to which question?"

"You know," she said, gazing blindly toward the windows beyond his shoulders.

"You're pregnant."

Silence. He waited, sitting perfectly still, his shoulders set and his fingers white around his pencil.

Meghan took a deep breath, then let it out in quiet defeat. "I—seem to be."

"Oh, God, Meghan," he said in hushed tones as he closed his eyes tight. "Thank you, God. Thank you."

Her head came up around with a snap. "He had very little to do with it! It was you. You did this on purpose, don't try to tell me you didn't! A gift for the woman who has Christmas every day, I think Christy said. Of all the nerve!"

"Christy?" He was startled.

"She came to see me, she and Annie."

"Annie? That was playing dirty."

"Not nearly as dirty as you, you low-down sneak!" she cried, narrowing her eyes as she came to her feet and stepped to poke a finger in his chest. "What in hell gave you the right to decide that I needed a baby? Or when I

4 BESTSELLING HISTORICAL ROMANCES BY YOUR FAVORITE AUTHORS CAN BE YOURS, FREE!

Kensington Choice, our newest book club now brings you historical romances by your favorite bestselling authors including Janelle Taylor, Shannon Drake, Rosanne Bittner, Jo Beverley, and Georgina Gentry, just to name a few! Each book is filled with passion, adventure and the excitement of bygone times!

To introduce you to this great new club which is part of Zebra Home Subscription Service, we'd like to send you your first 4 bestselling historical romances, absolutely free!   And once you get these 4 free books to savor at home, we'll rush you the next 4 brand-new books at the lowest prices available, as soon as they are published.

The way the club works is that after your initial FREE shipment, you will get our 4 newest bestselling historical romances delivered to your doorstep each month at the preferred subscriber's rate of only $4.20 per book, a savings of up to $7.16 per month (since these titles sell in bookstores for $4.99-$5.99)! All books are sent on a 10-day free examination basis and there is no minimum number of books to buy. (A postage and handling charge of $1.50 is added to each shipment.) Plus as a regular subscriber, you'll receive our FREE monthly newsletter, *Zebra/Pinnacle Romance News*, which features author profiles, contests, subscriber benefits, book previews and more!

So start today by returning the FREE BOOK CERTIFICATE provided. We'll send you 4 FREE BOOKS with no further obligation: A FREE gift offering you hours of reading pleasure with no obligation...how can you lose?

*We have 4 FREE BOOKS for you
as your introduction to
KENSINGTON CHOICE!
To get your FREE BOOKS, worth
up to $23.96, mail the card below.*

FREE BOOK CERTIFICATE

Yes! Please send me 4 Kensington Choice (the best of Zebra and Pinnacle Books) Historical Romances without cost or obligation (worth up to $23.96). As a Kensington Choice subscriber, I will then receive 4 brand-new romances to preview each month for 10 days FREE. I can return any books I decide not to keep and owe nothing. The publisher's prices for Kensington Choice romances range from $4.99-$5.99, but as a preferred subscriber I will get these books for only $4.20 per book or $16.80 for all four titles. There is no minimum number of books to buy and I may cancel my subscription at any time. A $1.50 postage and handling charge is added to each shipment. No matter what I decide to do, my first 4 books are mine to keep, absolutely FREE!

Name _____

Address _____ Apt. _____

City _____ State_____ Zip _____

Telephone ( ) _____

Signature _____

(If under 18, parent or guardian must sign)

KC0396

Subscription subject to acceptance. Terms and prices subject to change.

KENSINGTON CHOICE
Zebra Home Subscription Service, Inc.
120 Brighton Road
P.O.Box 5214
Clifton, NJ 07015-5214

should have one, for that matter? What kind of stupid, asi-
nine ego trip made you think it would be all right? I've
heard of 'Kiss and make it well,' but, believe me, this takes
the cake. Damn you, Rick Wallman, I could kill you for
doing this to me!"

"You're cussing me out," he said in wonder as a grin
spread across his face.

"You got it!" she said with hot color rising in her face.
"Though what's so damned funny about it, I have no earthly
idea!"

"It means it matters," he said with a shake of his head.
"I matter. You're sure you're pregnant?"

"I'm positive, and you can take that smug look off your
face, buster, because you didn't do it by yourself."

"No," he said, still grinning, "I remember."

"I told you to stop laughing!"

He sobered, at least a fraction. Reaching out, he brushed
his hand along her arm before closing his fingers gently
around it. "Oh, Meghan, I know you're upset and I don't
blame you, but you don't seem—you don't really mind, do
you?"

"No, I want this baby so—" She stopped, her gaze kin-
dling as she saw what he was doing. "Of course I mind,
you jerk! I am not one of your strays or orphans. I don't
need you to come along and take me in and make things
all better."

"I know that, and it never crossed my mind, believe me.
I was mostly trying to make things better for me."

The words were spoken with complete candor. Hearing
them, she clenched her fist and thumped his chest again, a
blow with little force behind it. "And I don't need you manipulating me or doing things for my own good. I can decide for my very own self what I want, thank you very
much. Yes, and when I want it."

"Can you now?" he said with a definite lascivious curl
to the corner of his mouth.

"That's not what I meant!"

"No?" He rose easily to his feet, the light in his eyes glowing bright blue. "What do you want, Aun' Mama?"

Tears rose suddenly in her throat, threatening to choke her. "I want you for the father of my baby, Rick Wallman, and I flat refuse to let you run out on me or this kid—who will probably be a boy and look just like . . . you and drive me absolutely crazy . . ."

"God," he breathed, smiling again with incredible tenderness as he moved closer. "I wish, how I wish, though an Annie would be fine, too."

"But I don't want you to make any more decisions for me or to—to fight my demons for me. I can manage on my own."

He gave a slow shake of his head as he reached for her. "I know, love," he said, "but why should you when I'll be there?"

She shivered a little at the warm touch of his hands on her arms, but she wasn't finished. "You can't take the place of my husband who died, and I don't need you to, don't want you to try. Our son will never be exactly like the son I lost, any more than he will be like the one you never had. But if I love you enough, then maybe one day you'll get over playing St. Michael or Sir Galahad or whoever, and then you'll love me, too. If that happens, we just might become a—a real family."

The last word was smothered against the front of his shirt. His voice vibrated deep in his chest as he said in whimsical wonder, "And live in the country in this fairly large house, I see." He added innocently, "Do you think five bedrooms will be enough?"

She laughed, a watery sound, because she couldn't help it. "Maybe. To start."

"Meghan, sweet Meghan," he said in husky tones as he rocked her slowly against his heart. "You are the light of my life and my only love. I'm absolutely crazy, blind, nutso, stupid—especially stupid—in love with you. If I wasn't, hadn't been from the minute I first saw you with Annie, I wouldn't have made such a mess of things. If I hurt you, I'm sorry. If I did wrong by trying to give you the child we both wanted, then I'll make it up to you every day the rest of my life. I'll build you your house in the country with my own bare hands if you'll just let me live in it with you and our children, if you'll give me even a small amount of the love you give them, and let me be a part of your family."

"The most important part," she said, crying into his collar. "I love you, too, Rick Wallman."

"Oh, Meghan, sweet Meghan." He cupped her face in his hands as he lowered his mouth to hers.

It was some time later when he opened one eye without breaking contact. "What," he said with some difficulty, "are you smiling about?"

Meghan chuckled and wound her arms tighter around his neck. "I was just wondering."

He stiffened warily, drawing back to look down his nose at her. "About what?"

"What Annie will think."

"She'll love it," he said, relaxing again. "As long as we serve garlic bread at the wedding and let her open the presents."

"She can do whatever she wants," Meghan said.

"I was afraid of that." He heaved a resigned sigh. "Some mother you're going to be."

She stood on tiptoe the better to reach his mouth again as she growled, "You'd better believe it!"

"Oh, I do," he said with utter sincerity, then grinned to himself as he kissed her.

The Yuletide Gift

Hannah Howell

One

As the maid laced up her blue velvet kirtle, Jessa Armstrong began to feel as if all the air was being slowly squeezed out of her body. She knew it was all in her mind, that the maids were not really lacing her in too tightly. Their happy chatter hurt her ears. Each cheerful word stabbed at her until her head throbbed painfully. When the maids set the orie on her head, the thick circlet made of two colors of silk twisted together immediately increased the tense aching in her head.

Jessa struggled to banish the feelings sweeping over her. This was her wedding day. Everyone praised the match. Colin MacDubh might not be the best of all men, but everyone agreed that he was an excellent choice for a husband. His pedigree was impeccable. He was related through marriage to the dukes of Albany and Rothesay, who everyone knew held all the real power in the country. He was thirty, not too old, but no callow youth, handsome enough, had proven his virility with—at last count—at least twenty-two bastards, and was a warrior of wide renown. He also had lands and wealth.

I should be pleased to have such a mon, she silently told herself, nervously twisting one fat lock of her dark auburn hair around her finger until her nursemaid, Glenna, lightly slapped her hand.

She was nineteen, far past marriageable age. The constant internal strife and warfare scarring the land and her own family's wavering fortunes had made it very difficult to arrange a match for her. Jessa knew that she should thank God that she was not going to be left a spinster. Instead she began to feel ill, to feel as trapped as if she were chained to some dungeon wall. The urge to flee grew so strong she shook from the force of it.

"Are ye ailing, child?" Glenna asked, lightly feeling Jessa's cheeks and forehead, her weathered face crinkled in concern.

"I think I must visit the garderobe," Jessa replied, her voice little more than a hoarse whisper.

"Here, I will fetch ye the chamberpot."

"Nay," Jessa cried, and she pushed through the small knot of maids watching her with open curiosity until she reached the heavy wooden door. "I think I need the privacy of the garderobe."

Glenna grabbed Jessa by the arm, her bony fingers painfully strong as she held her back. "Ye can have your privacy, lass. Here, within your own bedchambers. We are done and will leave ye be for now. I will come back to fetch ye when 'tis time for the wedding to begin."

Not trusting herself to speak, Jessa nodded and watched them all leave. She briefly fixed her gaze upon the young maid named Alice whose stomach rounded with Colin Mac-Dubh's twenty-third bastard. The girl blushed and, being the last one to leave, hurriedly shut the door after her. A heavy silence descended upon the room, a silence that demanded Jessa think about what she was doing.

She was about to become a man's wife, a duty she had been raised to accept without question or complaint. The marriage would bring her family power, prestige and an ally, all things of great value in the unsettled times in which they lived. Yet, the mere thought of vowing before God to take the lecherous, and sometimes brutal, Colin MacDubh as her husband was making her physically ill. She had protested the choice made for her, but no one had heeded her. Now she had no time left to protest.

A sense of panic gripped her so tightly she began to have trouble breathing. All she could think of was escape. As she rushed to shove a few clothes into a small bag, a little voice in her head urged her to think of her family. She viciously silenced it. When had her family ever thought of her? They pushed her toward the altar without once considering her wants or needs or even her very obvious and vocal distaste. Throwing her thick black cloak around her shoulders, she crept out of her room.

Her hood flung over her head in a thin disguise, Jessa was astonished at the ease with which she slipped through the halls of her home and out to the stables. The crowd of guests and their multitude of servants bustling around helped her immensely. No one noticed one tiny woman bundled in a cape and carrying a bag. Once she reached the stable she realized she could use that to her advantage. She claimed to be Lady Sarah's maid and said that she needed to ride out to find some herbs to cure her ladyship's headache. The distracted, overworked stable hands did not look at her closely, simply saddled one of Lady Sarah's horses and sent her away. Jessa suspected they were pleased that there would be one less person to beleaguer them.

It was not until she was deep into the woods to the north of the castle that Jessa was able to relax a little. The marriage ceremony was not supposed to begin for another hour or more. It would then take her family a little while to realize that she was not just hiding from them, but had actually fled the castle. If she could cover enough miles in that short period of time, she might have a chance of success. Any pursuit would be halted before nightfall, before they could run her down. As she spurred her horse to a greater speed, she decided to go to Edinburgh, to her aunt Grier. That sympathetic woman would surely help her.

* * *

Jessa cursed softly as the increasing darkness forced her to move more slowly. There was a damp, cold bite to the air which was making her uneasy. It felt too much like a winter storm was swiftly descending upon the land. She suspected the approaching storm was what was making it get dark so quickly. Even though it was December, she knew she should have had a little more time before it grew too dark to see.

She was so intent upon watching the rocky trail as she nudged her reluctant mount along, Jessa did not see the men until they were reaching out for her. *Catarans* she realized in horror as she looked around at the six filthy men trying to encircle her. She had blithely ridden into a nest of the thieves and marauders. Her screech of fright and sudden jerk upon the reins she held startled her mount. The horse reared up, causing the men to retreat a little. Although she knew she had lost all control of her mount, the panicked animal was racing away from the thieves, so Jessa hung on and prayed that she could elude the catarans successfully and safely.

A moment later, she knew her prayers were to be unanswered. Her terrified mount stumbled and fell on the uneven ground, tossing her out of the saddle. She hit the ground hard. As she scrambled fruitlessly to stop herself from tumbling down the hillside, she watched her horse regain its footing and run away. Jessa fought to shelter her body as she slid and rolled down the rocky hill, her only consolation being the knowledge that the men were chasing down her horse, thus moving farther and farther away from her. Their fading shouts were still echoing in her ears as, despite all of her efforts to protect her head, she landed hard on a flat area halfway down the hill. After one moment of blinding pain at the back of her head, she slipped into unconciousness.

* * *

Cold was the first thing Jessa was aware of as she slowly began to drag herself up from the pit of unconciousness. Her head throbbed and her body ached, but neither affliction troubled her as much as the cold. She opened her eyes and cautiously eased her battered body into a seated position, cursing viciously when even the smallest of movement caused her pain. There was no mistaking the soft white flakes floating down from the night sky. Jessa clutched her now damp cloak more tightly around herself and fought against the strong urge to panic. Panic was what had put her into such deep trouble.

With a hard-won calm, and fighting the dizzying effects of her pounding head, Jessa studied her situation. She was several hours' hard ride from Edinburgh. When her horse had bolted, it had lead the robbers away from her, but it had also taken her clothes and what meager supplies she had managed to gather in the midst of her reckless escape from marriage. Although she knew the road to Edinburgh, she knew very little else about the area. She was, she realized, in a very precarious position.

Inch by inch, fighting the weakening and unsteadiness caused by her head wound, Jessa stood up, then slowly brushed the snow from her clothes. Her sturdy cloak was dirty and a little damp, but still whole. Her fine wedding dress, however, was badly torn. She ripped off the dangling pieces of her skirt that could easily trip her and tried to think of what she should do next.

"There is but one answer," she said, as she straightened up and looked around. "Ye must walk and pray that some shelter will soon cross your path."

It was not easy to pick out a path to walk in the dark and the snow, but Jessa began to head north. There was no chance that she would be able to reach Edinburgh alive, but she decided that she might as well continue on in the same

direction she had chosen before disaster had struck. There
had to be someone living on the route to such a large place.
She heartily wished she had paid closer heed to what lined
the route the few times she had traveled to the city. Her
inattention could cost her dearly now.

Only a short time passed before Jessa realized that even
if there was shelter ahead, she might not survive long
enough to reach it. As she pulled her hood more tightly
around her head in a vain attempt to protect her face from
the stinging, icy snow, she was not sure she would be able
to see a place to shelter even if she walked right by one.
The storm was increasing in strength, the cold wind growing stronger and the snow falling more thickly. The wind
mercilessly buffeted her, and the heavy wet snow clung to
her boots and clothing, weighing her down. She stumbled
on, but increasingly began to wonder why she was troubling
herself with such a vain attempt to survive.

As Jessa picked herself up out of the snow for the third
time in less than an hour, she frowned and squinted, trying
to peer through the swirling snow and the dark. Her heart
began to beat faster. There was light up ahead. She was
sure of it. As she awkwardly increased her pace, she began
to discern a large, dark shape looming up before her. Pray-
ing that she was not suffering from some delusion brought
on by the cold and her growing despair, she pressed on.
She stumbled and fell time and time again, but the promise
of shelter gave her the strength to get up and keep moving.

Murdoch Graeme stood firm on the battlements of the
thick walls encircling his tower house. He ignored the sting
of the icy snow and the cold, fierce push and pull of the
wind as he scowled into the depths of the storm. It was
going to be another severe winter. There were too many of
them lately, and the summer growing seasons seemed to be
getting shorter each year. Even the weather tried to destroy

him, he thought morosely. When his sergeant at arms stumbled up to his side, he just grunted out a greeting.

"Ye shouldna be out here," complained Ennis Graeme. "Ye could easily catch a deadly fever from this cold. Aye, or be pushed right off the wall by this twice-cursed wind."

Briefly, Murdoch studied his cousin and closest friend, a man younger and, he mused, more charming and handsome than he. "Ye shouldna be here either."

"Weel, someone has to come and pull ye in from the cold."

"Nay, I meant that ye should have traveled to the king's court with your father and brother, not stayed here to rot at my side."

"What? And forsake such a high position? Where else would a mon of my meager years attain the post of sergeant at arms?"

"A great many other places once the laird realized how skilled ye are." He nudged his cousin when he realized that the younger man was ignoring him, leaning over the parapets and staring into the snow. "What is it?"

"Someone comes this way," Ennis replied, pointing into the storm.

"Are ye mad?" Murdoch asked, even as he looked in the direction Ennis pointed. "What fool would be out in this storm?"

"Ye can ask that when ye have stood here so long 'tis drifted up to your knees?"

Murdoch ignored his cousin and stared down at the small figure that was barely visible through the swirling snow. It was not until the staggering, stumbling unwanted guest was but yards from his gates that he realized it was a woman who approached so ungracefully. He cursed and pretended not to see his cousin's look of concern.

"We had best go and help her," Ennis finally suggested when Murdoch said nothing for several moments, simply glared down at the tiny, cloak-shrouded figure. "She is clearly alone."

"Aye. I can see that," snapped Murdoch as he turned toward the narrow stone steps which lead down off of the walls.

His fervent wish that some miracle would happen to carry her off to safety before he would have to deal with her was plainly not going to be granted, so Murdoch braced himself to confront this unwanted intruder. For three long years he had shut out the world, weary of the misery it brought him. Only family and a few old, faithful servants shared his isolation. Murdoch dreaded this intrusion into his sanctuary, but he knew he could never leave the woman out there to die.

When he hesitated at his gates, staring at them as the woman weakly pounded against them, Ennis swore and struggled to open the gates alone. Murdoch shook free of the sudden dread that had frozen him and helped his cousin. A tiny snow-encrusted figure staggered in, and he and Ennis quickly shut and bolted the gates behind her. He released a soft cry of shock when she suddenly collapsed against him, holding him tightly as she fought to stay upright.

"Oh, thank ye, sir. I feared I was doomed to be buried in snow and not be found 'til the spring thaw. When I saw your tower house, I was tempted to fall to my knees and thank God, but I feared I wouldna be able to get up again."

As she spoke she looked up at him, and her hood slipped back a little. Murdoch found himself staring into a huge pair of rich brown eyes. Long-dead feelings stirred deep within him, and he felt a distinct thrill of panic. He pushed her toward Ennis, who caught her as she stumbled into him.

"Take her to Old Margaret," he ordered his cousin as he gave in to the overwhelming urge to flee and started to stride away. "She will tend to the girl's needs."

"What an odd mon," Jessa murmured, but then collapsed into unconciousness before the slender young man now holding her could make any reply to her observation.

Two

Soft whispers and sporadic muffled giggles began to penetrate the thick darkness enclosing Jessa's mind. She winced as with returning awareness all her aches and pains made themselves known. As she eased her eyes open she realized she was dressed in a soft linen nightdress and tucked beneath several blankets in a huge bed. She started to look around, but her attention was immediately and firmly held by the two girls standing at her bedside.

One girl wore a soft gray gown, and the other wore a dark blue one. In all other ways, however, they were the same, from their big blue eyes to their thick black curls. They were stunningly beautiful little girls. When they both leaned closer, Jessa felt slightly intimidated.

"We feared ye would never wake. Ye have been asleep for nigh on to two full days," said the girl in the gray gown. "I am Isobel and this is my sister Lesley."

"Twins," Jessa mumbled hoarsely and knew, even before the girls smiled in a gently patronizing manner, that it was a rather foolish thing to say. "Where am I?"

"Ye have been given shelter by our father, Sir Murdoch Graeme, the laird of Dunstanmoor," replied Isobel. "And who are you?"

"Lady Jessa Armstrong of—weel—of nowhere." She inwardly cursed herself for being so truthful, for the Graemes could search out her family, returning her to her home and to Colin MacDubh.

"Ye canna be of nowhere."

"Aye, I can. I turned my back on my home, thus I dinna have one now." She cautiously eased her bruised body into a seated position, smiling her gratitude when the two girls plumped up the pillows at her back. "I am also verra thirsty." As one of the girls fetched her a tankard of mead from a large pitcher by the bed, she asked, "How does one tell ye apart?"

"I am Isobel. Lesley, who is serving ye the mead, has a weak eye. See? The right one droops a wee bit. 'Tis worse when she grows weary, but 'tis always a wee bit closed."

Jessa sipped at the mead, savoring the way the sweet liquid soothed her parched throat. "Ah, I see it now." She smiled briefly at Lesley. "I am sure ye are both greatly different in many other ways, but since I have only just met ye, I needed something I could readily see. How old are ye?"

"Nine," replied Lesley, revealing that her voice was somewhat deeper than her sister's.

"A fine age. Mayhaps ye could fetch your lady mother?"

"Maman died o'er three years ago," replied Isobel.

"Oh." Jessa inwardly grimaced, then soothed her brief embarrassment by reminding herself that she could not have known that. "I beg your pardon."

"Dinna fret. How could ye ken it? She was verra ill for a verra long time. Death was a kindness. 'Tis what Old Margaret says."

"Sometimes that is the way of it. Mayhaps ye could fetch Old Margaret for me then."

"I will," Lesley said, even as she hurried out of the room.

Isobel sat down on the edge of the bed and eyed Jessa with open curiosity. "Why were ye wandering about in the midst of the storm?"

"My horse tossed me off her back and then bolted when we were set upon by thieves."

"Ah, aye. Our father curses them a lot. They are a plague upon our lands."

"Here, lassie, dinna pry into the womon's business," scolded a dry voice.

Jessa looked toward the older woman striding into the room, little Lesley following and shutting the door behind them. Old Margaret was plump, homely and probably just past child-bearing age. When she had heard the word old, she had not envisioned such a buxom, strong woman, so Jessa assumed that there had to be another Margaret in the keep. It was the only reason she could think of to call such a woman old.

"It canna be prying to ask why she was stumbling about in the heart of the storm," protested Isobel, even as Old Margaret gently tugged her off the bed. "And we didna ken who she was or where she had come from. She is Lady Jessa Armstrong from nowhere."

"A lady from nowhere, eh?"

Jessa smiled a little weakly beneath Old Margaret's piercing stare. " 'Tis kind of ye to come so quickly. I just need to see if I can stand so that I may tend to myself, and I dared not try it without aid the first time."

"And ye willna try it until I say ye are strong enough."

Before Jessa could protest she was plucked from the bed. Old Margaret briskly helped her see to her personal needs while Isobel and Lesley changed the linen on the bed. She was then stripped, sponged down, dressed in a freshly cleaned nightdress and put back in the bed. Old Margaret undid her hair, vigorously brushed it out and was rebraiding it before Jessa gathered her wits enough to speak.

"I didna have much chance to test my footing," she protested.

"Ye need a wee bit more time ere ye start walking about. Ye were cold to the bone and had a bad crack on the head when they brought ye to me. E'en if ye dinna choose to admit it, I ken that ye still ache and suffer from a wee bit of dizziness. There is no need to rush the healing."

"I canna impose upon the laird's kindness for too long."

"And ye canna go anywhere whilst the storm still rages." Margaret finished braiding Jessa's hair and told the twins, "Go and fetch this lass some hearty fare. Bread, cheese and the like. Not too rich, mind ye, but something firmer than the broth we have been squeezing through her lips for the past two days."

The moment the two girls left, Jessa slumped against the pillows and closed her eyes. She knew Old Margaret wanted to question her, so she feigned weakness. It was not as much of an act as she would have liked, for Old Margaret's simple and swift administrations had indeed tired her. She listened to the older woman tidying up the room, and each time she dared to peek from beneath her lowered lashes, she caught Margaret eyeing her closely. The woman would not be pushed away for too long. When she heard Old Margaret step up to the side of the bed she tensed, not sure she could feign sleep well enough to fool her.

"I ken that ye arena asleep, child. I have me a few questions I need to ask," Old Margaret finally said.

"As do I."

The deep, rich, and very male voice startled Jessa so much that she forgot her ploy. Opening her eyes, she looked toward the door where the voice had come from. The big man striding toward her looked vaguely familiar, but it was a moment before she could pin down the elusive memory tickling her mind. He had been the first man she had seen when she had staggered through the gates.

When he stood by the side of her bed, she instinctively tried to burrow deeper into the pillows and coverlet. His expression was cold, remote and not at all welcoming, certainly not the face of a man given to rescuing wayfaring strangers. His startling blue eyes proclaimed him the father of Lesley and Isobel, and the thick hair that hung to his broad shoulders was a black so deep and glossy that the candlelight picked out highlights almost blue in color. His lean face held the promise of handsomeness, but lines caused by somber expressions, a dark spirit and bitterness stole it away. Jessa wondered what could have made the man so desolate, but one look into his eyes told her that she would get no answers from him. She wondered why the darkness she sensed in him and the knowledge that she would never be given the chance to disperse it should trouble her so much. When she told herself that it was simply because she hated to see anyone so sad, Jessa did not believe it, and that worried her.

"My lasses tell me that ye are the Lady Jessa Armstrong of nowhere," he said, placing his hands on his trim hips as he stared down at her.

Murdoch did not really want to be there, did not want to know anything about her, and certainly did not want to be staring into the biggest brown eyes he had ever seen. They were eyes that reached down inside of him and stirred up feelings he had thought were securely buried. When his daughters had told him what their unexpected guest had said, however, he had realized that he could not just ignore her. When she had first arrived, he had seen only the emotional danger of such a lovely young woman, one whose mere touch had roused him to painful life. Now he realized that it could be far worse, that she was either in danger or in flight from something. She could bring a great deal of trouble to his gates.

"I am verra sorry to intrude upon you during this festive and holy time," Jessa said, hoping she could talk around the answers he was demanding of her.

"Ah, do ye mean the Yuletide and all of the great foolishness which greets the new year? We dinna indulge in such nonsense here." He held up one long-fingered hand to silence her when she started to speak. "Dinna try to turn me from my purpose, m'lady." He gave her a faint bow. "I am Sir Murdoch Graeme. Are ye truly Lady Jessa Armstrong?"

"Aye," she replied with a hint of ill humor she made no effort to hide. "I dinna lie, sir."

"Mayhaps not, but ye hold fast to the truth, dinna ye. Where are ye from?"

Jessa really wanted to tell the man a vast array of lies, but she was tired, her head throbbed and she knew it would serve no purpose other than to annoy him. "I am from Dithismhac. I am the daughter of Moira and Duncan Armstrong."

"Dithismhac? That means two sons, doesna it? An odd name for a place."

"Why? Two sons built it."

"Of course," he murmured, but his expression briefly and clearly revealed that he still considered it a very odd name for a keep. "What were ye doing out in the storm?"

"I didna intend to be out in such a storm. I intended to go to Edinburgh to see my aunt Grier. Howbeit, a wretched band of catarans attacked."

"And what of the others who traveled with ye? Did only ye escape?"

"Ah, weel, there was only me. My horse stumbled as I fled the men, tossed me to the ground and ran off. Fortunately, the catarans chased my horse. I believe the storm ended any attempt they may have made to come back and find me when they discovered their error."

"No one would let ye ride o'er such dangerous country alone. What are ye fleeing from?"

"I grow verra weary, sir," Jessa said in a fading voice, extremely reluctant to answer that particular question. "My head still throbs." She fought the urge to cringe when he leaned down, placing one large hand on either side of her head.

"What are ye fleeing from?"

"A marriage, curse your eyes," she snapped, breathing an inner sigh of relief when he stood up again, for his nearness oddly increased her pulse.

"I see. Your family betrothed ye to a mon ye didna like

and ye ran away like some petulant child. Ye probably didna even try to talk with them or to ken the mon they had chosen for ye."

"Ye think yourself so clever, dinna ye. Weel, I did discuss it, over and over and over, and none would heed my words. As to the mon I was to wed, mayhaps I didna try to ken the mon he is. Howbeit, 'twas probably because I was weary from stepping o'er the twenty-two bastard children he has scattered about, or walking around the maid he got with child during our betrothal celebrations." Only by the slightest lift of his vaguely winged brows could she tell that she had shocked him. "I could wait no longer and so I fled."

"What do ye mean ye could wait no longer?"

"Weel, there was but an hour and a wee bit left ere I would kneel with Colin MacDubh afore a priest." This time there was no doubt that she had shocked him, for he gaped at her for a full moment before he recalled himself and closed his mouth.

"Ye left Colin MacDubh at the altar?"

"Weel, not at the altar exactly. We hadna stepped before the priest yet."

Murdoch muttered a soft curse, ignored Old Margaret's hissed scold and glared at Jessa. He knew of Sir Colin Mac-Dubh, and the thought of the lovely, delicate Jessa marrying such a man nearly turned his stomach. The depth of his distaste surprised him, and he fought it back. Even if he wanted to entangle himself in her affairs, it was not his place to do so.

"As soon as ye are weel enough and the weather is calmer, ye will return to your family at Dithismhac," he said and, not waiting for an answer, strode to the door.

"I willna!" she protested. "I canna. Ye dinna understand."

"Ye *will* return to them even if I must take ye back myself. I refuse to be dragged into the midst of a family squabble," he added, as he stepped out of the room and shut the door behind him with a distinct thud.

"Who does that mon think he is?" Jessa muttered.

"The laird?" Old Margaret said, a faint smile curving her lips.

"Oh, aye, there is that." Jessa grimaced, then glared at the door Sir Graeme had almost slammed. "Howbeit, he isna *my* laird. And, even if courtesy demands it, I willna bow to his wishes. Nay, not in this."

"I dinna think there is a muckle lot ye can do about it, lass."

"I can get strong again and continue on my way—to Edinburgh and my aunt."

Before Old Margaret could argue with her, Isobel and Lesley arrived with some food. It was a light meal of bread, cheese, honey and cider, yet Jessa found that despite her hunger, she soon grew weary of eating. When Old Margaret had to help her spread a little honey on a thick piece of bread, Jessa decided that she had had enough. She weakly waved away the offer of more and sagged against the pillows.

"Ye need to rest again, lass," Old Margaret said as she signaled the girls to collect up the tray and the remains of the meal.

Jessa only nodded as she watched the woman and the two girls prepare to leave her. There was a sadness at Dunstanmoor that seemed to infect everyone. It was evident in the quiet of the place and the people. Jessa knew exactly where the infection came from, too—the laird himself. It had only taken one meeting for her to see how weighted down he was with his own sorrows. She knew it was none of her business and certainly not her place to interfere. When the girls looked at her to faintly smile and softly wish her a good sleep, however, she also knew she would intrude. If she had time, she would root out the cause of the pervasive somberness of Dunstanmoor and then do her best to shake the children free of its tight grip.

Three

After gently scraping the frost off of the inside of the narrow window, Jessa peered out and softly cursed. There was snow everywhere. She could not really tell if it was still falling from the sky or was simply being swirled about by the icy winds. She had been at Dunstanmoor for a full week. It was her first day out of bed without the ever watchful Old Margaret watching over her, and her first thought had been of escape. The white frozen blanket coating everything for miles around meant that she was well and truly stuck at Dunstanmoor. She could still make plans to flee, but it would be a long time before she could act upon them.

A shiver rippled through her, and she quickly dropped the heavy curtain back over the window. Wrapping the thick robe she wore more tightly around herself, she moved to the fireplace and sat down on the plush sheepskin rug set before it. In minutes the heat of the fire seeped through her body and she welcomed it. Her ordeal had severely weakened her, and the slightest chill could easily send her back to bed. She needed to regain her full strength so that if any opportunity came to continue on to Edinburgh, she could grab it.

"At least if I reach my aunt and she refuses to help me, I will be returned to Dithismhac by family and not some arrogant, cold-eyed laird who doesna even have the courtesy to visit with his guests," she muttered as she glared into the fire.

Jessa was not sure why it irritated her so that Sir Murdoch

never visited. She had no lack of company. Sir Ennis often came by, even graciously reading to her as she recovered. Isobel and Lesley visited several times a day. And Old Margaret did the same. It made no sense to be almost hurt by the pointed absence of one dour man, a man she had only seen twice. Her total acquaintance with Sir Murdoch amounted to only a few tense minutes.

" 'Tis most like those thrice-cursed sad eyes of his," she muttered, groping for some explanation for her fascination with a man she had passed only a few curt words with.

"Talking to yourself?"

The sudden intrusion into her thoughts of that already familiar deep voice so startled Jessa that she nearly tipped over as she swiftly turned to look at the man stepping into her room. "I dinna suppose ye thought to rap at the door first?" she snapped as Murdoch shut the door behind him and strode toward her.

"If I had kenned what a foul temper ye were in, I might have."

Murdoch sat down beside her and prayed that she could not see the strain he was under upon his face, or hear it in his voice. When he had opened the door and seen her sitting by the fire, he had suddenly wanted to run away. Her bright red hair was loose, hanging down her slim back in thick waves until it pooled slightly on the sheepskin. The soft, pale skin of her small, heart-shaped face was touched with a faint rose blush of warmth from the fire. Although the heavy robe she wore was modest, the glimpse of her long, slim neck and her delicate wrists and ankles told him that she wore little or nothing beneath it. As he looked into her wide, dark eyes he struggled against the overwhelming urge to open that robe. The mere sight of her stirred him almost past reason. That terrified him, but he had decided he could not continue to run from it. Now he wondered if that had been a wise decision.

"What has put ye into such a foul mood?" he asked,

clenching his hands in his lap as he fought the powerful urge to reach out and drag his fingers through her lush, shiny hair.

Jessa briefly wondered how he would respond if she told him the full truth, that she was both hurt and angry that he avoided her and irritated because she did not know why she should even care. She decided she would only embarrass herself, so replied, "This cursed weather weighs upon my temper. It has been naught but white and gray for a week. The sun seems to have forgotten us." She grimaced slightly. "I fear that we shall soon be buried in snow. 'Twill be piled so high that any enemy ye might have willna need scaling ladders to come o'er your walls."

"I dinna believe the snow is that firm," he murmured and almost smiled. "It hasna been snowing consistantly since your arrival here. We have had but one other storm. Howbeit, the winds are so fierce that the snow is blown about almost constantly, and it does seem as if it has ne'er ceased to snow. The sky does remain gray and forbidding, so, mayhaps, there will be more snow to come.

"Ye need not worry o'er it," he assured her. "We have enough to remain warm and weel fed e'en if it snows for weeks. The only thing we may come to lack is an adequate supply of meat, but that, too, willna happen for many, many days yet."

"Ye believe in being verra weel supplied."

"Aye. I have suffered through a siege at a keep that didna plan weel, and I vowed then that I would ne'er be caught in the same trap."

Jessa only briefly considered asking him to tell her more about his experience. There was a look in his eyes that dampened her curiosity. Murdoch Graeme had suffered far more than an empty belly at that siege, she was sure of it. It was also not an experience he wanted to recall in any depth. If she wished to learn anything about this man, she would have to work very hard. He was not going to reveal anything about himself or his past easily. She wondered why she even considered trying to come to know him, then looked into his eyes. The why of it all might not be clear to her, but she knew she would twist herself into knots in an attempt to break through the tough armor he had encased himself in.

As she struggled to think of something to say to end the sudden tension between them, Jessa noticed a change in the look in his rich blue eyes. The cool distance began to melt away, a faint warmth replacing it. Even as he shifted his gaze to her hair, he lifted his hand. She sat so still she could hardly breathe as he slowly reached out to stroke her hair. It was a light touch, tentative, reluctant, but her heart began to pound so hard she could hear it throbbing in her ears. When he began to lean closer, she fought the natural urge to bend away. Instinct told her he was about to kiss her, common sense and propriety told her to put a stop to it all, and her heart told her to accept his advance. Jessa decided to obey her heart.

When his mouth touched hers, she shuddered faintly, all tension flowing from her body in a rush to be replaced by a heat that flooded her. She reached for him as he brushed his soft lips across hers, but he was too far away to hold. All she could do was rest her hands on his broad shoulders. He cupped her face in his hands, but the gentle restraint was unnecessary. Jessa knew she would not be the one to stop the kiss. As he deepened the kiss, she tightened her grip on his shoulders, sensing that he could flee at any moment.

He touched his tongue to her lips, and she obediently opened her mouth. A soft groan escaped her as he stroked the inside of her mouth. She murmured a plaintive protest when he suddenly drew away. As his lips left hers, she felt as if he drew all the warmth from her body. Cautiously, she opened her eyes and inwardly cursed. He looked stunned, but, worse, the coolness was seeping back into his eyes. He was retreating from her, running from the passion that had so briefly flared between them, and she did not know how to bring him back.

"Curse it," he muttered, dragging his fingers through his hair as he stared at her. "What am I doing?"

"Kissing me." she replied and met his disgusted look with a half smile.

"That isna what I came here to do. 'Tisna what I should be doing, or what ye should be allowing me to do either." He stood up and absently smoothed down his tunic. "Ye should have pushed me away."

"Mayhaps I didna wish to."

"And mayhaps ye should consider the dangers of such recklessness."

"A little recklessness can be a good thing. It can keep a person's blood from freezing in his veins."

Murdoch ignored her pointed look. "I came to extend an invitation to dine with us in the great hall tonight. 'Tis evident that ye have recovered from your ordeal and so ye need not remain secluded in these chambers."

"How kind of ye."

"Sarcasm isna a quality many men admire in a woman."

"My observations tell me that there isna verra much at all that most men admire in women."

"Ye arena old enough to have made many such observations."

"I am nineteen." She smiled faintly at his look of surprise and knew that some of it came from the fact that she was not already married. Although she wanted to keep him with her, perhaps even pulling a few morsels of information from him, she could sense his urge to leave and said, "I thank ye for the kind invitation and will indeed join ye in the great hall this eve."

Murdoch nodded, muttered a farewell, and fled. As he strode to his private chambers he tried to convince himself that he was not running away, but he was unable to swallow the huge lie. It had been such a small kiss, quickly ended, but he could still taste her sweetness on his mouth. The soft moan of welcome and pleasure that had escaped her still caressed his ears. He could still feel her silken hair beneath his fingers. The wealth of emotion that had flooded him at the mere touch of her lips had terrified him. He had thought he had killed all such feelings. The fact that he had not and that a tiny brown-eyed woman could bring them to such a full, fierce life was what sent him running to his room like some frightened child.

Worse, he mused as he entered his bedchamber and slammed the door behind him, he was sure that she knew. There had been a look in her eyes as he had left, a strange mixture of sadness, sympathy and determination, that told him that his fears were not as secret or as well-hidden as he would like them to be. Her eyes, he decided as he poured himself a large tankard of wine and gulped it down, were a dangerous weapon. He did not know if the shields he had put up around his heart were strong enough to hold against them.

"Murdoch?" Ennis called as he tentatively entered the room. "Is something wrong?"

"What makes ye think that something is wrong?" Murdoch asked, fighting to regain the calm he had lost in Jessa Armstrong's bedchamber.

"Mayhaps the fact that ye just shut this door hard enough to split the oak." Ennis examined the door as he closed it and shook his head. "I am truly astounded that it is still intact. The floor fairly shook when ye shut it."

Murdoch ignored his cousin's nonsense and silently offered the younger man a drink. "I was but lost in thought and didna realize how hard I shut it," he said, as Ennis filled a tankard with the sweet wine.

"Something our wee, bonny guest said?"

"What makes ye think she had anything to do with it?"

"I saw ye stride out of her room. I did call out to ye,

but ye were too lost in your own thoughts." He shrugged and sipped at his wine as he watched Murdoch pace the room. "I ken that ye have been troubled by the lass's presence."

Murdoch stopped by the tiny window and glared unseeingly out at the snow. "I kenned she was trouble the moment she stumbled in through our gates."

"Why? Because ye found that ye still have a spark of life left in your veins?"

Slowly, Murdoch turned to face his cousin. "Aye. Dinna look so pleased. I want no sparks, no glowing embers, no fire at all. Such things have brought me naught but grief in my life. When I locked the gates of Dunstanmoor to the outside world, I intended to lock all of that away as weel. 'Tis clear that it can still stumble inside, so now I must strengthen myself. Mayhaps this was a test I needed. It has revealed that although my mind has learned all the hard lessons I have been taught o'er the years, the rest of me needs a great deal more training."

"Ye mean to kill all that makes ye a mon."

"Unthinking passion? Reckless emotion? I believe there is much more to a mon than that and many a mon would be the better for not having them."

"I disagree, but ye ken that. I have made no secret of my opinion. Mayhaps ye ought to consider what your killing all that is alive in ye will do to your daughters."

"What do ye mean?"

"I mean that children mimic their parents. Do ye really wish your lasses to grow to be cold and unfeeling, to hold none of the softer or wilder emotions that often make life worth living?"

That troubled Murdoch, but he fought to hide his concern. "They will ken less pain in their lives."

"As ye wish." Ennis set down his empty tankard and started to leave, pausing in the doorway to look at Murdoch. "Ye are right in saying that they will ken less pain, but they willna ken much of anything else either. Kill all life within yourself if that is what ye wish, but I think 'tis the height of arrogance to decide that your daughters will wish to be the same." He quietly shut the door as he left.

Murdoch softly cursed and poured himself another tankard of wine. He was drinking too much of the heady liquid, using it to calm himself, to push aside painful memories and even to deaden all thought so that he could sleep at night. If he became a drunkard, it would be all Jessa Armstrong's fault, he decided crossly. The sooner that young woman was gone, the better. He cursed again when he realized that already a large part of him did not want her to leave.

Jessa frowned as she looked over the gown she was wearing. Despite all the hurried work she, Old Margaret and the girls had done, it still did not look as good as she had hoped. It was a lovely blue brocade, but it did not hang quite right. There had not been enough time to do a proper and thorough fitting.

She cursed when she realized why she was so concerned. Her appearance was of such great importance because Murdoch would be there. He had seen her wet and bedraggled, sick, and then dressed in old robes that were far too large for her. She wanted to show him that she could look presentable, perhaps even pretty.

"Foolishness," she muttered as she made one last check of her lightly braided hair. "That mon willna notice what I am wearing anyway."

The moment she stepped out of her room, the twins straightened up from leaning against the wall opposite her door. She smiled at them as they hastily brushed down their skirts. In the week since her arrival she and the twins had grown closer. Occasionally she had even made the girls giggle as young girls should. It saddened her to think that she had to work to make that happen.

"Have ye come to escort me to the great hall, then?" she asked as they fell into step on either side of her.

"Ye have ne'er been there," replied Isobel. "And we thought ye may be unsure of where ye should sit."

"Ah, there is that."

The moment Jessa entered the great hall of Dunstanmoor she began to wish she had stayed in her bedchamber. She inwardly grimaced as she was given the seat to the right of the grim-faced Sir Murdoch. Whatever had softened in him earlier had been ruthlessly quashed. She suspected she would find more warmth if she rolled about naked in the snow. What both dismayed and annoyed her was how much his icy politeness hurt her. She decided to leave him in his self-imposed exile and turned all of her attention to the twins and Ennis.

Only once did she catch a brief break in Murdoch's distant air, and that was when she mentioned how she would miss the Yuletide celebrations at Dithismhac. The twins glanced his way nervously, but when he said nothing, they eagerly listened to her tales of past celebrations. They were so entertained by her tales of mishaps and frolics that by the time she returned to her bedchamber, she was almost hoarse from talking and laughing so much.

She was also furious at Murdoch. He had said nothing to halt the twins' enjoyment, but his dark expression had definitely muted it. As Old Margaret helped her change into her nightdress and brushed out her hair, Jessa railed against Murdoch, complaining of his cold-heartedness and ill humor. It was not until Old Margaret was swiftly rebraiding her hair that she noticed that the woman was not pleased by her complaints.

"I realize that he is your laird and that ye have probably kenned him since he was a suckling bairn, but the mon is naught but one huge, blue-eyed storm cloud," she said.

"He has suffered a lot in his life," Old Margaret said in Murdoch's defense.

"So have many others and they dinna become brooding bears because of it."

"True, but Murdoch is a mon of deep, strong emotion, and mayhaps he feels the blows dealt and the pain of them more deeply."

"The mon in the great hall tonight showed little sign of that."

"Lass, ye dinna ken what he has endured."

Jessa turned to face Old Margaret. "Nay, I dinna, and I ne'er will unless someone tells me. Mayhaps I wouldna be so condemning if I kenned what had turned the mon into the cold statue that sat next to me throughout the meal tonight."

Old Margaret sighed and sat down on the stool next to Jessa's chair. "The mon not only lost a wife, but many of his kinsmen and a wee son."

" 'Tis sad, Margaret, but many have suffered such losses. I myself have seen many of my kin buried, some whom I dearly loved and many sent to their deaths whilst they were still young."

"I ken it and I canna fully pardon the way Murdoch has turned. He blames himself for each and every loss. He has burdened his heart and mind with guilts he hasna earned. His parents and brother were murdered by his enemy, and he blames himself for not being there to help them or die with them. 'Twas much the same with other kinsmen who were either murdered by Murdoch's enemy or lost in a battle with the mon. Aye, he finally killed the bastard, but a lot of Graemes were slain ere he could achieve that vengeance."

"Was it that mon who killed his wife?"

"Nay, 'twas the enemy of her people, but I fear Murdoch has twisted it all about in his mind until he believes he somehow brought that death to their door. He and his pretty little wife took their newborn son to her family's keep farther north. The lasses were suffering a touch of the ague and couldna go. 'Tis probably all that saved them."

"Aye, yet he finds little joy in that," Jessa murmured, her heart heavy with sympathy for Murdoch.

"He does, lass. He has just lost the ability to show it. But, let us return to the tale, for I shall only tell it once and ye willna get any others here to tell ye."

"I ken that weel enough."

"He and his wee wife had only but arrived at her family's keep when their enemy struck. There were not enough men at the keep to win an open battle and so their enemy was able to lay siege, and a tight one it was. Ill supplied, those within the keep began to suffer, yet the laird refused to give. Murdoch buried his wee son there. The poor laddie starved when his mother grew so weak and wan that all of her milk dried up. The siege was ended only when the old laird himself died and his wife immediately surrendered. Murdoch brought his wife home, but she ne'er recovered from the ordeal or the loss of her bairn. He buried her a few short months later."

"And when did all of this happen?"

"Three years ago come this Yuletide."

Jessa cursed, stood up and paced the room for a minute before flopping down onto her bed. "So that is why he doesna celebrate the Yuletide or the New Year."

"Aye, the mon finds it a time of naught but painful memories," Old Margaret said as she idly tucked Jessa in her bed.

"I understand now, but it still doesna make it right for him to inflict his sorrows upon Isobel and Lesley. If they have the ability to heal and forget, then they should be allowed to do so, not kept weighed down by their father's grief."

"I feel the same. The mon doesna see how he steals all

the laughter, all the life, from his wee girls, but there is no changing him."

"Mayhaps not, but that doesna mean that someone canna change the girls."

"I dinna understand."

" 'Tis past time that the twins' emotions, moods and ideas were released from their father's somber grip. Dinna frown so, Margaret. I dinna mean to turn them against their father, but 'tis time they pulled free of the morass he has sunk himself in. After all, ye can love your parents without being just like them. Aye, 'tis time those girls had a wee taste of how the rest of the world lives, and I mean to give it to them."

"Ye could pull a great deal of trouble down on your head."

"So be it. And, mayhaps it might just shake Murdoch free of his grief."

When Old Margaret just smiled faintly and shook her head, Jessa tried not to let that dim her hopes of success. After tonight she knew she had to do something. If Murdoch did not want to participate, that was his choice, but she was determined to give Isobel and Lesley a taste of a true, joyful Yuletide.

Four

Jessa laughed with the twins and shook the snow from her hair as they stepped into the great hall. After she had made her decision the night before to celebrate the Yuletide despite Murdoch Graeme, she had not been very surprised to find the sun shining when she awoke, although she tried not to read it as some omen or sign of divine approval. She had hopped out of bed, dressed and gone to rouse the twins so that they could take advantage of the change in the weather to collect some pine boughs. When the twins grew quiet and hesitated upon seeing their father sitting at the head table, Jessa marched right up to his table and dumped her armful of pine boughs on the newly polished wood, signaling the twins to do the same.

"What is this?" Murdoch demanded, quickly moving the papers he had been working on.

"I think ye have been shut away for too long, m'laird," Jessa murmured as she brushed the snow from her cloak. "These are pine boughs," she said, speaking slowly as if to a child who was just learning his words.

"I ken *what* they are. *Why* are they here, cluttering up my table?"

"I am going to use them to prepare the great hall for the Yuletide feast." She fought the urge to shift away when he rose from his seat and stood close beside her.

"I told ye that we dinna celebrate that nonsense at Dunstanmoor."

"Aye, I do recall ye said something of the sort. Howbeit, I am a guest, am I not?"

"Aye, though an uninvited one."

She decided to ignore that testy remark. "And is it not the duty of the host to satisfy all of his guest's desires?"

"Aye. The rules of hospitality require it." He leaned so close to her that his warm breath stirred the wisps of hair covering her ear, and he whispered, "But, I must wonder if my guest truly wishes *all* of her desires satisfied."

Jessa could feel the blush heating her cheeks, but when she met his gaze, she smiled calmly. "Aye, I do."

"Ye may not ken what ye are asking. Ye may get more than ye wish for or can deal with."

"Sir Graeme, I am no weak lass. I can deal with whate'er ye wish to toss my way. Now, if ye are through playing your wee game, the lasses and I are going to have some warm cider to take the chill from our blood and then begin to prepare this hall for the festive time ahead."

She watched him closely as he looked from her to the girls to the boughs and then back at the girls once more before scowling at her. "Ye dare a great deal, Jessa Armstrong."

"Ah, weel, we Armstrongs have e'er been a bold and daring sort."

"Then, as your host"—he gave her a small, mocking bow—"I concede to your demands."

"And so graciously, too."

Jessa bit back a smile at the disgusted look he gave her before he went to collect his papers. After one final cross look at her and the pine boughs covering the table, he walked out of the great hall. Inwardly, Jessa breathed a hearty sigh of relief. The confrontation had gone far more smoothly than she had anticipated. She knew the girls were the reason it had been so mild and quickly ended. Murdoch really did not want to make his children unhappy, and the girls, despite their efforts to keep their faces clear of all expression, had looked painfully hopeful. He did not have the heart to cause them any disappointment. Jessa wondered if Murdoch knew what a keen weapon he had just placed in her hand.

As a shy maid served her and the twins some hot, lightly spiced cider, Jessa told herself that she would not stoop to using the girls. Isobel and Lesley were not tools to use in molding their father, but children who could be sorely hurt by such tricks and deceptions. She would, however, make no effort to hide what she did with the girls in order to bow to Murdoch's self-imposed sensitivity. If seeing them prepare for the holiday ahead helped him pull himself free of the somber, even morose, mood he was so tightly caught up in, then so be it.

Not long after they began to spread around the pine boughs and hotly discuss what other things they might do to brighten up the hall, others slipped in to help. It was not only the children who missed indulging in one of the few festive times there were in the cold depths of wintertime. Soon people even ceased to look over their shoulders, afraid that their laird would catch them, and the planning expanded to the point where Jessa knew even Murdoch would not be able to ignore the celebrations.

Murdoch heard the laughter from the great hall and was drawn to the door. Hugging the shadows so as not to be seen, he watched his children and his people help Jessa Armstrong. He felt a sharp twinge of pain for times lost, recalling how his wife Anne had so enjoyed festive occasions, but the pain was neither as strong nor as lasting as he felt it ought to be. Seeing how much they all were enjoying themselves, he also felt guilty. Had he been depriving his children and his loyal people for all these years? And, if he had, why had no one complained? Murdoch did not believe he was such a fearsome man that his own people could not speak up if they had a complaint.

Cursing softly, he slipped away and walked to his bed-chamber. When he reached for the decanter of wine the moment he was in his room, he cursed again. He would not seek refuge there, not this time. If there was some truth that needed to be faced, he would face it with a clear head and not try to drown the revelation in wine.

"And curse that woman for intruding upon my life," he nearly snarled as he flopped onto his bed and glared up at the ceiling.

Even when he sent her home his life would not return to what it had been. She had only been with them for a week and a day, and already she had changed things beyond re-demption. The people of Dunstanmoor had forgone the Yuletide celebrations in deference to his long mourning, but now that he had not loudly forbidden Jessa Armstrong from celebrating, he could not stop anyone else. From now on Dunstanmoor would be filled with frivolity on the anniver-sary of the deaths of his wife and infant son.

Murdoch waited for the accustomed gut-wrenching pain to tear through him at the thought of their deaths. There was pain, but it was softer, a gentle melancholy rather than sharp grief. At some time during his hibernation from the world he had begun to heal. The guilt was still there, still weighing his heart, but that, too, was more of a regret than a shamed admission of culpability. There should have been some way to save them, yet he no longer felt as if he alone had failed them.

"Ye have two other children, ye great sulking laddie," said a coarse voice.

Only slightly startled by how quietly Old Margaret had slipped into his room, Murdoch turned his head to watch her as she shut the door behind her and walked over to the bed. He smiled faintly when she put her work-worn hands on her ample hips and scowled down at him.

"Did ye come to see how I fared?" he asked.

"Aye and nay," she replied and shook her head. "That Armstrong lass oversteps herself, but I willna admonish her for it. The lasses are enjoying themselves and I willna put a stop to that."

He slowly sat up and frowned at her. "Do ye mean to imply that I have kept the joy from my children's lives?"

"Not apurpose, nay. Now, dinna look so affronted. Ye arena a cruel mon and none think ye are. But, when ye wrap yourself in grief and despair, when ye shut us all away as if ye fear the plague, how do ye think that affects the wee lasses?"

There was no answer he could make to that, and he mumbled, "No one has complained to me."

"Of course they havena. They understand your pain, and they certainly dinna wish to stir it up afresh or appear to lack all sympathy for your tragic losses." Old Margaret shrugged when Murdoch said nothing, and she started out the door. "I just wished to say my piece. Ye may do as ye please."

Murdoch released a sharp bark of laughter as she shut the door behind her. Old Margaret had intended to do more than just state her opinion. She had meant to plant a seed of thought, and she had done just that. He suspected that beneath her words was also the soft threat that he would have her to deal with if he tried to put a stop to Jessa's activities.

Crossing his arms beneath his head, he sighed and stared at the ceiling. He had no intention of stopping Jessa, but neither did he intend to join in, at least not completely. It seemed disrespectful to the dead. Even as he told himself that, however, he knew it was not the only reason he would try to avoid the celebrations. Jessa Armstrong herself was a good reason to remain distant. When she had come into the great hall flushed from the cold and smelling lightly of fresh air and pine, he had felt an immediate attraction. Their brief exchange of innuendo had deeply excited him. Joining in any festivity with her, relaxing with good food and pleasant company, could be extremely dangerous. He would have no strength to resist her then and he knew it. The celebrations would go on unhindered by him, and he would do all that courtesy demanded, but no more. Jessa Armstrong had done enough to alter his life as it was. He would not, could not, allow her to change him as well. He had vowed never to let love for a woman enter his heart again, and he meant to hold firm to that vow. After the torture of grief he had suffered when Anne died, Murdoch suspected that firmly protecting his heart was the only way to keep his sanity.

Jessa covered her mouth to stifle a yawn and then frowned. She stopped in the hall only a few steps from her room and stared at her hands and laughed softly. They were streaked with pitch, and that sticky residue from the branches had clung tightly to every fleck of dirt she had drawn near to. She had thoroughly scrubbed her hands just before the evening meal, so she had to have gotten into such a state in the few hours since then, when she and the twins had eagerly put the final touches on their decorations. Shaking her head and smiling, for it was a small price to pay for the joy that had shone in the twins' pretty faces tonight, she diligently tried to rub some of the pitch from her palms.

Although she had heard nothing, some sense told her that she was being watched. A little warily she turned to find Murdoch leaning against the wall just across the hall from where she stood. The light in the hall was dim, so she could not be certain, but he appeared to find her amusing. She tensed a little when he walked over to her and took her hand in his to look at her palm.

"Disrupting people's lives is clearly dirty work," he murmured, the ghost of a smile curving his lips when she scowled at him.

"I am sorry if ye find the celebration of our Lord's birth a disruption," she said, struggling to look haughty despite the way his touch made her tremble inside.

"Dinna turn all pious on me, Jessa Armstrong."

"Pious?"

"Aye, pious. Ye have the look, but I dinna think that condemning self-righteousness runs verra deep."

"I wasna condemning anyone, simply making an observation."

"Then allow me to make one as weel."

"Ye look an odd mix of annoyed and amused, so I am nay sure I wish to hear it."

"Since ye first opened those huge brown eyes of yours within my walls, ye have diligently turned my quiet life wrong way round. 'Tis no longer so quiet here. Ye have all my people running about preparing for a feast when we are under siege by the cursed weather. The men who should be guarding my walls are tramping about in the wood searching for a Yule log. I must secure myself in my bedchamber to do my work. And my great hall now smells like a forest. Have I forgotten anything?"

"Nay, I dinna think so." Jessa only briefly considered defending herself or denying any of his complaints. She simply did not believe that she was doing anything wrong.

"I am surprised ye havena dragged some priest here to put his blessing upon all of this nonsense."

"I fear the one who served the village was away when the snows fell, and he willna be back in time. We shall each have to honor the holiness of the season in our own way, in our own minds and hearts. I was a little surprised that a mon of your standing doesna have any mon of the church right here within your own wee chapel."

"I used to have one, but he was sent away. He suggested that I find another wife for the sake of my daughters. True, 'tis a request any mon of the church might make, but this fool approached me on the matter when my wife was but three months dead."

Jessa inwardly grimaced, wondering how any man could be so inept at judging his laird's temper and mood or so tactless. "It matters not. I am sure we can all stumble through the day without the guidance of such a mon."

When Murdoch edged closer to her, she moved back only to come up against the wall. He swiftly cornered her there. She knew she needed to make only the smallest of protests and he would let her go, but she allowed him to lightly cage her between his strong body and the cool stone wall. The man ran hot and cold, pulling her close and then pushing her away. It was a painful dance, but she enjoyed the brief glimpses of his warmth far too much to turn away. She just wondered how long this particular moment would last.

"And why do we need a priest when Jessa Armstrong is here to lead us?" He slowly ran his hand down the length of her thick lightly braided hair.

"I would never attempt to tend to anyone's spiritual needs."

"And what needs would ye attempt to minister to?"

"Ye ask some verra bold questions, m'laird." Her voice sank to a low, husky level when he touched light kisses to her cheeks.

"Did ye not say that the Armstrongs are a bold and daring people? Surely ye can abide a few bold questions."

Jessa knew she should be responding with some clever, even witty, remark, but as he brushed his warm lips over hers, she found it very difficult to think clearly. She found the taste of the man to be as heady and as intoxicating as the strongest wine. When he pressed closer, their bodies touching from chest to thigh, she felt almost weak and curled her arms around his neck, both to hold him close and to support herself. A soft cry of welcome escaped her when he finally kissed her. He deepened the kiss with a speed that made her head swim, and Jessa knew instinctively that each time he warmed to her he grew less able to control himself.

The hunger of his kiss quickly infected her with an equal need. She shifted against him, her body asking for all he could give her. A low moan of need echoed in her throat when he slipped his arm about her waist and pressed their loins together. A sharp throb pulsated through her, and she savored the growl of pleasure that escaped him.

Although it did not surprise her when he suddenly pushed her away, she nearly cursed. She felt tight with wanting him, a greed he had inspired yet refused to placate. When he stared at her with a mixture of shock and curiosity, the coolness seeping into his eyes again, she fought against the hurt that look caused. He obviously thought she was doing something to tempt him into these lapses. She almost wished she was, for then she could use the skill to halt his retreat.

"Ye are a verra odd woman, Jessa Armstrong," he murmured, his voice still hoarse, as he took a few steps back from her.

"*I* am odd?" She made no attempt to hide her irritation as she absently brushed down her skirts and glared at him. " 'Tis not I who stops people in the hall, kisses them senseless, and then leaps away as if the one they hold has suddenly turned leperous."

"Weel, one of us must have some control."

"Is that what ye call it?" She walked up to her door, yanked it open and looked at him over her shoulder as she stepped inside. "I think, my dour laird, that ye had best take a closer look. What ye call control looks verra much like confusion to me."

Murdoch winced as she shut the door behind her with a distinct thud. She was right. It was confusion. In fact, he had to wonder if he suffered from some strange new insan-

ity. One moment he swore to keep his distance, the next he
was cornering her in the hall and stealing kisses like some
lovesick lad. He shook his head and laughed sourly as he
strode to his room. If he did not get a firmer grasp upon
himself and his tumultuous emotions soon, he just might
go mad.

Five

"So here is where ye have hidden yourself."

Jessa cried out softly in surprise and turned to frown at the man filling the doorway to the kitchens. She knew that deep voice as well as she knew her own, but wondered if she could ever become accustomed to the way he could approach without sound or warning. She softly harumphed her disapproval of his apparent fondness for startling people and turned her attention back to the delicate sweets she was making for the Yuletide feast. She tensed a little when he stepped up close behind her. It was not only his nearness that disturbed her. She still feared that he might try to halt the feast, even though it was all planned for tomorrow.

"I wasna hiding," she said. "To say that I was hiding is to imply that I was aware that ye were searching for me and thus was purposely trying to elude you. I wasna and I didna so I wasna *hiding*. Ye simply didna ken where I was." She glanced at him briefly and was certain that she saw the hint of a smile. The man did possess a sense of humor, and she found it very sad that he revealed it so rarely.

"Have ye driven everyone away from the kitchens, then?"

"Nay. There was naught they could do to assist me here, but a great amount of work to do elsewhere." She lightly slapped his hand when he reached around her to steal some of the sweetened fruit filling she was working with. "These are for the feast on the morrow."

Murdoch idly licked from his finger the meager amount

of sugary fruit he had stolen and studied the tiny woman he had cornered between himself and the work-worn table. She was diligently preparing food for a feast she knew he did not want and offered no apologies for her actions. Their bodies were close yet not touching, but he felt his hunger for her fill his blood, heating it and causing it to pound through his veins at a heady pace. She had worked a change in his people. He had not realized how subdued they had become in deference to his grief and dark moods. Jessa had freed them, and he knew that once she was gone, things could not return to what they had once been. She had also freed a few tongues if the lectures he had received from Ennis and Old Margaret were any indication. Murdoch began to wonder who had whom cornered.

He gently placed his hands upon her shoulders. She tensed, then trembled slightly. Murdoch slowly smoothed his hands down her arms, then curled his arms around her waist. As he pulled her lithe body close to his, he echoed the shudder that tore through her. She wanted him as badly as he wanted her. That knowledge made his passion burn all the hotter. Briefly he tried to tell himself that he was losing control so easily because he had not had a woman since his Anne died, but his mind scornfully laughed aside that excuse. He did not want just any woman; he wanted Jessa Armstrong.

When she turned in his hold, placing her small, sticky and floury hands on his chest, he ignored her weak push against him and looked into her eyes. The brown was dark and softly liquid with a passion he felt sure matched his. She was just murmuring a faint protest when he kissed her.

Jessa wondered why she bothered to protest as she wrapped her arms around his neck and fully returned his hungry kiss. She did not really wish to stop him, only to forestall the hurt he inflicted when he would bring their moment of heated closeness to an abrupt halt. Then the chill returned. The physical distance he would hurriedly put between them was not so hard to bear, for there were many good, inoffensive reasons to impose it. It was the emotional distance he imposed upon them that cut her as deeply and as agonizingly as any well-honed sword. There was only a small comfort to be grasped in the fact that he was finding that distance harder and harder to maintain. Each time they dined together, each time they met in the hall and each time they even looked at each other, his ability to hold her at a distance was chipped away. The change was slow, however, and time was not on her side.

When he slid his hands up her sides and cradled her breasts in his palms, she moaned softly and arched into his hold in silent welcome. She wondered how such a light touch could have such power. Every part of her tingled with the heat of desire. She ached, she burned, she was weak with an all-encompassing need for Murdoch. He slipped his hands around to her backside and pressed her against him. Jessa trembled as she felt the hard proof of his desire. Instinctively, she shifted against him, but even as she savored the sharp delight of that movement coursing through her body, she felt him start to wrench himself free of the tight grip of their passion. She inwardly cursed and then struggled to calm herself as he eased his hold on her and stepped away.

There was a little satisfaction in how ragged his breathing was and the flush on his high-boned cheeks. Jessa was irritated, however, by how quickly he overcame and subdued those signs of desire. She did not find her frustrated passions quite so malleable. The look she hated crept over his face, that annoying mix of accusation and surprise, and she fought the urge to slap it away. It also saddened her, for as long as he blamed her for what he felt, as long as he could convince himself that she was the sole cause of his lack of control and confusion, he would never look closely at what might lurk within his own heart. Unless he was willing to do that, she had no chance of making a place for herself within that imprisoned organ.

"I dinna ken how one tiny, wide-eyed lass can bring such confusion to a place as large as Dunstanmoor," he muttered as he needlessly smoothed down his jerkin.

" 'Tisna Dunstanmoor which is confused," Jessa snapped as she abruptly turned her back on him and returned to preparing the sweets for the celebration, "just its laird."

Murdoch walked to the other side of the table so that he might look into her face and cursed softly when all he was presented with was the top of her head. "I dinna suffer from any confusion." He scowled when she made a distinctly mocking noise. "My life was weel planned, calm, organized just to my liking."

"I didna realize that ye were the only one who lived at Dunstanmoor."

He ignored that snide remark, but was not so successful in shaking aside the discomfort it caused him. "This celebration ye are planning, despite kenning my distaste for it, is but one example of how ye have blithely disrupted my life." Murdoch resisted the urge to step back when she finally looked at him, her lovely eyes hard and dark with anger.

"Ye are an idiot." He opened his mouth to object to that insult, but Jessa rushed on, giving him no chance to speak. "Ye have shrouded this keep in a black cloud of your own grief, donned a hair shirt, and ne'er once looked outside of your own selfish misery to see how others felt or how much your dark moods weighed them down."

This time she knew that the flush upon his cheeks was not from passion, but from anger. Jessa ruthlessly subdued a sudden attack of timidity and continued, "As for this celebration which ye find so distasteful—"

"I ken that there are few secrets at Dunstanmoor so ye must now ken exactly why I ceased to consider this a festive time of the year," he interrupted, his voice cold and hard.

"Aye, I ken all about your losses and I do grieve for you. I also ken that in customary male arrogance and stupidity, ye have steeped yourself in guilt, as if somehow your mere presence should have stopped these tragedies from happening. Aye, the first year may have been too soon to be so festive, but it has been three long years."

"Some of us dinna cast off our pain as easily and as swiftly as others."

"And some of us cling to it like a starving bairn clings to its mother's breast. And why should your losses take precedence over this particular celebration? Why should ye deny all of your people, e'en your own daughters, the chance to fully celebrate this holy time? 'Tis not May Day or All Hallow's Eve, festive times easily cast aside, but the day on which we celebrate the birth of Christ."

"Ye sorely overstep yourself, Mistress Armstrong."

She shrugged, even though she felt chilled by his fury. " 'Tis past time that someone did, and I am the best choice for a messenger, the perfect one to tell ye things ye dinna wish to hear and which infuriate you. I am but a guest. Courtesy prevents ye from doing me any harm—"

"I shouldna lay any great wager on that."

She ignored his softly snarled interruption. "I will also be leaving. I can eventually walk away from whate'er ill feeling my words may bestir."

"Aye, and as the weather is beginning to take a turn for the better, your leave-taking will be soon, thank the sweet lord."

Jessa frowned and absently licked the sticky sweet fruit from her fingers as she watched Murdoch stride away. She was not quite sure what had possessed her to speak to Murdoch like that. The frustration born of his warm and cold treatment of her could easily have prompted such blunt speech, but she knew that was not all of it. She truly felt that he had oppressed his kinsmen with his grief for far too long. Sighing heavily, she returned to her work as she admitted that some of her fury was also caused by her inability to cut through his hard shell of guilt and sorrow.

It was hard to maintain any hope of reaching the man. She was swiftly running out of time and ideas. Jessa suddenly realized that she loved the man and cursed herself for her own foolishness. It had not seemed so bad to want him, even to want to stay at Dunstanmoor. After all, her only other real choices in life appeared to be MacDubh or spinsterhood. To give her heart to Murdoch, however, was the height of idiocy, for from all she could see, he neither wanted such deep emotion nor knew how to return it. Jessa did not know whether to laugh at her own stupidity or weep over the hopelessness of it all.

She shook her head. There was nothing to be gained from bemoaning the facts. What was done was done. Matters would settle themselves in her favor or they would not. The best she could hope for was that she had made some small crack in his armor, just enough to make him realize how he was depriving and hurting his daughters.

The twins tried to stop giggling and failed miserably, collapsing onto Jessa's bed as they gave in to their laughter. Jessa smiled faintly and sat on a stool by the fireplace. She had been teaching the girls *The Brus,* an epic poem chronicling the glory of Robert the Bruce, to recite at the feast. Their memories were excellent, and they had learned it quickly; but she was not sure they would be able to complete the recitation without giggling. They had been unsuccessful so far. She decided that if they became too silly at the feast, she would assume the recitation until they calmed down or it was finished. The people of Dunstanmoor would certainly be tolerant of their foolishness and would probably find the twins amusing, but she knew they would also appreciate hearing the end of the tale.

When the girls began to calm down and nervously

glanced her way, she gave them a sweet smile. Jessa was in a somber mood, but she did not want the twins to see that and think that they were the cause of it. The sound of water dripping, of the snow slowly melting away, deepened the sadness she was not able to shake free of. Soon her family would search for her. They would easily guess that she would try to reach her aunt Grier, for everyone knew how strongly she favored the woman. Once they discovered that she had never reached Edinburgh, it would not take them long to come pounding on the gates of Dunstanmoor. If nothing else, it was the perfect place to seek help in their search of the area. Jessa dreaded facing her parents almost as much as she dreaded leaving Dunstanmoor and Murdoch. She thought it grossly unfair that after several winters of cold, dark days when the snow remained deep upon the ground for months, this year fate blessed them with a spell of warmth and sun.

"Did we get the words right?" Isobel asked.

"Aye, child, ye did, save for the laughter," Jessa replied with a half smile.

"We shall be most somber and respectful when we recite it on the morrow. Do ye think Papa will like it?"

"How could any mon *not* like such a stirring tale? With your recitation and young Robert the stable lad's beautiful song, we shall be heartily entertained."

A soft rap at the door interrupted them, and even as Jessa rose to walk to the door, the twins rushed over and opened it. Jessa smiled at Ennis and said, "I hope ye have some good news."

"I think ye will be pleased," he replied, catching her by the hand and tugging her out of the room. "Follow us, my tittering lasses," he said to the twins as he led Jessa to the great hall.

The moment Jessa stepped into the great hall she knew why Ennis was acting so pleased with himself. Two men at arms flanked the huge fireplace, grinning at her as she gaped with delight and hurried closer. A massive log was proudly settled within the fireplace.

"Ye found a Yule log," she cried and briefly hugged Ennis. " 'Tis so huge it could burn 'til twelfth night." She glanced around at the pine boughs and mistletoe decorating the great hall and then back at the huge log. " 'Tis the perfect final touch. We shall have a splendid Yuletide feast with this to keep us warm."

Murdoch paused in the doorway of the great hall to watch the people gathered around the fireplace. Ennis, his men at arms and his daughters all beamed at Jessa. He realized, with a deep pang of guilt, that it had been a long time since he had seen such an easy, unfettered pleasure. Jessa's angry words had pounded in his brain from the moment he had walked away from her, and he had valiantly argued against them; but now he had to face their hard truth. He had oppressed his people with his fears and his sorrows. He had forced them to suffer with him. They had done so out of love and respect for him, but knowing that only added to his guilt.

When his daughters caught sight of him, hailing him and beckoning him to join them, he noticed how quickly the smiles left all the faces turned his way. He wanted to seclude himself so that he could think about all he had done and if he should, or ever could, make amends. Instead, he squared his shoulders and joined the small group by the fireplace, hoping the smile he gave them was enough to disperse their sudden reticence.

"Have ye e'er seen such a huge log, Papa?" Isobel asked, tentatively slipping her hand into his.

He lightly squeezed her hand. "Nay, Loving. I ne'er realized we had such a large tree upon our lands."

"We dinna now," Ennis murmured and grinned at the brief, mildly disgusted glance Murdoch sent his way.

"Arena ye going to set it alight?" Murdoch asked, looking

at Jessa and feeling stung by the cool, wary look in her eyes.

"We will do so this evening," she replied. "We shall light it whilst saying a prayer or two. 'Tis the way to make a proper start to the Yuletide."

"The great hall may grow a wee bit chill if ye wait 'til then."

"Aye, but a sturdy log such as this has the strength to burn away all the cold," she murmured and subtly watched him as he listened to his daughters' chatter. She wished the log was touched by magic, a magic that would cause the warmth it would give the great hall of Dunstanmoor to seep into its laird's heart as well.

Six

A soft grunt escaped Jessa as her bed bounced under the weight of the giggling twins. She cautiously opened one eye and looked at them, her attempt to appear cross and stern only bringing wider smiles to their faces. She eased herself into a sitting position and hastily smothered a huge yawn. Sleep did not come easy, and her night had been long and restless. She could not stop thinking about Murdoch no matter how often she tried and had cursed herself for a fool time and time again.

As the girls talked excitedly about the feast, Jessa sipped at the sweet cider and ate the thick buttered bread they had brought her. Murdoch had seemed a changed man at the evening meal, even joining in the ceremony of lighting the Yule log. It had been subtle, but there had definitely been a change. Jessa could not believe that her angry words had done it, and she fretted over how deep that change went. All night her mind had been crowded with questions about how such a change might affect her and Murdoch. It had been a wasteful loss of sleep, however, for the distance between them was still there. At times during the night she had pushed herself to tears with the thought that her outburst had actually made that distance wider and easier for him to maintain. What also saddened her was the certainty that such tortured nights would grow more frequent as her time to leave Dunstanmoor drew ever nearer.

Jessa took a long, deep drink of cider and forced all

thought of Murdoch from her mind, turning her full attention to the twins. "There is something for each of you set on the stool by the fire."

"A gift?" Isobel cried and hurried over to collect them. "I didna think we were to get a gift until after the New Year, on Hansel Monday."

"I may not be here then, so I thought it best to give it to you now."

"Oh." Isobel slowly sat down on the bed and watched Jessa closely as she said, "I wish ye could stay with us."

"That would be nice, but ye ken that I must return to my own kinsmen." She smiled crookedly. "I left matters a wee bit unsettled, ye ken. Come, let us not think on leave-takings. The white linen wrapped gift is for Leslie, the other for you, Isobel." A flush of pride colored Jessa's cheeks as the two young girls oohed and aahed over the delicately embroidered chemises she had given them. "Old Margaret gave me some help with the chemises themselves as I am nay verra skilled at cutting and putting together a garment."

"We shall go and thank her right now," Isobel said as she and Lesley each gave Jessa a kiss on the cheek before rushing out the door.

Jessa sighed and stretched as the heavy door thudded shut behind the girls. There had not been too much time when she had been alone, except to sleep, and she had used almost every precious moment of that privacy to do the ornate, delicate embroidery on the girls' chemises. Their pleasure had made those stolen work-filled hours worth it.

As she moved to dress, she wondered if Murdoch would take much pleasure in the gift she had given him. During her long, almost sleepless night, she had crept down the hall and left it outside his door. Again, with Old Margaret's help to make the garment, she had laboriously embroidered a doublet of warm, sturdy material for Murdoch. She had thought that the gold and silver embroidery colors had looked handsomely striking against the black tunic, but was

suddenly uncertain. Murdoch had not worn anything like it
in all the time she had been at Dunstanmoor.

She shook her head as she tidied her bed and then started
out the door. There was no sense in fretting over it. Despite
that admonition, she caught herself looking at his door as she
passed it and felt a stab of anticipation when she saw that the
package was gone. She sighed as she skipped down the stairs.
Now she would be waiting to see if he liked it or wore it and
probably be hurt if he did not. As she strode into the kitchens,
she decided she would work so hard that she pushed all
thought of Murdoch Graeme out of her mind. It could not
stop the hurt she knew she would soon endure, large and small,
but at least she would not torture herself waiting and wondering when and how he would next hurt her.

By the time Jessa returned to her bedchamber to dress
for the feast, she was almost too tired. For one brief moment
she considered just curling up in bed and going to sleep,
but that was not possible. After she had spent so much time
and worked so hard, she found it odd that she suddenly did
not really care if she went to the feast. There had to be a
reason, and she was not really sure she wanted to consider
what it could be.

As she dressed in a soft gray gown Old Margaret had
cut down to fit her, her mind refused to stop puzzling over
the matter. She cursed as she finally admitted to herself
what was causing her sudden reluctance. She was uneasy
about meeting Murdoch. He did not want the celebration.
This was the anniversary of his wife's and infant son's
deaths, and she had not seen him all day so had not been
able to judge his mood. He had not even taken a brief moment to thank her for the gift she had given him.

When a shaft of pain tore through her at the mere thought
of that slight, she could no longer ignore the truth. She
cursed herself and then cursed Murdoch. Jessa knew that
she was simply afraid to go to the feast, afraid of Murdoch's
disapproval, afraid to discover that he hated the gift she had

worked so hard to make him, afraid to see that he still grieved deeply for a wife who had been dead for three years, and even afraid that he simply would not attend the feast. The thought that she would wish to hide from the man she loved because she feared he would hurt her in some way so infuriated Jessa that she felt all of her reluctance leave her. She also knew that hiding in her bedchamber would not prevent a broken heart, no more than constantly worrying about it could.

"Pain is a part of life, Jessa Armstrong," she told herself as she took one last check of her appearance. "Skulking about in your bedchamber isna going to save ye from it."

Strengthened by her annoyance over her own cowardice and a determination not to shy away from any chance to reach Murdoch's armored heart, Jessa went to the great hall. She hesitated only a moment when she entered and saw Murdoch sitting at his place at the head table and wearing the jerkin she had given him. Jessa wondered, however, just how real his smile was as she cautiously approached the seat he had reserved for her on his right.

"I thank ye for this fine gift," Murdoch said as she sat down. "I am shamed to admit that I have nothing to give ye."

"If not for your kind hospitality, I would be naught but a frozen clump beneath the snow," she replied, unable to completely subdue a blush over his compliment. "My life is gift enough."

The cheers that greeted Old Margaret's entrance with the roast pigs diverted Jessa. Soon the feast was the center of everyone's attention. To Jessa's surprise, Murdoch was very gregarious. They had often talked as they dined; but it had always had the feel of polite conversation with only the tiniest slivers of intimacy intruding, and after even the smallest softening on Murdoch's part, there would follow long silences. This time Murdoch was congenial, even flirtatious. Jessa both savored it and mistrusted it. If she succumbed to his charm, believed in his sweet words and warm smiles, and he turned cold as he had every time before, she knew it would devastate her.

The determination to resist his wiles began to waver as the evening wore on. His pride in his daughters when they flawlessly recited *The Brus* and the praise he gave her for teaching them shattered it completely. This was the man she knew had always existed beneath the hard, cold shell he had encased himself in, and Jessa decided she would regret it if she did not enjoy it to its fullest.

"The lasses are clever, 'tis all," she demurred, knowing she could not take all of the credit for the girls' performance.

"Aye, they are," he murmured with a proud smile. "Howbeit, it takes patience and cleverness to teach children such a long tale and to help them tell it with such feeling and respect."

Jessa watched as he hugged both girls and praised them profusely, causing both of them to blush deeply. Murdoch did indeed love his daughters; he had just forgotten how much they needed to be shown that he did. A small crack had appeared in his self-imposed isolation, and Jessa prayed it was enough to allow his daughters to draw nearer to him.

It was late, the twins escorted to their beds a long time ago, when Jessa finally rose to seek her own bed. She readily accepted Murdoch's offer to walk her to her bedchamber, reluctant to end the evening. When she opened the door to her room and turned to bid him good night, the look on his face almost made her gasp. It was the look of passion, raw and uncontrolled. She knew Murdoch wanted her—now and very badly. Jessa took only a moment to decide that if he chose to act upon that desire, she would not push him away. He could easily turn cold and distant in the morning, leaving her with one night of passion and a shattered heart, but Jessa took one look into his eyes and knew she would risk it.

Murdoch stepped into the room, and when Jessa calmly stepped back to allow him in, he felt his heart race with anticipation. This time he had let his guard slip so far that he knew he was lost. Although she was an innocent, the look in her eyes was all warm invitation, and he felt what little control he had struggled to muster slip away.

It was wrong, unfair and perhaps even cruel, to savor her passion and offer nothing in return, but he knew he would do just that. All evening he had watched her, reveled in her company and ached with wanting. At first, he had been pleasant to her because he was deeply touched by the gift she had given him, and an effort to enjoy the feast she had worked so hard to prepare had not seemed to be too much to give in return. The smiles his small flatteries and pleasantries had brought to her face had only made him want to please her more. Each blush upon her cheek as he had complimented her, the light flush of pleasure she wore as the feast proved to be a complete success and her throaty laugh had all inspired him. He had truly enjoyed himself, had felt alive for the first time in years, and he did not want to leave her now.

"Jessa," he murmured as he shut the door and reached for her.

"Aye," she replied as she allowed him to pull her into his arms, and she knew she did not have to say or do anything else.

When he kissed her, Jessa knew this would be no gentle wooing. His hunger was too strong, his passion too long denied. She felt overwhelmed by her own desire, but she was not sure it could match his. Jessa prayed that she would not falter, that her untried state would not cause her to fear or hesitate. Instinct told her that if their passion was not consummated now, she would never have another chance to hold him so close.

Murdoch picked her up in his arms and carried her to her bed. Jessa blushed yet felt intensely excited as he removed their clothes with more speed than care. As their flesh met, Jessa knew that she would have no trouble keeping pace with him. Each flattery he muttered against her heated skin, each stroke of his large, callused hands, only enflamed her more. She clung to him, encouraging his fierce passion by returning kiss for kiss, touch for touch.

The pain that came when he joined their bodies only briefly dimmed the desire which held her so tightly in its grip. Her passion swiftly returned in full strength to push it aside. Jessa looked into his eyes, saw the glint of concern beneath the hunger that made his eyes such a vibrant, spellbinding blue, and wrapped her body around his. With one subtle movement, she told him there was no need to pause. She cried out her pleasure as he moved. In but moments, she was dragged down into the sweet oblivion of her release, a small part of her briefly aware of Murdoch crying out her name, before it, too, drowned in the intense feelings ripping through her body.

Murdoch looked down at Jessa as he eased his body free of hers. A chill immediately swept over him, and he fought the almost desperate need to return to her warmth. He had come to her bed to find passion, but he had found much more, too much. It had flooded every part of him, reached deep inside of him to stir up far more than the one need he had been trying to satisfy.

Suddenly he was overwhelmed. This was not what he wanted. This was all that he had tried to hide from for three long years, all he had struggled so hard to shield himself from. Murdoch knew he could no longer convince himself that all he felt was passion, the sharp pinch of a need left unfed for far too long, and that terrified him. He needed to get away from her, to think without Jessa's big dark eyes pulling him back to her and, he prayed, to revive that shield her touch had pulled away.

Jessa knew something was wrong the moment Murdoch sat up and reached for his clothes. She felt cold all over as all of her fears were realized. Instead of pulling him closer, their lovemaking had pushed him even farther away. She was so tense it hurt to turn her head to look at him, and she clenched her fists so tightly her nails dug deeply into the soft flesh of her palms. She dared not move, afraid that caught up in the fury of her battered emotions, she would cling to him, beg him to stay, and make a complete fool of herself or beat him senseless.

"I didna think ye would run away quite so swiftly," she said, her voice tight and rough as she fought to hide her pain.

A light flush tinged Murdoch's cheeks, but he continued to dress, turning to look at her as he laced up the tunic she had made for him. "This was a mistake. I shouldna have allowed this to happen." She paled, and he reached for her, feeling and regretting the pain he had just inflicted, but then jerked his hand back. "Nay. Nay, this isna what I want," he muttered and stumbled away.

Jessa contemplated saying something or moving to stop him when he hesitated briefly in the doorway and glanced back at her, but she did neither. As the heavy door shut behind him, she felt a tear wriggle across her cheek to dampen her ear and knew it was the harbinger of a flood. She had hoped to spend the Yuletide night wrapped in Murdoch's arms, the chill of the night held far away by the warmth of his passion. Instead, she knew that unless the pain tearing at her now could be turned to anger or pushed away, she would spend the night weeping.

She knew that a lot of the pain she felt was born of a deep disappointment and not simply over the miserable failure of all the gambles she had taken on the man. She had known that the man she was so much in love with was troubled, wary, his emotions locked away, and was not seeking a wife. Not once in all the time she had been at Dunstanmoor, however, had she thought of him as deliberately cruel. It added to Jessa's agony to be proven so terribly wrong in her own judgments.

Seven

"The stable master has just returned from the village, and he said that people are traveling the roads again," Isobel announced in a heavy voice as she walked into Jessa's bedchamber, Lesley quietly trailing behind her.

Jessa sat up in the bed as Isobel and Lesley sat on the edge. She was not surprised at how late in the morning it was. It had been three days since she and Murdoch had made love, since he had fled her arms as if she had suddenly turned into a wart-ridden old hag. He had become like the shadows in the halls of Dunstanmoor, always there yet elusive, untouchable. They barely even exchanged an occasional muttered greeting the rare times that they happened to pass each other in the halls. Each day that passed without him returning to her arms caused her to become more morose, slower to rise in the mornings, unable to sleep at night and unable to keep her mind on anything else but him. Jessa wished she had given more thought to how much it would hurt to lose when she had decided to place her heart in his hands.

"Ye will be leaving soon," Lesley said, the tone of her voice revealing how little she liked that idea.

"Aye, I will," Jessa replied in a gentle voice. "Ye kenned that I wouldna be staying forever. I have always been nay more than an uninvited guest."

"Weel, if we had kenned who ye were, we would have invited you," Isobel assured her.

"Thank ye. 'Tis kind of ye to say so."

" 'Tis but the truth."

"We shall ne'er see you again," Lesley said, plucking furiously at the bedcover.

"Of course ye will," Jessa argued. "Now that we have met, we can visit with each other. We dinna live so verra far apart." Jessa shifted down the bed enough to kiss each girl on the cheek and give each a brief hug. "Now, off with you. I have languished abed long enough and must dress and do my chores."

As soon as the twins left, Jessa sat back down on the bed and fought the urge to crawl back beneath the covers. There were a lot of things worth hiding from—the pain of having Murdoch treat her as if her mere touch could infect him with some horrible, incurable disease and the impending time of her departure. Despite the unhappiness her stay at Dunstanmoor had brought her, she did not want to leave. Jessa was not fool enough to think that staying would change Murdoch's feelings toward her, but she dreaded leaving Old Margaret, the twins, Ennis, and all the others, people she had come to love.

"Enough of bemoaning your fate," she scolded herself as she got up, tidied her bed and began to dress.

Just as she was about to leave, Old Margaret walked in. Jessa was startled by the woman's abrupt entrance, for she had always knocked before. When Margaret said nothing, just scowled and walked over to poke at the cold ashes in the fireplace, Jessa began to grow alarmed.

"Is there something wrong?" Jessa finally asked her.

"People are moving about again," Margaret replied, turning to frown at Jessa. "The roads are passable again, though still treacherous and 'tis slow work to go from one place to another."

"The twins have already reported that to me. I shall be sorry to leave."

"Will ye?"

"Aye." Jessa was a little puzzled by Old Margaret's attitude, one of belligerence with a hint of accusation. "Why should ye think otherwise?"

"I dinna ken what to think. I thought ye were trouble from the moment I set eyes on ye, a wee lass traveling about all alone. Weel, for a while, it looked as if ye were just the sort of trouble Dunstanmoor needed. Ye put a wee bit of life back into these old walls. When ye gave us the first Yuletide feast we have had in three long years, I was near to weeping with joy. Things have really changed, I thought to meself. Aye, 'tis a holy time, and I said my prayers; but my joy was more for the fact that we were celebrating the day than for what the day meant. I will do a penance for that and 'twill be worth it. But, things havena changed, have they? I thought the laddie was living again, had finally broken free of the grief and the guilt that was choking the life out of him and this keep. Sweet Mary, but now he is even worse than he e'er was. What did ye do to him?"

"I loved him," Jessa replied with quiet honesty and smiled crookedly at Old Margaret's shock.

"I dinna understand."

"I am nay too sure that I do either, but 'tis the way of it. Dinna worry o'er it. The mon will improve when I leave." Jessa inwardly winced at that admission, that the only way she could make the man she loved as happy as he might allow himself to be was to leave him.

A moment later Old Margaret's eyes slowly widened. "I think I begin to understand. I wasna wrong in what I thought I saw between the two of you, just in how I thought it would work." Her hands on her hips, she shook her head and muttered a gentle curse. "I thought that once ye broke that armor he has placed around all heart and feeling, all would be weel. Instead, the laddie has run away and hid himself, hasna he?"

"Aye, he has." Jessa shrugged. "He truly doesna want to love anyone. I think, like a wee bairn who burns himself and then shies away from the fire, Murdoch shies from any deep emotion, for it has, thus far, only caused him great pain. Mayhaps that fear of being hurt could be overcome, but I dinna have the time. If people are traveling again, then my kinsmen will soon begin to search for me, and I dinna think it will take them long to find me."

"Weel, ye arena far away. Mayhaps—"

"Mayhaps he will come after me?" Jessa smiled sadly and shook her head. "I willna be fool enough to wait for him."

"But if he loves you—"

"I didna say that he did. I said I loved him. Oh, aye, he feels something, for that is what has sent him fleeing from me. It may not be enough to make him seek me out later. And, I am nay sure I would want him to as I have had a taste of his cruelty and I dinna think I want another. Oh, I dinna think he means to be cruel," she added when Old Margaret began to protest. " 'Tis just that he is such a troubled mon that he can easily hurt others in his desperate need to protect himself."

"The laddie needs a good, solid knock offside his head."

Jessa laughed softly. "He does, and I have considered giving him one many times. Howbeit, I dinna think it will knock any sense into him." She hooked her arm through the older woman's. "Come, we waste the day trying to understand him, and there is a great deal of work to do."

As they walked toward the kitchens Old Margaret remained quiet, thoughtful and frowning. Jessa suspected that the woman was considering having a talk with Murdoch. For one brief moment, Jessa considered telling Margaret not to say anything, then decided to just leave the matter alone. She doubted that Murdoch would listen anyway, and if being lectured angered him, it could not make him any more distant than he was now.

* * *

Murdoch eyed his cousin Ennis warily as the younger man strode, unannounced, into his bedchamber, a look of determination on his handsome face. These intrusions had become more frequent since Jessa Armstrong had entered his life. He gave his cousin a stern look, a silent warning to tread warily, which Ennis ignored, and then turned to stare out of the narrow window that looked out on the heavy gates of Dunstanmoor.

"Ye may not listen to a word I am about to say," Ennis began, standing next to Murdoch, "but I intend to say them anyway."

"I rather thought that ye might," Murdoch murmured.

"For three long days ye have skulked about this keep, hiding in the shadows and eating all of your meals in this room. If ye think no one kens the cause of this mood, then ye are a fool. We all saw ye leave the Yuletide feast with Jessa, your spirits high, yet now ye sulk and hide. The whole keep frets o'er what might have happened."

" 'Tis none of their concern."

"Nay? Ye are their laird. Your health and your moods affect them. I am not so concerned about ye as I am about Jessa. There are many of your people who begin to blame her for this change in you."

"She had naught to do with it," Murdoch said, his voice sharp as he finally looked at Ennis.

"Oh, I dinna blame her, but I suspect she is the cause of your sudden seclusion. Ye felt something, didna ye, and ye ran from it like a whipped cur."

"This is nay your business, Ennis. Leave it be."

Ennis stepped back, but only to get out of Murdoch's way as he began to pace his room. "Nay, but ye are my kinsmon. If I dinna stop ye from cutting your own throat, who will? Are ye really so dimwitted that ye would let that lass return to her kinsmen and, quite possibly, to Colin MacDubh?"

Murdoch unsuccessfully tried to push aside the alarm he

felt at the thought of Jessa becoming another man's wife. "She left MacDubh standing at the altar. I dinna think he will be waiting for her."

"Ye canna be sure of that. Ye dinna ken what the marriage agreement is. MacDubh might decide that it profits him more to overlook any humiliation he suffered, at least until he can call Jessa his wife."

Before Murdoch could answer that there was a sharp rap at the door followed immediately by a flushed page stumbling into the room. Breathless, the boy stuttered out, "There are people at the gates, m'laird. The Armstrongs. They search for Mistress Jessa."

"Did anyone tell them that she is here?" Murdoch asked, a chill entering his blood.

"Nay, for they didna ask for her yet. They wish to speak with you."

"Have them settled in the great hall. Dinna tell them that Jessa is here, but do send someone to tell Jessa that her kinsmen have arrived. I will meet with the Armstrongs in a moment."

The minute the boy left, Ennis walked to the door, opened it and looked back at Murdoch. "I hope ye think hard ere ye hand them Jessa. I dinna think ye will be given the chance to change your mind later."

Murdoch cursed as Ennis shut the door behind him. He did not appreciate everyone knowing about his confusion or discussing it, and it annoyed him to be lectured by his young cousin. He had to admit that Ennis was right this time, however. Whatever decision he made now, he would have to live with for the rest of his life.

Jessa felt all of the blood leave her head when the page told her that her parents were seated in the great hall. She clung to the edge of the kitchen table for a moment as she tried to collect herself. Although she had expected this moment to arrive, she realized she was still unprepared. She needed time to tightly wrap all her emotion so that she could face the leave-taking with calm dignity and not let Murdoch see her pain. Fate had chosen not to give her any.

"Do ye want me to go with ye?" asked Old Margaret.

"Nay. I will be fine." Jessa forced a smile to her lips as she struggled to tidy herself, idly noticing that her hands were shaking badly. "I think ye had best find the twins and tell them."

It was not easy, but Jessa turned and smiled at the nervous young page and signaled him to walk ahead of her to the great hall. She knew she ought to be nervous about seeing her parents after running away from the marriage they had planned for her, but thoughts of leaving Murdoch made that seem like a very small problem. If her parents still wanted her to marry MacDubh and the man would still have her after she caused him such humiliation, she would deal with that later. Now her sole concern was to be strong. As she stepped into the great hall and saw her parents and Murdoch look her way, Jessa decided she was about to face the greatest trial of her young life.

Murdoch struggled to be polite to the Armstrongs. It was difficult, for he did not want them at Dunstanmoor and his mind was crowded with thoughts of Jessa. When she walked into the hall and began to move toward her family, he suddenly knew he could not let her go.

He almost laughed. He had done nothing to make her want to stay. With her parents sitting right there, he could not even approach Jessa and speak privately to her. There was no time to try and make amends for all of the wrongs he had done her, no time to find out if she wanted to stay, or even if she could forgive him. Even as he considered the possibility of allowing her to leave and trying to woo her back, her parents spoke, and he knew he would not be allowed that opportunity.

"Courtesy prevents me from saying all I wish to before our host," Lord Armstrong said as he scowled at Jessa.

"I understand, Father," Jessa murmured.

"Howbeit, ye are more fortunate than ye deserve to be. Lord MacDubh has chosen to forgive the humiliation ye caused him."

Jessa tensed and stared at her parents, chilled by the implication of her father's words. "He forgives me for leaving him at the altar?"

"Aye. We sweetened your dowry to show our gratitude."

"I will cost ye more, will I?"

"There is no cause for ye to be so impertinent. Ye are past marrying age. Ye should thank God that Lord Mac-Dubh has chosen to accept you."

"Ye ne'er listened to me, did ye?" Jessa suddenly felt very tired.

" 'Tis not your place to decide these things. Do ye truly wish to be a spinster?"

"If the choice is to wed MacDubh—aye."

"Cease this stubbornness," her father snapped. "If ye turn this mon down, no other will ask for your hand."

"I will," Murdoch said quietly, and he almost smiled at the way everyone gaped at him, including Ennis, Old Margaret and his daughters, who were halted by his words even as they stepped into the great hall.

"Ye wish to marry my daughter?" asked Lord Armstrong.

"Aye," replied Murdoch, glancing a little warily at Jessa, who was somewhat pale and glassy-eyed. "I believe I have more to offer ye than MacDubh, despite his illustrious and powerful kinsmen."

"I ken weel who ye are, sir, and what ye have to offer, but, mayhaps we could discuss it in more detail."

"Then ye accept my proposal?"

"I do."

"Wait," Jessa said, her voice soft and raspy as she fought to speak through the shock that had left her reeling.

"Nay, m'love," said Murdoch, and he kissed her on the cheek even as he signaled to Margaret, who hurried over. "Ye had best prepare for the wedding."

"Now?" She stared at him, wondering if this was some impostor, as Old Margaret took her arm in a tight grip.

"I will send Ennis for the priest. I had word but this morning that the mon has returned to the village. Is that not fortuitous?"

"But—"

"Come, lassie," Old Margaret said as she dragged Jessa out of the great hall. "We dinna have much time, and I want ye to look your best when ye become the lady of Dunstanmoor."

Jessa tried to pull free of the woman's grip, but Margaret was strong. She took one look at the smiling, excited twins and knew she could not get into a fight with the older woman. She was so shocked and so confused that she felt ill. There were a hundred things she should be saying or doing, a hundred questions she should be demanding the answers to, but she mutely allowed Margaret to drag her to her bedchamber. For the moment there was nothing else she could do. She needed time to collect her thoughts, time to try and understand what was happening and if there was any way to stop it, or even if she wanted to.

Eight

Jessa stared at the old priest, kneeling only after Murdoch tugged her down beside him. Only a few hours had passed since he had made his blunt announcement. Her family had agreed with such alacrity that a glimmer of embarrassment had eventually poked through her mind-numbing shock. She had been shoved into the care of Old Margaret and the twins, whose delight and excitement as they had dressed her had kept her from saying or doing anything to interrupt the course of events she was caught up in.

She glanced at her parents, who watched her closely as if they expected her to bolt again. Although she was so confused she felt dizzy, she suddenly realized that she had no urge to flee. When she looked at Murdoch, however, she saw no real reason to stay. He looked as cold and remote as ever. There was no hint in his expression to explain why he had suddenly decided to marry her. As Jessa absently repeated her vows, she prayed that Murdoch was not marrying her out of a sense of honor. She needed so much more from him. Although she had never asked anything of him the night they had become lovers, he could easily think he owed her something.

All through the hastily prepared feast, Jessa was unable to catch Murdoch's full attention. He used the high spirits of the group to shield himself from any questions and did not even meet her gaze directly the few times he did look her way. In fact, only the twins and Ennis paid her any attention, and she found that to be somewhat of a strain. They were so openly elated at the match that she was forced to hide all of her doubts, concerns and confusion. Even her parents almost completely ignored her until the feasting was nearly at an end, and the moment her father spoke, Jessa heartily wished that they had continued to do so.

"I hope ye fully appreciate the honor Sir Graeme has bestowed upon you," said her father, his rough voice heavy with reproach and warning.

"Oh, aye," she drawled. "I am fair overcome." Murdoch nudged her leg with his foot under the table, but she ignored him.

Her father shook his head, the movement shifting the few wispy strands of hair he had left on the top from one side to the other. "I hope, Sir Graeme, that ye have a tolerant and forgiving nature. I fear my daughter has an unbecoming spirit and sharpness of tongue."

"She is my wife now, Sir Armstrong," Murdoch said in a somber voice. "I have sworn before God to endure all such trials."

Jessa stared at him, but he took a long drink from his goblet, hiding his expression. Before he had obscured his face, however, she was sure she had seen the ghost of a smile. It took all of her willpower, but she finally subdued the urge to give him a sharp kick under the table.

It was all a strange sort of madness, she decided, as her father lectured her on the duties of a wife and the proper way to behave. When her father began to lecture her on her wayward tongue, she was so accustomed to the speech she suddenly found herself mouthing the words as he pontificated. She quickly pressed her lips together. When she peeked at the twins and Ennis she was not surprised to see them struggling to hide their laughter. Nor did it seem unusual to see that her parents were completely oblivious to her impertinence. What almost made her gape, however, was the way Murdoch stared at his empty plate, his broad shoulders shuddering with an obvious if silent laughter.

Suddenly, Jessa was afraid. This was not the Murdoch she was familiar with. There had been the occasional glimpses of a lighter spirit in the short time she had known him, but never to this extent. One moment he was still cool to her, still holding her at a distance as if somehow she could hurt him with her affections. The next, he was laughing, charming her parents and enjoying the wedding feast as if he had not a care in the world. Although he was still holding her at a distance, it was more a simple avoidance than rejection. Despite all of her efforts to repress it, an unsettling question began to form in her mind: just how well did she know the man she had just bound herself to for life?

That chilling question occupied her mind so completely that she was only faintly aware of Murdoch standing and tugging her to her feet. As he pulled her close to his side and joined in one last toast, she stared at his hand and fought to regain the feeling of safety and intimacy that had flooded her before at his mere touch. She began to wonder if he had some sickness of the brain that made him act like one kind of man one day and another on the next.

She remained consumed by that thought and paid little heed to the remarks called out to them as Murdoch led her out of the great hall. This was supposed to be all she could possibly want—Murdoch as her husband and Dunstanmoor as her home—but she was no longer so sure. Murdoch said nothing to comfort her or still her rising fears as he led her to his bedchamber.

The moment they stepped inside of Murdoch's bedchamber, Jessa pulled free of his hold, and whirled to face him. He watched her with a wary calm that made her nervous as he shut and bolted the heavy door. The glint of passion slowly warmed his eyes, and she took a hasty step away from him, her uneasiness growing when her own desire heedlessly stirred to life in response to his.

"Ye have gone mad, havena ye," she said, flinching out of his reach as he walked to the bed, sat down and began to remove his clothes.

"Quite possibly," he replied.

Murdoch saw her glance at the door and tensed. He would not allow her to run away. If he had to woo her, he would, but he would do it at Dunstanmoor. She looked so frightened and uncertain, it hurt him. The moment he had uttered the marriage vows, he had felt a sense of relief and a certainty that he had done the right thing. He knew it would not be easy to make her believe that, not after the way he had treated her. She had no way of knowing the soul searching he had gone through. To her it had to seem as if he had changed in the blinking of an eye, and he could not blame her for being afraid.

"I dinna understand," she muttered and dragged her fingers through her hair. "Why have ye done this?"

"Come here, Jessa," he said and held out his hand.

After a moment's hesitation, Jessa cautiously walked over to him, tensing slightly when he took her by the hand and pulled her down onto his lap. "Ye have married me because ye felt honor demanded it. Is that it?"

"Nay." He touched a kiss to the pulse point in her throat and smiled when the beat immediately quickened. She still felt something for him. "I married ye because I wished to have ye for my wife."

"What nonsense. Ye have not said but one or two words to me in three days. Ye fled my bed that night as if I had the plague. Aye, and ye said ye didna want this, whatever *this* was."

"*This* was love." He smiled when she jerked in his hold, grasped his face in her hands and stared at him.

"Ye have contracted a brain fever."

"Nay, bonny Jessa," he said, laughing softly as he pushed her down onto the bed and sprawled on top of her. "I do have a fever, though," he murmured against her neck.

It was not easy, but Jessa pushed him away. "Nay. I canna let ye do that, not until I have some answers."

"And why did ye let me do it three nights ago?"

"I will answer your questions when ye answer mine. After all, 'tis not I who is acting as if all her wits have been scattered."

"Aye, I realize it must seem that way to you, that all that has happened today makes no sense at all. 'Tis odd, though, I feel as if for the first time in a verra long time, my thoughts are perfectly clear."

"Murdoch," she said, her voice little more than a groan of frustration over his evasive replies.

He propped himself up on his elbows and smiled crookedly. "I have been a coward and an idiot. I dinna seek pity or sympathy when I say that my life has been naught but one tragedy after another, one loss after another. At times it seemed as if everything and everyone I loved were doomed."

"Ye still have two beautiful daughters," she whispered.

"I ken it, and God forgive me, I did ofttimes seem to forget that. I began to think that I cursed anyone I cared for. 'Twas a sort of madness, I think. At times I even feared revealing that I loved my wee lasses, as if some unseen fate would discover it and strike them down." He shook his head. "I locked them within these walls and then tried to lock away all sentiment within myself."

"Ye needed to protect yourself. 'Tisna madness to try and avoid pain."

" 'Tis foolish. When ye stumbled into Dunstanmoor, I took one look at you and kenned that I hadna shielded myself as weel as I thought I had. I kenned even then that ye were a threat to all of my carefully laid plans." He idly began to take down her hair. "Suddenly, I didna want to kill all that was inside of me, and I heartily resented ye for showing me that. I have been cruel."

Jessa started to deny that, then half smiled and murmured,

"Aye, ye have. I ne'er kenned what mood ye would be in, if ye would be warm or cold. 'Twas most confusing."

"And this day I confused ye even more."

"Aye. Ye ran from me, Murdoch, and ye ne'er once, not in three days, gave me any sign that that was not just what it looked like—an end."

"I ken it." He shook his head. "I will confess that that night I wanted it to be the end of it. I am shamed and embarrassed to admit that ye put the fear of God into me that night, Jessa." He laughed softly at her look of astonishment, but quickly grew serious again. "I have spent the last three days trying to understand myself, and it wasna easy. I stayed as far away from ye as I could, for each time I saw you I wanted to return to your arms. Aye, and that wasna a place where I could do any clear thinking."

Murdoch cursed softly and thrust his fingers through his hair. "I canna explain to you what I canna fully understand myself. All I am sure of is that when your father talked of marrying ye to MacDubh, I kenned that I couldna let that happen. I had just been thinking that I didna wish you to leave Dunstanmoor, but since I couldna stop your own kinsmen from taking you, I would come and woo you, to try and make amends."

"Ye were intending to come and woo me?"

"Aye, and I will understand if ye say ye need some time now, that ye canna simply become my wife now, tonight."

"Oh." Jessa sighed, not really paying attention to him, for he had already eased most of her fears. "It would have been nice to be wooed."

Murdoch laughed. "Woman, do ye think ye could pay heed when I am baring my soul?"

She curled her arms around his neck and lightly kissed him. "Many pardons, husband." She smiled when he tensed and looked at her intently.

"Are ye saying that ye need no time?"

" 'Twas never I who needed any time. I kenned what I

wanted when I first set eyes on you. I just needed a little time to ken how much I wanted it."

"I am surprised that my idiocy hasna killed all feeling ye might have had for me."

"I am made of sturdier stock than that, Murdoch." She trailed her finger across his mouth, shivering with delight when he playfully nipped at it. "Are your fears all conquered, Murdoch?"

"I should like to say they are, but one doesna cure such a sickness that quickly. I am done with hiding from life, with trying to lock my heart away. The few times I let my guard down since ye arrived, I was painfully aware of all I was denying myself. Aye, I am still afraid, but now that will just cause me to be more protective than ye might like."

"I believe I can live with that."

"And I think that ye are already planning to try and cure me of that as weel." He laughed when she blushed. "I dinna ken how ye can accept such an idiot for a husband."

"Because I love you."

Jessa grew wary when he said nothing, just stared at her. She did not really expect him to immediately return her sentiments, but she feared she may have misjudged just how much he wanted from her. A man did not necessarily want such emotion from the woman he married. Murdoch talked of no longer sheltering his heart, but that did not mean he now wished to have hers dropped in his hands.

"How can you?" he asked in a soft, hoarse voice.

"I dinna think anyone can explain such things. I just do." She felt her hopes rise when he suddenly buried his face in her neck and held her so tightly it was almost painful. He could not possibly reveal such emotion over her declaration if he felt little for her in return. "I willna embarrass you by listing what all of your good qualities are, but I think I must have seen them from the beginning."

" 'Twould be a short list," he mumbled and took a long,

unsteady breath before lifting his head to look at her. "Are ye sure?"

"Aye. I love you."

He cupped her face in his hands and gently kissed her. " 'Tis a good thing, for I realized today that I love you." Murdoch laughed shakily when she hugged him, but then frowned when he felt the dampness of her tears against his neck. "I thought ye would see that as good news."

"Oh, aye, I do," she said, finally pulling away and hastily wiping the tears from her face. " 'Tis just that today has been such a muddle, my emotions are quite high and tender." She gently caressed his cheek. "Are *ye* sure?"

"Aye. I kenned it the moment the page told me your kinsmen were here. There was no more time, and that knowledge cleared all the mists from my mind. I think I suspected it from the verra beginning and 'tis why ye frightened me so."

"I have been a sore trial for you." She smiled as he sat up and tugged off his tunic.

"That ye have." He winked at her, then smoothed his hand over the tunic before carefully folding it and placing it at the foot of the bed. "I still have no gift for you," he murmured, regret weighing his voice.

Jessa sat up, curled her arms around his neck and pulled him back down onto the bed. "We have found each other. We have love. There can be no finer Yuletide gift."

Naughty or Nice

Olga Bicos

For the unsung heroes of this, and so many others:
Barbara Benedict, Meryl Sawyer,
and my husband, Andrew.

One

All her life, Phoebe Nichols had wanted to do the right thing.

The way Phoebe saw life, a person traveled down a certain path only to reach a fork in the road. The question then became, which way to turn? Left? Right? Straight ahead? It was a choice that could change the course of your life forever—a choice that could mean the difference between happiness or misery, success or dismal failure . . . love or loneliness.

When faced with such a decision, Phoebe Nichols was always careful to take a Right Turn.

She earned her teaching credentials and gave up her fantasy of becoming an actress. She put aside ambitions of climbing the Himalayas with the Sherpas and accepted a position teaching Spanish at Bernstein's Academy in the suburban foothills of Sierra Madre. She didn't fill out the paperwork she'd filched from the principal's office for that position to teach in Sweden.

"And I'm going to marry Marshall," she told the face in the mirror.

Tomorrow morning, on Christmas day, Phoebe Nichols planned to make the biggest Right Turn of her life. She would walk down the aisle of Our Lady of Assumption Church to become Mrs. Marshall Drummond.

Phoebe turned on the chrome faucet and splashed a handful of water on her face. It was near midnight. She was in the fourth-floor rest room at Krueger's department store, the store having extended its hours for a special Christmas Eve promotion. She'd come shopping in an attempt to get over her pre-wedding jitters—to drown out that voice inside her head that kept shouting: *Left, Phoebe! For once in your life, turn left!*

The knocking started again. A bit more insistent this time.

"Are you all right, miss?"

"I'll be right out." For the last fifteen minutes, the man outside had been trying to coax Phoebe out the door. Taking a deep breath, she leaned both hands on the porcelain sink, feeling ill and rooted to the tile floor.

Half an hour ago, a chipper female had announced the store's closing over the intercom. Phoebe had come to the rest room thinking only to make a quick stop before heading home. She hadn't expected to look up into the mirror and see those black circles under her eyes. She hadn't anticipated this complete sense of immobility keeping her lodged over this sink as she mulled over the significance of Right Turns and Life Commitments.

Again the knocking. Louder this time.

"I'm afraid I'm going to have to come in, miss."

Phoebe pried her hands from the sink as an elderly security guard, love handles bulging over his gun belt, slammed inside the rest room like Rambo, his hat askew over a buzz cut of gray hair.

Catching her breath, she whispered, "Merry Christmas," at a complete loss as to what else to say.

The man's bushy gray brows beetled over hazel eyes. "Right this way, miss."

Phoebe fumbled to pick up her package from the floor and trailed behind the burly figure with keys jingling at his side. A series of apologies brewed inside her head. *Really, sir. I'm not the kind of person who brings security guards banging on bathroom doors. I'm usually no trouble at all.*

"I'm sorry I took so long," she said, falling into step next to the guard. The floor appeared embarrassingly empty now, no lingering sales people or recalcitrant shoppers. "I guess I'm a little nervous. I'm getting married in the morning." She clutched her Krueger's bag in both arms. "It's a big day. And Marshall, my fiancé, wants everything to be perfect."

She knew she had a bad habit of telling people more than they wanted to know. Over the years, she'd decided she just had trouble with silence, there having been so much of it in her life. Marshall had tried to curb what he called her "tendency to babble." But Phoebe considered it something innate to her, like her curly black hair and her green eyes . . . something she couldn't change without becoming someone other than Phoebe Nichols.

"Did I mention I'm Catholic?" she added. "So I'll be taking the till-death-do-you-part vow." She let out a slow breath of air. "Feels a little weighty."

For the first time, the security guard, whose badge read "Jack," smiled at her. "Been married thirty-five years myself, miss. I wish you a good one."

He gestured toward the elevator visible past a group of mannequins wearing robes. Phoebe looped her thumb over the strap of her purse and shifted her Krueger's bag to her right hand. Nestled inside lay a negligee and a bottle of champagne. Both items had been part of a display in the lingerie department. In a wild instant, Phoebe had pictured herself wearing the ankle-length sheath with its dramatically plunging back and peek-a-boo lace bodice, her heart brimming with honeymoon promises. On impulse, she had bought the nightgown and talked the salesclerk into letting her have the champagne.

Only now, when she tried to imagine Marshall clicking his champagne glass to hers as they lounged on some sultan-size bed, she couldn't get a fix on the picture. The image kept shifting in her head, swimming eerily out of focus until it coalesced into Marshall in his sensible plaid pajamas, his blond hair plastered back from his shower . . . while

Phoebe wore sweats and sat cross-legged on her purple beanbag chair in her Altadena apartment.

She could feel perspiration beading at the back of her neck. She was getting married in the morning, and she couldn't even picture herself enjoying anything as exotic as a honeymoon with Marshall.

She wondered if it weren't too late to just open the champagne tonight and drink it herself.

Sometimes, in the deepest recess of her heart, Phoebe dearly wished she'd taken that Left Turn.

"I should have gone to Sweden," she said.

"What's that, miss?"

"Sweden," she said, moving ahead toward the elevator. "There was this fellowship. I could teach a year in the Swedish school system. But I didn't fill out the paperwork."

Because she'd been afraid—afraid to take that left fork in the road—unable to disappoint her mother and father after all they'd sacrificed for her education. It would have killed her father if she'd risked her position at the prestigious Bernstein's.

"The wife and I went to Acapulco last year," Jack said, his voice not unkind.

Phoebe brightened at this mention of Mexico. "We were going to Palenque, to see the Temple of Inscriptions, which it is truly my deepest desire to see." She frowned, remembering how Marshall had nixed the idea. "Only Marshall wanted to go to the Poconos. He has this aunt and uncle back east who own a time-share there. It was really convenient. For the honeymoon, I mean."

Jack turned to face her, startling her a little as he held out a large, slightly liver-spotted hand. "Good luck, miss."

Phoebe shifted her bag to her left and took the guard's grip in a shake, seeing in his smile not so much a stranger, but a kind-hearted man who might just understand what she was facing this night.

"Thanks for listening, Jack," she said. And then, because

this was probably the last person she would speak to before the morning and the hectic pace of her wedding preparations, she added, "I just know everything will turn out all right."

He studied her a moment, and then he winked. "You bet."

The elevator chimed, letting Phoebe know the car had arrived. She took a deep breath, pressing her shoulders back to face her future as the doors slowly opened.

Santa Claus was waiting for her inside the elevator.

He was dressed in the traditional red suit and wore a fluffy white beard and mustache. Long, flowing hair cascaded over broad shoulders. *A wig,* she thought, seeing from what was visible of his face that he was younger than the usual Santa, possibly in his mid-thirties. He had the boots, the bag, the cap. Saint Nick in all his glory.

"Merry Christmas," he said to Phoebe, keeping his hand on the "open door" button. To the security guard behind her, he said, "I'll take her down, Jack. You finish up here."

"Sure thing, Mr. Cameron."

Phoebe stepped inside the elevator as Krueger's Santa Claus picked up a black leather briefcase and moved to the back. She had the insane notion that she might ask Santa for advice. She imagined herself on tiptoe whispering in his ear: *Santa, I've been such a good girl all my life, but lately I've been thinking of doing this really rotten thing to my fiancé.*

The doors shut before her. The unpleasant sensation that these were prison bars settled into her bones, screaming that she should never have left the rest room . . . that by doing so, she had somehow taken an irrevocable step down the aisle.

Phoebe bit her lip, trying to dredge up memories of Marshall—to gather up and wrap around her some confidence about their future together.

Marshall, who taught rhetoric at Bernstein's . . . a schoolteacher, just like Phoebe. Upstanding Marshall, whose Catholicism, intelligence, and quiet dignity had charmed both her parents. Marshall, whose perseverance had steered Phoebe into friendship, romance, and now matrimony.

Marshall, who didn't bring any fireworks.

Turn left, Phoebe! LEFT!

Phoebe's palm slammed up against the doors as the elevator began to descend. She thought she might be having one of those panic attacks, where people can't catch their breath and hyperventilate. She didn't know what to do . . . she just didn't know what to do.

In that blazing instant of panic, a solution rose incredibly past the chaos in her mind. Phoebe glanced back at Santa Claus. It was minutes before Christmas, the day Christ was born. She was in the elevator with Santa Claus, a symbol for a season of magic. Okay, so he carried a briefcase . . . but maybe, just maybe, she could ask for a bit of magic to help her. Perhaps—in this elevator with Santa watching her back—she could reach out and pray for guidance.

The elevator doors opened onto the third floor, but no one was there. They closed again and Phoebe squeezed her eyes shut.

Give me a sign, Lord, she prayed. *Please God. Tell me what I should do!*

As the elevator continued its descent, she knew that if only she believed enough, she would get an answer. She felt the hope of it blossom inside her chest like a wellspring of possibilities. Silently, she added her own plea that—no matter what the answer— she would find the strength to follow His counsel. Even if it meant telling a church filled with people that she wasn't ready; even if she had to face down Marshall's puppy dog eyes filled with despair.

But she needed something more solid than the last months of unease to let her know that yes indeed, she had missed that fork in the road. And so, with every ounce of faith she had stored in her Roman Catholic heart these past twenty-nine years, Phoebe opened her eyes and prayed: *God, should I marry Marshall?*

The lights of the elevator flickered.

Phoebe's heart pounded inside the wall of her chest. She vaguely heard Santa Claus murmur something under his breath. She licked her lips.

"All right," she told God, thankful that he was listening. "But does that mean yes or no?"

The elevator jerked to a stop, hiccuping under her feet. The motor wound down to a low purr, followed by an eerie metallic whine.

"God?" she whispered cautiously.

The lights blacked out.

"Oh, shit," she heard Santa say behind her—just as the floor dropped out from under her.

The elevator plunged into a free fall.

Two

Jeffrey Cameron hooked one arm around the woman's waist and braced himself against the wall of the plummeting elevator. He searched blindly for the operation's panel, found it, then fumbled over the metal casement. The woman's piercing scream threatened to blow out his left eardrum, but he managed to wrap his fingers around the distinctive shape of the emergency button. He yanked hard.

The elevator lurched, bucking wildly. The screeching of metal rent the air as he and the woman were hurtled across the elevator and the car slammed to a halt. Jeff's back smashed into the wall, taking the considerable force of both bodies. The air left his lungs in an audible "whoosh" as his legs buckled, and he and the woman were thrown to the floor.

The emergency lights flashed on.

Sucking in a breath, Jeffrey Cameron focused on the woman now lodged firmly between his two extended legs.

She had both hands in a death grip, one on each of his thighs. He could barely see the flowing curls of her hair over the padding of the Santa suit. But he knew distinctly that her head was buried in his groin.

He gripped her shoulders and helped her to a sitting position. "Are you all right?" What the hell had just happened?

The woman blinked, the pupils of her eyes two tiny pinpoints. She had unusual green eyes. And she was pretty, in a natural sort of way, without makeup. Dark hair tumbled to her shoulders in ringlets, contrasting with porcelain fair skin. He might have thought she was kind of cute, stuck there between his legs, if it weren't for the wild elevator ride they had just taken.

"Ohmigod," she whispered, staring at him.

"We're going to be fine," he said, hearing that flash of panic in her voice. "I'm the manager here at Krueger's and I can—"

"OH MY GOD!"

Instead of pulling away from her compromising position between his thighs, the woman latched on to Jeff and began scrambling up his body. She clutched fistfuls of the red velvet Santa suit, scaling a path up his chest like an athlete on a Nike commercial. Both her hands clasped on to his lapels as she knelt before him.

"It's a sign!"

"Take it easy, lady."

"It's a sign from God!"

"Hey." He grabbed hold of her wrists, trying to move her off him. He was getting a bad feeling about this. "Why don't you just take a couple of deep breaths and settle down. Someone will be here in a minute to let us out."

But her fingers remained locked around the fur trim of the suit. "God doesn't want me to go through with it."

This time she spoke in a little chirp of a voice. Her pupils had dilated considerably, leaving only a thin rim of green. Jeff stared at her, nonplussed.

"Pardon?" Was she on drugs?

Those awesome eyes filled with tears. "Do you have any idea how many family members alone that man has?" She gave another pained squeak. "I counted as many as sixty-five when I sent out the invitations. Sixty-five angry men and women. Every one of them looking at me. Hating me. Blaming me."

"Listen very carefully," he said in a low voice. "I'm going to help you sit down, and then I'm going to reach behind you and try and open the doors." He spoke slowly, trying not to spook her any more than she was. He'd seen some wild things in his days as a free-lance photographer, but he'd never been with anyone delusional.

He cautioned himself not to make any sudden moves.

"And then there's the people from Bernstein's." Her gaze turned introspective. "The principal is such a gossip. I'll have to quit—Marshall will quit! And he's worked at Bernstein's Academy forever."

"Lady." Jeff gave her a little shake. "Get a grip!"

She blinked up at him, her gaze clearing for the first time. She straightened in his arms, backing away a few blessed inches.

"Oh, goodness. You think I'm crazy. No, no," she assured him. "It's just that . . . well, I asked God for a sign. And then . . . oh, dear." Again, her eyes became unfocused. She shook her head. "Oh, dear, dear, dear."

With a little squeaking sound, she scooted out of his arms. Her hand covered her mouth.

And then she started to bawl.

She cut loose, really wailing. Jeff sat back on his heels, panic twisting in his gut. If there was one thing in the world he couldn't handle, it was a woman's tears.

Feeling intensely awkward, he patted her on the shoulder. "You know, the elevator door is going to open any second now. If you could just keep it together for a few minutes—"

"How can I even think of breaking things off now?" she asked, as if he might have an answer. "Marshall does charity work. He fasts before communion." She pressed her hands to her cheeks, her fingers trembling. "But I asked *God* for a sign! You just can't fool around with that sort of thing. Divine intervention."

The last two words slipped past in an ominous whisper.

She appeared to be contemplating some horrible fire-and-brimstone fate. It gave him the willies. Kinda made him want to check and see if a bolt of lightning might be coming her way and he should duck.

"I should never have asked God for a sign. Oh, why did I ever ask?"

As he watched, she curled up in the elevator's corner. He thought it was a pretty good thing she hadn't waited around for him to answer her questions. He didn't have clue what she was talking about.

Thinking every minute might count, he tapped the "open door" button a couple of times, then jabbed at a few floor buttons. When nothing happened, he grabbed the telephone in the operation's panel. It was dead. He opened his brief-case and rifled through piles of papers, finding his cellular phone. He punched in the number for security.

"Scott? Listen, it's Jeff. I'm stuck in the elevator. It just lost control and dropped a couple of floors." He tapped the "open door" button again. Nothing. "Looks like we're somewhere between the first floor and the lower level." More softly, he added, "Scott, there's a customer in here with me . . . the one Jack flushed out of the bathroom. She's really hysterical, and it would be an excellent idea to get us out—fast—before she really cracks . . . You're kidding," he said, as his head of security delivered the news that they were in the middle of a city-wide blackout.

He reached over and stabbed his finger against the floor buttons, harder this time. But he stopped when he realized how his actions might come across to the woman hiccuping with tears in the corner.

"Okay, well. You have my phone number on the portable. Call me as soon as you know how long this is going to take."

He turned off the phone and looked at the woman huddled just a foot away. She was a little thing, couldn't be taller than five-three. Though she was still sniffling, her mental meltdown appeared over. He hoped to God it didn't take long for the electricity to come back on.

Several minutes passed. The woman didn't budge, didn't say a word. Didn't even look at him. Shock, he figured. Of all his luck, to get stuck in an elevator with a head case.

He knew he should try to smooth over the experience. She could very well sue the store once she got out of here. The thought of an impending lawsuit made him nervous enough that he laid a hand on her shoulder, getting her attention.

"There's been a blackout in the city; it must have been what triggered the fall," he told her. "As soon as the electricity is back on, security will have us out."

She shook her head, turning her face up to his. She looked almost serene now, even though there were still tears brimming in her eyes. Jeff noticed her thick black lashes made her eyes appear almost iridescent, they were so green.

"The elevator didn't fall because of a blackout," she said. "Don't you understand? I asked God for a sign. I stood there—" she pointed her finger toward the door "—and I asked Him: 'God? Should I marry Marshall? Should I not marry Marshall?' " She ticked off the possibilities on two fingers. "And that's *exactly* when the elevator fell. I'm doomed. I'm absolutely doomed."

In a startlingly slow process, something akin to watching dominos fall against each other, her features crumpled. Her dark brows pressed together; her eyes shut. Her mouth quivered.

"But now—now that God gave me my answer—I don't have the courage to go through with it. Just like I didn't have the guts to go to Swe-e-e-den." The word came out in a hiccup, those lovely green eyes tearing up again. "I'll just go ahead and *marry* Marshall. And it will be like a sin, because I ignored God and what He told me to do. I won't get to see Palenque and the Temple of Inscriptions. And I'm going to go to the Poconoooos! I'm going to Pocono hell."

Jeff Cameron sat back on his heels. Her words zipped

around inside his head, falling into a pattern until he began
to understand what was going on. It was the Poconos that
did it, bringing the image of heart-shaped Jacuzzis and
round, frilly beds in honeymoon suites.

He realized he wasn't locked away with a loony.

He was penned up with a bride-to-be experiencing a case
of very cold feet.

Now, as he went over in his head the bits and pieces
she'd sputtered out loud, it all made an odd sort of sense.
Imagine, the elevator dropping like that just when she asked
God to give her a sign. What a weird coincidence.

And boy, had it ever shaken her up. He figured she must
be pretty religious. She was taking her message from On
High pretty hard.

With a sigh, Jeff sat down beside the woman, letting her
have her cry, figuring she was entitled after the scare they
had just been through. He even managed a little sympathy
for her. The fall hadn't lasted longer than a split second,
but it had been enough to stick his stomach in his throat.
He glanced at the door, wondering again how long this
could take. He would give it a little time before he called
Martha and Phil. No sense in worrying them.

"Too bad about Palenque," he said, completely at a loss
as to what else to say. "It's really a nice place."

She looked up at him in mild surprise. She wore one of
those old-fashioned dresses, the kind with tiny flowers all
over it and a hem that dropped to just above the ankles.
Very feminine. "You've been to Palenque?"

"About seven years ago. My wife did her dissertation on
the Mayan ruins in Mexico. Palenque, Chichén Itzá, Teoti-
huacán . . . we toured them all. I went along to photograph
everything, but Palenque was my favorite."

It appeared he'd said the right thing. For the first time,
she actually smiled.

It was a startling transition, one that his photographer's
eye could appreciate. He realized she had an interesting

face, the kind the camera would admire. Heart-shaped, with a sweet mouth and wide-spaced green eyes accented by the dark flare of her brows. Her expression lent a sort of timeless innocence to her features. She could pass for any age between late teens to early thirties.

He watched her sniff back her tears and wipe her cheeks with her sleeve. "I read all the guide books," she said, her voice sounding strangely melodic. "It was all so wonderful . . . so romantic. I could almost hear the frogs and insects chirping at night."

"It's a little more than chirping. More like a racket. Deafening. And it's hot there. Humid as hell."

But even as he said it, he recalled how magical it had been to sit on the verandah of the bungalow with Maggie, listening to that orchestra of jungle sounds. Soothing, like a lullaby. It had been years since he'd thought of Palenque. But now . . . oh, yes, he remembered.

"Yeah," he admitted softly. "It's very romantic."

Jeff stared at the elevator wall with its wood paneling, the memory tangling up inside his gut with other not-so-happy ones of his wife. His lips pressed together as the floodgates opened to the familiar black mood he'd been fighting all week. Of all the nights to mull over the past.

God, he hated Christmas.

Most of the year, he was okay with things. But December . . . the challenge of it; the mental struggle *not* to remember. And his daughter was getting old enough now that he was afraid she would sense her father's funks around the holiday . . . the time of her own birth. That it would affect her. Part of the reason he'd come up with the idea for tonight's special promotion and extended hours was because of Maggie. Krueger's Christmas Eve sale had at least kept him busy, his mind occupied. It had cut the edge.

He glanced over at the woman. She, too, was staring ahead, looking as if there was plenty on her mind. He studied her a little, thinking that her coloring reminded him of a painting of Snow White he'd seen in one of Kayla's picture books. That pale complexion and raven curls were really striking. Especially with her green eyes.

A little shocked, he realized he wanted to photograph her. Right now, just the way she looked, with her legs tucked up inside the dress and her arms hugging her knees. He thought of how he might capture her shy smile as she looked up at him. What F-stop would do justice to her eyes still luminous with tears.

It was a strange thought. Other than his daughter, he hadn't had the desire to photograph anyone in years.

"Forget the Poconos," he said, not really sure why he was giving her advice. Maybe she'd gotten to him with that melodious but husky voice when she'd described those tropical nights. "If you decide to marry the guy, make him take you to Palenque."

"Marshall is afraid he'll get Montezuma's Revenge if he goes to Mexico."

He shrugged. "Sure, I was sick as a dog when I got back. I had the worst case of the trots for a week. But it was worth it."

"I don't think I'm supposed to marry him." She barely whispered the words.

Jeff grimaced. The sign from God again. He *did* feel sorry for her. Snow White stuck in an elevator with her second thoughts.

He considered making things a little easier for her. It wasn't something he would normally do, get involved. But then, these were unusual circumstances. Just five minutes ago, she'd had her face planted between his legs.

"Look lady, we're in the middle of a city-wide blackout. Do you really think God blacked out Pasadena so you wouldn't get married tomorrow?"

She looked him dead in the eyes and said, "Why, yes. Yes, I do."

Jeff stared at her, a little shocked by her response. It

wasn't often that someone took him by surprise. Well, at least she wasn't going to sue Krueger's for an act of God.

"Okay, but how do you know God doesn't want you to marry the guy?" he said, asking the obvious. "So the elevator dropped. That could mean anything. It wasn't like some voice shouted, 'Dump the jerk.' "

She sniffed, thinking about it. "No. No I didn't hear any voices."

Thank God for small favors. "When did you say the wedding is?"

"Tomo—" She frowned, then glanced down at her wristwatch. "Today. It's Christmas. I'm getting married in . . ." she seemed to count mentally ". . . in less than ten hours."

Jeff thought she was cutting it close with the second thoughts. But then again, maybe that was all too normal. "Look, you're just having pre-wedding jitters. I would forget about signs from God and search your heart to see if you really love the guy."

He couldn't believe he was saying this sentimental claptrap. But what the hell. She really looked spooked . . . and kind of sweet, sitting there, worrying about her signs from God. And perhaps he even admired her faith. Jeff had stopped believing in much of anything since Maggie's death.

"You're right to be careful," he said. "Marriage is a big commitment. But it's also a great way to live your life, with someone beside you, making a family." He tried to say it lightly, not to let the words stick in his throat. "But skip the Poconos." He gave her a wink. "Palenque. Trust me on that one."

"Are you married?"

It always surprised him how much that question still hurt. It had been three years. "I'm a widower."

"I'm so sorry."

"Yeah. Me, too," he said, cutting off her sympathy.

The cell phone rang. Jeff picked it up. "So what's the

deal?" he said into the phone. "That long? Hell. All right. Keep me posted. No, don't call anyone in on it yet. Most likely, when the electricity comes back, this puppy will start up, no problem."

He turned off the cell phone. The bride-to-be was looking at him expectantly.

"I'm afraid we're stuck here a little longer than I thought," he told her quietly.

Phoebe watched Santa Claus hold out the cell phone to her.

"Security says it might be as long as an hour," Santa told her. "You want to call someone?"

She shook her head. "There's no one expecting me. At least, not until the wedding."

Santa grinned. "We'll have you out of here long before that."

Phoebe's gaze dropped to his smile surrounded by the fluffy white beard. He had dimples. Two beautiful dimples, one to each side of his mouth. And merry brown eyes.

And he'd been to Palenque.

She clutched her legs and rested her chin on her knees, thinking about what he'd said. Maybe he was right. She couldn't be certain God had been telling her not to marry Marshall—although she couldn't help attaching a big "No!" to an elevator falling out of control.

She sighed, feeling like Pandora after opening the box. For the first time, she realized just how much it would hurt if she was wrong about Marshall. All her life, she'd been so careful about the choices she made. To miss the boat on such an important decision . . . well . . . it was more than a little daunting. It made her question everything she'd ever done.

"If the power is off," she asked Santa, "why are there lights on in the elevator?"

"Emergency generator. Just enough juice to light up the stairs, the exits, and the elevator for added safety."

"But not enough for the elevator to work?"

He stood and punched the floor buttons uselessly. "Apparently not."

"I'm sorry about what happened before, crying like that, spilling out my life's problems. It was just . . . well . . . with the elevator dropping when I asked for a sign."

"Yeah. I could see how that might give you ideas."

Phoebe bit her lip, staring around the tiny confines of the elevator. "I . . . I always thought when I married I would be so sure. And I was for a while. Only, the last couple of months, I started wondering if it weren't Marshall who was certain enough for the two of us . . ."

If she hadn't let his persistence influence her. She'd begged off his proposals despite the fact that her parents had absolutely loved him. But after three years, she wondered if he hadn't just worn her down.

She glanced up at Santa. She recalled he'd said he was the manager here. She thought it was cute that he also played Santa Claus for the store. "Did you? Get cold feet, I mean . . . when you married?"

She wanted to hear that he had. Desperately. At the moment, some amusing anecdote about his pre-wedding jitters would go a long way to helping ease her mind. When she thought of what would happen if she called off the wedding, she realized she needed very much to go ahead with her marriage.

She didn't want to fail Marshall. She didn't want to ruin his life.

"Sorry, but no," Santa said.

"Maybe just a few misgivings?"

He stared at her for the longest time, then shook his head.

He looked like the kind of man who knew his mind. Whereas, Phoebe always doubted. Even when she picked chicken salad instead of tuna for lunch, there was always that niggling doubt that she had picked the wrong one. But the way Santa was watching her, returning her gaze without flinching, he appeared so self-assured . . . even dressed in a jolly red suit—which she thought might be a little difficult to pull off for most men.

"That's too bad," she said, disappointed. "I was certain there was a reason why you were stuck in the elevator with me," she continued, thinking out loud. "I mean, don't you think that's the kind of thing God might do?" She stared up at him. "Have a man dressed like Santa Claus steer me in the right direction."

He was looking at her a little funny. "I need to make another phone call," he said, reaching for the cell phone.

Phoebe settled back against the wall of the elevator as Santa spoke quietly into the phone, letting the party on the other end of the line know he would be later getting home than he'd expected because of the blackout. She could tell she was making him uncomfortable again. But what she'd said made sense. She couldn't shake the feeling that he was part of this crisis in her life. She was a deeply religious person, and she saw the hand of God in many things. Somehow, some way, Santa could be a vehicle to getting at her truths.

She felt the rightness of it slide home. If divine intervention were involved here, Santa must be a part of it.

The minute he hung up the phone, Phoebe asserted, "You know, I really think you're here for a reason." And when he just watched her with that unblinking stare of his, she added, "I mean, it seems so obvious. Stuck in an elevator with Santa Claus the night before my wedding—right at the moment of my greatest doubts. That *has* to mean something."

"The guy we hired came down with the flu. Unfortunately, I fit the suit."

"No," she said, certain there was more to this, "that's not why."

"I told you—I'm the manager of Krueger's." He pulled the beard and mustache down below his chin. "The only reason I'm in here with you now is because Jack called and told me there was a customer holed up in the bathroom. Sorry, lady. Whether you get married or not is completely up to you."

He sounded very adamant. Only Phoebe was having trouble listening at the moment. She was too busy staring.

All her life, she'd been a little intimidated by good-looking men. Perhaps it was because she'd always been shy about her own looks, being such a late bloomer. It wasn't until she was near twenty that Phoebe had shown signs of anything other than acute homeliness. Boys hadn't been part of the picture while she was growing up, particularly handsome ones.

But there was no other way to classify Santa. He was drop-dead gorgeous.

There was something very classic about his features, his straight and noble nose, his deep-set eyes a lovely shade of chocolate brown—his strong chin. And those lips, the kind that would appear under the Batman mask when Val Kilmer played the role.

Her mouth went suddenly dry as she remembered the dimples.

She realized she was staring. She glanced away, remembering that edge to his voice when he'd spoken earlier. Obviously, he wasn't the kind for soul-searching conversations. Which only told her he needed one. She remembered his expression when he'd said he was a widower.

With the intuition she'd come to rely on all her life, Phoebe said gently, "You must have loved her very much."

His eyes turned very dark, reminding her of the center of a storm. "I don't talk about Maggie."

The wall came down instantly. It startled her because she didn't normally have that effect on people. They usually smiled and humored her as she prattled on . . . until minutes later they found themselves speaking just as candidly. She sensed the barrier was shored up by the incredible pain of losing his wife. She wondered how Maggie had died, but knew enough not to ask.

"Yes, of course. I understand. I shouldn't pry."

They stared at each other. Finally, Santa pulled off his hat and shoved his hand through a shock of sandy brown hair. "I didn't mean to bite your head off just now . . . it's just that—"

"It still hurts."

"It still . . . hurts."

She nodded, studying the boots of his Santa suit. She thought the elevator felt different somehow . . . a little colder, as if his sadness had seeped into the air around them. She thought of how unfair it was that he'd lost his wife, when he'd clearly loved his Maggie.

Poor man. He hadn't been given a choice on which way to turn. God had just thrown a big curve and told him to deal with it.

The injustice of it weighed on her heart, driving her to do something to make things better. She thought this might even be the reason why they were stuck in this elevator together—that there was something *she* must do to help *him*. There just had to be something . . .

And then, she realized there was.

Squaring her shoulders, she stood and stuck her hand out. "Phoebe Nichols."

A slow grin crept up Santa's face, lighting up the dimples, making her breath catch in a peculiar fashion in her chest.

"Jeff Cameron." His hands were massive, as befitting a man over six feet in height. Phoebe watched as his palm swallowed hers in one big bite. "Nice to meet you, Phoebe."

"Have a seat," she said, indicating the floor, all business now. Before he could comment, she dropped down to sit cross-legged. She took a deep breath, balancing her hands on her knees, getting situated.

"Now, Jeff, I know you're uncomfortable with the topic of my upcoming marriage, so I'll do the talking."

It all made perfect sense to Phoebe. First, she would break the ice, open up to Santa, let him know all her terrible little secrets, her horrible doubts. Then, after this shared experience, Santa would turn to her for the same kind of guidance. They would help each other.

Phoebe smiled, thinking that at last she'd discovered the reason they had been trapped inside the elevator. It was, after all, very obvious that a widower might have a few things to work through. And the way Phoebe saw things, God might not let them out until he did.

She glanced at her watch, feeling very certain about this Right Turn.

"All right, Jeff. I'm sure between the two of us, we'll figure out in no time whether or not I'm supposed to get married in nine hours."

Three

"Is it animal, vegetable, or mineral?" Jeff asked in a tired voice.

Snow White shook her head doggedly. "You're supposed to ask only yes or no questions."

"Oh, yeah? Well that could take forever."

Forever—as in just about as long as they had been trapped in this damned elevator. He glanced at his watch. *Two hours.*

He didn't know how much more he could take of this. He should have never let his guard down those first few minutes, falling for that seductive smile, that sweet voice . . . the tears.

Snow White wanted to get inside his head. She wanted to probe around and dissect memories he'd stashed away, deep inside, where even he wouldn't find them.

Snow White wanted an encounter group.

Well, he wasn't having any of it. As soon as he'd figured out what she was up to, he'd made it perfectly clear he wasn't going to hold her hand or bare his soul. But the woman had persevered, volunteering information about herself and her life with Marshall—like Jeff should care or something. When that hadn't gotten a response, she'd actually started talking to herself, weighing the pros and cons of her upcoming marriage in some mumbled discussion geared to getting Jeff to open up.

But it hadn't been until she'd started humming Christmas

songs that he finally gave in to her suggestion that they break the ice by playing twenty questions. Hell, he could take just about anything but Christmas carols.

"It won't take forever," she told him in a crisp school-teacher voice that had replaced the husky tones he'd found so seductive. He could tell he was beginning to push her buttons. "If you haven't figured it out in twenty tries, I win. That's why it's called twenty questions."

She looked up at him as if he weren't particularly bright, which only irritated the hell out of him. Okay, so he was a little testy around Christmas—and being stuck here all frigging night in a Santa suit was adding new heights of joy to his memories of the jolly holiday. But at least he didn't hide out in department store bathrooms and ask for signs from God. At least he didn't pry into other people's lives, trying to "fix" a perfect stranger.

"All right," he said, with a smirk. "Yes or no—is it animal, vegetable, or mineral?"

Snow White pursed her lips. He could see the proverbial wheels turning in her head as she searched for a witty comeback. Cripes, she was annoying.

And pretty. Downright sexy with that delicious bow-shaped mouth and those cat eyes. He kept getting these visions of her wearing some off-the-shoulder dress, sitting amid a field of wildflowers, her black curls windblown around her heart-shaped face. She made him itch to have his camera in his hands. And that, he realized, *really* bothered him.

Snow White crossed her arms over her chest. "If you didn't want to play, you could have just said so."

Jeff reached for the top two buttons of the Santa suit, yanking open the collar, taking his eyes off the enticing sight of her dress clinging to her breasts. The last thing he needed was to get turned on by Snow White.

Unfortunately, that was becoming increasingly easy. He couldn't seem to help himself, watching to see how the thin cotton of her dress draped over her hips and breasts . . . catching a glimpse of her shapely legs. It was freaking hot in here. He thought that might be part of it, the heat. He would probably boil in this getup if the blackout lasted much longer.

"No, I'll play." What the hell. It might take his mind off the fact that the five-by-nine-feet area of the elevator was steaming up like a furnace with their body heat. Good old Southern California. "But you ask the questions."

Yeah, that's the ticket, he thought. Make her do the work; keep her busy. That would nix the Christmas songs and the probing questions about his personal life. He figured there was no way anyone could guess what he was thinking in twenty questions.

Glancing up at the elevator lights, he decided: *A light bulb.* "Go ahead. I have something in mind." He leaned back against the wall of the elevator, trying to get comfortable. When she ran out of questions, he would call Scott again. Get an update.

"Is it alive?"

"Nope."

She nibbled on her bottom lip. "Is it useful?"

"Yeah. Yeah, it's useful."

"Does it run on electricity?"

He looked at her sharply. He nodded.

A sudden excitement lit up her eyes. "Is it a light bulb?"

She must have seen the surprise on his face because she said, "Well, it was a little obvious, given the blackout and all. And you did look right at the light just before you said you were ready."

"It's a dumb game," he told her.

"Yes, of course. It's a silly game." She was seated on the wall perpendicular to his, her feet tucked up under her dress. She shrugged, giving him a glance. "Only . . . usually, it lasts a little longer than that."

He couldn't quite understand his reaction. Sure, he was

never himself on Christmas, but the hostility steamrollering through him was incredibly disproportionate to the situation. It wasn't as if she were commenting on his sexual prowess or anything.

And yet, the way she said it, it was almost as if . . .

"Are you trying to rile me?"

She didn't say anything, but he could *swear* she was biting the inside of her cheek to keep from laughing.

"Because I'm going to point out that you are stuck in this elevator with me."

"Jeez, you have a terrible temper."

And Jeff knew it would only get worse as the night wore on. Just as he knew it wouldn't be Snow White's fault, although he was likely to take it out on her. No, it wasn't her fault that he found her attractive . . . that a part of him wanted to respond to that lovely empathy she offered up, to spill his guts about Maggie.

But he also knew he would keep quiet, as he had all these years. He was afraid to talk about the memories that haunted him on this day, making him retreat from everyone, even his daughter. Afraid of what would happen if he let go. He always made certain he was alone on Christmas for that very reason.

The cell phone rang. He snatched it out of his briefcase and turned away from Snow White, accidentally kicking the case so that some of his papers spilled out. With a soft curse, he ignored the mess.

"Fill me in," he said, speaking into the phone. He listened to Scott, then let out a sigh of relief. "Thank you, God. All right . . . No. Don't worry. This will work."

He turned off the phone. "They're saying in just a few minutes—what the hell are you doing?"

Snow White was leaning over his briefcase. She was making a neat pile of the papers that had fallen out, tapping them straight against the floor. She reached back into the case for another batch.

"Oh, I'm just straightening things up a bit," she said breezily. She finished with the papers and clamped her fingers around his calculator, tucking it inside one of the accordion pockets. "You know, you can really discover a lot about a person from the way they organize their things. And I don't want you to take this the wrong way, Jeff, but you're not much of a talker. Jeez, it's a wonder you find anything in here," she said, peering inside his briefcase. "You must be an artistic type. Most right brain—"

He grabbed up his papers and dumped them in the briefcase, then snatched the case out from under her hands.

She remained kneeling, looking up at him with her green-eyed stare, her lips slightly parted.

"I'm really quite good at organizing people," she whispered. "Marshall always says so." And when Jeff didn't respond, she sighed. "You probably don't feel comfortable with my going through your things. I guess that was a little presumptuous of me. I do that sometimes, misjudge situations. I should have known that getting locked up in an elevator gives a false sense of intimacy."

He just couldn't help it. He had to say it. "Lady. You are a case."

She raised her chin an inch, looking oddly regal. "Yes. I suppose I am."

Another blanket of silence fell over them. Jeff took a deep breath, telling himself to calm down. He wasn't going to let her get to him. He was the manager here. And no matter what, this woman was a customer.

"I've decided I should marry Marshall, after all."

Jeff closed his eyes, stifling a groan. She was, if anything, persistent.

He put the briefcase down. With the tip of his boot, he pushed it across the elevator, watching the leather case slide out of the way. He crossed his arms over his padded stomach, and stared at her, taking her on.

"That might be a wise choice," he said. "If you can irritate me this much in just under three hours, you might not have too many marriage proposals coming down the pike."

She looked at him sharply. But she didn't say anything, ignoring the jibe.

"I think what you said earlier was right," she said instead. "I was just having a bad case of pre-wedding jitters."

"Oh, no. Leave me out of this, Snow White. What happens between you and—"

"What did you call me?"

He realized suddenly he'd spoken the name out loud. He hadn't meant to do that. He shook his head. Imagine, calling her Snow White like that.

He had to admit there was something about her. She'd had a strange effect on him, the most obvious being anger. But there was something else there, too. A more subtle emotion.

He glanced over at the briefcase. Maybe she was right. Maybe getting locked up like this *did* give a false sense of intimacy.

He shrugged, trying to make light of it. "It's just that you have that—" he pointed to her curls "—black-hair, pale-complexion thing going for you."

"My father used to call me Snow White. When I was little." Her eyes became unfocused, as if capturing a special memory. "I liked it."

A tiny smile crept over her mouth. It reached her eyes, making them glow and look even more almond-shaped. Very alluring. She tilted her head, glancing up at him as if she might be flirting with that smile. He realized it was a big turn on, the way she was looking at him.

Jeff whipped around and banged on the elevator buttons again, starting to feel the sweat drip down his back. *Come on. Come on.*

"I'm sorry if all those questions I asked you earlier made you uncomfortable."

He tapped the buttons again. Scott had said only a few more minutes.

"But I don't see why you have to be so angry with me."

Jeff sighed. He glanced at his watch. Two in the morning. "Look. Christmas doesn't happen to be my best day."

He could already feel that clenching starting in his chest. He should have been home by now, should have kissed Kayla good night and disappeared with his bottle of Scotch, keeping himself and his temper away from others.

"You're not particularly religious, I gather."

"Not in the least—"

The lights overhead flickered, then flashed on as if the elevator had just received a hit of juice.

"Wait." A grin spread over his face. "I may be getting some religion here. Come on, baby," he whispered to the elevator.

The elevator lurched, bouncing beneath their feet. Both he and Snow White grabbed on to the railings. The hum of a motor wound up, purring under them . . . then fizzled out.

Nothing.

He grabbed the cell phone and jabbed Scott's number. "Now what? The power is back on? Well, we're still stuck here," he said, giving the floor buttons another go. Each lit up at the touch, but the elevator failed to move. He tried the "open door" button. No response.

"All right, Scott," he said, pinching the bridge of his nose where he could feel the mother of all headaches beginning. "Call the fire department."

Scott Bainbridge hung up the phone and stared across his desk at Jack. He pushed his blond hair out of his eyes, remembering that he'd told his wife he'd get a haircut before the big Christmas feast tonight at his in-laws and that he'd forgotten again. That meant Connie was going to take the scissors to him herself. He was going to get one of those bowl cuts, like the kids. Connie, the budding beautician.

"He wants me to call the fire department," Scott told Jack.

After patrolling the building, the older security guard had kept Scott company throughout the blackout. They were the only two left at Krueger's—if Scott didn't count his boss and the customer stuck in the elevator.

"Boy, it's hard to think of Mr. Cameron stuck in there like that." Jack puckered his lips. "Tonight of all nights."

Unconsciously, both men glanced at their wristwatches.

"Two o'clock," Scott said.

"Christmas morning," Jack finished.

Silently, each man contemplated the significance of the hour for Jeff Cameron.

"Maybe being stuck in there will keep his mind off it?" Scott said hopefully.

But Jack shook his head. "No, son. That's not how it happens."

Jack hitched his hip onto the top of Scott's desk. His pale eyes looked very serious. Krueger's was like a small family. Everyone knew everyone's business. And everyone knew about Mr. Cameron and Christmas.

Jack heaved a sigh. "What Mr. Cameron needs is to get on with his life. Find someone else. Someone who can be a mother to that little girl of his—"

Jack stopped mid-sentence. He glanced back at Scott. Scott had known Jack enough years to recognize that light in his eyes.

"What?" Scott asked. Though Scott had been head of security the last year and a half, he respected Jack a great deal. The older man had taken Scott under his wing when he'd first gotten on board at Krueger's six years ago, showing Scott the ropes. It was only after Jack turned down the promotion, saying it was a job for the young, that Mr. Cameron had offered the position to Scott.

"What about calling Nelson?" Jack asked. "Before you go through the hullabaloo of the fire department. If anyone can get the elevator to work, it's Nelson."

Scott picked up the phone. "It's worth a shot."

* * *

Santa Claus was stripping.

He'd started with the stuffing, unbuttoning his suit to remove the large pillowlike pad that had been strapped around his stomach. Now, he was taking his arms out of the red velvet sleeves, letting the suit drop down to his hips as he paced back and forth inside the elevator, talking heatedly into the cell phone clamped between his ear and shoulder. She noticed he wore Calvin's.

"So is Nelson there yet? Look, I'm ready to call 911. Okay, okay. But he better get here soon. Yeah, I know . . . he could make this puppy work with spit and string. All right. We'll hang tight."

She watched him shut the antenna against his chest. She'd been trying not to look there. Honestly, she had. But now her eyes focused on the T of dark brown hair, the muscles of his chest, all gloriously defined. Suddenly, she understood the beauty of the male body. Like Michelangelo's David, he stood gorgeously before her.

Marshall was rather on the thin side. Taller, yes. But much, much thinner. And pale. Santa had wonderfully tanned shoulders—

Phoebe shut her eyes. *Don't compare. Do not compare them!*

She had to remind herself that this was one of those crisis situations where people could really have a lapse in judgment. She'd already determined she was well on her way to getting over her cold feet, ready to go through with her wedding. The last thing she should do was check out some poor unsuspecting man's anatomy as if he were a centerfold.

Just the same, she peeked.

Boy, she thought, staring now. *He must work out.*

Santa pushed his hand through his hair, continuing to pace. "Looks like we're in here for at least another half hour. Hell."

Or maybe he just has good genes, she thought, watching the ripple of muscles as he threw his hands up in exasperation. *Nah,* she thought, *you have to sweat to look like that.*

"Sorry about the clothes," he said. "It's just that I was starting to cook in that suit."

"It is a little warm," Phoebe said, fanning her face with her hand. But she hadn't noticed the heat until Santa had started discarding his suit. Now, she was roasting.

Santa sat down and rested his head against the elevator wall. "Nelson runs maintenance for Krueger's. He's an engineering genius. He can make just about anything work, and this elevator has been his baby for years. God, I can't wait to get out of here."

The way he said it, well . . . maybe she was taking things a little personal . . . but he'd made it sound as if he couldn't wait to get away from *her.* She knew she'd been annoying him. Her idea that she would open herself up to him by talking about Marshall, then help Jeff sort through his own grief over his wife, hadn't quite worked out the way she'd imagined. If anything, the man had become downright hostile.

Now, he was staring straight ahead. She wondered if he was warming up for another zinger comment or if she was in for a second bout of the silent treatment.

"I know I talk too much," she said, trying a preemptive strike on his possible attack. She spoke in a metered voice, attempting to come off unemotional about the subject, which she wasn't in the least. "I know that sometimes people think I'm silly or ridiculous because of the things I say. I just don't happen to like silence. I suppose that's because I was an only child."

She glanced up, judging his reaction. For once, he was watching her with only mild surprise. She took that as encouragement.

"There was always so much silence around our house. Because both my parents worked. I used to talk to all these imaginary friends." She shrugged. "I guess I thought I was improving when I started talking to people. Whether they wanted to hear me or not, at least they were real."

She'd meant it as a joke, and he smiled, showing a shadow of those dimples, making her pulse soar.

After a moment, he said softly, "I'm only mean on Christmas."

She thought it was a rather strange comment. On Christmas? Why would someone be rude on Christmas of all days?

"But that's exactly the wrong day to be angry," she said. "Christmas is a time of joy . . . a time for making memories and following tradition. That's why Marshall made such a fuss about our wedding day. Even as a little boy, he'd dreamed about getting married on Christmas."

"Yeah? Well, I hate Christmas."

There was such acid in his voice, she instantly swallowed any response she might have made. She supposed holidays *could* depress people. But still, he sounded like such a scrooge. There was no reason to hate Christmas. Not unless—

Not unless something really bad happened to him on Christmas Day. Something that would make him pace like a caged animal and lose his temper as the hour drew closer to Christmas morning . . . something that would make him loath to be trapped in an elevator with nothing to do but think. Something truly dreadful.

Like losing his wife.

Even as the thought struck her, she dismissed it as too awful. She was letting her imagination run away again. His wife couldn't have died on Christmas . . . could she?

Phoebe curled her arms around her legs, knowing she wouldn't ask, even as a morbid curiosity begged her to find out. Imagine, what a horrible thing to happen on Christmas.

She leaned her head back against the elevator wall, subdued by the direction of her thoughts, wondering. What would happen if she lost Marshall? If on Christmas Day, or any other holiday, he should die unexpectedly? Tears filled her eyes, and she turned away, not wanting Santa Claus to see her crying again.

What would she do if Marshall were gone from her life forever?

A tiny voice inside her head answered: *You would be free.*

Phoebe tensed, feeling a little sick inside. Is that really how she saw Marshall's demise? Freedom? No, she couldn't be that terrible—someone who lacked the character to call off a wedding, but if a twist of fate should take the decision from her . . . so be it. That little voice had just been one of those terrible thoughts that sometimes pop into people's heads. She didn't really feel like that.

Did she?

Suddenly, there didn't seem to be enough air in the elevator. She tugged at her dress, realizing the elevator was *really* warm. Stifling, even. She made a little mewling sound in the back of her throat, telling herself to calm down.

"Are you okay?"

Santa Claus was staring at her. He only intensified her panic. Here was this saintlike man mourning the loss of his wife, while she envisioned poor Marshall's death as some sort of ticket to freedom.

Phoebe thought she might be hyperventilating. The elevator was terribly hot. And small. She hadn't really thought of it as being so small before.

She glanced down at the floor, measuring in her head. It couldn't be wider than five feet. The length wasn't even twice that. "How soon did you say we would get out of here?"

"Half an hour. Hey, how about another game of twenty questions? I'll let you think of something this time."

He was trying to humor her. That almost made her smile. Only, the queasy feeling was still with her, making it impossible to do anything but concentrate on catching her next breath.

Was it her imagination, or was the room getting smaller?

"You know, you don't look so good," Santa said.

She hugged her arms around her stomach, staring up at the ceiling, telling herself to keep breathing.

And then the ceiling seemed to move, slipping down, slowly coming down to crush her.

Four

Snow White was banging a champagne bottle against the elevator door.

"Help!" *Bang, bang, bang.* "Someone. Anyone! Help!"

The cell phone dangled uselessly from Jeff's hand. Somehow, he knew it wouldn't make any difference if he offered it to her.

She turned around, the champagne bottle she'd taken out of her Krueger's bag gripped in both hands. There was a wild look in her eyes.

"I think I'm claustrophobic," she whispered.

He could see the pearls of sweat forming on her upper lip. He put down the cell phone and shrugged into the sleeves of the Santa suit, not bothering to button it. "Listen to me. I've been sitting with you here for over two hours and you've been fine." He reached her in one step. She was visibly trembling, and he could see a huge problem unfolding if she cracked.

He gripped her shoulders. "You are not claustrophobic." He said each word slowly. Decisively.

"Yes. I am. Only, I wasn't thinking about it before. And then, all of a sudden, the walls started closing in—"

"It's just a little warm in here. Think cool thoughts. Imagine a placid mountain lake—"

"I even have these dreams sometimes," she said, her voice slightly hoarse. "I'm in a tunnel, going forward. Only, the tunnel gets smaller, so I have to crawl on my hands and knees. And as I move ahead, it gets smaller and smaller."

"This is really a very large elevator. Fifteen people could stand in here comfortably. Look," he said, stepping back from her. He stretched his arms out, reaching for the opposite walls of the elevator. "I can't even touch both sides at the same time."

Snow White started sliding down the elevator door, her dress pooling around her. "Oh, God." She spoke in this tiny, squeaky voice, clutching the champagne bottle to her chest. "Oh, God."

Jeff knelt down beside her. He uncurled her fingers from around the champagne bottle. "You know what you need?"

"What?" she asked, the whites of her eyes showing around her pupils.

Jeff tore off the foil from the champagne bottle and twisted free the metal wires that kept the cork in place. He'd always been good in an emergency—all that lifeguard training as a kid. He figured now was as good a time as any to step up to the plate.

"You need a nice stiff drink." The cork made a resounding pop.

"A drink?" She blinked, staring at the bottle. "Yes. All right." She took the opened bottle and stared at it. She glanced up. "But we don't have any glasses."

"Improvise," he said, tipping the bottle up to her lips.

She took a sip, then grimaced. "I thought this stuff was supposed to taste good."

Jeff glanced down at the price tag hailing the bottle a vintage $4.99. Funny, he didn't think they sold champagne at Krueger's. Certainly not bad champagne. "It's just warm. Think of it as a tranquilizer," he said, urging her to take another drink.

She closed her eyes. And then she started chugging down the champagne as if it were soda.

"Whoa. Hold on there, sport." He took the bottle from her. "Easy does it."

"I feel a little better. You were right. Liquids help. Why don't you have some?"

"I think I'll save it," he said, thinking he might need this form of ammo later, in case she wigged out again.

She took the bottle out of his hands and drank another good belt. "Yes. This definitely helps." Before he could stop her, she downed a few more mouthfuls, then cradled the bottle to her chest, making it clear she was keeping custody.

His gaze dropped to where the bottle nestled up against her cleavage. He'd already noticed some time ago that beneath that demure gown she hid a very fine pair of breasts. She smelled good, too. Like lilacs, or something.

Stop right there, he warned himself. Snow White was spoken for . . . and a pain in the neck.

"Tell me about Palenque."

There was a hushed quality to her request, as if she were searching for more comfort than the champagne. She was staring straight ahead, still looking a little spooked. He thought he should probably make this good. Keep her thoughts occupied.

He settled down beside her, thinking of how to describe the countryside he'd visited so long ago, a land that had left such a lasting impression. He smiled, remembering.

"It's like falling into another world. You know, *Journey to the Center of the Earth*. Exotic, beautiful." Yes. It had certainly been all that. "A tropical jungle."

"You make it sound wonderful."

"It is. Everything is so green; you come in by prop plane to Villa Hermosa to see this sweeping carpet of color. From there, you rent a car to get to the ruins. It's incredible country. Lush, with swaying palm trees and thatch-roofed homes."

She sighed a little, leaning back so that her spine grew

supple, curving into the paneled wall of the elevator. She held her hands wrapped around her stomach, hugging the champagne bottle. "I love the tropics. I've never been there, but I just know it must be marvelous. Sometimes, I drive over to the Orchid House at the Arboretum, and I close my eyes and listen to the water falling down the fountain and smell the flowers. And I just pretend."

He could see her doing that, the schoolteacher who longed for Palenque but settled for the Poconos, trying to find her tropics in a greenhouse. Sitting there in front of him, she kept her eyes closed, as if she might be pretending right now. He obliged her.

"Outside of Palenque," he said in a low voice, "the jungle gets very dense. Insulating. It's like, there's nothing around you. No civilization."

"And at night, the noise is deafening," she said dreamily. "Like an orchestra."

It surprised him that the memories didn't hurt. He thought maybe that was because he was concentrating on her crisis, not letting this be about him. She looked so sweet, her arms curled around her champagne bottle as she dreamed.

He realized he liked looking at her. With her eyes closed, he could take in every inch of her without her knowing. Indulge himself.

"There's this flower," he said. "White ginger. It grows everywhere, the stalks almost as tall as a man. The Spanish name for it is *mariposa.*"

"Mariposa," she whispered. "Butterfly."

"You speak Spanish?" In Mexico, Maggie had been their translator, completely fluent.

"And French," she told him. "The romance languages."

He could tell the champagne had kicked in. She didn't quite slur her words, but they slipped into each other like music. Her voice had been the first thing he'd noticed about her, a sound that reminded him of crushed velvet—when she didn't speak like a schoolteacher, that was. She kept her eyes closed, as if trying to visualize everything he said, and there was a slight smile on her lips as she swayed her head to the rhythm of some imagined song. "What does it smell like, *mariposa?*"

"Exotic. Spicy. Very sweet."

"Tell me about the temples."

Her voice had attained a throaty quality. It was sexy as hell . . . like her smile. A few wisps of hair clung to her cheeks in tiny curls while the rest haloed her face in ringlets. Her lips were a very deep pink, and she had these really sooty lashes.

He realized he hadn't looked at a woman like this since Maggie. Oh, sure, he'd noticed a few; he wasn't dead. And recently, there had been the parade of eligibles his well-intentioned friends had brought his way.

But their good looks registered only faintly, like passing scenery. He was beginning to see this woman in layers of beauty. First, there was the over-all picture. And then, bit by bit, there followed the fine details.

For the first time, he let himself think: *Maybe if things had been different* . . .

"You walk down a long path choked with vines," he said, giving her the dreams she asked for. "It's hot and you can hear the chirping of the cicadas. And then, suddenly, the jungle opens up and you come across this vista. The temples seem to rise up from the very trees, almost as green as the leaves. The stones beneath are only tiny glimpses through the thick vines. But then you come closer. And the temples are huge, dominating everything."

"You said you went to take photographs. For your wife?"

"Nah. Though I took plenty of her." He smiled, remembering Maggie, always in shorts, searching through her treasure of hieroglyphs. "I sold a few things to a travel magazine."

"You're a professional photographer?"

"I . . . was. But after Maggie died, I had our daughter to

think of. I needed to settle down, stay here, where she had both grandparents nearby. I started working for my father-in-law. He's part owner of Krueger's. I'd worked for him before—summers and right after college."

She opened her eyes, blinking up at him, looking excited, like a kid, as she whispered, "I bet you've been to the most wonderful places."

He smiled, because there was such awe in her voice. It brought back a little of the magic of those times. "Yeah. I've seen a few things."

"It must have been difficult, leaving all of that to manage a department store."

He realized they'd segued into talking about him—but for some reason, it seemed all right now. It was easy to talk to her. Too easy, maybe. She had that quality about her, that you could confide in her. She was so forthcoming about herself. You knew she wouldn't hold anything back. It made it okay to do the same.

"I did what I had to do."

She nodded. "You took a Right Turn."

"Right Turn?"

"It's my philosophy of life. Every once in a while, we come to a crossroads. We have to choose . . . do we turn left or right?" Her voice had grown very soft, but there was a severity to her words, the schoolteacher lecturing again. "You've always turned left. That's what artists do, take chances like that. They can't help themselves. It's in their soul. But now, because of circumstances, you had to take a Right Turn."

He didn't know what to say. He was still trying to figure out what the hell she was talking about, making right turns, when she said, "Tell me about the Temple of Inscriptions."

Of course she would ask about that. "The burial chamber?"

She lifted the champagne bottle to her lips and took another long drink. "Please."

She closed her eyes again, but this time, they were shut tight, as if she were trying to keep out reality rather than fall into her dreams. It made him a little angry to see her like that. What the hell was this crap about right turns? If she wanted to travel, why couldn't she just get on a plane and go somewhere, for Pete's sake?

But then he remembered she'd said she was an only child. Perhaps her parents had poured too many of their hopes and dreams inside her, making their child scared to disappoint them. Making her grow into a woman who might devise a rigid philosophy of life—one that didn't allow mistakes.

"Does it really look like a man in a spaceship?"

She was asking about the carved sarcophagus, made famous when someone claimed it was evidence that extraterrestrials had visited Earth in ancient times. Everyone who visited Palenque went to see the famed burial chamber. The tomb was inside the temple, five feet below the plaza level. To reach it, he'd descended down a dark and dank stairwell that made this elevator seem like a claustrophobic's vision of heaven.

But once inside the chamber, the sight of that enormous carved slab of stone had made it all worth it. The Mayan lord depicted in the carvings captured the imagination, indeed appearing to recline in some mythical spaceship, surrounded by stars.

"Yes. I guess it does look like a spaceman."

"I would really love to see that some day."

There was such longing in her voice. And the tears were there again, brimming in her eyes, making them shine incredibly green. He'd never seen eye color like hers, not hazel, but a true clear hue, like peridot. Her expression reminded him of one of those paintings that plastered the walls of the museums in Italy. A Madonna. She appeared incredibly fragile. A woman who would cry for her dreams.

At that moment, he realized he was beyond creating the photographs he'd first imagined in his head, those visions of

Phoebe with windblown curls and wildflowers that had made his hand itch to hold his camera again. Instead, he could picture himself leaning down to kiss her tears away. To comfort her.

He told himself it wasn't what he wanted, to confuse her even more the night before her supposed wedding. Phoebe didn't need this. Stuck in this elevator together, they could make mistakes.

"You cry a lot," he said.

He'd wanted to break the spell between them, keeping his voice clipped and unsympathetic. And it worked. She looked as if he'd hit her. She actually pulled away physically, leaning farther away from him.

She grabbed up the bottle and downed another drink. "I'm sorry I'm not the pillar of strength your wife was."

Now it was his turn to flinch. "What the hell are you talking about?"

"I bet she never cried."

He stared at her, telling himself not to say what was on the tip of his tongue. To keep things cool. But he was angry, and the words tumbled out.

"Maggie never let anything hurt. She didn't have that luxury. But she cried. Oh, yes. She cried."

Right then, the phone rang. Neither of them moved. Phoebe clutched her champagne bottle in her hands, staring at him, her eyes filled with apologies. Jeff felt trapped by that look, an expression that said she would take all his pain inside herself if he would let her. And he almost believed it was possible, that for the first time in too many years he'd found someone who could help him remember Maggie without the pain.

That's when he figured out what was going on between them.

It scared the hell out of him.

* * *

Phoebe watched Jeff pick up the phone. She couldn't imagine what had possessed her to say the things she'd said.

She took another sip of the champagne, a little ashamed. She should never have compared herself to his wife. The more she thought about it, the worse she felt . . . because she knew she was envious of Maggie, a woman Phoebe imagined had known her own mind. A woman who had loved and married—even if it had been for only a short while.

She brushed back a tear impatiently. She didn't know what was wrong with her. She had always been emotional, but now, everything seemed so close to the surface. Too intense.

She looked up at Jeff. He was speaking into the cell phone, ignoring her. She could still see his magnificent chest where he hadn't bothered to button the Santa suit. He kept brushing back his sandy brown curls with his fingers, making her want to reach out and test to see if his hair really was as thick and soft as it looked. His eyes could melt a spinster's heart.

He was the kind of man a woman would dream about having an affair with . . . an adventurer who traveled around the world finding his photographs with his artist's vision and his artist's heart. A man who could sweep you off your feet.

A photographer with no roots—no security. A man Phoebe would only dream about, but never dare to make part of her life.

She wondered how long he would be able to work at Krueger's before that spirit inside him drew him away, back to his camera. Though Marshall always accused her of being too quick to judge people, Phoebe knew she had good instincts about these things. And she suspected it wouldn't be long before Jeff Cameron left his post here in search of foreign climes.

Jeff put down the phone. "That was Scott, my security

guy. Nelson just got here. He'll have us out of here in less than an hour." He looked steadily into her eyes. "Do you think you can make it that long, Phoebe?"

She took another long drink from the bottle. She closed her eyes, feeling the champagne fuel her courage, daring herself to say more. What difference could it possibly make? She'd already made a fool of herself with this man too many times to count.

"Call me Snow White."

There. That hadn't been so bad. A lightning bolt hadn't come down from the sky to annihilate her. She peeked open one eye and glanced up at him. "Please."

"Can you handle it, Snow White?"

"You have such a wonderful voice," she whispered. "So deep. I love the way you make it sound. Snow White, I mean." She realized she was starting to feel a little woozy. Was she drunk? "I asked my father once why he'd stopped calling me that. He told me I was a grown woman, much too sensible for silly nicknames."

She remembered how she'd wanted to cry when he said it, because she knew what he meant. She was sensible. Sensible Phoebe—not an actress, but a teacher. The kind of woman who would marry Marshall because he was Catholic, just like her. Because he had a good heart and loved her. Because he would save his money to buy a house and someday earn the post of principal.

Her parents had taught her these were the things that mattered. These were the things that made a good marriage.

Phoebe took another drink. She hated feeling like this, as if she were suddenly living someone else's life, a life she didn't want anymore.

"I'm going to ask you a question," she said, holding her bottle. "It's very personal—but I would like you to consider answering."

She licked her lips, telling herself she wanted to know the answer to this question—enough to embarrass herself

by asking it. And she knew Jeff with his artist's heart coul[
give her what she needed.

She glanced up, meeting his eyes, eyes that could turn [
simple image into art. "Tell me what it feels like to be i[
love?"

He shook his head. "I can't tell you whether or not t[
marry the guy."

"That's not what I'm asking. I take full responsibility fo[
my own decisions. I just want to know . . . I *need* to know
You see, I'm so afraid I don't . . ."

"That you don't love him?" he said, finishing the question when she couldn't.

This time, she fought her tears. She didn't want to b[
weak now. She didn't want to put her head in the san[
anymore. She was beginning to suspect that what she'd la-
beled as claustrophobia was just a good old-fashioned attack of nerves. She hadn't wanted to believe that she coul[
equate Marshall's demise with freedom. She didn't want t[
know there could be such ugliness inside her.

There came a long sigh from Santa Claus. "Snow White
you're going to break my heart if you keep looking at m[
like that."

"It's just that—"

"Yeah. I know." Jeff sat down beside her, resting his hea[
back against the paneling. "Hell, you make something that'[
so easy seem so incredibly hard."

He took the champagne bottle from her and drank a few
sips before handing it back. "Look, I can't speak for everyone. Maybe, for some people, love means getting to know
someone and growing to love them. But that wasn't how i[
was for me. I knew from the first time I saw her in school,
Maggie was special. I did everything I could to get her to
notice me . . . to ask her out. But when I kissed her, I knew
then for sure. Because it was like fireworks."

"Fireworks," she said, echoing the words. That's how
she'd always imagined love. Rockets. A kiss that would se[

off Fourth of July sparklers inside her head. "When I was fourteen years old, I went to church and I prayed—I begged God to make very certain I would fall in love only once. I didn't want to make any mistakes. I didn't want any false starts."

Jeff frowned. "Is that what's going on? You think you can't back out because of some vow you made as a kid? Do you really believe you had one shot and blew it?"

"I think I'm . . . committed."

"Let me tell you something, you aren't committed until you walk down that aisle and say 'I do.' And even then, if you don't have kids to think about, those ties can be pretty flimsy."

"No," she said, knowing in her heart it wasn't true. "When I marry, I'll marry for life."

He was silent after that. Perhaps it was the champagne, but it took her a moment to realize how her words might affect him—as if, even now, young as he was, he'd had his one chance at happiness and it had died with his wife.

"I'm sorry," she said. "I didn't mean—"

"I know what you meant."

He'd said it coolly. He wasn't looking at her anymore, and the dimples were gone.

He held all his pain dammed up inside him. He didn't want to talk about his wife's death, with Phoebe or anyone. But even without the words, she could see it—feel it. The way he held his shoulders, so stiff—his expression—she could guess at the ache in his soul.

She tried to think of something she might say to make things better, to ease that hurt. Empathy was something that came only too naturally for her. She wanted to make things right for other people.

But the only thing that came to mind was that he should *talk* about Maggie with someone—with her—no matter how much he wanted to fight it. Wasn't that what confession was about? Good for the soul?

Only, all her little tricks to coax him to talk had accom
plished exactly nothing. And so this time, she simply asked
"How did she die?"

She didn't think he would answer her at first. He wa
staring straight ahead, as if she hadn't even spoken. She
thought of trying to persuade him. But then she thought i
might be better if she just waited. If she let him decide fo
himself.

It almost surprised her when she heard him say, "She
died giving birth to our daughter. On Christmas. Three year;
ago. It was five o'clock in the morning and she died."

Phoebe closed her eyes, the words reaching past the cour
age of the champagne to form a painful lump inside he
chest. She couldn't imagine the conflicting emotions o
such a tragedy, how he might reconcile the joy of birth with
the devastation of his loss.

Without thinking, she reached out and grasped his fin
gers. "Oh, Jeff. I am so very sorry."

"You think life is made up of simple choices, right turn;
and left turns," he said, his voice low and monotone. He
wasn't looking at her as he spoke, but he hadn't pushed her
hand away. "You believe all you have to do is make the
right decision, marry or not marry." He turned to look a
her, his eyes very intent. "You are so afraid of making the
wrong choice, that your life can be ruined forever by tha
single decision. But that's not how life is. It's never tha
simple."

"Will you tell me about her? Please." Squeezing his fin
gers, she added, "I think it would help."

"Yeah. Yeah, I know you do. And you almost make me
believe it's true . . . which is so goddamned strange."

"You can try. Tell me."

His gaze never wavered. They both sat there in the ele
vator together, holding hands, looking at each other. And
then suddenly, it was so right. And she knew he felt it

too—how special the moment was. And she knew he would finally trust her.

"Maggie had myasthenia gravis," he said softly. "It's an autoimmune disease. Unfortunately her condition was complicated by other medical problems. She was in remission when we met, leading a pretty normal life for once. But she thought she couldn't get involved with anyone. She didn't think it would be fair because she couldn't promise me a future."

"But you didn't care," she said, knowing it was true.

"I told her she was crazy to live her life as if she were dying. I wasn't thinking marriage or anything—I was pretty much thinking with my dick. But I loved her. And I married her, when I figured out what was what."

"Did she die from the disease? Because of the baby?"

"Not in the way you mean. Sure, she wasn't supposed to get pregnant. The doctors told her it might incite her condition. But you see, I'd convinced Maggie that she shouldn't live her life always thinking she was sick. And when she really believed it, she wanted it all. Husband, children. A family."

She could see he was trying to hold back the emotions the memories brought. But his gaze never left hers. Her own throat tightened as she looked at him.

"I begged her not to do it. I told her we could adopt. But once Maggie got something in her head." He shook his head. "She told me it was an accident. Something about the diaphragm not being one hundred percent effective. I believed her." He smiled. "Most of the time, I believed her. She was something, my Maggie. She told me it was all my fault—that I had given her this thirst to lead a normal life. She told me a few moments of wonderfulness were better than a whole life of nothingness."

"She knew the risks, Jeff. She must have wanted a baby very badly." She watched as he closed his eyes.

"Yeah. Yeah, maybe. But it seemed so unfair. You see, it

wasn't myasthenia that got her. She came through the pregnancy with flying colors."

She could feel her breath catch in her throat, but she didn't make a sound. She just waited.

"It was a one in a million thing, a risk any woman takes when she gives birth." He opened his eyes again. "After she gave birth, she started bleeding. They couldn't stop it. Her veins collapsed. And it had nothing to do with the disease. She died of something very normal . . . just a one in a million complication you never expect."

He turned to her then. He reached up and touched her cheek. He brushed a tear from her face, a tear she hadn't realized was there. Then he started wiping away all the others streaming down her cheeks, using both hands.

"And I'm scared, Snow White. Because she gave me this beautiful child. A child that she wanted more than my love or life itself, and now—I'm afraid I'll never be there on my daughter's birthday. That it will always be a day I hide out with a bottle of Scotch and my anger at that God you believe in so much."

"Don't," she said to him, smiling through her tears, even as he kept brushing them off her cheeks. "Don't blame yourself. You gave Maggie such a gift, Jeff. One bad day—" she reached up and grabbed both his hands, squeezing them "—I think you're allowed that. Let your daughter celebrate Christmas and her birthday with her grandparents. If you give her every other day of your life . . . she won't hold one day against you."

"Her birthday—"

"Pick another day to celebrate it with her. Make New Year's special. And when she's older and she can understand . . . just tell her how you feel. You love her. That's what really matters."

The way he was looking at her, it did something to Phoebe. He'd reached a place so deep inside her, she didn't even know it existed.

And then he smiled, dimples and all, looking so incredibly beautiful, she thought no man had a right to smile like that.

"Maybe you're not so bad at that organization stuff," he told her.

Phoebe laughed, letting go of his hands. "I could give your briefcase another go."

"I might just let you."

"What's your daughter's name? Do you have any pictures?"

He pulled the briefcase over and, after a long search through the piles of papers, took out an envelope filled with photographs. "That's Kayla."

The pictures were exquisite. Not the normal childhood photos you see in albums. These were works of art. Some were black and white, using shadow and light to make the child they portrayed an angel. Others were in vivid color, showing a tow-headed little girl dressed up in a woman's dress flowing to her toes, a china cup held to her lips. In another, she was caught in the act of spinning, her arms held wide open, her face laughing up at the sun.

"She's beautiful."

"She's the best," he said with a father's pride. "And smart. She could talk like an adult by the time she was two. And no baby speech either, I mean with perfect diction. I think she's going to start reading soon."

"I wouldn't push that," she said, automatically falling into teacher mode. "You know, in Sweden, they don't even begin to teach children to read until the third grade, and they have the highest literacy rate in the world. You're very talented."

"Maybe." He was looking at her and not the photographs. "If I'm inspired."

She handed the pictures over reluctantly. For some reason, she wanted to keep them, as if she could somehow steal a little of their magic and make it part of her life. She grabbed up her champagne bottle instead, watching Jeff put the photographs back in the briefcase.

"I hope your father-in-law has someone in line to take over Krueger's when you leave," she said.

He frowned, turning back to her. "What's that supposed to mean?"

"You'll go back to your photographs soon."

"You have a crystal ball now, Snow White?"

"No, but I can recognize a right brain person when I see one."

He watched her with that penetrating stare that was so Jeff, his artist's eyes giving her the kind of look that made Phoebe feel as if he were seeing so much more than a dark-haired woman with shoulder-length curls who cried too easily.

He lifted her face up, his fingers feeling warm against her skin. Phoebe caught her breath. Her heart began beating so hard, she thought he must see it pounding there against the wall of her chest.

She had this incredible thought. *Please, let him kiss me.* And then, she thought she might faint.

But Jeff released her and took the champagne bottle. He drank a sip as he watched her. "Maybe you're right, Snow White. Maybe you're right."

In the security office on the third floor, three men sat around the telephone, now set on speaker mode. Each was perfectly silent, listening intently to the conversation taking place inside the elevator.

"Hell," they heard Jeffrey Cameron's voice blare from the speaker phone. "I left the phone on. God, if the battery is dead—"

The voice was suddenly cut off, Jeffrey Cameron having discovered his failure to properly disconnect the cell phone after his last conversation with Scott. But the three men in the security office had heard enough.

Nelson, an African American man with a receding hairline, was still dressed in his best suit, Scott having beeped him at his daughter's house. After a wonderful dinner of glazed ham, Nelson and his wife had been watching Trina and her husband set out the toys for their girls, his two granddaughters.

Nelson hadn't been in the best of moods when he'd arrived at Krueger's, but he had a soft spot for Jeff Cameron, a man he'd seen go through the worst nightmare imaginable when Maggie Cameron had died. And now, having eavesdropped on that touching moment, Nelson found himself wiping a tear from his eye, hoping the other guys hadn't seen it.

"I didn't know he was a photographer," Scott said.

"What did you think all those photographs hanging in his office were for, son?" Nelson asked, pushing aside his coat as he dropped down into the chair next to Jack's.

"The ones of the rhinos and lions? You're kidding. He took all those?" Scott asked, seeing a new dimension to his employer. Over the years, he'd never really thought about what Jeff Cameron had done before he'd taken over at Krueger's.

"A wildlife photographer," Jack said. "One of the best."

"Wow." Scott glanced back at the speaker phone. "But she's getting married," he said, completely dumbfounded by the softness he had heard in Cameron's voice. Scott had never known the details surrounding Maggie Cameron's death. But everyone at Krueger's knew how Jeff celebrated Christmas—with a bottle of Scotch.

Jack the security guard smiled. "Well, now. She might be getting married." He glanced over at Nelson, his hazel eyes gleaming. "Then again, she might not. What do you make of it, Nelson?" he asked his long-time buddy.

"I think I'm getting my tail over to the elevator to fix it."

"Nelson . . ." Jack grabbed the engineer's arm, stopping him from getting out of his chair. "It's Christmas morning. Don't you think that boy deserves something else to think about on this day?"

"You know something, Jack. You can be a real pain sometimes."

Both men turned to Scott sitting behind his desk, letting the head of security make the call. The younger man sighed. "Well, shoot. How could an hour . . . or two, hurt anything?"

Nelson shook his head. "It's probably my job if he ever finds out, but all right. I'll keep them in that elevator a bit longer."

All three men looked at each other. After a few seconds, each broke into a smile.

Five

Fifteen minutes after he'd made his incredible confession about Maggie's death, Jeff Cameron discovered another fact about Snow White.

She was a really bad drunk.

"So maybe it's not fireworks," she told him, sounding both weepy and angry. She waved the champagne bottle at him—a bottle that was now half-empty. "You said yourself it doesn't have to be like that for everyone. What about those arranged marriages? Some of them turn out just fine."

These were the pearls of wisdom that had been coming his way. Incredibly, she was trying to talk herself into going through with the wedding. But the more Jeff thought about it, the more he realized Snow White would never be happy if she did.

For the last fifteen minutes, he'd been scrambling through his brain for every bit of information he had on Marshall, and those first two hours, Phoebe had gone into excruciating detail about the man. The picture Jeff got was disturbing. Marshall was a manipulator, a man who—from what Jeff could gather—had romanced Phoebe's parents into pressuring her to marry him. A man who would willingly take away her dreams of Palenque.

"If you haven't noticed," Jeff said, jabbing his finger into her breastbone, "in the twentieth century, we're a little beyond arranged marriages."

Snow White swatted away his hand. "But the principle still stands. I could *learn* to love Marshall."

"Ah, for Pete's sake. Are you telling me that you're going to marry the guy knowing you *don't* love him?"

"I did not say that. You're making me all mixed up."

"That's damn well exactly what you said. You have to *learn* to love the guy. As in a future possibility."

"Well, I misspoke," she shouted, managing to raise her voice above Jeff's. She glanced down at the champagne bottle she was holding, staring at it as if she couldn't imagine how it got there. She blinked up at Jeff. "Am I slurring my words?"

She had in fact been slurring for some time now.

"Nah," Jeff said.

She looked at him suspiciously, then set the champagne bottle down on the floor. "It's just that I care very much about Marshall. We are entirely suited for each other."

"Look, Snow White. You can't just tick off a bunch of facts—Catholic, teacher, play duets on the piano—and say it's love."

"And why not?" she asked, once again raising her voice to match his. "Besides, you forgot that Marshall is loyal. Marshall is dependable. Do you think dependability isn't important?" She took her turn at jabbing Jeff in the chest. "I suppose you believe that just because a man is drop-dead gorgeous *that's* reason enough to fall in love? That being this really hunky guy is more important than being loyal—"

"Not to mention Roman Catholic. Hey, don't they require that for marriage licenses these days?"

"I suppose you would have me marry some artist type. Someone who bounds around to these incredibly wonderful places, snapping exotic photos, never knowing where his next meal check is coming from!"

"Not that it matters, but I don't remember asking you if you wanted to get married."

Phoebe fell silent. She turned perfectly red. And then, just as quickly, she lost all her color.

She didn't say a word. Not one word.

"Look," he said, sorry he'd embarrassed her by saying that last bit. "It just seems to me that this Roman Catholic, Chopin playing, gonna-be-a-principal guy isn't for you. I would bet that measly meal check I earned with my camera—" a check that had amounted to six figures a year "—that all those things you listed were dished up for you by Marshall."

She pursed her lips, refusing to look at him.

"You see!" Jeff said, now getting somewhere.

He told himself he wasn't trying to talk her out of the wedding because he wanted to clear the field for himself. Despite the fact that what was happening between them felt incredibly intimate, Jeff figured he hadn't lost all objectivity. He'd just known that stoic laundry list of love Phoebe kept spouting didn't sound like her. Hell, this was a woman who cried at the drop of a hat. Someone who could look inside your heart after knowing you only a couple of hours and find the words to help it heal.

"I'm right, aren't I?" Jeff asked. *"He's* telling you that you should marry because you share all these things in common. How long did it take the guy to talk you into this wedding, anyway?"

Again, no response.

He didn't quite know why he was pushing. *He* certainly wasn't drunk. But just the same, he said, "Is that how your life is always going to be? Marshall talking you into things. Like the Poconos?"

"Give me that phone." Her voice was so soft, he wasn't sure he'd heard her.

"Why?" he asked, suddenly suspicious.

"Give . . . me . . . the . . . phone."

She thrust her hand out, nailing him with this virulent stare. He reached into his briefcase and handed over the phone.

She punched out a number and waited, glancing back at him every so often as if any minute now she was going to take a swing at him.

"Marshall?" Instantly, her voice dropped into honeyed tones. Her expression softened, making her eyes almost glow. "It's Phoebe, pumpkin."

Jeff groaned. He dropped to the floor, holding his stomach. "Oh, man. Pumpkin? I'm going to be sick."

"Darling," Phoebe continued, doing her best to ignore Jeff. "There was a blackout a few hours ago. I'm trapped in the elevator at Krueger's. I've been in here since . . . I went shopping."

There was a pause. Phoebe wrinkled her brow. Jeff sat up, hope coming to life inside him. *Let him be a jerk about this. Let him be a real prick.*

"I needed to buy a few things, Marshall."

Another pause followed. This time, Phoebe pinched the bridge of her nose, as if she might be getting a headache.

"Well, I'm sorry I'm trapped in the elevator the night before our wedding. But believe me, Marshall, it was no design of mine—what? Have I been drinking?" She glanced guiltily at the champagne bottle. "Ahh, just a little. You see, I had this attack of claustrophobia—"

Jeff laced his fingers behind his head and leaned back against the paneling of the elevator. Oh, this was going to be good. He winked at Phoebe.

She turned away, whispering into the phone, "No, Marshall. It doesn't happen to me all the time, but since this is the first time I've been trapped all night in an elevator—"

Jeff watched Phoebe fall silent once more, obviously listening to Marshall on the other side of the line. He could in fact hear the buzz of Marshall's words blaring through the phone. *The guy must be yelling into the mouthpiece.*

An expression of pain darkened Phoebe's eyes. Slowly, her shoulders slouched forward; she leaned against the elevator wall, still listening to Marshall's tirade. As Jeff watched, the spark left her gaze as the hum of Marshall's anger reached Jeff where he was sitting.

Though Jeff couldn't make out the actual words, he could see their effect on Phoebe. She looked like something was dying inside her. How could this guy talk to her like that, knowing she was so sensitive? Who the hell did this guy think he was?

Before he could think better of what he was doing, Jeff rose to his feet. He grabbed the phone from Phoebe.

"Marshall, this is Jeff Cameron," he said, using his best imitation of an I'm-the-guy-women-go-for voice. "I'm the manager at Krueger's. And I'm happy to report that your utterly gorgeous fiancée is completely safe. In fact, I would say she has never been better. She did have a small attack of the jitters. Understandably. Marriage is such a big step. All those doubts to deal with the night before . . . well, you know. Luckily, we had a bottle of champagne—"

Phoebe snatched the phone from Jeff, staring at him with utter disbelief. He tried real hard not to smile.

"Marshall—yes, yes, Mr. Cameron is trapped in here with me. He was kind enough to give me the champagne to calm my nerves . . . No, Marshall, there's no one else in here with us . . . Of course he is not drunk. I didn't mean to make it sound as if we're having a party in here—for goodness sake, Marsh, listen to me!"

This time, Jeff couldn't stop his grin. He slapped his hands together as if dusting them off after a job well done.

Phoebe snagged his elbow just as he turned away.

"Marshall, I called to tell you I'm stuck in here, but the maintenance engineer is working on the problem as we speak." She was enunciating her words carefully now, looking at Jeff meaningfully. "And Marshall. I wanted you to know. I've been thinking real hard about this, and I don't want to go to the Poconos. I want to go to Palenque."

Atta girl, Jeff thought, seeing that spark return to her eyes. But then he had another thought. It came like a shock, unexpected and stinging. He realized he didn't want Snow White going anywhere with Marshall. Not to the Poconos . . . and not to Palenque.

Before he could analyze why, Phoebe frowned, the light in her eyes fading. She whispered into the phone, "I realize all the arrangements are made . . . No, of course not. I don't want to make your aunt and uncle feel as if we don't appreciate them offering their summer place. Marshall, I'm trying to tell you something, for goodness sake . . . Good. Thank you. Now, it's very important to me that we go to Palenque. It's a dream of mine, like your wanting to get married on Christmas . . . No, I will not come to my senses in the morning—well, maybe I've had an epiphany of sorts stuck in this damn elevator for three hours! . . . Yes. I'm glad. We'll speak in the morning."

She pushed the "end" button and handed the phone back to Jeff. She smirked and crossed her arms over her chest. The effect was ruined only by a very loud hiccup.

She thought she could do it, Jeff realized. She thought she could marry this guy and find happiness.

But Jeff didn't see things that way. Not anymore.

"That guy is taking you to the Poconos, Snow White," he said quietly.

She hiccuped again, then covered her mouth. She tried to stand regally, but lost her footing, almost dropping to the floor before Jeff steadied her. She brushed his hands away, then crossed her arms over her beautiful breasts and leaned one shoulder against the wall for support.

"You're wrong," she said. "You'll see. He just didn't know how important Palenque was to me."

Across town, in the hilly suburb of Altadena, Marshall Drummond was sitting in bed. He had broken out into a cold sweat.

All along, he'd feared this would happen. That Phoebe

would wake up one morning and change her mind about marrying him.

Panic surged through him. He threw his legs over the side of the bed and scrubbed his face with his hands. It had taken him three years to convince Phoebe Nichols to marry him. It had been a campaign he had set upon with the calculation of a four star general.

He'd always felt a little guilty about the guerrilla tactics he'd employed during their three-year courtship. He knew Phoebe had a soft heart—and he'd used that to his advantage, manipulating her by appealing to her sensitive nature. It hadn't taken long to realize that if he made it very clear he couldn't live without her, that his life would be meaningless if she weren't there beside him, Phoebe would accept his proposal. Phoebe, with her great heart, couldn't bear to be the source of anyone's misery.

And then there was her father, who loved Marshall. Her father had a great deal of influence over Phoebe—another man who knew how much she hated to be responsible for another's unhappiness.

But there was a part of Marshall that truly believed Phoebe and he were meant to be together. They both spoke several languages. They shared common values. Phoebe Nichols was intellectual, sensitive and nurturing. She was beautiful.

They were both Roman Catholic, for goodness sake.

And he wanted her. He'd wanted Phoebe Nichols from the first moment they'd been introduced at Bernstein's.

Marshall slipped his feet into leather mules he kept at his bedside. He started to pace, haunted by images of Phoebe drunk in that elevator. He could almost see the man with her, that manager from Krueger's, putting doubts in Phoebe's head when she was almost Marshall's wife.

He should have said he would go to Palenque. He shouldn't have yelled at her.

But he'd heard the hesitation in her voice. And he'd been angry.

Marshall glanced back at the telephone, picturing that mysterious man walking toward Phoebe, some Pierce Brosnan clone who would take her into his arms and seduce her, stealing her away after all of Marshall's hard work.

An incredible rage rose inside him with those pictures in his head, drowning out his better sense. His hands shaking, Marshall sat down on his bed and opened the nightstand drawer. A small personal telephone book lay inside. He searched for the number he'd jotted down just last week, one of many contacts he'd made to publicize Bernstein's annual music festival. He reached for the phone. He dialed.

He realized what he was doing was slightly unbalanced. As he listened to the phone ringing, he felt a little disassociated from his actions. He knew he was acting out of sheer desperation.

But he also knew that he couldn't lose Phoebe. He'd worked too hard to get her down that aisle.

"Mr. Holden? This is Marshall Drummond. From Bernstein's Academy? I'm so sorry to call you at this ungodly hour." Marshall knew Holden—a young reporter who looked absolutely bored with the possibility of writing up Bernstein's music program—would bite. "But I'd like to speak to you about a breaking story. It's happening right now, and I'm certain it's front page news."

Marshall waited patiently as Holden woke up enough to respond. Marshall's heart beat a mile a minute. He had only one thought echoing in his head: He was not going to lose Phoebe!

"I just heard from my fiancée. You won't believe this, but she's trapped in the elevator at Krueger's. Yes, the department store. And if you can imagine this, we're getting married in about six hours. That's right. A Christmas wedding. I'm on my way to give her moral support, but I thought this might make a good human interest story locally for the paper—not to mention an incredible tale for our grandchildren. The ceremony is set for ten A.M. at our Lady of Assumption, so it will be touch and go to see if we make it . . . well, I'm so pleased. I'll see you there."

Marshall hung up the phone, then reached for his phone book again. He remembered how cool the reporters had been when he'd called about the music festival. Well, he had quite a different story for them now.

He dialed again. He was going to fight for the woman he loved. And he knew for a fact—even if all else failed him—with enough reporters there to commemorate their upcoming nuptials, he could shame Phoebe into going through with the ceremony.

After finishing his calls, Marshall held his face in his hands. He was suddenly very cold. He reached for the robe he kept at the foot of the bed. Guerrilla tactics—that's how he'd always dealt with Phoebe. And, as always, he was just a little ashamed. But the media coverage would lock his hold on her. If it was in print, he knew Phoebe would stand by her word.

Tomorrow, they would be on their way to the Poconos as man and wife.

One last time, he picked up the phone. This time, he punched the numbers 911.

They all three heard the sirens.

But it wasn't until Scott brought up the paramedics that Jack and Nelson knew their goose was cooked.

The reporters turned up five minutes later, cameras flashing.

Now Scott stood beside Jack, his arms crossed over his chest as he listened to Marshall Drummond—the professed fiancé of the woman inside the elevator—continue his impromptu press conference in front of the cosmetic counter.

"This is equal to kidnapping!" he shouted. "Krueger's

never notified the police. They failed to contact me! I Phoebe hadn't called on that cell phone, I wouldn't ever know about this. Good Lord—" Drummond glanced meaningfully at Scott as the reporters either feverishly jotted down the man's every word or held a mini tape recorder up to his face. "She's been trapped in that elevator for over three hours!"

"I'm working on the problem," Nelson said to the fire chief as he pushed away the tape recorders now jammed in his face. "Really, Chief. Everything is under control."

"That is absolute poppycock!" Drummond said.

"Who the hell uses words like poppycock?" Scott whispered to Jack beside him.

Nelson shot Drummond a withering stare. "If this guy would just let me go down to the control panel to do my job, she'd get out of there a lot faster."

"And what have the people at Krueger's been doing for the last three hours, I ask! This is nothing short of kidnapping. I'm going to sue! Do you hear me? I'm suing!"

Several reporters snapped Drummond's picture as he threw his hands in the air in a dramatic gesture.

Scott shook his head, leaning closer to Jack. "You know. That guy is a prick."

Jack only smiled, watching Nelson lean his considerable bulk into the skinny Drummond fellow, backing Drummond away before Nelson skirted past the reporters and headed toward Scott and Jack.

Jack said, "I learned a long time ago, you don't pick a fight with Nelson."

They both watched as Drummond continued his soliloquy, the reporters closing their ranks as they huddled closer hanging on his every word. Nelson came to a steaming halt in front of Scott and Jack. He glanced down at his wrist watch, a determined expression in his brown eyes. "Five o'clock, right?" he asked Scott.

Scott stared up at the chaos of reporters setting up equipment and hovering over the fire chief, who now held court while Drummond took a breather. Scott nodded. "Mr. Cameron isn't going to be thinking about his wife's death on Christmas morning this year. Not if we can help it."

Nelson nodded once, then headed for the stairs. Scott looked up at Jack. "Not that it should matter, but on a scale of one to ten, how good-looking is this woman?"

Jack smiled. "Nine. Maybe nine and a half because she's young and I'm just an old geezer."

Scott grinned. "That'll do."

Six

Phoebe stared across the elevator at Jeff. He was sitting on the floor next to his briefcase, the Santa suit still unbuttoned halfway down his chest, making him look incongruously sexy in the red velvet. He'd been silent for an uncomfortably long period of time. Brooding, no doubt. And the way he kept glancing at her and shaking his head . . . she had the distinct notion that he wanted to say something to her, but was forcing himself to remain silent.

Phoebe huddled back against the elevator wall, feeling a little sick. She could just imagine what he would say.

"You're a wimp, Phoebe."

Yup, she thought. That's exactly what she thought he would say.

"You and I have been stuck in this elevator for almost four hours," Jeff continued, "talking over this wedding. We both know there's no way in hell you should go through with it."

"I thought you didn't want to give your opinion," she said.

"Let me stick my neck out here and say that it is very much my opinion that you are not ready to march down the aisle in—" he glanced at his watch "—six hours."

Phoebe could feel all that wonderful champagne start to sour in her stomach, the magic of its effervescence drifting out of her reach like so many bursting bubbles. She kept replaying her conversation with Marshall. She'd tried to be strong . . . to be like Maggie. But she wasn't Maggie. She was just a very drunk Phoebe Nichols.

"I took my Right Turn," she whispered, knowing in the deepest part of her soul the truth. She lacked the courage to back out now.

"Are we back to that again? You know, that stuff about right turns and left turns is about the nuttiest thing I have ever heard you say tonight. And believe me, that's saying a lot."

"Why are you yelling at me? This has nothing to do with you. Remember?"

"Because I can't stand to see someone make such a crock out of life." He jumped to his feet and walked over to drop down to one knee before her. "Listen to me. You get one shot at life. No one tells you to get ready, the end is coming. Maybe tomorrow, stepping off the sidewalk to cross the street, it could all be over. Be very certain you don't have any regrets, Phoebe," he murmured in a low, urgent voice. "Don't throw it all away because you think you need to make right turns."

"And will it make me happy to tell Marshall we shouldn't get married?" she asked, voicing out loud all her weaknesses, parading them out for Jeff to see as easily as she had her tears. "I'll be thirty years old next week. Don't you see? You were right when you said I don't have a lot of marriage proposals. I've had exactly one."

"Yeah. You have spinster written all over you."

"I'm serious," she said, rising to her knees to take him on. Only, the motion brought her nose to the level of his chest. And it was such a wonderful chest. All sculpted and tanned. It made it really difficult to think. She wondered if he spent a lot of time in the sun taking photographs.

She shook her head, trying to make sense of her scattered thoughts, to clear away the champagne haze. She forced her face up to his, tearing her eyes away from that marvelous expanse of chest. "Don't you understand? I always thought

I would be married by now. That I would have my house and my children. Haven't you heard about the biological time clock? What if I'm just expecting too much out of life? What if Marshall is as good as it gets?"

"Do you make this stuff up?" He grabbed her shoulders, giving her a little shake. "Look, life isn't like that—some crossroads where you make decisions that you have to live with for the rest of your days, even if they make you miserable. There's a million and one ways to get that family you want so much. Phoebe, listen to me. Life's full of pitfalls and riches, horrors and high points. It's all part of the process . . ."

He stopped. Their eyes met.

"You're thinking about your wife," she whispered, knowing it was true.

"I'm thinking I'm full of shit to be giving this kind of advice to you." He pushed his hand through his hair, a habit she was beginning to think was absolutely endearing. "Listen to me. 'Make the most of things.' 'Life is a process.' " He shook his head. "I sound like those people at the grief sessions after Maggie died."

"You're really angry with her, aren't you?"

His eyes searched deep into hers, making her part of the anger she sensed ripping through him. The pain. "Yeah. I guess I am."

"Because she chose having a baby instead of living the rest of her life with you?"

"I'm angry because she made me want it, too. The baby . . . the family. She made me believe we could beat the odds and have it all. And then, it turned out we couldn't. And she left me all alone, with only Kayla to take care of, wondering each day if I didn't sacrifice my wife to have her."

She reached up to stroke his face, needing to touch him. "You didn't even know she was trying to get pregnant. Can you really blame yourself because—after the fact—you were happy? Jeff, it must have been an awful decision for her. But I think I understand why she did it."

"Yeah?" For the first time, she saw a suspicion of tears in his eyes, making them shine with his anger. "You want to fill me in, because I never did."

She brushed her fingers across his cheek. She knew he wouldn't cry, and she wondered if he'd ever allowed himself that release. "Yes, you do," she said, her fingertips searching for places where his dimples would appear when he laughed. There. At the corner of his mouth. And here. "You said it yourself. All those years, she had to limit her life because of her illness. But you came and gave her a taste of what the future could be like . . . and she wanted more. She wanted it all. You gave her wings to fly away from her disease, to feel love—to feel life growing inside her. Can you imagine? She felt Kayla *moving* inside her. She knew and loved that baby, even before Kayla was born. I don't know why Maggie died, Jeff. But something tells me, you know in your heart, she died happy."

He still held her by her shoulders. Only, somehow his touch had gentled, becoming more of an embrace. She found herself leaning into his arms, coming closer so that she could almost rest her cheek on his shoulder.

"You're right. All her life, people only talked about Maggie's limits," he said gruffly. "She hated it. And I loved seeing that look of joy in her eyes when she finally let go of all of that. I *needed* to see that hope in her eyes."

He tilted Phoebe's face up to his. She knew she was on the verge of tears, but that he wouldn't mind this time. And the champagne made those emotions poignant, but distant, so that when she looked into his eyes, all she could think was: *Please. Let him kiss me this time. Just once, and I'll never ask again.*

"Sometimes, you just have to take chances," he whispered, talking about Phoebe now.

She shook her head. "But I'm not like you. I don't have

the strength to give people wings. I can't go off and take pictures for a living and never worry about where my next paycheck might come from, living day to day. I'm like an ant. I find my path. I need to know where I'm going."

"And then, one day, it all blows up in your face, and nothing makes sense anymore. And then what? What happens if your Right Turn brings you up against a brick wall?"

"I . . . I don't know."

"Trace your steps back," he murmured, coming so close. "Look around. You may have more options than you think."

He was so beautiful. So earnest. For an instant, she tried to believe in the things he said. But she thought she was too drunk to make that kind of decision right now. She had to wait and decipher the complicated emotions coursing through her.

She pushed away from the temptation of his arms and returned to her corner. She thought about taking another drink of the champagne, but rejected the idea. It was all slipping away from her anyway, the good feelings, slowly turning into a dull ache at the back of her head. Instead, she reached for the Krueger's bag. She took out the black lace gown, slipping the coolness of the silk through her fingers.

It was so beautiful, the nightgown. Daring and provocative in a way that she could only dream of being. And she didn't think she would ever wear it.

She twisted the gown in her hands and closed her eyes. "Would you kiss me?" she whispered.

When Jeff didn't respond, Phoebe opened her eyes, wondering what she might find. Would he be appalled . . . or just a little tempted?

She found only that he was staring at the gown in her hands. She didn't know why she did it, perhaps it was the champagne—or perhaps she blamed too much on the champagne. Regardless of the reason, she slid the gown up, fitting the spaghetti straps to her shoulders and hugging the black lace and silk so it molded to her body.

His eyes turned impossibly dark. No one had ever looked at her like that . . . with such obvious hunger.

"I don't think this is a good idea," he said, his voice suddenly hoarse.

Phoebe rose to her knees, still holding the silk against her. "I just thought. In the last three years, I've only kissed one man." She stood and stepped toward Jeff. "And once I marry him, I'll never be able to kiss anyone else again." Very slowly, she raised her hand and did what she'd been dreaming of doing all night. She placed her palm on his chest where the suit lay opened, allowing herself to feel the warmth of his skin. "And I think this is my last chance. Please. Will you kiss me?"

He closed his eyes. When he opened them again, there was a fire burning inside his gaze. "Yes. I'll kiss you. But I'm going on record. This is a really big mistake."

Very gently, he pulled her to him. She didn't close her eyes, as she always did with Marshall. She kept staring up at his face, seeing that he, too, was keeping his eyes open. She dropped the silk gown and placed both her hands on his chest so that one hand felt only the rich fabric of the velvet suit, but the fingers of her other hand brushed against hot skin, feeling the firm muscles and the curling chest hair.

His mouth inched toward hers. He grinned, showing those delectable dimples. "Are you sure? There's still time to back out."

She shook her head, closing her eyes as she brought her mouth to his.

Fireworks, Jeff thought. Fourth of July . . . and then some.

He'd known it was going to be like this with Snow White—he'd worried it would be like this.

He would have given anything in the world for it to be like this.

He buried his hands in the dark curls of her hair, forcing her mouth firmly against his. She tasted like champagne. And life—all the living he'd denied himself these last years with his grieving.

When she'd pulled that black gown out of her bag, he'd known he was in trouble. He just hadn't realized how much until she'd fitted it up to the curves of her body and looked up at him, her expression filled with an incredible expectation.

Now all that expectation was swirling around them, sparking into unbelievable bursts of fireworks, heating up their bodies with its sizzle and pop. Making them both burn and explode as their mouths discovered each other.

Fireworks. Like he'd never thought would be part of his life again.

She still had her eyes closed when he pulled away. That luscious pink mouth curled in a smile of pure satisfaction. She blinked her eyes open.

"You're a very good kisser," she whispered.

He nodded, because that's what he'd expected her to say. Something cute and naive. And meaningless. Hiding from what was really going on. But he wouldn't let her hide. Not this time.

"Is that all you have to say?" he asked. "That I kiss well?"

She looked mildly surprised. And then she murmured a soft, "Oh." She smiled again. "Thank you. Very much."

Jeff shook his head, his fingers once more curving around the back of her neck to draw her to him. "I can see this is going to take the sledgehammer approach."

His mouth opened over hers, his tongue coaxing until she moaned and fell into the rhythm of the kiss. He realized that he had probably set himself up for this kind of crash and burn. He hadn't been with a woman since Maggie. He had shut those needs deep inside himself to the point of letting himself starve, so that when he kissed Phoebe— Phoebe of the tears, Phoebe of the Right Turns, Phoebe of the dreams—there had been too much hunger.

But even as his hands caressed her, drawing her to the floor of the elevator, lowering her beneath him as he covered her body with his, he knew that was a lie.

This had nothing to do with grief or need.

This was the kind of kiss you waited a lifetime to experience.

Fireworks.

It was a simple thing to unbutton her dress. She even helped him, slipping her arms through the sleeves, offering her nakedness to him as she twined her arms around his neck and pressed her heart against his. He lay on top of her, almost startled by how wonderfully her tiny body fit against his. *So right. So right.* He kissed the strap of her bra off her shoulder, smiling as he smelled the lilacs.

"Do I need to make love to you in this elevator," he whispered against her mouth, "or do you get the message?"

She seemed to wake up with his words. And then she was scrambling out from under him. He sighed, knowing this was coming, too. When he moved away, she shot up, ramrod straight.

"Ohmigod." She stared up at him as if she was seeing him for the first time, then glanced down at her dress pooling around her hips. "OH MY GOD!"

"I believe this is where I came in."

But she was shaking her head, holding her hands up as if she might somehow ward him off. "No," she said, crawling back, away from him. "No, no, no."

"No, what?" he asked, following her, prowling forward as he stalked her on hands and knees. A man on a mission. "No wedding at ten o'clock?" He snapped the elastic strap of her bra, the only thing she was wearing from the waist up. "Because this is what I'm thinking."

Snow White covered up, clutching her dress against her. "But I can't marry *you*. You're a photographer, an artist. Living hand to mouth. Never knowing what tomorrow will bring, much less which continent you're going to be on."

Just a little irritated by her characterization of him, he said, "Not that I'm asking, but for the sake of argument, let me point out that I am the manager of a very successful department store."

"No," she said, stabbing her hands into the sleeves of her dress as she shrugged it back on. "Oh, you may be a store manager now, but soon enough, you'll go back to your camera." Her eyes met his for the first time since their kiss. "Don't you realize the way you look at me?" she whispered. "I can already see the photographs you're conjuring in your head."

"So you're saying I'm unreliable?" As she fastened the buttons of her gown, he undid them just as quickly. He smiled, because she didn't even notice.

"Oh, very, very unreliable."

"Again, let me just point out—for argument's sake—that if you do marry Marshall, we're not even going to date, much less marry."

Finally realizing what he was doing with her buttons, she slapped his hands away. She kneeled up before him. "But I don't want to date you! I don't even want to be near you." She looked around the elevator. "I need to get out of here. I need to get out of here now."

But he took her hand, and laced their fingers together. She just stared at their twined fingers, mesmerized as he pulled her back into his arms.

"You're just scared. Which is okay. I was scared, too. And I got over it," he said, rolling down to the floor, tucking her beneath him as his mouth covered hers.

She melted. Just melted. It made him smile as he kissed her, enjoying the hot taste of her tongue against his. His palm reached up and covered her breast under her dress, playing with the lacy rim of her bra. She wore a pink bra. Somehow, he'd thought Phoebe was the kind who wore only white. And then just as suddenly, he saw her in so many other colors. Yellow, ice blue . . . a black lace nightie.

She blinked her eyes open again. "This is just sex. It fizzles out." She bit her lip to keep back a moan as he stroked the tip of her breast, making the nipple reach up for his touch. "Everyone knows you can't base marriage on sex."

"Well, sex just happens to be my favorite basis for a relationship." He nibbled on her ear. "And I promise, Snow White. It's not going to fizzle out."

"I can't make a life decision based on a kiss," she nearly yelled at him.

"Hmm." His hand crept up to her bared shoulder, rounding the skin with his palm, once again easing her sleeve down her arm. His mouth brushed against her neck. "Then I better try harder."

She slapped his hands away. "Stop that. I can't think straight when you touch me."

There was a loud banging, like doors opening. The elevator seemed to rock a bit. From afar, Jeff could hear a voice calling. The sound of it came winding down from the elevator shaft above them. It reverberated into one word, echoing over and over plaintively, until it came in loud and clear.

"PHOEBE!"

Snow White gasped. She stared up at Jeff. "It's Marshall!"

"You know, sir, it's really not safe to hang over the elevator shaft like that," Scott said in a slow drawl, really tempted to give the guy's rear a little shove with his foot. "Maintenance is down at the main switch. The elevator could start up any minute now."

"I'm not holding my breath," Drummond said snidely. He had bullied the firemen now standing around the elevator shaft until they'd finally conceded and forced the elevator doors open just to shut him up.

"PHOEBE!" he yelled down the elevator shaft once more. "It's Marshall, darling. Hold on! I'm going to get you out."

Scott glanced at his watch. Casually, he stepped over to Jack. "Ten to five."

Nelson had radioed Jack some time ago, telling them that he'd found the problem. A couple of loose connections, cables shaken loose when the elevator had slammed to a stop with the emergency brake. Nelson had already reattached the wires and was ready to reset the elevator. Now, he waited at the lower level, his hand on the main switch.

They'd decided on five o'clock as the exact time to flip the switch.

It was almost as if the fiancé could smell their conspiracy. Drummond had looked at each of them with suspicion, accusing them of keeping his "Sweet Phoebs" locked away with their lecherous boss. Scott was almost certain he'd used the word lecherous. In the end, Drummond had settled on regaling the press with torrid descriptions of his love for his fiancée, and the years they had planned for this blessed wedding. Now, he was yelling his fool head off down the elevator shaft, no longer content to wait.

The fire chief came up, pulling Drummond away from the opened doors. "Sir. I think it's best if you wait back here. I've checked with the maintenance engineer. Everything seems under control now. We don't want to add any accidents to the event."

"But she's down there. She could be hurt," he said, watching the elevator door close.

"We've been in constant communication by cell phone with Mr. Cameron and your fiancée," Scott said. "No one is injured."

"Can I call her now?" Marshall asked.

"Unfortunately," Jack said from beside Scott, "the phone battery appears to be dead."

Keeping a straight expression, Scott echoed the lie. "Stone dead."

Marshall took his wire-rimmed glasses off and fastidiously cleaned the lenses for the fifth time in ten minutes. He then carefully folded his handkerchief into squares before placing it neatly in his pocket. "How much longer will this take?" he whined.

Scott glanced at his wristwatch. He caught Jack's eye. They both knew Nelson was prepared to pull the switch at exactly five o'clock.

"Any minute now," Scott whispered.

Seven

Meanwhile, back in the elevator.

Jeff paced across the floor. "So you're telling me, your husband being Roman Catholic is more important to you than having great sex together? Boy. Are your priorities screwed up!"

"Will you listen to yourself?" Phoebe argued back, dogging his steps, something that was a little difficult to do since the elevator was smaller than most walk-in closets. "You're going to build an entire relationship on having the 'hots' for someone?"

"At the moment, it looks like I'm building shit here."

"Keep your voice down."

"Why?" he asked, turning on her savagely, feeling a little desperate since he'd heard that voice calling her name down the elevator shaft. "Are you afraid Marshall might hear me?" Then, raising his voice, "Are you scared Marshy might find out I have half your clothes off and that we almost did it on the floor of the elevator?"

"Why are you doing this? You don't even want me!"

He grabbed her wrists and pulled her flush against him. "Sure, I don't want you." Taking her hand, he placed it very purposefully over his erection. "Like hell, I don't want you."

"That's just sex!"

"Oh, no, Snow White. I'm not going to let this be easy for you. Remember what I told you?" He cupped her face in his palms. "Fireworks," he whispered, lowering his mouth to hers. "Tell me you don't feel them right now."

He kissed her as if his very life depended on it, and he thought it just might. The photographs in his head no longer focused on Phoebe's beauty . . . they had shifted to more intimate portraits of her in his arms. Phoebe naked in his bed. Phoebe holding Kayla . . . loving him and Kayla both. And he remembered that once, before they had married— when Maggie still thought only about the possibility of death and the limits of her disease—she had made him promise that he would remarry. And she had asked only one thing of him. Smiling, she had said, "Find someone wonderful."

Phoebe was wonderful. She tasted wonderful; she smelled wonderful. She kissed wonderfully. And she would love wonderfully, with all her heart. These things he knew about her as his mouth caressed hers and they heated up their own personal fireworks, making them burst into a shower of sparks. He'd been called a wizard with a camera. And just as surely as he knew the photographs he snapped would develop with his own special sorcery, he recognized that he held magic in his hands. And he wanted it forever.

"What about shared priorities?" she protested against his mouth. "Being like-minded."

"Honey, you have it ass backwards," he said, continuing their kiss.

He was lost, totally and completely. In the smell of her, the taste of her, the feel of her. And the fireworks just burned incredibly hotter, bringing those images in his head into greater focus. Making him want it all again. Making him want love. Phoebe's love.

I'm in love. He pulled away, looking down at her dreamy expression, her closed eyes and the lush pink of her lips. He threaded his fingers through her shoulder length curls, envisioning himself doing it every day for the rest of his life. He'd always thought of love as something automatic—

instinctual—like the instant you captured an image on a frame. He hadn't thought it would ever happen again, and yet . . .

He was in love with a woman who could possibly be getting married in a few hours. To another man.

"You can't marry him, Phoebe."

But she was shaking her head. "Love isn't like the things you said. It's not an instant thing. It can only come from time spent together, knowing each other. It's like nurturing a seed, watching to see if it will blossom. If it's white hot . . . it can burn out."

"And if it doesn't?" he asked, brushing his thumb across her mouth.

"Are you saying you love me?"

"Phoebe, I can tell you that I love you . . . but I know enough about you to believe you won't trust those words." He held her tighter, speaking from his heart. "Isn't it enough that there's something here between us . . . something that deserves a chance?"

"You're asking me to ruin Marshall's life, back out of my wedding, for a man I've known only a few hours? This will never work out!"

"And if next year we're standing in this elevator as man and wife?"

"You can't promise me that—"

"So nothing is certain in this life!" he said, raising his voice. "Boy, is that a lesson I learned the hard way. Well, maybe it's time for you to learn the same lesson. That out there, in all your security, Marshall can't promise he'll make you happy . . . that your life won't be endless trips to his aunt's time-share in the Poconos."

With a moan, Phoebe pulled away. She sat down on the floor, hugging herself. "I wish I wasn't drunk. Aren't you ashamed of yourself? Taking advantage of a drunk woman?"

He slid down beside her. "Are you? Drunk, I mean?"

She shook her head. "I don't know. Nothing seems to be

making much sense right now." She looked at him. "I'm hoping it's the champagne and not the fact that I'm losing my mind."

He took her hands in his. "Phoebe, you asked for a sign from God—what if this is it? What if that's why you were trapped in here with me? On Christmas, my wife died. Maybe, just maybe, God is giving a guy like me a second chance. Something good to remember on Christmas. Something to bring back the joy."

"Now you believe in God?" she whispered.

"I don't know what I believe. But you have to give us a chance, Phoebe." He pulled her into his arms, his mouth easing over hers as they slipped to the elevator floor. "Give us a chance."

Standing before the main control panel, maintenance engineer Nelson Barkley glanced at his wristwatch. At the stroke of five, he flipped a switch, smiling as he saw the light indicators show that the elevator was slowly rising to the first floor.

He took a deep breath and said a small prayer.

Inside the elevator, Phoebe and Jeff lay in each other's arms, completely lost in a blaze of fireworks.

"Jeff?" Phoebe whispered against his mouth. "Jeff, I think I just felt the earth move."

"For me, too, baby," he moaned back. "For me, too."

Huddled outside the elevator door, the camera crews and reporters jumped to alert. The lights above the door showed the elevator would arrive momentarily. They grouped around the door, reporters and firemen, each trying for a better view.

Pushing them aside, Marshall Drummond made his way to the front, shouting for the crowd to give him room. He patted the perspiration from his forehead with his handkerchief, then waited anxiously. Some of the reporters focused their lenses on Drummond's face, trying to capture the exact moment when he would see his beloved fiancée.

In the back of the crowd, Scott and Jack waited. They glanced at each other just as the elevator door chimed.

Together, they turned to watch the elevator door open in a hushed whisper.

Immediately, the flashes of cameras spotlighted the couple inside the elevator. They were on the floor, the woman's dress hiked up to her hip, one sleeve dripping off her shoulder to expose a lacy pink bra. The man, wearing a very rumpled Santa suit, looked up from his position covering the luscious female body beneath him. He appeared slightly disoriented.

Catching sight of the lone man wearing glasses and a cardigan standing in front of a bank of reporters, Santa had only one thing to say.

"Oh, shit."

"Phoebe?" The name came out as a feeble murmur from Marshall's lips, barely audible over the clicking of cameras.

The woman with Santa seemed to slip out of her dreamlike state. Her eyes widened, showing shock—quickly followed by utter mortification.

"Marshall?" She shot up, ramming her head into Santa's chin. "Ohmigod, Marshall!"

At that moment, Santa lunged to his feet. He hit the "close door" button to the elevator. The door slid shut.

The cameras continued to click, this time focusing on Marshall. He turned slowly to face the crowd. And then he fainted.

"Paramedics!" one of the reporters shouted.

As a fireman pressed through the crowd, Scott and Jack

made their way to Drummond's side. They both dropped
down beside the prone figure.

"Is he going to be all right?" Scott asked anxiously.

"He'll be fine," the fireman said, breaking open a capsule
and waving it under the man's nose.

Marshall sputtered awake. Scott swallowed the knot in
his throat as he watched Drummond sit up. After a quick
nod from Scott, Jack stood up.

"Okay, folks. Show's over. Give the man some air," Jack
said, herding the reporters away from Marshall.

Watching Drummond moaning into his hands, Scott almost felt sorry for the guy. But then be remembered Drummond had threatened to sue Krueger's, that he had brought
the media here in the first place. The architect to his own
humiliation.

"If you don't mind," Drummond said pointedly, sounding
like his old sour self.

"No problem," Scott said, glad to get away.

He found Jack arguing with reporters, trying to drive
them out of Krueger's. Letting the fire chief take over, Jack
glanced at Scott and made his way to a private corner. Scott
met him there.

"Maybe this wasn't such a good idea," Jack said, looking
over to Drummond still sitting on the floor.

"But then again." Scott glanced down at his watch. "It's
fifteen minutes after five."

Jack broke into a grin. Scott raised his hand shoulder high.

"Merry Christmas, Jack," Scott said.

Jack slapped the security chief a high five.

Outside Krueger's, one of the reporters slipped a film
roll out of his camera. Beside him, a reporter from a rival
news agency said, "You know, this is turning out to be a
pretty good story."

Eight

Keeping his finger jammed against the "close door" button, Jeff turned to look at Phoebe. She was sitting on the floor of the elevator, staring straight ahead.

"Are you okay?" he asked.

She shook her head. "No. I am most definitely not okay. But I'm sober. Oh, boy, am I ever sober."

She dropped her face into her hands. Her shoulders started to shake. He thought she was crying. But then he realized she was laughing.

"Phoebe?"

"I'm sorry," she said, laughing harder now. "I know I shouldn't be laughing. This is so inappropriate—but I can't help it. I just had this really funny thought. You're dressed like Santa Claus." And then the tears started, filling her eyes as the hysteria of her laughter transformed into grief and regrets. "You're suppose to ask me if I've been naughty or nice." The tears began in earnest, slipping silently down her cheeks. "Oh, Jeff."

"Phoebe." He reached for her, drawing her into his arms. "Come here."

He hugged her with one arm, leaning his head against hers. He just let her cry, knowing she needed to. After a while, she stopped trembling.

He kissed the top of her head. "Was that so bad?" he asked, sensing the storm was over.

"Yes," she said, wiping away her tears. "That stunk." She

looked up at him. "This isn't me, Jeff. A woman who hides out in the bathroom of Krueger's. Who buys black negligees and champagne bottles, then makes out with a perfect stranger while her fiancé waits outside the elevator doors." She shook her head. "This just isn't me."

He held her tighter, whispering, "Are you so sure?"

She sighed. "I'm not sure about anything anymore. Ever since I was little, I had my whole life mapped out. And now—now I don't know what to do next." She glanced up at Jeff and whispered, "I keep thinking, what if after you get to know me, you don't like me? A woman who cries all the time . . . a prissy schoolteacher who wants to organize your briefcase."

"Shh. Phoebe." He cupped her face in his hands. "You had so much faith when you asked God for your sign—you even thought he would blackout all of Pasadena for you. Have a little faith now."

She sniffed, brushing away her tears. "It's just so hard to believe that someone as wonderful as you could be meant to love me."

"Ah," he said, kissing the top of her head. "Now I get it. The martyr thing. Boy, you Catholics. Well, let's see. Maybe if you spend the rest of your life bringing me breakfast in bed, darning my socks, fattening me up on gourmet dinners—and let's not forget wearing really sexy clothes when you're serving them—"

She punched his arm, making him laugh. She curled up against him. "What about Marshall? I've hurt him terribly."

He tipped her face up to his once more. "Or just maybe you saved him from a whole lot more hurt."

She bit her lip, then nodded. Jeff granted one last kiss of reassurance, sending up his own silent pleas to Phoebe's God that when she stepped out of the elevator, no amount of guilt or badgering from Marshall could change her mind.

"Are you ready?" he asked.

Phoebe nodded. She stood as she wiped the last of her

tears. After she fixed her dress, she took a deep breath. "Ready."

The doors opened. Marshall was waiting outside.

He was leaning against the wall, his hands tucked into his pockets. He was dressed in what Phoebe considered his uniform, Docker pants and a cardigan sweater over a button-down shirt. She'd given him that particular sweater for his birthday. It was a lovely light blue that matched his eyes.

Phoebe stepped out of the elevator. She could see a handful of reporters being kept back by a fireman and three other men. A camera flashed in her direction. Phoebe recognized Jack, the security guard she'd spoken to earlier, as he grabbed the photographer's camera, threatening to expose his film, and anyone else's, if they didn't let up.

Phoebe turned toward Marshall. "I am so sorry—"

He covered her mouth. Grabbing her hand, he pulled her away from Jeff and the elevator, guiding her to a secluded corner away from the press.

"Listen to me, Phoebe. Listen very carefully," he said in a feverish voice she didn't recognize. "I am prepared to overlook what's happened here tonight. I can understand you were scared in that elevator . . . drunk. That you weren't yourself."

"Marshall, I'm afraid I was very much myself. And whether I was drunk or not, I knew what I was doing."

Marshall clutched both her arms, holding her too tightly. "I am not going to let you throw away three years on some pre-wedding jitters snafu—"

Before he could say anything more, Phoebe threw her arms around Marshall and hugged him tight. She whispered, "Please, don't try to fix this. We *can't* fix this. I am so sorry."

Slowly, Marshall's arms rose. His hands hovered over her back, then settled gently around her waist. "Phoebe," he told her. "We were so perfect for each other."

But Phoebe shook her head. "No, Marshall." She stepped back, knowing she owed him at least the backbone to look him in the eye. "You can't make a list—Catholic, both teachers—and say it makes a marriage."

His eyes narrowed behind his glasses, his expression growing ugly. "But a few hours making out on the floor of an elevator can?"

But Marshall's words had the opposite effect from what he'd intended. Almost without willing it, Phoebe's gaze found Jeff. He was still in the Santa suit, all rumpled, looking absolutely adorable. And his eyes were filled with all his love and all his fears.

She looked at Marshall. "I don't know if you can understand this, but I think God wanted me to give someone back their joy for Christmas."

Even as she said the words, she knew in her heart she spoke the truth. She realized that Jeff in his Santa suit had never been in that elevator to give her advice about marrying Marshall. God had put him there to give her a choice. *Left, or right, Phoebe?*

Suddenly, she didn't need assurances or promises. She wanted to reach out and grab for the adventure of it all.

She straightened his sweater, pressing it neatly against his shoulders as she had done so many times in the past. "I think you knew, Marshall," she said, speaking the truth for him. "I think we both knew."

She took a couple steps back and wrapped her arms around her waist. "Don't hate me," she whispered. "Unless you really need to. Then it's okay."

And then, she left.

Marshall watched Phoebe walk away. Don't hate me, she'd said.

Boy, he wanted to.

He rammed his hands into the pockets of his trousers,

trying to fire up that enmity she had warned against. The problem was, he *couldn't* hate Phoebe. It was impossible to hate a woman whose very vulnerabilities included a big heart—one he'd tried to use to his gain. And he had to admit, maybe he deserved his humiliation, bringing the press here, trying to manipulate her one last time.

But still, it hurt.

He heard someone clear their throat. "Excuse me."

Marshall turned, unexpectedly finding a woman standing behind him. She was an attractive blonde with a bombshell figure almost hidden behind what looked like army fatigues, a khaki T-shirt and baggy pants. She'd even tucked her pants into chunky black shoes, the kind a marine sergeant might wear.

"Want a cigarette?" she offered, holding out a pack of Camels.

Good Lord, was that a tattoo on her wrist? "I don't smoke."

She grimaced. "I'm trying to give it up myself." Taking one last puff of her cigarette, inhaling for all she was worth, she blew out the smoke through her nostrils, then tossed her cigarette to the floor. She ground it out beneath her shoe.

She kept staring at him. She had these pretty eyes—golden brown, almost the yellow of topaz. She looked as if she wanted to say something.

He realized she must be one of the reporters. A woman with enough tenacity that the security guard hadn't managed to hustle her off with the others.

"I'm sorry," he said, his voice clipped with anger and hurt, "but if you want a comment of some sort, I really don't feel up to—"

"No," she said. "I just thought . . . well . . . that was kinda tough. What just happened. Been through one of those myself. Only, my guy just forgot to show up, and I was enough of a schlock to wait five hours at City Hall with a wilting bouquet." She paused. "I know it can hurt."

She watched him with an unblinking stare, waiting. As if in slow motion, his vision seemed to zoom in on her face. There was almost this aura about her, like a shining light.

Turn left.

Marshall shook his head. He glanced around. He could have sworn—

Turn left!

There it was again. This little voice inside his head. Only he hadn't a clue what it could mean.

And then he recalled Phoebe's Philosophy of the Crossroads. What had she told him? Something about right turns and life choices?

He hadn't really paid that much attention. In fact, he'd developed a terrible habit of tuning Phoebe out. *A mistake, that.*

"Hey, you want a cup of coffee or something?" The blonde in fatigues shrugged. "A shoulder to cry on?"

She was really quite lovely, if you didn't count the tattoo and the clothes. And it was nice for her to be so concerned.

"I should call my mother," he said without thinking. He felt himself turn beet red, knowing he sounded like a momma's boy, a little worried he might be exactly that. "I should tell her to call the guests," he added to explain.

She looked at her wristwatch. It was huge and black and looked like it could give you the hour in three time zones. "Kinda early to start calling people."

"Yes. You're right. There's plenty of time."

She smiled again, pulling a lock of her sleek page boy behind her ear—an ear that wore no less than four earrings. "How about that coffee?"

"What's your name?" he asked.

"Sally, but everybody calls me Sal."

"Sal, you're not Roman Catholic are you?"

She raised both her brows. "Sal Bronstein. I'm Jewish. That's why I'm here. The guy you called wanted to celebrate Christmas with his kids."

Marshall smiled, feeling better for the first time that night.

"Not Catholic? Well, that's at least a start," he said, taking her hand.

"He hates me," Phoebe said against Jeff's chest.

Jeff was holding her, having listened to what had happened between her and Marshall, trying to help her sort out her feelings, her guilt . . . and the sense that she'd just been run over by a Mack truck.

Out of the corner of his eye, he caught sight of Marshall. Unbelievably, the guy was walking with some blonde toward the exit, smiling down at her. As Jeff watched, reporters broke past the security guards and followed Marshall as he set his hand to the middle of the woman's back and guided her out the doors.

"Something tells me he'll get over it," Jeff said.

Phoebe sighed. "Now what do we do?"

"I want you to come home with me." He brushed her hair from her cheek and kissed the top of her head. "Meet my daughter. Eat Christmas dinner."

Phoebe smiled up at him, that wonderful curl of her lips that could turn him completely inside out. "I'm afraid I have a few phone calls to make. A lot of people are going to be very disappointed in me—starting with my own mother and father. But after that, I would love to," she said softly. "Very much."

He kissed her mouth, stealing that smile inside himself, thinking of what it was going to be like to make love to her and wake up next to her every morning, her arms and legs entangled with his. To have Kayla run into their room and jump on their bed. To make them a family.

It was something he really looked forward to. Something he could see so clearly in his head. Like a photograph.

"Well, then, why don't I tag along with you and go to your place," he said, grabbing up the Krueger's bag. He showed her the champagne bottle and the negligee nestled inside. He winked. "No sense in letting these go to waste."

From the pocket of his suit, he took out his Santa hat and beard, having stashed them there earlier. He put both of them on and lowered his voice. "After all, you never did answer the question."

Phoebe looked like she was doing her best not to laugh. He liked that . . . seeing her happy again, knowing that with time, she would be okay.

"Don't tell me," she said coyly, trying to bite back a smile. "You want to know if I've been naughty or nice?"

He grinned, flashing his dimples. "If I'm lucky, Snow White. You'll be both."

Epilogue

One year later, the headline Christmas morning read: *Storybook Wedding . . . In An Elevator?*

Pasadena, Ca—Looking for a truly unique place to set your wedding? Well, look no farther than your friendly neighborhood department store elevator. That's what Jeffrey Cameron of San Marino and Phoebe Nichols of Altadena did. Exactly one year from the day they were first trapped inside the elevator at Krueger's department store for five harrowing hours, Jeffrey Cameron and Phoebe Nichols returned to that same elevator to tie the knot. The ceremony was held on Christmas morning inside—you guessed it, folks—the elevator. A religious ceremony will take place this Saturday at Our Lady of Assumption Catholic Church.

Acting as best man was the good sport who lost the lady just one day before their own marriage was to take place. But the ill-fated groom isn't shedding any tears. He is now an engaged man himself, to one of our own reporters, the woman covering the story the night of the elevator incident!

Jeff Cameron lost his first wife due to a one in a million complication during childbirth. He believes it was divine intervention that brought him and Phoebe together in that elevator. "God's way of giving me back my faith in him and in life," he said during an interview. He added that Phoebe believes God blacked out all of Pasadena to get them together. "So I guess we owe the town an apology."

Jeff recently retired as manager of Krueger's, a business

owned in part by his family. He will pursue his previous career of free-lance wildlife photographer. Phoebe, who speaks three languages and is learning a fourth, plans to travel along as an interpreter for her husband. After their honeymoon, the couple will be heading to Kenya, taking Jeff's four-year-old daughter with them into their adventures in the bush.

The happy twosome are planning an extended honeymoon in Palenque.

ABOUT THE AUTHORS

Fern Michaels is the beloved author of over thirty bestselling novels, including the TEXAS series, the upcoming VEGAS series, and the *New York Times* bestselling Zebra romances, *Dear Emily* and *Wish List*. She lives in Summerville, South Carolina.

Jennifer Blake has been writing bestselling romances since 1977, when *Love's Wild Desire* became a *New York Times* bestseller. Twenty million books later, she continues to break records and to win hearts. She lives in Quitman, Louisiana.

Hannah Howell is the award-winning author of many books, including three Zebra historical romances—*Only For You, My Valiant Knight,* and *Unconquered.* She is currently working on her next Zebra romance which will be published in August, 1997. She lives with her family in Georgetown, Massachusetts.

Olga Bicos is an attorney turned romance writer and an award-winning author of six books, her most recent entitled, *Wrapped in Wishes.* She asks for readers' indulgence for a Roman Catholic wedding on Christmas—Marshall had his heart set on it—and for an elevator that probably defied all rules of engineering. In Olga's words, "I believe God was in control of that elevator at all times." She lives in California with her husband, two children, and a menagerie of animals. She loves to hear from readers.

FOR THE VERY BEST IN ROMANCE—
DENISE LITTLE PRESENTS!

AMBER, SING SOFTLY (0038, $4.99)
by Joan Elliott Pickart

Astonished to find a wounded gun-slinger on her doorstep, Amber Prescott can't decide whether to take him in or put him out of his misery. Since this lonely frontierswoman can't deny her longing to have a man of her own, she nurses him back to health, while savoring the glorious possibilities of the situation. But what Amber doesn't realize is that this strong, handsome man is full of surprises!

A DEEPER MAGIC (0039, $4.99)
by Jillian Hunter

From the moment wealthy Margaret Rose and struggling physician Ian MacNeill meet, they are swept away in an adventure that takes them from the haunted land of Aberdeen to a primitive, faraway island—and into a world of danger and irresistible desire. Amid the clash of ancient magic and new science Margaret and Ian find themselves falling helplessly in love.

SWEET AMY JANE (0050, $4.99)
by Anna Eberhardt

Her horoscope warned her she'd be dealing with the wrong sort of man. And private eye Amy Jane Chadwick was used to dealing with the wrong kind of man, due to her profession. But nothing prepared her for the gorgeously handsome Max, a former professional athlete who is being stalked by an obsessive fan. And from the moment they meet, sparks fly and danger follows!

MORE THAN MAGIC (0049, $4.99)
by Olga Bicos

This classic romance is a thrilling tale of two adventurers who set out for the wilds of the Arizona territory in the year 1878. Seeking treasure, an archaeologist and an astronomer find the greatest prize of all—love.